LEAD ME NOT

LEAD ME NOT

A ROMANCE OF AVIATION

JAMES B. JOHNSON

THE BORGO PRESS

MMXIII

LEAD ME NOT

FIRST EDITION

Published by Wildside Press LLC

www.wildsidebooks.com

DEDICATION

For Beverly: You're the Best!

CONTENTS

CHAPTER ONE
HER

She was the kind of girl your mother warned you about. She was the kind of girl boys think about at night. She was the kind of girl they whisper about at school, in the locker room and under the bleachers.

She had urges, mostly sexual urges, she could neither control nor understand.

It was 10:30 that fateful night. She wore a short beige dress, no panties and a touch of black lace showing from her bra.

She was sitting on the top step of his ladder, right in the middle of his living room, and listening to old records. Eric Burdon and the Animals. Her name was Aloha Blaze, for which she alternately would never, ever forgive her parents, or loved them for the uniqueness it bestowed upon her. At times, it made her feel like a stripper. Dollops of red paint splotched the ladder.

Height was her friend and refuge.

He would be here soon. What would he think of her, a patch of thigh showing, sitting atop the ladder in his living room? She was afraid her plans would prove fruitless again. She didn't think she had the guts to try this one more time. She wanted desperately for him to like her as much as she liked him. At one time, she'd had a crush on his son—but nothing like this.

He was good looking, a pilot, a businessman—and the father of her best girlfriend.

Rudyard Kipling Six walked in the door from an office party, tie loose and jacket thrown over his shoulder. As an ex-Air Force officer, he did not affect the long hair and pork chop sideburns of the mid-seventies, even though now, in '78, those styles were dying out.

Aloha needed something in her life, she wasn't quite certain what, and her fantasies made her believe Rudd would fill that void.

Burdon's bluesy version of "The House of the Rising Sun" came on the stereo and the lights were low.

He saw her on the ladder and stopped. His sports jacket fell to the floor. He stared. The whole scene took on a fantasy twist. His eyes raked her appreciatively.

They locked eyes. Her arms became hungry and her eyes heavy. Words were not necessary.

She knew what he was seeing. She had champagne-colored hair, dark brows, and deep, deep forest green eyes. A touch of ruby lipstick. And her hourglass figure belied her age. All of which gave her the appearance of a tall, sensual animal. Most people mistook her for twenty-one or older.

He came toward her as if against his will. He was seeing how incredibly desirable she really was.

Familiar with each other, they'd talked occasionally as she came and went from visiting his daughter. Nor did he know that Aloha had contrived to have Denise away from the house at this time.

He stopped at the foot of the ladder. Her legs were together so that he knew she wore no panties, but modestly, so that naked thigh and a flash of inner leg mesmerized him. Her nipples strained against the fabric.

She opened her arms self-consciously and he took her from the ladder. Their eyes remained locked. Their mouths touched. Her dry tongue became moist.

She wrapped her long legs around his hips and his strong, hard arms went around her and held her tightly against him. The blues of New Orleans flowed between them and fused a sensual bond. He began to move with the rhythm, their mouths still only touching, feather-like and aching.

She trembled in his arms, fire burning through her body.

They danced slowly around the old paint-splattered ladder, her legs clutching him. She could feel this virile man was aroused. Her arms went around his neck and his hands moved to cup her naked buttocks.

The music evoked a primal urge within her and their mouths no longer simply touched, they were locked together. She growled her pleasure and clutched him rhythmically with her legs. He tasted all masculine, add a little gin and lime flavor. Their tongues danced together.

He groaned into her and pulled her more tightly against him, grinding his groin against her.

"If I ever die?" Rudd said into her ear, tongue darting, teasing. "Kiss me like that one more time. That's what I want to remember when I kick down the gates of hell."

"I will," she whispered. "Promise."

"Something to carry with me through eternity."

The Animals were now singing "Bring It on Home to Me."

The music was raw and the dollops of red paint on the ladder seemed to pulse and glow with their emotions.

He stood her on her feet. At five-seven, she had not yet reached the height everybody said she would.

Smoothly he pulled her dress over her head and she stood there clad only in her dark lacy bra. He drank her in for a moment and she was glad her body belied her age.

Urgency overwhelmed her and with awkward arms, she unbuttoned his shirt and pulled his tie out of the knot. She felt her bra unsnap and his gasp of appreciation.

He kicked his shoes off and she unbuckled his belt and he quickly stepped out of his slacks.

"Ummm," she mumbled, eyes glazed.

Then they were down on the deep carpet, one of her legs overlapping his buttock and thigh. She captured him. "Oh, my God."

"Aloha," he said her name magically.

Their mouths touched again, hers hungry.

Their coupling was long and slow until she reached her very first screaming orgasm. Her entire body was filled with love and she exploded, pure pleasure throbbing through her. He continued, more urgent and demanding, and her craving increased again until they climaxed together, she screaming again, he straining against her and into her.

The wordless emotion-filled noise she made embarrassed her; but she couldn't wait to do it again.

They were rigid against each other for a few minutes, the hair on his hard chest titillating her nipples. Their mouths were touching again. She felt drugged, out of control, aching for him.

A gust of wind blew the front door shut with a slam.

He was startled and tensed his body arousing her again.

"Denise?" he murmured in afterthought.

"Gone," she said into his mouth and felt him move inside of her.

"Umm, good." He tasted her nipple.

She couldn't believe she was ready again. Never had she done it more than once. Then she was on top of him, rocking gently as he sucked her nipples one by one.

This scream wasn't as loud, but it was into his mouth and throat. It was the sweetest orgasm of her life.

She knew then that she was no longer infatuated with him. She was in love with him. Or so she thought.

She tried to say "I love you," but in only came out as a three-syllable moan.

"Say again?" He talked like a pilot.

"I liked that. A lot." She was regaining her breathing along with her senses.

"Umm. Me too." His hands were roaming her back, her buttocks, learning her. "For too long I've wanted to taste you. Your mouth, your nipples, the sweat under your breasts, your belly button, your vagina. And more."

"More?"

"The salt in your ear, dried tears on your cheek, rain in your hair."

Her green eyes locked onto his steel gray ones and she wondered, "What next?"

His mouth captured hers again.

Later, as he nuzzled her hair, she said, "That leaves just the rain in my hair."

"I look forward to that," he murmured.

* * * * * * *

"Oh, my God! You didn't!" said Denise, waving the slice of pizza.

"I didn't say anything." Aloha looked defiant.

"My father!" The slice of pizza hung suspended in front of Denise's mouth, the tip sagging.

Aloha did not respond.

"Look into my eyes," Denise commanded. "Promise me you didn't touch him." Denise was an attractive brunette.

Aloha shrugged and took a bite of pizza.

"He's been so vulnerable since Mother and him split up." A mushroom dropped onto the kitchen table and Denise sat the piece of pizza down. "You're gorgeous, and you radiate sex. You're dangerous."

Aloha sat back and looked at her friend. "I am not."

"You used him." Rudd's daughter's voice was accusing.

"I did not."

"Then how do you explain that cat-that-just-ate-the-mouse and very satisfied picture on your face?"

"I don't have to explain anything."

"You do so."

"Nu uh, I'm a grown girl." Aloha felt her face redden.

"Are you?" Ice dripped from Denise.

"We didn't do anything neither one of us didn't want to do." She bit into pizza but it didn't help sidetrack Denise.

"Just exactly how old are you?" demanded Denise.

They were across from each other in the kitchen. It was two

in the morning. Rudd was asleep in his bedroom. Denise had come home with pizza. Aloha was dressed, her hair fixed and makeup repaired.

"Old enough."

"Proverbs 17:17. 'A friend loveth at all times.' You were my friend."

"I still am, goddamnit." Anger was replacing her embarrassment.

"Do *not* take the Lord's name in vain." Denise was a born-again fundamentalist Christian.

Aloha had known Denise before her recent conversion and still liked the girl. "Stop yelling at me then."

"I am *not* yelling! And you set it all up. You schemed to have me out of the house at the most likely time."

Aloha was uncomfortable. It had taken three attempts before circumstances worked to her advantage. On this, her fourth attempt, Denise had left the house at the right time and Rudd had come home soon thereafter. Not to mention she, Aloha, had been in the right mood. Of course, she usually was in the right mood.

"You set up that study date for me and got me to have you order a pizza for that exact time so you'd know when I was gonna come home."

"I thought you liked that boy?" Aloha asked.

"Don't change the subject." Speculation ripped across Denise's features. "Lemme see. How old are you?"

Aloha did not answer.

"Jail-bait. Do you understand? You could put my father in jail!"

"Not if nobody tells the law."

"Jeez. Not to mention violating some of the Ten Commandments. That was a morally reprehensible thing."

"Nope," Aloha said doggedly. She was infatuated with Rudd. Having sex was not wrong...was it?

"Thou shalt not—"

"What?"

"Commit adultery."

"Rudd's divorced and I'm not married."

"It's adultery anyway, darn it. In Galatians, it says, 'The works of the flesh are manifest, which are these; adultery, fornication, uncleanness, lasciviousness.' Don't you understand?"

"It was beautiful—"

"There. Admitting—"

"I admit nothing."

"You're so darkly intelligent; you're going to get away with it."

"There's nothing to get away with, Denise." Aloha tried to make her voice reflect patience.

"I always figgered you were old for your grade level." Triumph lighted in Denise's eyes.

Aloha thought, *Sometimes I'm too old for myself.* But she treasured what had happened tonight. There was a spark, a light, a hope, an enthusiasm she'd never, ever thought would happen to her. Certainly not as a result of getting laid. She used to think that sex was just a feel-good time. She knew she had little control over her craving for sex. It had certainly been satiated tonight.

"Reprehensible," Denise repeated.

"No. It was beautiful and natural."

"So you admit your reprehensible actions?"

"Denise, I admit nothing. And stop showing off by using those big college words."

Denise was eighteen and a sophomore at Florida State across town.

Denise pulled one finger off her fist at a time. "I always thought you were a year or two behind everybody in our age group. But that doesn't explain why you're so bright. If a street smart girl like you were academically inclined...."

"I leave that to you intellectuals," Aloha lied. Aloha could read something one time and remember it. She did not have to study. She always got straight A's in school, but did not broadcast that fact.

Denise didn't notice her sarcasm. "Like I said, suppose I've got it backwards. Suppose you're not eighteen in the eleventh grade, a bit behind kids your age—"

"What are you trying to say?" Aloha's voice became low and dangerous. This goodygoddamntwoshoes was accusing her of being *too* young. This got Aloha's dander up.

"Suppose, like we really know, that you are very smart, but just don't show it. Suppose you were bright enough to skip a couple of grades—"

My God! Denise thinks I'm keeping a secret. That I'm fourteen or fifteen.

Aloha had been born in July, just beating the Florida August first cutoff for the next grade year. One thing her parents had done was to let her go through schools, more than a few, at her own pace, and end up wherever the she felt comfortable.

This ongoing situation made her very lonely.

Aloha carefully pulled another slice from the pizza and took a large bite, avoiding Denise's glaring eyes. "You're full of shit, Miss Six." It came out mumbled through pizza.

Denise continued to glare at her. She shook her head emphatically. "You're probably right. Because if what I was thinking is true—"

"It isn't," Aloha lied.

"You would be maybe fifteen? In eleventh grade."

"I am a junior, but you're wrong about my age." And she was.

Denise shook her head. "Maybe I'm dreaming. It can't be true. My father is forty-seven—"

"Eighteen is the age of consent in Florida," Aloha said impulsively. At her age, she failed to see the relevance of the age disparity.

"You'd have everybody think you're eighteen."

"I don't care what everybody thinks."

"Obviously. But you are, um, well-developed."

Aloha tilted her head. "Voluptuous?" She was baiting Denise now.

"Not exactly. You've a regal sort of way about you. But you

exude sex. All the boys say—" She looked up guiltily.

"I've known some of the boys. And I don't care what they say. I like men better. Like your father. He *exudes* virility."

Denise sucked in air. "Don't talk like that about my father."

Aloha had successfully changed the subject, but Denise had not caught the thickening sarcasm.

"I'm glad your father did not change into a hotshot religious nut like you did. You used to be my friend, now you quote the Bible all the damn time. Are you some kind of body-snatcher from outer space? What have you done with my friend Denise?"

Denise sat back astonished. "Why, I, uh, found the Lord. And He comforts me in my times of trial and tribulations—like now. He would not be a traitor like you. His rod and His staff, they comfort me."

Aloha was breathing hard now. "We haven't been very good friends since you quote found the Lord unquote. Seems to me this religion stuff has changed you, maybe for the worse."

Her mouth pursed, Denise said, "No, sireee." Denise took after her mother. Pretty but not stunning like Aloha. But Denise had the same strong jaw as her father.

Denise ripped a bite of pizza. "I *knew* you were bright. First you seduced my father through a series of machinations, then you successfully distract me by making my religion the issue." She wagged her pointy finger at Aloha. "My father's been divorced for years. He's vulnerable, very much so—"

I hope he stays so, thought Aloha. I'd counted on it. All my maneuvering....

"—and he hasn't dated much at all since the divorce."

"What was the real reason for their divorce?"

"I will not again be distracted."

"Machinations? Reprehensible?"

Denise ignored her. "He's at a point where he needs companionship, a stable relationship—"

"He needs a woman."

"He needs, umm—"

Me.

"He needs a wife, a woman, who is not so clever, dark and coldly Machiavellian."

"I appreciate the compliments, Denise, but—"

"He needs a nice...."

"A nice girl?" Aloha's tone was soft.

Denise clenched her jaw. "It is not my intention to insult you. But tonight you've revealed yourself as a —"

"Harlot?"

"That's what the Gospel says." Denise pushed the pizza box away.

Aloha rose. "I'm tired of you wearing your religion on your sleeve. And I'm getting more and more pissed at your accusations."

"God will forgive you for saying that." Denise paused. "Daddy was the one who connected me with the Lord—"

"Oh? How?" Aloha couldn't keep the ice from her voice.

"Every night he put me to bed with *'Now I lay me down to sleep, I pray the Lord my soul to keep.'* It was my first step to salvation, thanks to Daddy."

"If I want to see Rudd, I will."

Denise stood and stepped toward Aloha. "Not if I can help it."

"You can't."

"I'll tell him all about you," Denise spat out.

"Oh? What will you tell him?" Aloha said in a dangerous whisper.

"I'll tell him about you and all the other boys."

"Hearsay."

"Hearsay, theresay, *I* will say."

Even if not completely true, Aloha thought about what they said behind her back, there's plenty of truth, enough to make Rudd hate her. "It's not very Christian of you."

That stopped Denise. After a moment of thought, Denise said, "I have to protect my father."

"From what?"

"From you."

Aloha forced herself to laugh. "Get real, Denise. Do you think I have designs on your father?"

That threw her. She stepped backward, thinking. Then: "You don't?"

I do. "Whatever gave you that idea?"

"The fact that you seduced him tonight. The fact that your parents don't ever care about anything you ever do. The fact that you always get the boy you go after—"

"That's not true."

"I can bring in some of my girlfriends to swear to it. I thought *you* were my friend. The fact that you worked hard to arrange the events of tonight. And now that I mention it, it occurs to me that there have been a couple of other occasions you've come over and I wasn't here but something came up."

"Please. You are imagining things." Until tonight, Aloha's strategies had not worked.

"Am I?"

It was late and Aloha suddenly found herself no longer elated but weary. "I don't want to fight, Denise. You're my friend. Look. How about if I promise to stay away from Rudd?" Like hell I will.

"You'd do that?"

"For you. For our friendship." So you don't poison your dashing, handsome pilot of a father against me. Somehow somebody had poisoned Rudd's relationship with his ex-wife. Why had they gotten divorced?

"Well, maybe."

"And don't be telling any tales out of school about me." Damn, shouldn't have said that.

Denise cast an appraising eye. Denise had leverage over her now. "Maybe, maybe not."

Aloha knew that Rudd was impressionable now, and whether he believed any rumors about her or not, they would be damning just in the telling. Especially coming from Denise, the apple of his eye. And, while Aloha knew hers was probably just a school-girl's infatuation, something special and different had happened tonight and she didn't want to lose Rudd so soon. She'd been in heat before. But this was different. She'd even dated Denise's brother Buddy, but they'd never had sex.

"Maybe I won't tell him if you reveal your age," said Denise.

CHAPTER TWO

HIM

Rudyard Kipling Six banked his aircraft. The Gulf of Mexico glittered beneath the Beech. He pulled back the yoke and performed his turn.

He settled back and sighed. His eyes swung back and forth metronome like. Too much traffic today. Up here with the muted engine noise and wind blowing past, he could think.

Rudd was obsessed. He didn't want to think of his infatuation. He'd been alone for so long. His son was long gone, thank God, and Denise had a dorm room at Reynolds Hall on campus. She visited home to do her laundry and spend weekends away from school. And whenever she wanted to get away.

Aloha Blaze. What a name. It caught your attention. Just as she caught your attention. She was getting under his skin. Rudd knew she'd been a schoolmate of Denise's, over at Leon High. Denise had graduated and gone on to FSU in town. Aloha Blaze was now a junior. A damn teenager in high school! He, Rudyard Kipling Six was having an affair. Forty-seven and she—? From something Denise had said, Rudd assumed Aloha was eighteen. Legal but—Rudd was a relatively moral man. He'd served in Southeast Asia, killed more than his share of fellow human beings and knew that life did not conform to any secular or moral rules. Whatever worked within the cultural dynamic. He groaned. He was starting to use uncommon terms as did Denise.

He'd not wanted to continue with Aloha after that first night; but he was trapped. God, she was so young. But he had no control over his own body, his own will. Not now. Not with her. Not anymore. A fatal flaw, he realized. She was an ache in the pit of his stomach, an ache which refused to go away.

It was something that had grown over the last few months, triggered one day by Aloha herself and her frank, appraising look. He liked her voice, her piercing green eyes, her hourglass figure, and the sensuous invisible smoke she exuded. While her unique attractiveness wasn't enough to sway him, her character was. She was very bright; she had a quick, wide smile; and she had a special self-deprecating sense of humor.

And now he could not get her out of his head.

This attraction was against his will. He was a moth to her flame.

Denise had gone back to FSU Monday morning.

Monday evening there was Aloha, boldly knocking on his door and weaving around him as he stood astonished in the doorway. They had not talked. He was mesmerized. They made love for two hours. He fell asleep and she was gone when he awakened.

He did not see her on Tuesday and was relieved.

Wednesday night he'd already been asleep when she awakened him, naked body hard and demanding.

"How'd you get in?" he asked.

"You've a drawer full of keys," she said into his mouth, her tongue slashing, seeking. Her supple hands moved, sought.

"We have to talk," he mumbled, pulling her closer, surrendering his will.

"I'd rather do this."

"Um, me too."

She spent the entire night.

Never needing an alarm clock, he awoke at five-thirty, having an early charter to Birmingham. She was up like a cat when he rose. When he came into the kitchen, the coffee pot was perking and she was stirring oatmeal on the stove. She gave him an apprehensive smile.

"Domestic, huh?" she said, giving him a shy look.

She wore jeans and a denim vest buttoned twice. No bra, no shirt. He had to bite the inside of his cheek to suppress his desire. Under her champagne hair, her dark brows and deep-set forest-green eyes added years to her. The only makeup she wore was bright red lipstick. It all gave him a warm and fuzzy feeling: one he knew was more dangerous and damning than the gut level attraction he felt for her.

"Sit down. How do you like your coffee?"

He sat. He gulped air. Do it, he demanded of himself.

"Black." He stared at her as she handed him the cup. "Listen, Aloha. We can't...."

"Can't what?" Her smile was impish.

"Can't go on like this."

"Why not?" Her voice innocent now.

"You don't even know how I like my coffee, yet we've shared the most intimate of experiences."

"Your point being?"

"We shouldn't be having this affair." Coffee scalded his throat, and it was strong.

"Why not? I like you. You like me, don't you?" Coyly.

"Well, yes, but—"

"You like the sex, don't you, darlin'?"

He wanted to snap at her not to call him darling. She hadn't earned that right. But he didn't say anything.

"It's pretty obvious you like the sex, Rudd." She sighed and shivered at a memory. "God, how you like it."

She handed him a bowl of oatmeal. It was too runny but he shrugged it off and doused it with butter and sugar and cinnamon.

"You're too young for me, Aloha—"

She turned away from him. "Eighteen is too young? Call a lawyer."

He felt awkward. "It's still very young." She was eighteen? Except she hadn't really said so. Did he really want to know?

"Again, your point being?"

"You're younger than my daughter."

"You got some sort of father-daughter hang up?"

"No, but it doesn't seem right."

"I like you a lot, Rudd. Do you like me?" Her eyes flashed brightly, alternating pure intelligence and sex.

"Plenty." That's the trouble, he thought, but could not say.

She moved behind him and began massaging his shoulders. "You're tense. Let it go, darlin'. Let's just enjoy."

A last thought. "How about your parents? What do they think about us?"

"Who cares. I hate them. They named me Aloha."

He didn't know how to respond.

"They don't care about me, they never have. I do anything I want."

"Not here, not with me."

Her smile was sly. "Oh?" She moved liquidly to the stove.

His face colored. "I have to fly to Birmingham and won't return 'til tomorrow and then Denise will be here for the weekend."

"I can wait." She ate oatmeal from the pan with a soup spoon.

"I don't know if I can," he said, pushing his chair back. "My resolve is dying." He was surprised at himself for being honest—and vulnerable. He stood.

She came gently into his arms and he tilted his head and kissed her gingerly, licking a spot of oatmeal from her upper lip. She was inches short of his six one, but would grow three more inches in the next few years.

Her vest came open and he was late for his charter to Birmingham.

Rudd shook his head at the memory, checked his heading and the altitude controller. The trim wheel moved automatically.

He was staring himself in the soul. He had a growing realization that he cared deeply for Aloha Bonnie Blaze. Certainly, the sex was almost obsessive, but something deeper was beginning to emerge. Yet she was so goddamn young!

A game he enjoyed playing to himself: He'd imagine how a certain person would look and act in ten, twenty, thirty years.

Aloha was not just interesting in those future terms, she was intriguing. He envisioned her at forty: The prime of her life, a knockout. And she'd be a Real Woman. Another game his mind played was to categorize people as a Real Man, a Real Woman, or not making the grade.

At forty, fifty, sixty, Aloha would be at the top of her game, a commanding presence, a woman with whom he'd love to be involved. Not a trophy, but a woman with her own agenda. Her future was bright—given the right opportunities. He could point the way for her, he realized.

At sixty, seventy, eighty, her hair would be more silver, her face smooth and classic, her quick wit and intellect still raging. This vision haunted him.

Long ago he'd made a pact with himself: Disregard what the woman looks like, it's character which counts. But Rudd could not ignore Aloha's regal beauty and her demanding presence. He had a gut-level, biological imperative for her. He was finding he had to be with her, not necessarily sex, but just be near her. He'd tried to tell her as much while dancing with her, but had become tongue-tied and decided silence was golden.

He landed in Tallahassee no closer to the answer.

Denise was already there when he got home.

After his shower, they settled in the family room, he with a gin and tonic, she with a glass of iced tea.

"Daddy, I've found blonde hair in my bathroom and a girl's vest in the hall closet."

"Champagne."

"What?"

"Not blonde, but champagne."

"Oh. I see. Well, we've always been frank between each other since you and Mother—"

"Tell me about Aloha Blaze."

Denise sank back into the sofa. "Very frank. May the Lord have mercy upon our souls."

"Our? Or just mine?" he asked.

"I was being diplomatic."

"Who is she?"

"Just another kid in the group. Well, not really *in* the group. Part of it, but a loner. Gets along only with certain people. Not a part of the group-think, the teenage thing where they all want to be alike, but different. Deceptively smart. Very enterprising. She's different. She doesn't care what others think. Does her own thing."

"Family?"

"She's an only child. Her parents are what they call original hippies. They still have long, scraggly hair, wear beads, smoke dope, stuff like that."

"Christ." He remembered meeting them once or twice, just in passing.

"Daddy! Do *not* take the Lord's name in vain."

"Sorry. I can never get used to you being—"

"Born-again?"

"Yeah, that."

She shook her head. "I'm not one for self-analysis. But you know full well it's your fault."

"Because of me and your mother?"

"Yep. You both drove me to it, probably in self-defense."

"I don't want to talk about it."

Denise took a sip of tea. "You will have to, one day. It's something which needs purging—"

"Pop psychology, young lady."

"I've some of Buddy's combativeness," she said grimacing. I've tried to channel it into my love for the Lord Jesus...."

"Buddy will grow up one day," Rudd said and prayed he was right, "and come to his senses. Take the edge off that boy and the world beware." Buddy was something akin to a male Aloha: very sharp with a raw edge. That rawness Rudd hadn't been able to blunt and had led to a falling out between father and son. Rudd and Buddy had butted heads too often.

"Even before I was born again and really took Jesus as my savior," Denise continued. "Remember you always prayed with me?"

"I do. Not bad for a heathen."

"I didn't say you were." Her tone was defensive.

"Your mother wouldn't take any interest."

"I know, Daddy, I know. It was your influence...."

How will I ever know if I did a good job? he scolded himself. But by God, I tried. He stirred his now-warm drink with his pointy finger.

"Every night it was, 'Now I lay me down to sleep, I pray the Lord my soul to keep....'" Denise shifted her right leg under her left leg and faced him on the couch. "That was always a very special time to me. I liked praying."

Well, how about this one, Rudd thought abruptly. *Lead me not into temptation—*

"We've always had that special relationship," Denise continued. "That's why I'm concerned now."

"About Aloha?"

"Do you have any idea of her age?" asked Denise pointedly.

Now he felt defensive. He eyed Denise. His voice was level. "She is eighteen, isn't she?" Aloha hadn't really said her age. Her language had been evasive.

Why?

CHAPTER THREE
DENISE

"She *is* eighteen, isn't she?" her father asked.

Denise didn't know what to say. So she didn't say it.

Her father fixed her with a stare. "Well?"

"She says she is, Daddy." Which was true, as far as it went. It wasn't what Denise thought anymore, not since the pizza conversation. Aloha had been elusive. Dread seeped through Denise. *Why did not—or could not—Aloha drive??* Should I mention this to Daddy? It was basic: if Aloha was eighteen she could drive. If she was under sixteen, she could not drive. OhmyGod!

"It's important," he said. "I don't think I mind the age differential. But if the girl is not yet eighteen—"

Denise seized her opportunity. "You don't trust what she says?" Why didn't he just ask her?

Six looked up at his daughter sharply. "You trying to say something?"

"A simple question, Daddy. From what you said, you were implying she might not be telling the exact truth." And we've been good friends, Dad, and this is so uncomfortable, talking to me about your love life which I don't want to know anything about. All of which Denise thought, but instead, she said, "Aloha is still my friend. This is awkward."

"I don't think she'd lie to me, she was just sort of evasive."

Denise didn't want to hurt her father with her suspicions. On the other hand, she was too Christian to condone the situation between Aloha and her father. Which led her to fear that the relationship between the two would continue, which wouldn't be good for her father or her friend. Or Denise's own Christian sense of rightness, not righteousness, she amended, but what was really right in the world in the ways things like this should work. She was glad you don't have to diagram thoughts like sentences in English class.

Her father sat back and put his drink down on the end table. He was thinking. Usually he was so up, not introspective. But now he was brooding.

And that made Denise angry. Her father was a good man, one who'd raised two children himself with little help from his wife.

Now along comes a teenage floozy and turns his head big time.

Could he weather the storm?

Anger grew in Denise. Her father deserved better. He'd paid his dues. Fighting for the red, white, and blue in Vietnam. Raising his children despite his wife, her own mother. Forgive me, Lord, for what I might do.

"Somebody's not doing you right," Denise blurted.

"Oh?"

"Oh. You bet, Daddy. I'm beginning to get mad."

He fixed her with his gaze again. "Don't get involved in this one, little girl."

"I'm no *little girl*. I'm a freshman in college."

"Which gives you no right to interfere."

"Who said I was gonna interfere, Daddy?"

"Your demeanor. Your history. This conversation. This is me, now. My personal collision avoidance system is blaring. Stay the hell out of my business."

"*You* are my business. You're my father. *I'm* all you have left. *She* is my business. *She's* my friend." Or she was. "Besides, *you* were the one who was asking me the questions, I was simply answering and now you're taking offense."

"Drop it. I know you, Denise. You'll attack what you perceive as a problem and gnaw it like a dog with a bone until you've chewed it to death."

"I'm worried about you, Daddy."

"Forget it."

"I won't. By gosh, the Bible says honor your parents. I do honor you. I care about you. It's my fault *she* was ever over here. I feel responsible."

"For that I thank you."

"She's nowhere near your age. Look what's happening to you."

"Nothing. And it's none of your business. Nor anybody else's business."

He was so serious about Aloha. Mom always said he was flawed, but Denise had never seen a major flub on his part. Until now.

"Ain't love wonderful," he quipped in a parody of his old self.

Love? Dear Jesus, let it not be so.

Nor was she disarmed by his flippancy. "And you blew it so very well your other time with Mom, didn't you?"

"Poison doesn't become you, *little girl*."

"But I'm right, aren't I?"

He sank back. "Maybe, maybe not. Look what came of it. Namely you."

"And my brother." What would the volcanic Buddy think?

"If I have to go through hell one more time to produce a couple of kids like you both, well—"

He had gone through hell. Daddy deserved better. Forty-seven years, unlucky in love and he still was paying his dues to society. She knew, too, that many of his wartime experiences were the stuff of heroic chronicles. He'd done his job, killed a bunch of the enemy. And come home to her—Marge. Denise had to admit that life hadn't been fair to her father.

Desperation. Denise knew that Aloha wasn't good for her father. And the more that she thought of it, the more she was certain that Aloha Blaze was lying about her age. More problems for Daddy. He didn't deserve the grief that was headed his way. Maybe even legal problems if Aloha was—too young. There, she admitted it.

And her anger grew. The determination that had made her into a hardcore Christian against everything she'd known in her life boiled out of her.

"Not even Mom would let that slut into this house." Denise surprised herself with her own venom.

"Watch you mouth, girl. And, damn it, leave your mother out of this."

She grabbed control of herself. *I pray thee, dear Lord, let me be strong and please please please help me control my big mouth and my anger because I will surely lose him if I do not. Oh, sweet Jesus, come and help your faithful servant, for I need you now as I never needed you before. I* must *save my father.*

"Daddy? I'm sorry. I got carried away. I do not wish to sound shrewish like Mother. And you deserve better, Daddy, never mind what I said. She's not a slut. I wanted to hurt you and get what I was thinking across to you." *Was Aloha a slut? All the boys said so.*

"What the hell's going on here, Denise? We used to get along so well. We used to agree on damn near everything." He brooded. "It's those goddamned evangelists you hang out with."

"I shouldn't be so judgmental," Denise said. "Look here, Daddy. You're a mature man, you've been alone a long time—"

"Even when your mother was here."

"And your biological clock is trucking right along—"

"I thought we were going to skip the pop psychology. I leave you alone with your religion. So I want some reciprocity. Leave me and...her alone."

No way, Daddy. Because I love you. I will do everything in my power to kill your romance with one each Aloha Blaze. "What's up with you and Amanda?" Denise asked coyly.

It almost knocked him back visually. He picked up his warm gin and tonic, barely touched, and drained it. "I haven't seen her lately." His reaction was like a kid caught with his hand in the cookie jar. The cliché fit so well she thought of it again.

Amanda McMullen was a professor at FSU. She was relatively new there, over in the English department, where Denise intended to major in English Lit. In fact, Amanda and Rudd had met through her.

While waiting for her father to pick her up one day, Denise had been standing in front of Bill's Bookstore on Copeland Street, right across from Wescott, FSU's main administrative building. Amanda McMullen was her English instructor and had been walking home from class. Amanda was known to walk miles a day. She stopped to talk to Denise for a moment and that's when Rudd had come along. They wound up going to lunch, the three of them, and then taking Amanda home. Rudd had gotten along quite well with the attractive brunette, who had been recently divorced over in Gainesville and had accepted a position in Tallahassee to get away from her previous situation. Amanda was maybe thirty-three or so, with that rounded cuteness surrounded by short hair, and a thick Georgia accent.

Denise knew her father had dated Amanda a few times. Amanda sometimes asked Denise about her father before or after class. After all, he was a handsome, dashing and unmarried pilot, a war hero, a magic combination to some women.

"Daddy?"

He looked at her.

"Don't take this wrong, okay?"

"Take what?"

"Put the rush on Amanda. You need something. I think Amanda can provide it, give her a chance."

His jaw clenched.

"She's a fine woman. Really. She asks about you. You won't be sorry."

He stared at her for a long moment. Then he laid his head back and closed his eyes. "Easy for you to say. Sometimes I don't know what the fuck to do."

Denise felt his utter despair. His personal hell had bubbled out. He was trapped. By that trash-mouth slut. Denise Six saw her father's haunted appearance and made a vow.

* * * * * * *

She walked quickly. Into the breach, help me, Lord, for Thou art with me all the days of my life and especially tonight.

Her father had fallen asleep on the couch, and Denise had let herself out quietly, anger driving her.

Denise liked to walk. The humid Tallahassee air seemed to provide a barrier through which she forged. Aloha's home was only a few blocks away—it was one of the reasons they were friends. They could walk to each other's house.

The neighborhood was growing. Her father had said that he was thinking of moving elsewhere, now that she was in school and Buddy gone. And Mom. He didn't need such a big house; he just hadn't gotten around to finding a new place, somewhere less crowded, and selling this one. Denise wished he'd done so and perhaps this thing with Aloha would never have occurred.

The tortured look on his face had told Denise that her father would not avail himself of the graceful Amanda. Genesis addressed "instruments of cruelty." Perhaps Aloha was one. Denise decided to leave her father's fate in the Lord's hands— right after she spoke her mind.

The Blaze house was well lighted, but Denise could see colored lights in the living room. She rang the bell and no one answered, obviously because the Rolling Stones were singing so loudly. At least it wasn't Michael rowing his boat ashore or everybody going to San Francisco. Peter and Mary Blaze were stuck in the sixties. And this was 1978, after all.

Mick Jagger wasn't getting any satisfaction and neither was Denise. Her anger made her knocking into a real pounding.

In a moment, Mary Blaze opened the door and the pungent odor of marijuana drifted out. Mary had a handful of her hair and was involved in pinning it up with hairpins.

"Hello, dear. Aloha is in her room studying. Come on in."

"Thanks, Mrs. Blaze."

"Mary, call me Mary." They always went through this same scene. Denise refused to use their first names; she was supposed to respect her elders. Wasn't she?

Mick Jagger went away and James Brown came on, doubtless sweating rivers on vinyl.

As Denise walked down the hall, she waved to Peter Blaze, a slight man with an out-of-style ponytail. He was sitting in a beanbag chair in front of the stereo and the television was on with the sound turned down. Atop the television was a lava lamp. The air was stifling.

"Tell your father I'll talk to him soon," said Peter.

Denise nodded and the import of what he said hit her. Peter wanted to talk to Daddy? That limp-wristed hippie couldn't know about Daddy and Aloha, could he? He didn't sound urgent or angry, so Denise forgot about it. Fatefully.

Aloha's door was closed and Denise knocked lightly. Even though she was furious at the girl, she minded her manners.

"Yes?" was enough for Denise so she pushed the door open.

Even though the air-conditioner was on, Aloha's window was wide open and a window fan was blowing air into the room.

A fleeting look of guilt raced across Aloha's face. She closed a history book and left her finger in to mark her place. She was sitting cross-legged atop a small desk which was clean except for the history book and a framed picture of—Rudyard Kipling Six.

It stopped Denise in midstride. She recognized the photo. It was one of her father in his flight suit with the SIXGUN AIR logo alongside a Cessna 172 Skyhawk. It contributed to Denise forgetting about Peter's comment.

"That's one of *our* pictures," Denise said. "Where'd you get it?"

"It followed me home," said Aloha.

A rack of vests hung at the foot of the bed, the one on the end fishnet and see-through.

The room was spotless and Denise couldn't smell the pot smoke in here. A couple of teddy bears and a stuffed tiger sat atop the chest of drawers. On the wall above the desk was tacked a print of an OV-10, one of the aircraft which Rudyard Six had flown in Vietnam.

"How do you explain the picture to your folks?" Denise was frankly curious.

Aloha shrugged. "I don't. They seldom come in here and I hide it when I leave. So what?"

"I don't know so what." Now that she was here, Denise didn't know how to go about this. "We got a problem."

Aloha lifted those dark brows. "We?"

"We. You, me, and my father." Her anger was returning.

"Sounds like *you* got a problem. Not me. Not Rudd."

Lord, please help me in this time of trial and tribulation. I need Your strength and wisdom. And I'm sorry I used the word bitch in my mind before and please help me to not use it again though I surely feel like it. Denise sat on the neatly made bed.

"My father is smitten or something with you. I feel you are taking advantage of him."

"I'm not and it's mutual."

"And you're jailbait, Aloha. You're lying through your teeth about your age and—"

Aloha put her book down. "Please leave. I don't want to talk."

"Don't you understand?" Denise was desperate. She didn't want to shout or threaten; that she knew would get her nowhere. "We've nosey neighbors. If anybody finds out about you and Daddy, he will go straight to jail and they'll mail the key to Antarctica. And it's wrong in the eyes of the Lord."

Aloha looked upset. "I don't want any trouble for Rudd."

"Then stay away from him."

Aloha's face contorted. "I can't." Her voice was a hoarse whisper.

"Oh, dear sweet Jesus."

"What I'm gonna do, Denise?" An age-old plea delivered in a plaintive voice.

Denise's heart went out to her friend. Her anger evaporated immediately. "I don't know, dear. I don't. We could pray?"

Aloha shrugged. "God's never helped me. Prayin's no good."

"Give it a chance. Jesus loves you."

"Shit. How come He gave me parents that don't care? I do whatever I want whenever I want. Big damn deal. I've been alone too long. My friends aren't real deep friends; you're the best. I don't have any girl-friends, 'cept you. That's why I prefer boys to girls. All the girls hate me and they're jealous of my looks." She unconsciously tossed her hair. "Jesus doesn't care if I'm lonely."

Dear God, lookit You've done. Daddy's been so lonely so long; Aloha's been so lonely so long. This woman-child is a knockout and he's handsome. Both are bright. Both are alike in their own ways. Both have physical desires and needs. Nature took its inevitable course. Dear Lord, why do You work in such mysterious ways?

She fell to her knees and steepled her hands. "Join me?"

"If it'll make you feel better. But it doesn't work for me."

"Our Father, Who art in Heaven...," Denise prayed. Through almost closed eyes, she watched Aloha watch her. Her heart went out to the young girl. For a brief moment, empathy flowed. Each shared a personal grief with which neither could deal. "...But deliver us from evil—"

Denise continued to pray, Aloha continued to watch—not detached, but not involved—looking down from her perch.

Denise shifted from her knees and sat on the floor with her back to the bed. "Well, that's that. What's next?"

"Ion't know."

"There's a problem, we've got to solve it."

Aloha sighed. "*You* have a problem. *I* am happier than I've been in a long time."

"How old are you, really, Aloha?"

"Umm, almost eighteen."

Was it the truth? "Why is it you do not drive?"

"I don't like to. I'm scared."

"You don't strike me as being frightened of anything."

"Thanks. But I am. Denise? There's something you ought to know. My Mom and Dad applied for positions overseas. We'll find out soon. Things will be different."

Denise's spirits soared. An out! Was it too easy? Later she would understand Aloha's wording; and Peter Blaze's earlier comment would finally make sense. Also, she would realize that Aloha had successfully changed the subject again, avoiding the age question. However, the prospect of the Blazes moving—overseas, no less!—overwhelmed her. God was smiling down this night. After all, from her point of view, things could get no worse.

CHAPTER FOUR
HIM

He tried to avoid her. He really did.

He went to work before dawn and returned late. When he came home well after dark one evening, she was sitting patiently in the big live oak tree in his front yard. His headlights captured her dangling legs.

"Hello, Rudd." Her voice came to him from ten feet up in the dark.

"Aloha, what's the story with you and heights?"

"Beats me." She swung off the limb and dropped lightly next to him. "But I do. I take refuge in them. How about an airplane ride?"

"Sure. When I get a free day."

"Can I have my key back?"

Taking her key away was the only control he had over her. "Maybe later."

She followed him inside and he didn't have the strength to send her away. She went home at dawn.

That night, to dodge Aloha, he called and got a date with Amanda McMullen. They went to dinner and a movie called *Close Encounters of the Third Kind*.

Amanda was a bright woman, very attractive and seemed to like him more than as a friend or acquaintance. When he dropped her off just before midnight, they kissed long and hard in the hall in front of her apartment door. He got the feeling that if he wanted, things could go further. But while it was arousing, he found no spark for Amanda that night. There was no clinging urgency, mental and physical, between them. Not like that which he shared with Aloha.

But he made another date with Amanda anyway.

Thirty minutes later he drove into his driveway. He looked around. No Aloha. He squelched an involuntary disappointment.

Dogged in his determination, he set his alarm for a change, and rose at four. Groggy, he made it out of the house in twenty minutes. As he drove off, he saw Aloha on the first intersecting street skipping like a little girl. He pretended he did not see her. Maybe she wouldn't recognize his car. It struck him that *she* cared enough to come to him at four thirty in the morning. He suppressed his guilt feelings.

At the Tallahassee airport, he went to the SIXGUN AIR hangar, went right to his office, and collapsed on his couch and was asleep in five minutes.

It was a Saturday, so the receptionist and mechanics were not at work. His partner, Ward Zekowski, was to fly donated relief supplies to Haiti for a church sponsored organization. When Zeke came, they loaded his aircraft and he flew off to the south. The relief flights were something they'd decided to do, it cost them only fuel and time on their aircraft. They usually performed this volunteer service on weekends or when they were free and sufficient supplies had accumulated.

So Rudd was alone and asleep in his office.

At high noon, Aloha Bonnie Blaze walked into his office.

Rudd swung himself up, still groggy with sleep. His hangar was part of the security perimeter and the doors from the office to the hangar were locked on the inside in accordance with security. But not the main, public access door into the office. But he thought that Zeke would have locked it.

"How'd you get in?"

"I got off the bus over at the terminal and this nice guy gave me a ride on his fuel truck." She preened.

"You vixen."

"You rat."

He knew what she was talking about. He went to a refrigerator and got both of them Cokes. "You broke security? You were on the flight line?"

"It was the shortest way."

"You have talent, Aloha." And a smile to steal hearts with and a body to beguile.

"You've been dodgin' me," she accused. Her hip jutted out. She was alluring in cutoff jeans, an FSU SEMINOLES shirt, and her denim vest helped conceal the obvious fact she wore no bra.

"I've been working long hours."

"All of a sudden?"

"Yes, dammit." He drained his Coke. "I don't have to explain my work hours to you."

She dropped her head. "I'm sorreee. I don't want you mad at me." She looked up from under her dark brows and those eyes chopped him to pieces. Some women twenty years older than she couldn't do that. It wasn't a feminine technique, it was a natural gesture.

He responded gutturally and she melted into his arms.

He was finding that when she was near him, his gut ached and the anticipation and desire melded into a warm and comfortable and fuzzy feeling. And, he recognized unable to do anything about it, and *that* was really dangerous.

When she came up for air, she said, "When do I get my airplane ride?"

"How about right now?"

"You're on, flyboy."

They went into the main office. He picked up the hotline to the tower. "Sammy? Yeah, this is Rudd. Listen. I'm gonna take the Beech Baron up for a check flight. Maybe a couple of hours, out over the Gulf and back. No, I'm not going to file a flight plan. Just wanted you to know." It had to be a two-engine aircraft. No way he'd trust *her* to a single engine. He got two headsets and they went out through the hangar to the flight line.

"This is a Beech Baron," he told her. "It's the stretched version, Model 58. Twin engine, cruises two ten, two twenty...."

He went through the preflight checklist religiously. Fuel level. Fuel sumps and filters. Oil. He removed the chocks and they climbed aboard.

The Beech had the pilot and copilot's seat up front and, instead of the seats behind those two, had a carpeted interior configuration for the next scheduled cargo flight Monday. If necessary, the seats could be installed quickly.

He strapped them in, ran up the engines, performed his checks, saw the radio was correctly set to 121.9 MHZ—Ground Control. He keyed the mike. "Hello tower, this is SIXGUN AIR Beech seven five six requesting taxi." He was using the radio's speaker instead of headsets so he could talk to Aloha.

"Go ahead seven five six, there's no other traffic. Just you and your passenger. Use runway 36. Winds 340 at ten knots. Altimeter three zero zero five." Rudd set the altimeter.

Aloha glanced her query at Rudd.

"Likely he has nothing to do up there, so he had his glasses on us." Rudd laughed. "Sammy wouldn't have said anything except he wanted me to know that he knows I've got a good-looking female on board."

She made a dimple. "Thank you, sir."

When they reached the end of runway three six, the tinny voice came from the tower, "You're cleared for takeoff whenever you want, seven five six."

"Roger." Procedure was lax on weekends.

Rudd did his final checks, ran the engines up and released the brakes. As they lumbered along, he said, "Nothing to it. When you get going fast enough, pull the stick or yoke back and up you go. They call it rotation." He did so and they were airborne.

"Have fun," said Sammy in the tower. "Turn left to zero nine zero heading then contact Departure Control. Ground control out."

Rudd set the radio to 132.15.

Tallahassee is only about thirty-five miles from the Gulf of

Mexico.

He stayed low and when they hit the Gulf, turned northwest and flew up the coast to Panama City under the control of Miami Center. They flew far out from the starkly white beaches. "You have to pay more attention around here—Tyndall Air Force Base and you never can tell what those hotshots'll do."

He banked and headed directly out over the Gulf, gaining altitude quickly. In a few minutes they were over ten thousand feet.

Aloha was leaning forward, eyes darting about, eager anticipation on her face.

"Want to fly her?" he asked. He held his hands off the yoke. "Good aircraft—even without autopilot, they'll fly themselves straight and level." The Beech did so. "Try it?"

"Just a minute," she said enigmatically.

She unbuckled her seatbelt and looked behind the seats, then scrambled into the cargo section.

"Hey! What are you doing?"

"Something I always dreamed about." Her vest hit the floor, followed immediately by her SEMINOLES shirt. Then she kicked her tennis shoes off and tugged her cutoffs and panties down at the same time. Soon she climbed back into her seat clad only in gym socks.

"Jesus," Rudd said.

"Sometimes I dream of flying," she said, looking far over the horizon, "and I'm not dressed. It seems so natural." Her breasts were firm and nipples up.

He had to force words through his strangling throat. "Now you're doing it for real. Is it natural?"

"It is, it is." She put her hands on her yoke. "What do I do?"

"Look at my hand." He held out his right hand, dipped it up and down on its longitudinal axis. "That's pitch." Then he kept his hand level and moved it from side to side. "That's yaw." Then he turned his hand and wrist over. "That's roll. We control all three. The rudder controls the yaw by these pedals and the yoke controls the pitch and roll. Actually, all three together is how...."

"Never mind the lecture, lemme fly her."

Aloha was a quick study. Strangely, at first she was apprehensive, then after a few moments, she relaxed. She flew for a while, banking and turning. Finally, he looked at his watch and they turned back and headed for the coast.

"You fly," she said and leaned back, releasing the yoke.

He thumbed on the autopilot. "You could go ahead and get dressed before my eyeballs pop out and I get ideas."

"Like what?" Her voice was not coy. "Heights make me horny. You've probably noticed by now. And this is *high*." She was staring at him with an intensity he wasn't used to. Her nipples were hard and erect. *All* of her hair was champagne.

He slid his seat back and she pulled his pants down and climbed on him, facing him. He reached around her and adjusted the trim to account for the shifted weight. Then he checked the altitude hold and the heading select.

Shortly, she was breathing deeply and hoarsely, and an urgency rose in both of them. His sensitive pilot's hands roamed with need.

"This is as close to Heaven as I've ever been," she said softly.

He wanted to share, not comfort nor conquer, and he did so.

When they were finished, Aloha said, "I will never, ever forget that." Clinging to him, she kissed him deeply.

"Me, neither," he mumbled and she moved against him, body taut, and then they were doing it a second time.

Shortly, she had a major screaming orgasm.

His powerful body rippled against her. Her every touch seared him.

She stayed on him, hanging on tightly, until he said, "The coast is coming up. I gotta fly." His hands stopped rubbing her buttocks.

Reluctantly, she crawled in the back and dressed.

After they landed and swung into the parking slot, Sammy in the tower responded to Rudd's transmission about shutting down. "Roger seven five six. You a member of the club now?"

Rudd stared at the speaker, clicked the mike button twice and hung it in its receptacle. He killed the engine and they dismounted. She followed him around during his post flight.

As she helped him attach the tie-down cable, she asked, "What did the tower guy mean, 'the club'?"

Rudd blushed.

"What?" she demanded.

"It's called the 'Mile High Club.' It, um, means you've um, made love while airborne."

"You mean got laid?"

"I mean that."

"I'll be darned," she said bemused.

He hid his grin.

"You didn't answer Sammy's question."

"It wasn't any of his business." Though he had clicked the mike twice, which in some circumstances means "roger."

Aloha grinned slyly at him and walked out from under the wing. She stood in front of the Beech and faced the tower. She waved her arms in a windmill motion for a moment, then raised her right hand high with her thumb up, her other hand provocatively on her hip. "Reckon he sees me?" she asked conversationally.

"Unless he's blind. Doubtless he's been watching us since we hit the ramp."

Then Aloha took her left hand and raised it, too, thumb high in the air, with a great, big, wide grin on her face. "Twice!" she shouted at the tower.

"*I'll* be goddammed," Rudd said.

At that exact moment he knew he was no longer simply enamored with Aloha Bonnie Blaze. He was fully and irrevocably in love with her.

And he had a date with Amanda in a few hours.

He wished he knew what the hell to do.

CHAPTER FIVE
HER

That two-timing son-of-a-bitch was sneaking out on her!

When he'd dropped her off from the Saturday afternoon flying, she'd suggested they spend the night together. Rudd had begged off evasively. He had a couple things to do and then much needed sleep.

She bought his story because she was tired, too. She was almost in a dream state. What a day. A new member of the Mile High Club. The after-sex euphoria.

Not only that, but she'd really enjoyed flying, the aloneness, the altitude, the silence, the background hum of strong engines. The different perspective she saw from high was striking and led her to think. And afterwards they'd shared an extremely comfortable silence. She could tell he was feeling good about the day, too. The more she thought about it, the more she decided it was the best day in her life so far.

The way Rudd acted was special, too. He'd treated her very gently, very softly, and his goodbye kiss, usually perfunctory if at all in front of her house, was sweet and tender. They didn't care if anybody was watching, which they probably weren't. The neighbors of the Blaze family were used to unusual comings and goings, not only from the teenager, but more so from the parents. Long ago they'd stopped paying attention.

"Today was super," Rudd said. "I don't remember when...."

She remained quiet in his arms.

He shivered. "I want to tell you...well, this will be one of my fondest memories. I've already got it stored."

Was he not ever going to declare his love for her? After all they went through, and the current tide of feelings, now would be the time. "We shared some stuff today, huh?"

"We did. And it fills an empty ache inside me."

"Me, too." He was so good with words. Aloha wished she could express herself so well. She vowed to study harder, to learn more, so she could be like him, on his level.

Finally, he shooed her out and went home.

At six-thirty she called him. No answer, not even Denise.

Once she'd told Rudd he'd be surprised at what she knew about him. One of the things she'd gleaned from Denise was Rudd's favorite restaurants. What else do you do on a Saturday night when there's not a Football Game at Doak Campbell Stadium? Too early for the movies, so—

She went through the restaurants in the yellow pages and marked the ones she remembered Denise saying or Rudd mentioning.

The Silver Slipper, the third one she tried. Perhaps the most expensive and exclusive restaurant in Tallahassee, except maybe The Governor's Club.

Aloha called the reservations number.

"Silver Slipper, this is Mark."

"I'm supposed to meet R. Six over there, but I forgot what time the reservation is." She pitched her voice level and businesslike.

"Let me check the—ah, there it is. Eight, Miss..?"

"He told you the correct number of people in the party?"

"It says here two—"

"Thanks for your help. Us secretaries can't trust the boss to do things by themselves, you know?" She hung up.

That goddamn Rudd had a date!

After all they'd been through today. Maybe the most wonderful day of her life. A cloud of depression settled upon her.

God damn it. Life wasn't fair. She'd been so high on life

today. Until now. No fair, damn it, no fair, damn it, no damn fair. She took several deep breaths.

Sometimes her alter ego, Bonnie, kicked in.

—Lissen to yourself, sweetie, observed Bonnie. You done everything yourself for yourself to the present. Nobody ever helped. Get your admittedly cute ass in gear. *Do not* go down without a fight.

—But it's so discouraging, replied Aloha.

—Shit, you only been chasing him for a few months. And nothing really started until a couple of weeks ago. Bonnie was usually level-headed.

—Yeah, right. Easy for you to say. You're the tough one. I just want to be held. I just want to be loved. I just want to be wanted. Aloha wrung her mental hands.

—By Rudd.

—Well, yeah.

—Long term, darlin'. Think years. Not months, not weeks, not days. Especially not *hours*.

—I'm glad there's a smarter me inside me, said Aloha.

—You been alone too long, sweetheart, said Bonnie.

—I have, I have. And watch your grammar. You're going to act like a fucking adult, talk like one.

—A point to note, sweetie: You make a conscious effort to speak clearly and with correct grammar, no?

—So?

—That's a long term thing, too. It don't bother you to screw up—you just keep plugging on, don't you?

—Yes—I do! Aloha agreed.

—Same deal. You win some battles, you lose some. The war's the thing. Learn something when you lose. Bonnie was making a lot of sense.

—I won today and I learned a lot.

—Goddamn right, Aloha Bonnie Blaze. You're one hell of a special person and deserve the best in life. You almost got it, too, babe. Keep fightin'.

—By God, I will.

—Lissen. About tonight. I got a idea—said Bonnie conspiratorially.

Aloha smiled to herself. If you're gonna lose a battle, do not go quietly. They shall all know you were there.

Peter and Mary Blaze had gone out for the evening. Not even a note. As usual. That made it easier and more difficult at the same time. Transportation would be tricky. Her education had always been most important to her. She'd rather study and read and forgo having a car if she'd spend her time working for the money to pay for the darn thing.

Not to mention that she was frightened of driving. Something she'd never admit. The always capable Aloha Blaze, afraid of driving? Spin another tale. Nobody would believe it. Not to mention number two: her vanity wouldn't let her admit her shortcoming.

—Yeah, but you took to flying immediately.

Bonnie, that had everything I like: sex and inordinate height.

—Altitude, corrected Bonnie. Regardless, think about it. You done good. It was a machine and you pointed it in the right direction and made it go there.

—Well, maybe.

The easier part was the dress. She had a demure, but sexy, black satin dress with straps and a plunging neckline. She'd bought it at Gayfer's one day on a whim, thinking it would make a good prom dress, even though it was probably too daring for high school. It would do tonight, she saw in the mirror. Quickly, she piled her champagne hair atop her hair, in a casual, rich-bitch, regal sort of look.

A touch of makeup, lipstick. No jewelry. Simplicity is best. Besides, she had no jewelry. Just a fancy watch she'd gotten for her birthday a couple of years ago. That works.

Paint the nails, quick, wave them dry.

Raid her stash. Since she'd been alone for so long, she'd learned to hoard cash. She had thirty-some dollars. Would it be enough? Maybe, but better be sure. She went and took some cash from her parent's pot jar. They kept their marijuana in a cookie jar to insure freshness. Next to it was another cookie jar with the cigarette paper and about a dozen twenty dollar bills. Aloha took three and hoped Peter and Mary wouldn't notice. She could lie out of it if she had to. She'd done so before.

She finally faced the fact: she was going to have to drive. Her parents had taken their VW bus. Which left Aloha the yellow and blue VW Beetle.

She removed her stiletto heels and tossed them into the back seat. That's when she almost backed out. It was difficult to face her fears.

—What I'm gonna do? she asked Bonnie.

—Looks like *you* got a problem, sweetie.

—Call a cab! I can do that, Aloha realized.

—You're flat out of time, Bonnie pointed out.

Aloha glanced at her fancy watch. "Damn."

—Gut check time. You can do it.

Aloha agonized.

—What if I wreck?

—Nobody'll notice the dents in this car. Look, dear, you drove an aircraft today. Just goddamn do it.

—I want to go there badly, Aloha admitted. "Fuck it," she said. She climbed in careful to protect her dress.

She pulled the gear into neutral even before she started the car, knowing this was safer. Once she had the car started, she went to the far right, past the H layout of first through fourth gears.

The damn thing wouldn't go into reverse. She stamped on the clutch and jammed the shifter to the right in every combination. No reverse. She put it in first and let up on the clutch and the car lurched forward, banging into the garbage cans in front of her which in turn saved the front of the garage wall. And the VW Bug chugged and stalled.

She got it going again and still no reverse.

"God*damn* it!" Aloha got out of the car and pushed it backwards. Once it got rolling good she jumped in a tried to steer it but the car rammed into the mailbox and the edge of the driveway.

"Shit."

She managed to shift into first gear and jumped forward, stood on the brake while still in first and the car stalled immediately.

—This ain't going very well, she observed drily.

—Why me, Lord? said Bonnie.

Aloha got out again and straightened the mailbox, climbed back into the front seat. "Oops." She got back out and went and pulled down the garage door.

Finally back in the driver's seat, she started the car smoothly this time, clutch in, shifted into first, chugged a little going into second, and wound the engine too high with too many RPM's, a term she'd just learned today, missed the shift to third and hit fourth anyway. She looked up in time to swerve away from a yellow and white '57 Chevy.

—*Lights!* screamed Bonnie.

"Oops. There."

She approached her first stop sign timidly. She killed the car, restarted it and lurched into the intersection, narrowly missing a kid on a bike.

She knew Tallahassee's street layout well, so she headed for North Monroe on all the back streets. "Just as a public service, you understand," she alibied aloud.

—Thank God, said Bonnie, her seeming voice strangled.

The worst was the heavy Saturday night traffic on North Monroe. She drove a couple of stumbling blocks in the slow lane.

Thankfully, it was cool enough to keep her from perspiring.

Aloha Blaze swerved into the Silver Slipper parking lot with relief. She even had enough sense to circle, and then park in a space pointing out so she wouldn't have to push the damn car out again.

And that's when she realized. She remembered her parents *depressing* the shifter on the far right of the H to get into reverse. She tried that thing.

"I'll be dipped in sh—"

—Aloha! Bonnie interrupted. Time to start being a lady.

"Here we are and I feel ragged as hell," Aloha said.

—You're running out of time.

"But," Aloha went on. "Not one crash, and we are *here*."

She checked her fancy watch. It was pushing eight. Well, whatever happened would. She was frazzled from the driving experience, but elation started within her that she'd actually driven and done so successfully—successfully by her definition.

Plan A: Fight for your man. Down and dirty. It fit her personality and mood right now. Beat them to the restaurant and occupy the reservation and when they showed up, act surprised and confounded and hurt. A nagging thought told her that wasn't the first class approach. And what would she do if they were already seated? Well, Plan B, of course. Plan B was: To be developed if necessary.

—Just be cool, dear.

—Yeah, sure.

If nothing else, *he* would know that she cared enough to go through all this trouble for him. Wouldn't he?

—Maybe, said Bonnie. Men are coarse and disappointing.

She hurried under the awning and into the front door. Before she headed for the reservations clerk, she turned to check her appearance in the door glass. Partially because of her vanity, but mostly worry that her driving travail had disheveled her.

Oh, shit.

Rudd and a woman were walking out of the parking lot coming this way.

Too late!

Quickly, she went to the ladies room and killed a few minutes. She reapplied her lipstick and breathed deeply to calm herself. There was no waiting line so they must be seating reservations pretty well on time.

—What to do? Plan A is no longer operational. Aloha.

—Okay, do Plan B. Bonnie.

—Which is?

—Beats me. Bonnie was dodging.

—Don't chicken out now, look at all the trouble you've gone through to this point.

—Bluster it out. You're pretty well composed now.

—Got it. Execute Plan B. Confrontation possible, but not part of Plan B. Aloha.

Besides, she realized, the elation at conquering her fear of driving was flowing through her like a tornado. This was a different kind of high.

Aloha Bonnie Blaze marched up to the reservations desk. "Sorry I'm a few minutes late. Reservations for Biggs, please."

She raced her memory for his name...Mark.

Plastered black hair and horn-rimmed glasses. He checked his list. "I don't have reservations for Biggs."

"Eight o'clock." She looked into the open-dining room she could see. Suppose she conned her way in and they put her in a different room? Or Rudd was in one of the many individual curtained rooms?

"Nothing, ma'am." He looked at her expectantly.

She fixed him with her glamorous smile. "You are Mark?" At his nod, she went on. "I confirmed these reservations with you a couple of hours ago."

He squenched his face. "I seem to remember—" He checked his reservations list. "Ah. That was a Mr. R. Six."

She shook her head emphatically. "No, Raymond Biggs. You confirmed it."

"I misunderstood, please forgive me." He was glancing around in the dining room behind him.

"It happens," she said, casual voice belying her racing heart. "It figgers. My first dinner with the new boss and—"

Mark waved a waiter over, and soon a table was set up at a far wall. She smiled her thanks to Mark. He melted visibly and that pumped her up.

Now what? She was seated, and turned slightly and could survey this dining room.

Bingo!

Rudd and a brunette, not a sexpot, but shapely and attractive, especially the way her hair framed her face. And worse, the woman was closer to Rudd's age.

About forty feet away, Rudd facing offset away from her table.

Aloha ordered a ginger ale in a champagne glass while she studied the menu. She gulped at the prices.

When her drink arrived, she hadn't yet decided what the rest of Plan B was. But the waiter did not know about Raymond Biggs, so she determined to simply order and eat alone and not pretend as if she were waiting for her date who was becoming increasingly late.

She felt on display, for many of the men had watched her entrance frankly. And some women with envy.

Rudd still hadn't noticed her. Aloha could tell that he was very tired. At least he hadn't lied about that. Plan B was dying with no action.

Damn.

Self-consciously, she ordered a chef's salad.

—Let us engage the battle, Bonnie ventured.

—Done.

Aloha rose, straightened her dress and walked to their table.

The level of conversation in the restaurant dropped off significantly, but maybe that was her imagination. The tinkle of dishes, flatware, and ice in glasses rang louder than the noise warranted.

She breathed deeply, stepped around a table of eight, and into his line of vision.

"Rudd! I *thought* I saw you over here. How are you, sweetheart?" She stepped over to him, bent over so that he could see her breasts were unconstrained, and kissed him on the cheek.

The woman could see what Rudd was staring at, too. And it wasn't her bare shoulders.

Half the room was watching.

"Aloha," he stammered. "What are you doing here?"

She extemporized as she straightened up. "I had an absolute great day and was topping it off with a celebration—but it seems my date isn't going to show up." She pouted. "What are *you* doing here?" Would he take the bait and ask her to join them? And if he did, would she accept?

The woman was watching closely, eyes alert to some kind of subtext to which she wasn't privy.

Avoiding the question, Rudd stood as he was supposed to. "Er, ah, Aloha, I want you to meet Amanda McMullen. Amanda, this is Aloha Blaze."

Amanda stuck out her hand. "My pleasure. What a wonderful name you have."

The compliment startled Aloha. "Thank you."

"Won't you join us?" Amanda was being polite, following protocol, but clearly curious.

Aloha sat quickly before Rudd could change the invitation. "Well, okay. Maybe until my dinner arrives."

—Should I nail the bastard?

—Wait. See what happens. Roll with it.

"What were you going to celebrate?" asked Amanda innocently.

Aloha shrugged. "Something very special, but very personal. I don't really want to say here."

"Oh, certainly. Forgive the intrusion." Amanda sounded as if she were from South Carolina or Georgia. She smiled at Aloha.

Dammit, I want to hate this woman. Aloha felt crushed. It wasn't turning out as she hoped it would. Amanda was personable. Aloha could see how men could be attracted to her. Especially Rudd. Who needed someone. Someone Aloha hoped was herself. But might not be. And this someone was within shooting distance of his own age. Shit.

She turned to Rudd. "It's surprising to see you here."

"I don't think so. I've had this scheduled."

"Scheduled?" Amanda said. "That, sir, is a strange term for a date."

"Poor choice of words," Rudd said, his steel gray eyes cutting into Aloha. He drank his entire gin and tonic. "Pilot lingo," he said lamely.

Aloha saw the waiter delivering her salad.

"My salad's come," she said. "Guess I should go back and eat."

Amanda was obviously trying to follow the interplay between Aloha and Rudd. "Would it be better if I went to the ladies room for a few minutes?"

Aloha found it hard to hate Amanda. So Aloha nodded vigorously.

Rudd obviously hadn't known what to say, but his eyes widened and changed from cloudy to clear. He laughed aloud. He stood. "That would be so very kind of you." He pulled her chair out.

As they both watched Amanda wend her way across the room, Rudd said, "You got guts, young lady." He sat and leaned toward her. His arm scrunched up the immaculate table cloth and he paused to straighten it. "I give you that. You know what you're doing is legally considered stalking?" The twinkle in his eye belied his words.

"Yeah, right after your statutory rape charges." Oh shit, she'd admitted something.

He stared into her eyes and covered her hand with his big one. "*That* is not something I haven't suspected but am unable to do anything about."

He knows! He knows something anyway. No, he's just best-guessing. Under the table, Aloha slipped off her high heels.

She made her voice small. "You're not angry at me?"

He rolled his shoulders. "I don't think I could ever be angry with you." He gestured at the restaurant in general. "You are resourceful, bright, and determined. You did not come in here with a challenge in your eyes—fire, yes; blood, no—you are wise beyond your years. Not only that, but you are one hundred percent knockout gorgeous."

She couldn't slow her heart.

"Who is Amanda?" she asked in a small voice.

Rudd leaned back in his chair and crossed his arms. "I'm not sure it's any of your business."

"I'm sorreee."

"What are you going to do now?" he asked. "It's your party."

"Rudd," she whispered urgently, "don't do this to me!"

"Do what?"

"This. I don't know what's going on."

"At least you finally admitted that."

"Here she comes!" whisper lower yet.

Rudd's smile was strained. "You've gotten this far. See what happens."

—Damn him! He is infuriating. This isn't going anything like I thought it would.

CHAPTER SIX

HIM

First he'd been surprised. Then angry. Then bemused. Now he was simply exhausted.

Since he'd made this date with Amanda, he'd been thinking about it. And Aloha. It had been his intention tonight to diplomatically tell Amanda that it wasn't working and maybe sometime in the future he'd look her up again. Not hedging his bets, but simply stating the truth. He liked Amanda a great deal. However, he had a passion for Aloha, and only today on the flight line had he admitted that he was in love with her.

What was Aloha going to do? Should he suggest something so she could follow his lead? Nah. See what she's made of.

Amanda returned to the table just as their salads arrived.

Out of habit, Rudd rose and held her chair.

Aloha shot him a knowing and challenging look. "I will accept your invite—invitation-to join you-all." She motioned to the waiter. "My chef's salad at the wall table?"

"Right."

"And add a two-pound Porterhouse, rare, and baked potato with all the fixins. And I thank you." She smiled and he nodded vigorously, anxious to do her bidding.

That answered that.

Amanda took on an uncertain look. Then she appeared to accept the situation. "Sometimes you sound Florida cracker, sometimes not. Where are you from, Aloha?"

"Tallahassee. My parents are the original hippies from Up

North, but I've grown up in Leon County, which accounts for the dichotomy of my diction."

Dichotomy of diction? Who was she trying to impress?

"Are you a student at FSU?"

Aloha paused. "No, ma'am."

"Please don't call me ma'am, it makes me feel old."

"Yes, ma'am." A glint of humor in Aloha's green eyes.

Amanda ducked her head into a forkful of house salad.

"Well Mr. Kipling," said Aloha, "what'd you do interesting today?"

"Went to work for a while." Guarded.

"Fly any special missions?" That tough little broad.

She was leaping into the breech. "As a matter of fact, I did. It was real pilot fun. I flew some baggage around."

"I hope you got paid well for working on a weekend?" said Aloha.

"Hell, I was *overpaid*," he said, "*darlin'*."

"Hey, I'm over here," said Amanda with an uncertain smile.

Aloha seemed to notice Amanda. She shook her champagne hair about her shoulders. "She's right, Rudd. We've been rude." Aloha touched Amanda's arm. "I'm sorry. We'll mind our manners, won't we, Rudd?" Her voice turned coy.

Aloha had taken charge.

"Tell me how you got your wonderful name," Amanda said.

"It's kind of personal and I'm not sure I like it; I change my mind on it a dozen times a year. I'd rather not say right now."

"I don't wish to pry."

"Don't apologize. It's a natural question." She chuckled. "Most of us have deep, dark secrets." She didn't look at Rudd. Statutory rape? Jesus.

Their food came, Rudd and Aloha had steaks, and Amanda chicken breast.

Aloha dug into her steak with gusto. That girl had an appetite tonight.

"I understand you're a professor of English," said Aloha.

"I don't think there are any secrets around here," said

Amanda, watching Aloha eat with amazement.

Big steak for a growing girl, thought Rudd. She's got to feed that indomitable energy.

"Denise told me," said Aloha.

"I see. Now I understand why you and Rudd were so, ah, easy with each other. Er, I mean, friendly, considering your age difference and all—" Amanda tried to smile. "I kind of didn't say that very well, did I?"

"It's okay," said Rudd. "Aloha's got thick skin."

"You wouldn't know it, though," snapped Aloha. She held her hand up without looking and the waiter appeared immediately. "Refill on the ginger ale, please."

How did she do that? Rudd wondered.

"My tastes in literature are eclectic," said Aloha cutting vigorously on her steak. She dipped a piece in the bloody juice and ate it enthusiastically. "The end of the nineteenth century in American lit doesn't get the publicity other periods do. Frank Norris, Twain of course. William Dean Howells. Crane. I know he and Norris were naturalists. Most of the others come under the realist category. And I like Jack London a bunch. Horatio Alger made his characters work hard and they all come out winners. But it's difficult not to like Blackmore's *Lorna Doone*, even though the English have a dry and stilted manner of writing."

"I like that book, too," said Amanda.

Aloha nodded. "John Ridd goes through hell and thinks Carver Doone killed Lorna, but she was really alive. Sort of an early potboiling romance novel."

"I never thought of it that way," said Amanda. "Same for the Bronte sisters."

"How about Rudyard Kipling?" Rudd asked.

Amanda said, "Well, he was all right."

"His writing turned much better," said Aloha, "after he married an American girl. Caroline Starr Balestier in 1892. 'Course, after that in 1907 he won the Nobel prize. Took her influence a few years to take hold."

Rudd was astounded at Aloha.

Aloha finished her steak and pushed her plate away. "Sorry, folks, didn't mean to monopolize the conversation."

"Your insights are different," Amanda said, picking at her uneaten chicken.

"Guess my date ain't gonna show. Reckon I'll see him later?"

"Beats me," said Rudd.

"Boy I sure hope so. 'Bye, Amanda. Maybe we can visit again sometime." Aloha stuck her hand out.

Amanda took it. "If you go to college, and it's FSU, I'd like you to be in my American lit survey class."

Aloha looked startled and regained her composure. She did her big, wide grin. "Thanks for dinner, Rudd." She was fumbling under the table. She'd taken her shoes off. A supremely self-confident move, under these circumstances and in the Silver Slipper.

As she was pushing her chair back, Rudd rose and pulled it our for her.

She leaned over to him as she did on her arrival, but this time she kissed him lightly on the lips. Then she turned and walked out of the dining room, obviously enjoying the fact that every man in the room had his eyes locked on her and their heads all swiveled as she went.

Amanda moved her barely touched food aside. "Six, who the *hell* was that and what the *hell* was that all about?"

Rudd usually did not avoid the truth, but in this case he certainly wasn't going to admit having an affair with a girl more than likely underage.

"Aloha is a very bright person and she's playing some kind of game," he said. But he thought, With Aloha's potential, she's rough-cut right now and needs some polishing.

"That bombshell is pure sex," Amanda said. "And every man in this room has a hard tongue. Look, it isn't any of my business. But there were undercurrents that I almost drowned in." She raised her eyebrows.

Rudd was self conscious. Usually he was glib enough to talk

his way out of most situations. "Some kind of game," he said lamely. "It's all I can figure."

Amanda stood. "Cut the crap, Six. When you grow up and want to play with the big girls, call me. Maybe I'll be there, maybe I won't. C'mon, pay up and take me home." She picked up her purse. "Not only that, but she stuck you with her supper check."

"She did, didn't she?"

"Me, too. Let's go."

* * * * * *

When Rudd got home, he drank until midnight. Aloha never came over as she'd hinted.

After a half a fifth of Gordon's gin disguised as martinis, he fell asleep on the couch.

Only to be awakened by Peter Blaze ringing the doorbell and pounding on the door at eight in the morning.

When Rudd groggily opened the door, Peter handed him a box of folded vests. "This is the first load of Aloha's clothes. I got more in the car."

Oh, shit.

CHAPTER SEVEN
HER

Carrying a suitcase, Aloha passed her father on the sidewalk. Rudd was standing inside the doorway looking not very romantic at all, as if he'd slept in his clothes. Aloha wondered what had happened between him and Amanda. If Rudd and the English professor had got laid, Aloha fervently hoped he'd been too drunk to remember it; Amanda sure looked like she'd be great in bed. But right now, Rudd certainly didn't *smell* like he'd been with a woman. At least he was here and not at her place. Aloha decided not to mention Amanda. One because it might upset him and she wanted him in as good a mood as possible and, two, because sometimes if you don't want to know the answer, don't ask the question.

She stopped in front of him. "Denise here?"

He shook his head. "You going to tell me what's going on?"

"I thought Denise would have said something," Aloha said adroitly. Not that she'd told Denise anything—except the overseas part. Certainly not this part, the part about her staying in Tallahassee. If everything worked out according to her plan, nobody'd know she had conned everybody; not her folks, not Rudd, not Denise. And the way Aloha had worded her statement only implied she'd spoken to Denise with all the details.

"Denise didn't tell me anything."

"Oh. See my folks are going overseas and I want to stay in my class at Leon High. So I need a place to stay in Tallahassee."

"Don't you have any relatives somewhere, Aloha?"

"A stuffy old aunt in Kansas City. But I'd have to move there." A not-so veiled threat. Either or. This made it *his* choice. If he chose in favor of her living with him, it signaled more than that choice. It obligated him to a form of commitment, one she so badly wanted.

And while he might be hung over and somewhat ragged this morning, he was no dummy and would figure most of this out. He could keep up with her and that was one of the things she loved about him. She was a very bright girl. No one noticed because of her body and looks; so she didn't wave her intelligence about. She simply used it like she used her beauty.

Rudd cocked his head. Aloha gave him her most engaging smile. She wore jeans, FSU garnet and gold tee shirt, and her denim vest, same as yesterday at the airport, all calculated to evoke a positive response in him. But this time she wore a bra and her hair was pulled back into a pony tail, both to project the image of an all-American girl. The pony tail was designed to be quite fetching rather than accentuate her beauty.

"This is another one of your games," Rudd said flatly.

"Nuh uh. The spring semester will be over in a couple of months and I'll go away," she said. Give him an easy out. Let him think she'd leave for the summer. That might make his decision easier. "Whatever you want, Rudd."

"I don't know what I want." He looked down into the box of vests he was holding.

Likely it was unfair to crowd him in his obvious condition of a hangover and having just awakened, but Aloha determined that if she didn't take charge and push, things wouldn't happen according to plan. Had he and Amanda gotten drunk together? Aloha wondered. —Jealousy doesn't become you. Bonnie again.

—Sure it does, sweetie, just like that streak of vanity.

—Anyway, that doesn't seem Amanda's style, no?

—Excellent point. Aloha cheered up.

She glanced behind her. Her father was coming back up the driveway with another load. She looked boldly at Rudd. "Time to shit or get off the pot, Rudd. What's it to be?"

CHAPTER EIGHT
HIM

She'd told him plainly that he had a choice: she either moves in right here and right now, or he *loses* her and she's off to Kansas City permanently.

As her father slowed to a stop behind her, she said in a louder voice, "Yes, Buddy's room will be fine." She pushed past Rudd and headed for the hallway, her father following faithfully behind.

Oddly, Rudd wondered what genetic turn of fate had produced Aloha from two people such as Peter and Mary Blaze. Peter was slender and Mary was a big-boned blonde with slim hips. Perhaps their DNA had arranged a compromise.

Rudd knew he was stalling, not dealing with the situation. He'd have to say something in the next minute or go along with this—convoluted machination. If nothing else, the past few weeks and especially yesterday at SIXGUN AIR and again at the Silver Slipper, had proved was that Aloha was not only a fine tactician, but a superb long-term strategist. Put her in a war room someplace and the enemy might as well simply surrender. With her on his staff, Custer would still have his hair.

On the other hand, he could construe her threat to move to Kansas City and thus away from him forever as undue pressure, and he didn't respond to threats. But he didn't want to lose her. On the other hand—there were too damn many on-the-other-hands.

His mind raced. Denise. What would her reaction be? Rudd

doubted that Aloha had coordinated this with Denise. Probably, Denise knew only part of the deal.

Rudd wanted Aloha. All the time. But did he need her?

He was still standing by the door with the box of vests in his hands when Aloha passed him with an innocent smile. Followed by Peter.

He'd talked to Peter Blaze only occasionally. And twice Peter had told him he should have named his daughter "Paula" so that they could say they were "Peter, Paula, and Mary."

He didn't have long now to decide. Then it would be too late.

Jail. Jesus. He could go to jail.

But her parents approved, not knowing of his and Aloha's relationship. They thought that she was going to stay with a family, namely her girlfriend, and that he, Rudd had approved the move. They probably did not even know Denise spent most of her time on campus.

Denise would have a fit. And Buddy? If he ever found out.... My God, Buddy....

But this was legitimate. What an opportunity.... Too lonely too long, a refrain now. It's okay to be selfish sometimes, isn't it?

Through the doorway he saw Peter hand Aloha an armful of hangup clothes and pick up a box of teddy bears and stuffed tigers.

This was it. He had to decide.

Right goddamn now.

It occurred to Rudd if he went ahead with this, he'd be assailed by doubts and anguish.

Yes or no?

Aloha passed him again, anxiety pasted all over her. She could see he hadn't moved and still held the box of vests.

Peter came along oblivious to the byplay.

Aloha set her jaw and went down the hall.

Aloha returned before her father did.

Rudd watched her consciously remove the worried look on her face and replace it with what she hoped was a salacious one, but didn't quite work. That alluring bit of vulnerability swung Rudd.

Never mind that she'd threatened him. She was using everything she could. If Colonel Travis had had her on his staff, they'd have lasted at least a week after their ammo ran out, and probably escaped to fight again.

In a moment of extreme clarity, he knew that right now he absolutely could not get along without Aloha Bonnie Blaze. He *must* have her in his life. He answered his own question: not only did he want her, he needed her like nothing he'd ever needed before in his life. Another thought which had been worming through his mind for weeks: this rough-cut gem needed polishing.

A few times in a man's life he is required to make an instant decision that he knows will affect the rest of his life and that of those around him. Most such decisions you have plenty of time to reflect on and think about. Not this one. In some ways, this was akin to a battlefield decision which could change the course of the war.

To hell with doubts and anguish.

So be it.

Aloha stopped in front of him. "Well?" Panic tugged at her eyes and tears were in her voice.

So be it.

Peter was coming from the hallway.

Rudd handed the box of vests to Aloha. "Here put these up. I disremembered that today was the day. You need to open the windows in there so the room can air out."

Aloha stood there, mouth agape, relief visibly washing over her.

"Peter," Rudd said, "Aloha can finish. Let's talk." He gestured for Blaze to follow him into the kitchen.

He had to push it here, see if Peter was really serious. He moved the almost empty Gordon's Gin aside on the counter. He opened the refrigerator, took two Budweisers out, popped the tops and handed one to Peter. He downed his own in one long gulp and got another.

"Boy, eight o'clock Sunday morning!" Peter said appreciatively. "Real guy-stuff." He sipped his own beer.

"Hair of the dog," Rudd said. Obviously this hard-drinking pilot bit didn't bother Peter. So now Rudd knew that Aloha's parents weren't worried about him getting drunk and robbing her virtue. "Sit down, Peter."

Rudd straddled a chair at the kitchen table and took a long swallow of Budweiser. He admitted that it did taste good and cleared his furry mouth and cloudy mind.

"In case you're wondering," said Peter, "I know you are divorced. I know also that Aloha is a street-smart girl who can handle herself very well and she can also exist pretty much on her own. Your daughter is very Christian, and that helped. And, of course, you have a sterling reputation both here in the neighborhood, and in the business community. I checked around."

Jesus.

"And you're a genuine war hero, which didn't used to matter to me because I fought hard against that war. And you, according to the local gossips, raised both of your children almost on your own."

Rudd said nothing, but was uncomfortable being the object of so much scrutiny.

"You probably think that I'm a limp-dicked, long-haired dope-smoking, commie, left-wing, old-hippie fucking scum pervert. I might be some or all of that; but I know what I want. I've a decent job and pay the mortgage regularly. I've always dreamed of being in the Peace Corps and doing my part. Mary, too. Finally, we agreed we weren't getting any younger and we decided to go ahead. We applied and were not accepted. We found an international peace foundation which works in a similar fashion. We might be old and crazy but we're doing what we want. Aloha is my daughter and I do care about her. She should be able to do what she wants, too. What she wants is paramount, and what she wants right now is to stay in the school she's been in with all her friends. And she gets straight

A's of course. So we agreed she could stay." He drank half his beer. "This *is* good. Mary and I agreed that Aloha couldn't stay alone; she had to find, ah, proper accommodations." He drained his beer. "You buying?"

Rudd unstraddled the chair and got them both another beer. His sixth sense and a slight breeze caused him to look at the kitchen door. It was a quarter of an inch ajar, but when he glanced at it, it closed gently as if nobody had been there. He sat back down and handed Peter a beer.

"When do you leave?" Rudd didn't indicate that what Peter was saying was new to him.

"Tomorrow morning. We're going to drive to Virginia. The house is leased for two years and Aloha will get the rent check and pay the mortgage. The difference between the two is two hundred dollars. That's for her, for spending money, clothes, the like. And most will be for her to give you for her share of household expenses and whatever you think her rent to be. Have you thought about it?"

"Not really."

"A hundred a month?"

"Maybe less," Rudd said.

"Aloha is very good with money. She can work it out."

"Fine."

"By the end of the school year, she is supposed to decide if she's going to stay here in Tally for her senior year next year, or go to Kansas City. To do that, she is going to spend the summer in KC. I suspect if she wants to stay with you—and if it's all right with you—next year too, that's okay. I think the girls get along famously and they'll wind up like sisters."

"You've got it all figured out, sounds to me."

"I hope so. Aloha has all her necessary documents—"

"Birth certificate, the like?" Rudd asked, keeping his voice casual.

"Yep." Blaze pulled an envelope out of his pocket and handed it to Rudd. "This is a limited power of attorney, mainly for medical purposes. While she has her own doctor, sometimes accidents happen and parents must okay emergency surgery or treatment. One of the things this does is give you that authority."

Peter Blaze went on to tell Rudd about their hopes and dreams. They wanted to be assigned to one of the emerging African nations, or maybe the Philippines, or maybe serve their time on some crisp, cool Latin American mountain country, where you travel with llamas and pack animals. "The most exciting thing," Peter concluded, "would be learning some new language, maybe Bantu or Tagalog." They finished two six-packs of Budweiser, mostly Peter talking and Rudd listening.

Aloha had the good sense not to intrude. When Peter was leaving, Rudd saw that Aloha had made the most of her time. She'd completely unpacked and cleaned Buddy's room. It was now hers as if she were a homesteader.

Peter and Aloha left, Aloha being circumspect.

She whispered, "I have to stay with them the last night. But think about tomorrow, Rudd, think about tomorrow and tomorrow and tomorrow and after all those tomorrow." She leered. "And tomorrow I'll pay the rent *with* interest."

Rudd wondered only momentarily where she intended to sleep. Rudd worried whether he could contain the explosion named Denise that was headed this way.

CHAPTER NINE
DENISE

Friday afternoon, with classes over and two weeks worth of laundry tied up in a sheet, Denise came home.

Her father was still at work. She opened the windows in her room and then the common living areas. She dumped her dirty clothes in the laundry room. And there hanging were a red lace bra and panties.

Denise shook her head. She shouldn't be surprised. She knew that Aloha was sleeping with Daddy. Denise had hoped that the affair would be short-lived. It wasn't Christian. It was indecent.

Then Denise recalled something about the Blaze family moving overseas.

In the kitchen, Denise noticed things were...not exactly as they'd always been. Her father living here alone during the week was a creature of habit. He never put the salt and pepper on the counter; it was always on the table. In the refrigerator, bottles of milk and ginger ale crowded the tall shelf. Daddy didn't drink milk or ginger ale.

Something tugged at her memory. She went back into the living room. It was neat—and, for goshsakes, dusted. Denise usually performed those chores when she visited on weekends. It wasn't something her father usually thought to do. She checked the master bedroom. More pillows on the king sized bed and it was made, not in the square corner military fashion of her father, but rounded corners with the bedspread tucked in under the pillows.

Okay, okay, Denise. No cause for surprise. It's a natural consequence of a woman visiting occasionally.

But alarm seeped through her. With great fear, she walked, in spite of herself, through the house noting differences where there shouldn't be differences.

She saved Buddy's room for last.

She swung the door open apprehensively.

"Sacrilege!"

The stand with the arms from which hung many vests. Teddy bears and stuffed tiger. Picture of Rudyard Six on the table which served as a desk. Thereon, too, a new dictionary, thesaurus, algebra text, and a paperback copy of *Lorna Doone*.

Oh, Dear Sweet Redeemer, the apocalypse has come.

She had heard nothing.

"Hello, Denise," said a low throaty voice.

Denise spun around. "You!"

"Me."

"What are *you* doing here?"

"Isn't it obvious? I live here."

"Oh, Dear Lord, forgive me for I have terrible thoughts."

Aloha stepped past Denise and set her backpack down. She removed books and notebooks and arranged them neatly on the table. "I have to do a book report. Want to help me?"

"You, you *Jezebel*. You're wicked. You're evil. You're a symbol of idolatry."

Fire came into Aloha's eyes. She ducked her head and glowered from under her dark brows. "I have fought too hard and too long and put too much of my soul on the line to get to where I am and no goddamn Bible-thumper is going to run me off."

"But, I—"

"But nothing. The way things work these days, I have just as much if not more right than you do to be here. It's even on paper."

"You *married* my father?"

"No, silly." Aloha's eyes darted furtively. "He's got a power of attorney over me."

"*Whatever* are you talking about? Your parents *gave* you to my father?"

"Limited power of attorney."

Denise wondered if she'd been wrong all along about Aloha's age. She was so adult, you'd never guess how old she really was. And bright, too, wielding legal terms. Denise slumped into a chair and toyed with the stuffed tiger. "Tony, I thought Aloha was my friend."

"I was and I am."

"You lied to me. Overseas job or something. You-all were going to move overseas."

Aloha levered herself to a sitting position on the table. "I only said that my folks had applied for a position."

"You led me to believe—"

"You jumped to a conclusion and heard what you wanted to hear."

Denise knew that Aloha was right. And that explained the passing remark made by Peter Blaze. "If you knew this weeks ago, why didn't you tell me? Why the big secret?"

"You reaction today, Denise."

"I was your friend. You could have trusted me?"

Aloha smiled wanly. "Trusted you? Me, Jezebel? Lookit the way you're acting now. Geez, Denise."

"Doesn't matter," Denise said doggedly. "We could have talked. We were friends. Like Jonathan and David in First Samuel."

"I'd like to remain friends. But no way could I talk to you about Rudd. You are overly protective. And me being here now would never have happened."

"So you went behind my back and worked your sex on him and he agreed to take you in?"

"I wanted to stay at Leon High, Denise. My parents were leaving town. I want you to stop and think and tell me who else would put me up for the rest of this year and maybe next?"

"A year and a half?"

"Answer me."

Denise rubbed Tony's back for a while and thought. "Nobody I know of."

"There you go. I ain't the most popular person around."

"Maybe with the boys."

"That's not fair," Aloha shot back.

Denise thought some more. Then she spoke in a low and deadly voice. "You've been chasing my father, using your body with him, so that you could *stay* here in Tallahassee?"

"No. I've always liked Rudd. But I didn't know about this peace foundation thing with my folks 'til a few weeks ago. It's the other way around. I'd of—I would have been out of Tallahassee and Florida like a scalded bat if it wasn't for Rudd."

"Oh."

"You can't not know that the girls don't like me because I'm, um, cuter than most, and the boys don't like me because I'm smarter than all of them. They only want one thing—"

"'Cuter' is putting it mildly."

"Listen, Denise. Rudd is the only man or boy who never wanted anything from me to start. And he has given me just as much as he's taken from me. Do you understand?"

"You're telling me this is not just an accommodation for you?"

"Hell, no. I love the son of a bitch."

"Blasphemy—"

Aloha leaned back against the wall and wrapped her arms around her knees. "Self-righteousness ought to be against one or more of the ten commandments. Reckon we can amend them and not piss off Moses?"

"I know you're trying to be funny and take the edge off this, but your mouth can be down in the gutter with your morals sometimes."

Aloha shrugged. "Some guys like it when you talk dirty."

"Not Daddy."

"He doesn't really care. But I'm trying to learn to be a class act for him."

"Maybe it is that you're simply looking for a father."

"Naah. One thing Rudd isn't to me is a father figure."

Denise tried again. "Aloha. You are living in sin with my father, made worse by the fact that you are underage—"

"Is it any worse than when your mother was living here? Me and Rudd get along and care for each other. Can you say that about her and Rudd?"

No, Denise admitted. But this was against the Gospel. "Since we're being so honest, tell me. Just how old are you, really?"

Aloha gave Denise a calculating look, then shook her head. "Sometimes I feel like a hundred and eighteen, but it's none of your goddamn business. You come marching in here and try to ruin a beautiful relationship—"

"I'm trying to protect my father. What you gonna do, girl, when all the nosey neighbors figure out that you are living here in sin with a man and are not married?"

"This is nineteen seventy-eight," said Aloha.

"One day one or more of those jerks who make everything their business is going to tell a cop, call the state's attorney, something. Add it up yourself. You'll be long gone and where does that put Daddy? The Leon County Correctional Facility."

Aloha made a pistol with her hand and went, "Bang, bang, bang. I usually have a plan for almost everything. The only one I can come up with is that my parents arranged this and it is legal—"

"You living here is legal; the illicit sex part is *not* legal, Aloha."

"I'll run to my room and act innocent."

"I have no doubt you can do that thing. Do not, do not get my father into trouble. And even if you slink out of it, you'll ruin his reputation. As soon as a cop walks into that front door, the entire city will know. Business associates and friends alike."

Aloha shook her head. "I don't have all the answers, Denise. What I know is I love Rudd and—and that's that."

"We'll see what he has to say when he gets home."

"He's already said, Denise. Else I wouldn't be here."

Denise was feeling lonely and left out.

"Buddy?"

"What about Buddy?"

"You and he used to date—"

"We went out a few times." Aloha shrugged. "He was too old for me—oops!"

Denise cocked an inquiring eye. "Are you using my father as a surrogate for my brother?"

Aloha shook her head. "He was a boy, just another boy trying his best to get into my pants. I didn't let him. There was nothing between us—then or now."

"Buddy is an engaging, good-looking guy. I'd think—?"

"Nope," said Aloha. "He needed to grow up."

That was true, Denise admitted to herself. But Buddy had really liked Aloha. Upon reflection, Denise could construe Buddy to be the male equivalent of Aloha.

Denise had a frightening thought. Suppose Buddy came home? Not very likely, she thought. But if he did finally decide to face the devil in his past, watch out!

Denise needed to pray and pray and pray some more.

"Hello," Rudd called and the front door closed loud enough for them to hear it. "Aloha? Denise?"

He came down the hall wearing slacks, a beige shirt with a tie, his normal work outfit. "Hi girls. Denise I saw your car. Glad you're home."

Denise stood. "I don't think so, Daddy. I don't wish to disturb your little love nest."

He regarded her calmly. "Is this how it's going to be?"

Aloha went past them and into the hall. "I gotta do some laundry."

"You don't have to go," said Rudd.

"I think I do." Aloha disappeared.

"The *number of the beast*," said Denise. "Six six six, Mr. Six." She held out her fist and popped out one finger. "Mom gone, the first Six." Another finger. "Buddy gone, a second Six." A third. "Now me. The last Six."

"You're not gone, Denise. You're here."

"Not for long."

His face hardened. "It appears you've made up your mind without any facts again. Well, so goddamn be it."

"She's turned *you* against *me*, Daddy."

"Nope. *You* have turned yourself against us. Aloha," he looked surreptitiously down the hall and dropped his voice, "speaks so very well of you. She's said she can't wait for you to come home this weekend, that maybe you and she can do things together. A movie. Shopping."

It startled Denise. But she couldn't help herself. "Because we're so much closer in age?"

Rudd looked at her for a few moments. "You sound like your mother now. I'll forgive you because I know you did not mean that."

"Aloha is taking advantage of you—"

"Did you stop to think, maybe it's the other way around?"

"You're a man. You take what comes your way and that's that."

He breathed deeply. "This is difficult to say when Aloha is so much younger. But if I did not care a lot about her, more than you can imagine, I would not have allowed this to happen. I tell you, Denise, it is more than physical."

"Real love?" Frost edged her words.

"I can*not* not do it. I've fought it and fought it, Denise. I found I have no choice. Do you understand? I have no goddamn choice—"

"Do not take the Lord's name in vain—"

"No *goddamn* choice. My gut and my heart and my soul are driving me. Not my goddamn brain. It's as if it were a physiological imperative. I don't know how old she is and I don't *want* to know. I am attracted to her as I've never been to anyone in my entire life. She is a compulsion to me. So much so that I make no excuses nor will I deny her. It's like an addict or an alcoholic—"

"Second Corinthians tells us to cleanse ourselves from all filthiness of the flesh and spirit."

Rudd stuck his face toward hers. "See my haunted eyes?

"What are you going to do when Mrs. Leverenson or some other busy-body calls the authorities?"

"I don't know."

"What are you going to do when she gets pregnant?"

"Maybe it won't happen."

"You better let me teach you how to pray, Daddy, because that is one fertile female. She's got ovum waiting and rubbing their little hands in anticipation of your sperm."

"Don't talk like that—"

The doorbell rang and Aloha called out, "I'll get it."

Rudd and Denise stood there glaring at each other.

"Daddy, I think you'll have to choose. Me or her. I feel strongly—"

"*Don't* make me choose between you."

"Oh?"

"You might not like my answer."

"Rudd?" Aloha appeared at the entrance to the hallway. "We got a problem."

"You bet," he said, voice angry.

"There's a detective from the Sheriff's Office here."

"Oh, shit." His eyes locked on Denise as if to accuse her of willing this to happen.

"She's from the Criminal Investigations Bureau."

CHAPTER TEN
HIM

He knew damn well what the law wanted.

"Did you?" he asked Denise.

"No," she said emphatically. "How can you think I'd do something like—?"

"I don't know what to think with you anymore, Miss *Six*." He headed for the living room. "I'm coming."

Aloha stood indecisively at the door to the living room.

Rudd walked over to the detective. "Hi there." He forced himself to be cheerful and curious.

She reminded him of a vulture on a fence post.

The woman opened her purse and pulled out a badge and a Sheriff's Department identification card with her picture on it. "Sergeant Ebert, Criminal Investigations Bureau. You are Rudyard Six?"

"I am, what can I do for you?"

At least she was in civilian clothes, Rudd thought. Maybe her car was an unmarked unit, because if it wasn't, the entire neighborhood would know about the visit in an hour. He chastised himself for worrying about his local image. He didn't like this neighborhood anymore anyway. His ex-wife had chosen the location because of school for the kids.

Sergeant Ebert was dressed in a gray skirt and a matching jacket over a white blouse. She was as tall as he was and perhaps twenty pounds overweight. Her hair was in a bun atop her head and she reminded Rudd of the stereotype you think of when someone says "matron."

"Mr. Six, we have a citizen complaint that you are cohabiting with a member of the opposite sex who is underage. Florida statutes are specific and we must investigate all such complaints."

"Who called it in?" he asked, keeping his voice level.

She checked her clipboard. "The party requests anonymity."

"I do too."

"What? You can't do that." She looked at him and he smiled. "Oh, a joke."

"Look, Sergeant Ebert." He nodded toward Aloha. "You mean her?"

"I don't know who I mean, Mr. Six. Is your name Aloha, dear?"

"Yes, ma'am," Aloha said and straightened her shoulders. She stepped forward. "Do I look underage?"

"Everybody under twenty-five does to me," said Ebert. "Are you right now living at this address?"

"I am staying here temporarily."

"For what purpose?"

"To finish school. My parents are in Virginia in training, from there they are going to an assignment for an international peace foundation overseas."

"I see." She consulted her clipboard. "Do you have ID with a birth date on it? A birth certificate?"

Aloha did not lose her composure, Rudd noted. So far he'd kept himself from searching her room for one of those documents: if you don't want to know the answer to the question, don't ask the question.

"I have something better," Aloha said and went out.

"Even if this is legitimate," said the sergeant, "you have to be very circumspect."

"Sergeant, there is nothing untoward going on here. Some neighborhood gossip is playing games with you people."

"That may be so, be we're required to investigate all such complaints."

"Tell me who made it?"

Ebert shook her head. "If we couldn't do it this way, we wouldn't get half the tips we do."

Aloha returned and handed the officer an envelope.

Ebert opened it and pulled out the long legal document. "Limited power of attorney for Rudyard Six concerning one Aloha Blaze. Witnessed, stamped, seal, holy water, everything right." She folded it and returned it to the envelope and handed it back to Aloha.

Aloha handed the detective another piece of paper. "The name and number of the lawyer who drew up the document if you doubt it. The other phone number is where you can reach my parents."

"I don't think that will be necessary now."

"Rudd's reputation has been soiled," Aloha said. "And that's it?"

The sergeant's eyes narrowed. "How about *your* reputation, dear?"

Uh oh, Aloha had gone one step too far. Rudd interrupted, "You can tell whoever made the complaint to mind their own damn business." He determined he'd better show some anger.

"You have every right to be angry, Mr. Six. *However*, you will have to admit that you living here alone with Miss Blaze is worthy of remark and doesn't look kosher."

"Alone?" said Denise from the doorway. "What do you mean? Aloha is my friend, else she wouldn't be here." She held up her Bible. "Psalms 133 says, 'Behold, how good and how pleasant it is for brethren to dwell together in unity.'"

Rudd thought the Bible quote overdoing it; but it was a superb performance. Idly, he wondered how Denise remembered all those quotes.

"Who are *you*?" asked Ebert.

"She's my daughter," said Rudd.

"And my friend," added Aloha.

"Oh," said the sergeant. "This puts a different light on it. I wasn't aware there was anyone else living here."

"Wanna see my room?" asked Denise. "It's not as neat as

hers."

The sergeant said, "Yes, yes I do." It was obviously a response to Denise's challenge.

They all trooped down the hall. Rudd swore to himself, remembering the red lace bra and panties hanging in the laundry room. Ebert glanced in there on the way past and when Rudd looked in, he saw that somebody had removed the possible damning evidence.

Aloha's room was neat as usual. Rudd knew that most personal things were gone from Denise's room but it was always ready for her unscheduled visits home.

They all stopped at the end of the hallway and Denise ushered the deputy in. Dirty clothes were everywhere. Two weeks worth of dirty laundry: clothes, sheets, towels, everything.

"Excuse the mess," said Denise. "I was sorting laundry."

Rudd noticed the framed photo of himself that Aloha kept on her desk-table was now on the dresser in here.

"Now I'm a believer," said Sergeant Ebert.

Rudd and the deputy went back to the living room. He held the front door for her.

"Everything appears on the up and up," she said. "Sorry to bother you." She paused. "You know something, Mr. Six. That girl isn't eighteen—"

"Nobody said she was, and so what?"

"The so what is that if you accidentally see her in the shower or changing clothes and she yells, you're in trouble."

"I'll try to avoid that."

"Even if you have consensual sex, that's statutory rape, to the legal system it falls under sexual battery."

He didn't answer.

Ebert eyed him speculatively for a moment. "It occurs to me that the response I got here was too pat, too many perfect answers to my inquiries." She tilted her head.

"What can I say to that?"

"What *I* can say to that falls under Florida statutes. If I recall correctly, starting with Chapter 794 going through Chapter

800, maybe. The age of consent is eighteen. Penalties are stiffer under twelve—but you don't have that problem—"

"I don't have *any* problem, Sergeant."

"See, some of the language says, oh, for instance, and I quote, 'Engages in any act with that person while the person is 12 years of age or older but less than 18 years of age which constitutes sexual battery under paragraph etcetera commits a felony of first degree' so on. If the kid's under twelve, then that's a capital or life felony."

Rudd didn't know what to think. "Listen, Sergeant Ebert, you know your law—"

"The next section is something about you can't claim ignorance or belief as to the victim's age as a defense."

This was becoming depressing.

"Farther along comes another section: 'Any person who has unlawful carnal intercourse with any unmarried person, of previous chaste character, who at the time of such intercourse is under the age of eighteen years, shall be guilty of a felony of the second degree, punishable...,' and so on. Another one about 'Living in open adultery.' Here's a real kicker. 'Lewd, lascivious, or indecent assault or act upon or in presence of child.' This one says you touch any kid, they call it handling, fondling, assaulting, any kid under sixteen. Second degree felony. To hell with it, I'm tired of talking."

"One thing I can say," Rudd observed, "is that you care. Thanks for caring."

"I think you mean that."

"I meant it."

"I do a lot of work in the schools and with young people," the detective said, looking him straight in the eye, "it's why I'm here on this call. But back to my point. That girl in there is dynamite, nitroglycerine in a bombshell housing, I mean ready to go off big time. I bet half the guys in school are running around after her, tongues out, having wet dreams about her. Watch yourself. If she gets angry with you, all she has to do is shout rape or attempted molestation. Anything."

"Yes, ma'am. I don't know what else to say."

Steel came into her eyes and she dropped her voice. "You trip over your dick, Six, and they will hang your ass. Me first."

"Oh?"

"Just a word to the wise."

She walked out the door and closed it gently behind her.

A tough woman in a tough job, he reflected.

"Daddy?" said Denise coming into the room. "I just want you to know I love you."

"I know, Dennie." Now.

* * * * * * *

Monday morning, Rudd was in his office going over the mail and billing notices.

Ward Zekowski, his partner, walked in and sat on the leather couch. "You old dog. Who is she?"

Zeke was a short, heavyset ex-Navy pilot who'd flown F-4 Phantoms from Yankee Station North off the coast of Vietnam. He had the requisite pork chop sideburns which he hoped distracted from the fact that his hairline was "advancing to the rear," almost even with his ears. Rudd's own hair was no longer GI-short, but it wasn't long, either. He had it so that all he had to do was comb or brush it over and nick in a part. When he'd gone to a faculty party with Amanda, he'd caused quite a stir; but the buzz died down when the word went out that he was a pilot and a war hero years earlier. His good looks swayed the women at the party and the pilot and war hero background won over most of the men. Amanda McMullen was beaming that night, and later she told him that while he was ex-military and all the negative feelings that culturally evoked, his presence had broken the ice for her: she was accepted thereafter and no longer the new kid on the block. "You were eloquent and handsome," said Amanda, "and really punched up my standing."

Rudd shook his head and came back to the present. If he weren't attached, that Amanda....

"Yeah, Zeke, what?"

"Sammy, over at the tower? He said you went for a ride the other weekend—"

"That's old news."

"It's the first time I've seen him in a while. Carlos, the fuel truck driver? He told me the other day about this drop-dead gorgeous blonde—"

"Champagne colored."

"Whatever. You in heat? Or is it love?"

Rudd shrugged. He didn't want to admit anything in public. "I'm comfortably involved."

"Jesus. Bureaucratic horseshit, partner. What happened to Amanda?"

"We sort of broke up."

"On account of this doll?"

"Several reasons."

Zeke grinned, Hollywood-even teeth flashing. "You never took Amanda flying. Sammy said the blonde about knocked his eyes out. Hell, I been flying longer than you and I never got screwed in an aircraft. Well, once, but it was in a hangar and not airborne."

"You're dreaming, Zekowski."

"Though I did take a Russian SAM up the rear over Haiphong."

"It's not the same," said Rudd.

"Sammy said she was very young, as good as he could tell through his binoculars, you old satyr. What's her name?"

"Aloha."

"Hello to you, too."

"That's her name, really, Zeke."

"Jesus. When I get to meet her."

"Sometime."

"I'll throw the bachelor party, just lemme know when."

"That is not in the cards."

Zeke stood. "Something oughta be, Pard. From what Sammy and Carlos said—Not to mention, anybody knocks Amanda out of contention gotta be super special. If you want, I'll make that run down to Tampa."

"Done. I've got to call a realtor."

"Moving?"

"The neighborhood's too crowded nowadays."

Zeke left and Rudd telephoned a realtor he knew. "Put the sign in the yard this afternoon if you can," he finished and hung up.

Remembering Sergeant Ebert and tying that in with what Zeke had said and had not said, made him think.

He reached back to his credenza and picked up his Webster's.

Let's see. He thumbed through the book. "Pedophile. See pedophilia." Okay, pedophilia. Sex perversion in which children are the sex object. Not me, he thought. He wondered what the definition of a child was. By age? So he looked up "child." "A young person between infancy and youth," or "a person not yet of age." What age? Draft age? Driving age? Shaving? Puberty? If female, the onset of menses?

Looking further he found "youth." The period between childhood and maturity.

Well, hell. From what he could tell, he wasn't a pedophile. Rudd wasn't certain if this were reassuring or not.

The rest of the day went smoothly and several overdue payments came in. He was doing well in business. They were going to buy another aircraft, and maybe hire another pilot. There was an old DC-3 Douglas Dakota, known to a million GI's as a C-47, or Gooney Bird, for sale down in Miami. They could haul some cargo in the DC-3. He soon would have to convert some of his cash. Too much sitting around doing nothing.

SIXGUN AIR was self-financing. His house was paid off and when he sold it, he was going to buy a much more expensive place, but would get a mortgage for the tax write-off and, consequently, have many thousands left over. He had to do something with that extra money.

Not to mention he'd been salting away several thousand dollars a month that for years had gone to alimony.

Pleasant prospects. He thought about these and other matters on his way home. Nearer home, he found himself driving faster, anxious to see Aloha.

As he drove into the driveway, he saw the new FOR SALE CALL LEON FIRST REALTY sign in the front yard. He got out and punched the garage door down as he went in the door into the front hallway next to the laundry room.

He pushed his happy thoughts aside as Aloha came to meet him.

He grabbed her up, swung her around, and gave her a long, deep, and wet kiss.

After a moment, she pushed away. "Wow."

"People said good things about you today."

Her raised brows said, "Who?"

"Carlos and Sammy."

"That's nice."

"And Zeke. He doesn't even know you. But he wants to."

"Rudd?"

"And...." Something in her eyes. She was deathly worried.

"Rudd? I'm pregnant."

CHAPTER ELEVEN
HER

Shame. She felt shame, pure shame.

She didn't know whether to tell him or not. But it wasn't something she could or would hide. Aloha Bonnie Blaze had never, ever failed to meet a problem head on.

When he came in, he was so up.

After the kiss, she separated them. "Rudd, I'm pregnant."

It stopped him dead. "Uh, oh. Denise warned me—" He paused. "I thought you were taking precautions?"

"Well, I do. Generally. Sometimes it's so spontaneous, so urgent...well, there isn't time to go find the damn diaphragm."

"Come here." He put his arms around her. She hadn't known what to expect, some acrimony maybe. Not this. She realized her surroundings: half in and half out of a residential laundry room, washer and dryer going full blast. And the dishwasher cranking away in the kitchen and the oven preheating. She squeezed him in relief. She'd been prepared to fight. But that was Rudd, often doing the unexpected.

"Ain't love wonderful," he said.

And her shame disappeared like he'd turned a switch.

He led her to the living room, away from the noise of domestic machinery. He held her again.

"I love you. You're holding me like this...aw, Rudd."

"I couldn't help but notice all the work you're doing, and don't you have an algebra test or something tomorrow?"

"I study while machines do the work. Ain't technology

wonderful?"

"It is, especially when most of this isn't necessarily your job."

"I do my share. You won't take any rent, I have to work it off."

He disengaged them and removed his jacket, tossing it over the back of a chair. "How was your day?"

She climbed onto the couch and sat on the top of the backrest, leaning against the wall. "You're avoiding me."

"Yeah. Okay, spill it."

"I missed my period last month and went to the doctor and she did the tests and lo and goddamn behold, I am with child."

He stood in front of her, her position atop the couch keeping them eye to eye. "Are you happy?"

"Happy? Shit, Rudd, I'm scared to death."

He took her hand. "Don't be. It's natural. I've had a couple of kids already and—"

"*You* stood around. A woman *had* them."

"It's an everyday occurrence," he continued, ignoring her interruption. "You and I even went through it ourselves when we were very young."

She couldn't stop them, so the tears plunged out of her eyes and fell unimpeded on her Buckskin fringed cowgirl vest. "It's not funny! Rudd, I am *so young*! I'm not ready for this. My *body* is not ready for this." Oh, were I religious like Dennie, God, for You could comfort me all the days of my life.

—There's no easy way out on this one, dearie.

—It's unfair!

He sat on the couch, back against the armrest and looked up at her. "You don't want the baby?"

"I don't know what I want. I'm just miserable. I've been worrying about it for weeks and then all day today, I thought I was going to die."

He began massaging her left leg. "The world is still going around, people still function. We'll live through this."

"The baby might not live through this."

His hands stilled. "Abortion?"

She shrugged. "Doctor Parkinson, she said if I'm gonna do that thing, the sooner the better and especially in the first trimester." It sounded so academic, the way she'd put it.

"You're in the last month of school—"

"Fuck school."

"If that's the way you feel—"

"I can get an abortion on Friday and be back at school Monday."

"I see."

"I don't think you do, Rudd. You talk around it. What do *you* want?" He'd been noncommittal so far.

"Um. Whatever you want, Aloha."

"Wrong answer, Six. You got to commit yourself."

For days she'd worried and worried and had finally decided that if she were pregnant that she would do whatever Rudd wished. Have the baby or get an abortion. She based this decision on the fact that she loved him totally and therefore would go with his decision to please him.

—Not any more, Aloha.

—Yes, ma'am.

—Lissen, sweetie. It's *your* body. You got your entire life ahead of you. You want to be chained to a kid?

—No, Bonnie, no.

—Suppose Rudd wants the child?

—Talk him out of it. Or ignore his druthers.

Seconds, then a minute went by. He spoke carefully. "I've had two children and I learned to love them then I had to learn to raise them. In retrospect, those were good times, regardless of *her*. I am proud of my accomplishments, fathering and raising two fine children, never mind Buddy's outlaw status. It also occurs to me that I would kill to have a child with you, that's how much I love you. Another thing, but not a major factor with me, is what Denise continually preaches: that abortion might well be murder. I don't know that answer. That's hard to go along with, especially at first when you've just got a lump of protoplasm growing." He paused and began rubbing her feet.

"But it is your body and you will have to do the hard part."

"I'm scared it will change our relationship."

"No."

"You wouldn't love me when I'm big and fat."

"I'll love you more."

She was silent.

"You're a very clever person, Aloha. I know you've thought about what kind of impact it will have on your schooling and your reputation, walking around the halls pregnant."

That downside had indeed gone through her mind.

"So you want me to have the baby?"

"I do."

"You haven't known about this for even an hour yet, and still you can make that quick a decision?"

"I've done it before, I'll do it again."

He had. She recalled using that against him when she conned him into her agreeing to her living here.

"But I want you to carry the baby to term under one condition only."

"That is?"

"Marry me."

Wham! The blow hammered her in the solar plexus and she couldn't breathe. She slid down the couch into his lap. "Rudd."

She couldn't withhold the tears this time, either. "The best thing I could ever give you, your child," she said choking.

—Alert! Alert! screamed Bonnie. You're folding. Down deep you'd decided *against* bearing the kid. And *I am* down there, deep. I know what's going on down here.

—I know, but Rudd wants—

—Tell *him* to bear the kid. You are too young, you got too much to do before settling down.

—If I go ahead with the abortion, I'll lose Rudd!

—If he deserts you now, he ain't worth keeping.

—No matter how much I love him?

—No matter.

Aloha Blaze found herself fighting against a strong biological imperative. She desperately wanted Rudd's child. On the other side of the issue is that she did not want a child herself, and was bright enough to see how it would forever alter the course of her life. She could have kids when she was old, like twenty or thirty. Not now.

—*I want to realize my dreams, not just dream them.*

—Right on, girl! said Bonnie proudly.

The most difficult thing she'd done in her entire short life was right then. She left the embrace of Rudd, got unsteadily to her feet, and said. "I've thought about it a lot. I'm sorry. I don't think so." Tears would not come. She'd turned down his marriage proposal in the doing.

His face fell. "Honest to God?"

"Cross my heart, Rudd. You don't know how this is tearing me apart."

"More than just you. And my proposal?"

"Until this minute, that was the single thing I've wanted most in my entire life."

He said nothing, he simply looked at her with dispassion.

That bastard! He was using this to force her to marry him. She hated him for it, but admired his machinations. It was something she'd done before: maneuver the situation to where he had to make a major decision and the consequences of that decision were exactly what Aloha had wanted all along. Very clever.

"Aloha," his voice was surprisingly level, "have I not treated you as an adult, with the utmost respect?"

"Yes." Where was he leading?

"Keeping that in mind, be advised that I have a kind of proprietary interest in your welfare—"

"I'm not your goddamn chattel."

"I did not say you were. That's why I prefaced my words as I did. My position would be to do what's in your best interests."

"According to you, not me, Rudd. You think it's best for a—a teenage girl to have a baby? Think again, buster."

"Fuck me to tears," he said, and pushed himself off the couch. She followed him to the kitchen and watched him pour a large glass of gin. He drank it in two quick gulps.

Then the dishwasher gurgled, draining noisily. "Down the drain with you, too, Six."

She went to her room, climbed on top of the dresser, and crossed her legs. She put the two teddy bears and the tiger in her lap. "At least I have some friends left."

She forced herself to study algebra and after an hour, couldn't remember a thing.

She went down the hall and folded the clothes in the dryer and transferred the wet clothes from the washer. Doing laundry always helped her relieve stress. She went into the kitchen and put up the dishes. She noticed that the Gordon's gin bottle was significantly lower.

She looked into the living room. Rudd was sitting there, glass of gin in hand, staring at the blank television screen.

She didn't know what do to, so she did what used to help.

She went into the garage, hit the door button to open it, got Rudd's old ladder she'd used to seduce him, took it outside into the side yard, and propped it next to the house. She climbed up on the roof, and went to the peak and sat down. She popped a can of ginger ale and sipped at it.

—What now, Bonnie?

—Keep on, dear. You done good so far.

—I got pregnant.

—Oh, yeah. Other than that.

—Don't you understand? He asked me to marry him. I said no.

—I understand. I hurt, too.

—I ache. I'm dying.

—You're not back to where you started. Months ago you were just another hot date to some pimply-faced jerk-off. You've grown. You've learned.

—Maybe Rudd will see it my way, maybe?

—Anything's possible. But he's sorely disappointed down there.

—I still love him.

—He'll come around, sure.

A cool May breeze blew down from Georgia and Aloha Blaze lay back against the roof pitch and watched stars come out and play.

Maybe she should just finish school and go to Kansas City and forget Tallahassee.

After a couple of hours, she went down the ladder. Back inside, she saw Rudd was asleep on the couch. There wasn't much gin left in the bottle.

She folded the last load of laundry from the dryer, showered and went to bed—her own bed.

At three o'clock in the morning, about an hour after she'd forced herself to sleep, she was awakened by a gentle shaking.

"Go away."

"I don't want anything," he said. "Wake up, Aloha."

Finally, she rolled over and opened her eyes. Light splashed from the hallway. He hadn't changed clothes, so he hadn't been to bed yet.

"Can you hear me?"

"Yes."

"I love you. I didn't want you to go to sleep without knowing that." And then he was gone and the light died.

* * * * * * *

The Woman's Centre was in an office park off Thomasville Road. Rudd drove them into the parking lot. He parked and they got out and locked the doors.

Aloha could see the obligatory pickets. At this time it was a desultory crowd, six or seven women and one child, all just kind of wandering around in front of The Centre with their signs dragging. All of whom raised their attention to a new level when Rudd and Aloha went up the steps. But the momentary commotion died down.

Rudd signed them in and they sat in the waiting room. One middle aged couple and two single girls, likely FSU students, were waiting.

Rudd filled out the forms and gave them back to the receptionist.

"Your daughter?" the woman said, scanning the forms.

"No."

"We like to have parental approval. You can't even send your child on a field trip without signed authorizations, you know?"

Rudd handed her a copy of the medical power of attorney that Peter Blaze had given him.

"Most excellent."

Then she took his check for two hundred and fifty dollars.

Next they found themselves in a joint counseling session with the other people waiting.

"I'm the nurse. My name is Jill Jillson. They call me JJ." JJ leaned against a cluttered desk and addressed those sitting around her. "Today we counsel you, tomorrow the doctor comes from Pensacola and performs the procedure. You have overnight to think it over." JJ had weak red hair, thick glasses and was wearing jeans.

As JJ went over the procedures, she flipped pages on an easel. She talked about alternatives. She listed the methods. "Menstrual extraction. Prostaglandin—that's IV or injection. Then there's dilation and curettage, the old D and C. Finally, what we're doing tomorrow, vacuum curettage. That's cannula suction after cervical dilation, local anesthesia. All of your pregnancies are twelve weeks or less. This is the one with the fewest complications, minimum of bleeding and discomfort. Although you do face the possibility of hemorrhage, infection, uterine perforation. These things happen. Not frequently, but they do. Vacuum suction is guaranteed to work unless you've got a double uterus or something weird in there. Bleeding is going to be like a very heavy menstrual period, a bad one. Maybe some cramps, but nothing you can't handle."

Aloha didn't want to hear any more. But she did.

JJ continued. "Don't use tampons for a few weeks. Do sanitary napkins." She glared at Rudd and another man. "That's like

Kotex." She went on. "Your period will start again in a month, maybe six weeks. No sex for at least a couple of weeks, then see how you're healing. Most importantly, strenuous activity: Don't. Not for a few days. Don't carry in the groceries. Don't kick the dog. Don't toss your five year old in the air."

There was more. But at the end, JJ reminded them. "Abortion is final. You cannot undo it. Think about it and we'll see you tomorrow. Or not. And remember. Two-piece outfits."

As they got up to leave, Rudd whispered, "She reminds me of a biology teacher who loves to lecture."

When they left, there was a whole new crew of pickets. Their signs were Bible quotes, and slogans such as MURDERERS, MURDER IS A FELONY, and THOU SHALT NOT KILL.

"Sobering," Rudd said as they drove off. "If they know the schedule, and that's very likely, then they'll be out in force tomorrow."

"I'm scared, Rudd."

"Of those Christians?"

"Not at all. About this whole thing."

"You can change your mind. That's what the delay was designed for."

"I'm more scared to have a baby. Gosh, I didn't expect to have to make such decisions."

"Life one oh one. I admire your stick-to-it attitude."

"Could we go home and you hold me?"

"Yes."

"And hold me all night, too?"

"I promise," he said gently. She slid over next to him and dropped her head and felt oh so small.

And he did. He held her tight the entire night. Occasionally, one of them would sleep, or exchange a few words. They did not have sex.

Once, Rudd said, "I love you. I want to marry you anyway."

She wept for a while. "No. Not out of pity."

"It's out of love, not pity."

"Oh, Rudd. I do love you. Ask me again in a year."

He didn't answer, and she turned over and they spooned for the rest of the night.

As Rudd drove them back down Thomasville Road in the morning, he said, "My offer still stands. I want to marry you."

"I want to marry you, too, Rudd. But not under these circumstances—"

"Under any circumstances."

"Thank you, dear. And don't worry." She smiled. "Think of this as a test of character."

"I already have enough character," he said.

"It's a simple surgical procedure."

"I already bought a dozen boxes of Kotex."

"One would have been enough, you crazy man." She giggled for the first time in days. "I bet you looked funny at the checkout counter."

Again they parked. This time they had to push through a line of picketers, and this time they were the objects of derision and catcalls.

As they went through the door, Rudd said, "It's early. There will be more of them when we come out."

Aloha straightened her shoulders and marched in The Woman's Centre like a soldier.

* * * * * * *

Aloha went into the procedure room alone. Rudd had to sit in the waiting room.

JJ was washing up. She eyed Aloha's clothes. "Good. Most of them forget." The two piece outfit. "Strip your shorts and panties. Hop up on the table, feet in the stirrups."

As Aloha stepped out of her panties, JJ said. "Scared?"

"Hell, yes."

"You don't show it." JJ eyed Aloha as Aloha folded her shorts and panties. "Guys follow you around and fight over you?"

"Um, sometimes?" Then Aloha got it. JJ was trying to make her feel at ease.

JJ handed Aloha a pill. "Tranquilizer. In case of pain and helps relax."

On the OB table, feet in stirrups, Aloha felt exposed to the world and the impact of what she was doing hit her.

—Oh, my God.

—Steady, dear. This is the right thing.

—I know. But Jesus. It's me. It's happening to me.

—You been growin' up fast lately. Time for another giant step.

—I'm scared.

—Me, too. I wonder what else life's got in store for us?

—Bonnie, I don't even want to think about that.

JJ threw a surgical blanket over Aloha. It covered her from the waist to her knees and she felt less exposed. Then JJ took Aloha's temperature, pulse, and blood pressure. She noted them on a form.

A woman in a surgical outfit came in the back door to the procedure room. She was maybe five eight and very slender. She had coal black hair and a high forehead.

"This is the doctor," said JJ. "She's a gynecologist."

Aloha had read a schedule on a clipboard and knew the doctor was named Graham. "Hello." But they never introduced the doctor by name, so Aloha thought of her as The Doctor.

"Paracervical block?" said The Doctor.

"I tranked her."

"Looks all right."

The Doctor worked. JJ assisted and handed The Doctor instruments, stuff that Aloha didn't want to know about.

"These two rods?" The Doctor held up two curved metal rods. "I'm going to use them to dilate the cervix."

"That's nice," said Aloha. She realized the tranquilizer had kicked in.

The Doctor worked for a few minutes.

A machine went on and a narrow plastic tube disappeared under the surgical blanket.

The Doctor worked slowly for about ten minutes. "Got to take your time here," she said, "get all the fetal and placental tissue. Really important to get all the placental tissue. So this." The plastic tube was gone and The Doctor held up a weird looking spoon. "A curet. It'll tickle, but I have to scrape the lining of the uterus."

She worked for a few minutes and then moved back and stood. "Finish up and clean up, JJ."

"Sure thing, Doc."

The doctor started peeling off gloves and looked down at Aloha. "You are very young, Miss Blaze. And those dunce-heads outside wonder why we do abortions." She shook her head sadly. "I was young once, too." She turned and went to wash up.

Suddenly, Aloha understood why the woman came all the way from Pensacola. Suddenly, The Doctor was human.

* * * * * * *

Aloha rested on the table for a little while. Then she got up and dressed slowly and awkwardly.

"You can sit in the waiting room until you feel you're ready to go home," said JJ.

"I'm ready now."

"Remember. No strenuous activity. There will be some bleeding."

"JJ? Thanks. Thanks very much."

"You know what, Aloha?"

"What is that?"

"You're all right. I hope we helped."

"You did," said Aloha.

She walked out of the operating room gingerly, and Rudd was immediately at her side.

"I can walk."

"Lean on me."

"I am, oh I am."

It didn't hurt like she thought it might. She felt strange in her womb, probably more psychological than anything else.

"How do you feel?"

"Funny. Strange. Like they sucked out my insides. Slightly disoriented. Fuzzy."

The sunlight struck her like a blow and was very uncomfortable.

She allowed Rudd to help her down the stairs. The building was atop a short hill, the sidewalk and parking lot at the bottom.

The noise level from the picketers rose significantly. They knew what had happened. A healthy young woman had walked into The Centre and the same one came limping out, walking carefully.

"Killers!" A fat woman was in their way.

"Please excuse us," said Rudd, pushing the shouting woman aside.

They stepped off the sidewalk into the parking lot and came face to face with Denise Six holding a sign on a stick which read: MURDERERS.

"Oh, my God!" said Denise and fainted.

CHAPTER TWELVE
HER

Denise fainted and someone in the picket line screamed. The crowd surged around them.

Rudd knelt to check Denise. She looked lifeless and was sprawled askew against the stairs. Had she hit her head?

"Get away from her, you filthy scum!" screamed a woman.

Rudd stood immediately, picked up Aloha and ran for his car. He put her behind the wheel. "I've got to help Denise. If they come over here, start the car and leave. If they threaten you, drive slowly through them. Or run over the motherfuckers, I don't care."

He locked the door and slammed it. Then he ran back to the growing crowd. Aloha watched him rip people out of the way. Soon he was swallowed by the swirling crowd.

Aloha felt weak. That damn Denise. Wouldn't you just know it was meant to be? Maybe there is a God and this is a trick He was playing on all three of them.

Aloha had to twist to see. Denise was her friend; she ought to go help Rudd. But Rudd wanted her here, out of harm's way. Give him a minute. Wooziness came and went. Today there were men in the now-large crowd. Aloha breathed in the stifling air of the closed car and wondered how really Christian those people would be.

Then she saw Rudd emerge, carrying Denise. He was going *up* the steps to the abortion clinic! Of course, that's where the nearest doctor was.

The crowd realized what he was doing and two men leapt after Rudd. One, a big blonde man, grabbed Rudd by the arm and the other, wearing an Atlanta Braves baseball cap, jumped on his back. Rudd kept going, shifting Denise to his left arm in front of him. He jerked his right elbow out of the grasp and swung it back viciously. The man who'd been holding him stopped immediately, and Aloha saw blood and teeth flying from his mouth in a rainbow spray. Rudd did not stop. With his free right hand, he plucked the other man with the baseball cap off his back, slammed the man to the ground and whirled in a martial arts movement of some kind and kicked the man backward as he started to rise.

Rudd continued his turn until he was facing the clinic and went swiftly up the remaining stairs.

The second man had lost his cap and was rolling slowly down the grass embankment alongside the stairs; the first one was puking blood into his cupped hands; it had even stained a strip of his blonde hair. People in the now-silenced crowd hurried to their aid, the picket line completely forgotten.

Aloha lowered the driver's side window and slid down, her brain fuzzy and feeling giddy. She reached up and tilted the rearview mirror so that she could watch.

Three other men were scrambling up the hill and running to intersect Rudd.

Aloha hit the horn three times sharply in warning.

She slammed the door open and started across the parking lot. She saw that her warning had alerted Rudd. Denise still in his arms, he stood atop the hill and the three men slowed to approach him. Aloha could see nobody was saying anything.

Rudd turned to face them and therefore couldn't see two other men angling up the hill behind him.

Just as Aloha shouted another warning, the first three attacked. Rudd's right leg lashed out and one went down, the other two dodging their friend and diving for Rudd. Rudd buckled as the two tackled him. Denise fell limply.

The final two had not yet reached the scene of the melee yet, but were coming cautiously, obviously waiting to jump on the unsuspecting Rudd.

Denise's body was lying there and Rudd was struggling with the two men. His arm was lashing out, not punching, but slashing.

Aloha sprinted up the hill. She felt a new wetness between her legs. She shook off the wooziness.

The two men sneaking up behind Rudd were almost to him, and she could tell they were going to ambush Rudd.

Women and children were screaming warnings to their cohorts as Aloha shoved a male bystander in her rush. He staggered aside.

Rudd had disabled a fourth man, leaving one on the ground with him still engaged in combat. Rudd was handicapped by trying to protect Denise's body.

Aloha didn't know what she was going to do when she reached the two men and she didn't think about it.

The bigger man had a white shirt and tie on and she reached around and grabbed the tie.

"Hey!" she shouted at them and jerked the tie hard, hoping it was not a clip-on. His head ripped around and his body followed. He was easy to trip and push down the hill, no longer in the action.

Her second opponent was short and compact and had fanatical eyes.

—Oh, shit.

Aloha faked a clawed hand at his eyes and when he raised his hands to protect himself, she put everything she had into her kick and her foot slammed into his crotch. He lifted a foot off the ground and his eyes bugged out like ping pong balls and she felt something rip inside her. And that pissed her off more so she kicked the son of a bitch one more time, this time with her other foot and the ripping in her womb wasn't as bad, but she knew she shouldn't have done it but, God, it felt satisfying to nail the bastard.

She felt moisture run down the inside of her left leg.

—Oh, Christ.

—Yeah.

The human fireplug had turned blue and was folding forward, arms across his abdomen, spittle and puke flowing from his nose and mouth and his face was down at his knee level and Aloha felt liquid running down the inside of her right leg, too, so she kicked the son of a bitch once more, this time in the face. He flipped back over, crashed, and rolled slowly and clumsily down the hill.

Aloha fought against doubling over, it was just psychological she reassured herself.

Rudd scrambled up, bodies lying all over around him. There was blood on his shirt and hand and Aloha bet herself that somebody had a busted nose.

Rudd hurried toward her, apparently no worse for the fight. "Aloha—"

"I'm okay. Get Denny inside."

—Will my sex life ever be the same?

—If not, you'll have some real memories.

—Bonnie!

Rudd snatched up Denise and went inside.

Aloha climbed the final two stairs and turned, standing sentinel in front of the door, eyes challenging.

She surveyed the carnage. It seemed men were strewn all about the hill and on the grass below. There were puddles of vomit and splashes of blood on the green grass.

Women and children stood below, hands to mouths and regarding her and the scene with awe and consternation. A man crawled down the hill on two knees and one elbow, dripping blood and an arm askew.

Aloha heard sirens and knew it was over.

The crowd forgot her and had turned into a disorganized group of people all wandering about aimlessly, yapping like a gaggle of jazzed-up geese. The quick and sudden violence had seemed to render an immediate character change in the crowd.

The door opened and Rudd appeared beside her.

"You put them in their place. I never saw one man dominate so many."

"They give Christianity a bad name."

"Denise?"

"She just fainted. Right now she's lying down on a couch drinking orange juice, jaws clenched tightly from finding herself *inside* that den of iniquity." He looked Aloha over. "I'm glad you're on *my* side." His eyes paused as he stared at her white shorts and legs.

"Aloha?"

"Yeah, I know. I'm bleeding."

Rudd slammed open the door and dragged Aloha inside. "Doctor! She might be hemorrhaging."

In two minutes she was back on the OB table, feet in the stirrups, The Doctor and JJ huddled in front of her.

"I said no strenuous activity," JJ pointed out mildly.

"I don't follow orders well." Aloha felt cold and clammy and dizzy. She said so.

"Minor shock," said The Doctor.

"I'll be okay in a minute."

"Vital signs," said JJ. "Pulse 120, going down now. Blood pressure 105 over 70 and rising."

"She's coming out of it," said The Doctor.

"I saw you through the window," said JJ. "Oh, how often I've longed to do that." She touched Aloha's hand. I don't know who your man is; the relationships are like spider webs. But he is a Real Man."

"Thanks," replied Aloha, feeling better by the minute.

"You're one hell of a Real Woman, too," continued JJ.

"JJ, you're in that club?"

"Yep. You, too, Aloha."

"I'm trying."

"Surprisingly, everything's okay," said The Doctor.

"It would've been worth it anyway," said Aloha.

"Most of them are only doing what they think is right," the Doctor observed. "You cannot fault them for that."

And Aloha learned more from The Doctor's attitude than she learned in school.

Sheriff's deputies came in and Rudd talked to them for a while, and The Doctor, JJ, and some other patients gave statements.

The Doctor let Aloha go and deputies escorted them out.

Denise was gone.

As they were leaving, JJ said, "Aloha? I *don't* want to see you again."

"Me, neither." Aloha gave JJ a wide smile and a hug.

Shortly, they were driving home.

"What are we going to do about Denise?" Aloha looked down at her blood-ruined white shorts.

"Nothing we can do. It's up to her. Perhaps I should have discouraged her when I realized how hardcore that church is." He smiled wistfully. "But raising a teenage daughter, I was scared to death she'd get in trouble, so what harm could religion do? I mean, it could only help. That's what I reasoned."

"It looks like you were right. I didn't do the religion bit and look at me."

He did. "I enjoy looking at you. It gives me much pleasure."

"What I'm trying to say, silly, is I'm living illegally and in sin with an older man, and I've just had an abortion. I'd say the difference between Denise and me is striking."

"Everybody's different. I like you the way you are."

"Even though I didn't have your child?"

"Even though." He looked at her strangely. "I will never, ever, forget you charging up that hill and taking out those two men. You've many surprises in you, Aloha. When we choose up sides in life? I'm picking you first on my team."

She dimpled. "But I do learn from my mistakes. I am now in possession of a prescription for birth control pills."

* * * * * * *

Aloha was right. By the next day she felt okay. She recovered even from her alleged strenuous activity except for a pair of white shorts which would not come clean. Monday she went to school and got an A on her algebra test.

When she got home from school, Denise's car was in the driveway. Inside were some boxes and a couple of suitcases.

Alarmed, Aloha went straight to Denise's room. She was loading a final box, the room no longer sprouting those personal items and now it looked vacant.

"Denise don't."

"I hope you are proud, Aloha. It was inevitable you'd get pregnant. I told you-all so." She stuffed a clock into the box.

"This appears permanent."

"Very much so."

"Lemme call your father. He'll want to talk to you."

"No."

"Denise, I know he'll at least want to kiss you goodbye and tell you he loves you."

She shook her head. "He loves only you, and sex with you."

"That's life, honey." Immediately, Aloha regretted her flippant remark. "Look, the semester at FSU is over in a couple of weeks. Come live here, with us—"

"You are *so* gracious."

"You are my best friend."

"Not any more. Find somebody else."

"I got Rudd, and that's all I need," Aloha said savagely. "I never had any friends, other than you." Aloha sat on the bed, totally dispirited. "What are you going to do?"

"The Church of the Redeemer is going to send me on a missionary trip."

"Will you be back in time to start your sophomore year in September?"

"I don't know; I don't think so. I don't care."

"Don't throw away your college education, Denise."

"Advice from *you*?"

"Call it what you want. You and Rudd, you both always talk school and college and education, that's the first thing that attracted me to you-all."

"Fine. Then *you* go to college."

"I fully intend to."

Denise slammed the box down. "And Daddy will pay for that, too!"

"I am no chattel," Aloha said for the second time recently. "I have my own money, too."

"Bully for you. How much do you charge for a trick?"

God, that hurt. She flipped her hair and spat out, "Twenty-five bucks for boys, Real Men get it free."

Denise looked uncertain, as if she didn't know Aloha was toying with her. Oh, well, thought Aloha.

"You have split this family," said Denise. "Before you seduced my father, we were very happy."

"You could still be."

"You, Aloha, have just committed *murder* in the eyes of God and man alike. *Thou shalt not kill!*"

"Denise, I have some money, if you need any."

"I want nothing from you, much less your filthy money."

"Maybe you will cool down. I'll have your father call you tonight over at the dorm."

"Don't bother. Six, Six, Six. I will never talk to him again." She glowered. "And you are the Daughter of the Devil."

"Jeez, Denise, you're making this terribly difficult. Are you aware of what your father went through when he thought you were dying?"

Denise picked up a photo album out of the box. "I just remembered, I don't want this anymore." She tossed it at Aloha.

Aloha snatched it out of the air and put it down. She said nothing.

Denise grabbed the box and walked stiffly out the door, down the hall, through the living room and out the front door. "You've driven me out of the house I grew up in."

Aloha followed her. This will kill Rudd. "You didn't see your father at The Woman's Centre," she said. "He went berserk when he thought something happened to you—"

"He beat up many people—"

"He was rescuing you, he didn't know what was wrong with you, and he had to get you to a doctor."

"So what?"

"He loves you. Hell, he even ignored me then. You were all he could think of." Aloha was exaggerating. Anything to stop Denise. Rudd would wilt away and die. First his wife, then his son, now his daughter.

"One of those he brutalized was my boyfriend."

"Life sucks sometimes, Denise. You've got to roll with the punches." She winced at her poor choice of words.

"Maybe Mom was right," Denise said. She got in the car and started it. "I am grateful to you for not marrying him. For that would make you my stepmother."

"Denise, please don't do this," begged Aloha.

"Get out of my way, murderer, seductress. Jezebel. Daughter of the Devil."

Denise backed out, not checking for traffic, which, fortunately, there was none, and sped off down the street.

Aloha was depressed. Because of her, Denise was gone. Because she'd wanted Rudd and went and got him. Then she'd ignored proper precautions and had an abortion that was the last straw. Exit one each Denise Six. Would Rudd blame her? She didn't know, but she was afraid. Even if he said he didn't blame her, would he really? Would it eat at him from inside until it burst forth?

Aloha was miserable.

So she went and climbed the live oak tree as high as she could and wedged herself between the trunk and a branch until Rudd got home.

Apprehensively, she climbed down.

She reached the ground at the same time as he was retrieving his briefcase from the backseat of the car.

He saw her face. "What's wrong?"

She told him as they went inside.

"Goddamn them! They've turned my own daughter against

me."

Aloha couldn't hold back. "I did my part."

He shook his head angrily. "You might have been the trigger. But you didn't do it. You and I cannot live our lives by her expectations."

"We could have observed propriety more."

"I'm forty-seven years old and I don't want to know how old you aren't, I'd say there ain't any propriety involved. We have to live our lives the way we want, here and now, because here and now will become there and then and the time will have gone away forever."

His wording was convoluted. "I understand."

He held her by her shoulders. "I'm not sure you do. That is the reason I agreed to us living together. Not just true love. You are the one most singular thing that has come to me in my life, and I did not want to lose you. In a flash of clarity, I knew true love and I knew that specific time and place was our one opportunity, choose wrong and the door would shut forever. Period. Right or wrong, and it's mostly wrong, I realized a few things. I learned a long time ago to look past the packaging. You're beautiful, the whole world knows that. But it doesn't matter to me. What does matter, is that you have a surprising character that attracts me. That we are compatible in bed is part of it. That we get along so well is another part of it. That's complimented by your intelligence, not only that but you use your intelligence quickly when you need to. I like your judgments, your values. I admire greatly your ability to step back and do today what's important for tomorrow, not just today. Like that abortion. Next year and the year after that, they don't matter. But year after year, they do matter. I can tell you're blaming yourself for Denise. Well, we all share the blame. But this is us and she has no business taking it so hard."

She hugged him fiercely.

He tried to telephone Denise at Reynolds Hall, but she wouldn't take his call.

Then he called the Church of the Redeemer and talked to the

pastor.

"What'd you people do to my daughter?"

Aloha couldn't hear the other side of the conversation, so she just watched.

"No, I did not beat up anybody. They were preventing me from getting Denise to medical help. I thought she needed it."

Pause.

"None of your damn business."

Pause.

"You realize you're kidnapping her? She's not twenty-one, yet." Rudd looked stricken at what he'd said. He glanced his apology to Aloha. "Never mind that. If she wants to go, I won't stop her."

Pause.

"Where?"

Pause.

"Look, give her a message?"

Long pause.

"She's welcome home anytime, under any circumstances. If she needs money, just call. Thank you." Rudd hung up.

He turned to Aloha. "At least Denise did not tell them specifically about us—our situation." He cocked his head at her. "Maybe we dodged another bullet there. Somehow it doesn't seem important, now."

"Denise is important now." The self-righteous bitch. Aloha was still angry that their friendship had meant so little to Denise.

"He said they were probably going to send her to Costa Rica. At least it's safe. Wouldn't it be funny if that's where your folks ended up? Anyway, I thought that I had screwed up yet again. See, since I'm a pilot and sometimes fly to Mexico, Yucatan, Haiti, the Caribbean islands, lots of places, I always had my kids have a passport in case I'd take them with me. So that is one obstacle the Church of the Redeemer doesn't have with her; consequently, I think they can get away with doing it without parental permission."

Aloha thought. "And Denise knows you could raise hell with

the authorities and stop them sending her—"

Surprisingly, Rudd grinned. "She reminds me of you. If I raise a stink that I haven't given my approval, then she can do the same about you and me living together."

"If you and I were not, um, together, and she simply wanted to play missionary now, drop out of school and all, would you let her?"

"Probably. I let her get away with murder anyway."

"If she wanted to move in with some guy, would you let her?"

He closed his eyes. "I don't know, hon. I really don't. I'm finding my 'druthers don't matter." His head dipped to his chest and he whispered, "Now I lay me down to sleep, I pray the Lord my soul to keep."

* * * * * * *

The school year ended and Aloha Blaze had the highest grade point average among juniors at Leon High. She wrote her aunt in Kansas City that she was staying in Tallahassee in order to attend summer honors classes, and that she intended to finish school at Leon High and would not right away pack and move to Kansas City. She got a letter from her father which said their training was going fine and they'd been assigned to Mauritania and Upper Volta, two countries not adjacent, but nearby.

At least once a week he sent her flowers.

It became a practice between her and Rudd to spend their time together when he came home in the evening. They would address current events or talk about the books she was reading. Or he would tell her about aviation, how to fly, the characteristics of different aircraft.

She knew the definition of a reciprocating engine, that the empennage on an aircraft is the tail assembly, or she could discuss pneudraulic systems, and the hybrid design between an aileron and an elevator is called an elevon. She knew that the contrail behind a jet way up in the sky wasn't smoke, but ice: water is a by-product of air compression which is the main event for jet engines, and water precipitated into the atmosphere at certain temperatures you find at thirty thousand feet freezes immediately into ice crystals.

* * * * * *

One day she came home to find Rudd in the garage. Rudd had only one car, and in the other bay she found a large exercise mat and a large cylindrical rubber bag hanging from the ceiling, approximately head height to about a foot off the floor.

He came through the door in shorts and a T-shirt. "Go change. Wear a bra."

"Then I should assume the game isn't going to involve sex?"

"You are incorrigible."

She favored him with a leer and a grin.

When she went through the house, she noticed the flowers, carnations, which Rudd had brought home. It was Flower Day.

In the garage, she kissed him. "Thank you for the lovely flowers, darlin'."

He returned her kiss then held her at arm's length. "You showed good instincts at the Women's Centre," Rudd said. "This thing is called a heavy bag, or a kick bag. Weighs maybe sixty pounds." He steadied the bag. "Never give your opponent time to think, time to plan. Keep him off-balance." Suddenly, he swiveled, lashed out with his right foot, striking the bag about five feet up. He turned with a backhand slash, slammed the bag with the heel of his hand. Then his left hand banged into the bag. "No time to think. I kicked him in the chest, chopped at his neck, and cold-cocked him with an All-American haymaker, just to make sure." The bag was swinging wildly, the attaching chain clinking, and the swivel attachment to the garage ceiling groaned and complained.

"Wow. Karate," said Aloha.

"Yes, and no. Karate, t'ai chi, savate, judo, jujitsu, aikido, tae-kwan-do, kung fu. You don't need to learn a discipline, you need to know unarmed combat. Techniques, moves, pressure points, self-defense. Skip the mystic bull shit."

"If you say so."

"Pay attention, there will be a pop quiz later. When it happens, move to a loose and ready stance like this, mobile and ready. Body sideways—less target and you protect vital organs. Feet shoulder width, even weight, short steps, arms and hands ready."

Day after day, week after week, month after month, they practiced daily and Aloha became proficient. She knew the four principles of self defense: prevention, awareness, release, escape. She learned defense against kicks while lying on the ground, how to kick, how to take an attacker down to the ground, turn and lifts, parries, knee and elbow strikes, head butts, front and rear holds and protection from front and rear holds, throws, chokes, wristlocks, armlocks. More.

Her favorite was the reverse elbow strike and she practiced that with a fury and finally the kick bag was spinning like a top.

"You got it," Rudd observed. "You know the basics, practice, hone your skills, practice, and practice some more."

"We worship the god of repetition?" asked Aloha.

"Over and over. Until it becomes automatic."

* * * * * * *

She began to read *The Tallahassee Democrat* every day, cover to cover, sometimes **The Florida Times Union** from Jacksonville, or the *St. Pete Times* or *The Miami Herald*. When Rudd flew elsewhere, he always brought home out of town newspapers and she enjoyed seeing the concerns of people from different places and it was interesting to compare sale prices, and what businesses were doing what. She also read weekly news magazines, though the more newspapers she read, the less she agreed with the magazines' interpretation of the news. And she studied, for she was taking an advanced summer history course. Since she had no social life other than with Rudd, she had plenty of time. She'd always gotten good grades and didn't have to put a lot of effort into it. Her parents had indicated that measuring knowledge wasn't an accurate science, and what was important was how she got along with her classmates, and what she thought about the school-thing experience. Consequently, Aloha did not get along well with her classmates, and she did get superior grades, for herself in rebellion and to show them she was good at the disdained academic life.

One night they were talking, and Rudd asked her about her parents. "You said you hated them. Why is that."

She felt self-conscious. "That was then. I was trying to make a point. I don't really hate them; I just didn't like them at the time." She was finding she liked them more now that they were several states removed. "At least my father wasn't one of those 1950's judgmental fathers controlling everything and always saying stuff like 'Because I said so.' He and my mother were more 60's beatniks than the hippies they're usually painted as."

"Peter seems to be the action agent, mostly." He sipped his gin and tonic. "It is my guess that you have encountered the usual mother-daughter friction."

"So what?"

"Just curious, Aloha. I want to know what makes you tick."

"Trade you even. You tell me about your ex-wife."

"Marge? Done."

"My mother is the one who named me. Everybody knows my father wanted to call me Paula. Peter, Paula, and Mary. But my mother insisted. And she has never told me why. I suspect why."

"What's your guess?"

She curled her legs under her. "Keep in mind their generation. They were in the original wave of hippies and haven't really grown out of it—another reason for my, ah, distaste. Anyway, I think she had an affair or the free love was flowing, and thereupon I was conceived."

"Raising the possibility that Peter is not your biological father."

"Exactly. I will say they've never admitted anything, and Peter has always done more than his share. Both shares being not much effort. It, um, this is hard to say, you know?"

"Don't talk about it if you don't want. We can discuss football."

"It's time, Rudd. I have to say it, okay?"

"Go ahead."

"Their free and easy attitudes—I was adult long before my time."

"It's one of your endearing qualities and you had the intelligence to use it right."

"Thanks. Sometimes, I did all right. With their example, I, well, I always regarded sex in sort of a casual way. Free love and all that. Until I met you and I found out what sex was really all about."

He clinked ice in his glass, eyes hooded, unreadable. "Hell of a thing to do to a kid."

Her eyes downcast. "If we ever have children? I vow to raise him, her, or them like you raised Denise. And I don't know Buddy these days."

"You would not believe Buddy. He's one giant problem we don't have to deal with, thank God. So where do you speculate the name Aloha came from?"

"In Hawaiian, aloha means hello and goodbye. I've guessed that my mother was trying to recall those days. Maybe she still carried a torch for whoever impregnated her. Maybe not. Maybe it was to welcome me to the world and wash her hands of me at the same time."

"I see. Sometimes when *I* think of the word aloha, it evokes sort of a sadness, one surrounded by bright and varied flowers. Sort of a bittersweet leave-taking."

She nodded. "I've thought of that. Or just the image the different flowers give you. Lots of white plumeria with the yellow centers and red hibiscus. Bunches of jungle green. Another term used back then was 'flower child' and that might have been Mom trying to wax poetic as many of the beat generation were supposed to have done."

"Didn't you ever ask them?"

"Several times. Peter told me he didn't know and that Mom insisted and he just went along. He feels that Aloha was simply an extraordinary name, that Mom was avoiding Jennifer or Betty or Susan."

"And what did your mom tell you?"

"She wouldn't. She always said I'd figure it out someday. Another possibility occurred to me. When they asked her what name to put on the birth certificate, she was stoned and said 'Aloha.' And her comment that I'd figure it out was meant to be cryptic and cover up the fact that she didn't remember."

Rudd laughed. "I don't know them very well, but that explanation fits what I do know."

"So that's why sometimes I like the name and other times I don't."

"From the unknown to tropical beauty. I choose the latter. Verdant, lush, colorful, bright, grabs your attention. Smells good, too."

"You mean fragrant," she teased.

"Another thing?" he said, voice turning serious. "You cannot stop tropical vegetation. It just keeps growing. You got to nuke it to change its course—"

"Jeez, Rudd, that's kind of deep. But that's the deal with my folks. I don't take after Peter very much, if at all. So the different father theory might explain why. And they never did the kid things. They never took me to church—who knows, I might have liked it. They never gave me a birthday party. I got a present or two, but never a party. And I always had to listen, when they bothered talking to me, to a bunch of mindless crap about everybody being the same and we all ought to help each other out. Whyn't they help out their daughter, the hell with the rest of mankind for a while. Then they just didn't have time for me—or make time. Damn. I'm getting angry thinking about it."

"Don't." He turned her sideways and began massaging her back and shoulders. Since she was wearing only a black lace vest, his hands went under the fabric and kneaded her flesh.

"Maybe I'm fortunate, because of them, I will never smoke

anything or do any drugs." His hands felt good.

"You turned out okay from what they say about smoking and pregnancy."

"I don't think Mom smoked much, Mary Jane especially, while she carried me."

"I'm glad she did," Rudd said. "As bright as you are now? Else you'd be a brain surgeon or rocket scientist already and not here with me."

"Thank you—I think."

"These things drive me crazy." He flipped the vest up and out of the way.

"Is that all you ever think about?"

"It's all I can think about with you dressing like this around here." His hands roamed. "It's indecent."

"You love it."

"Well, yes."

As the summer wore on, their lives fell into routine. Occasionally, they went to a movie or out to dinner, careful not to do so anywhere near home. By mutual consent they kept a very low profile. Aloha practiced her unarmed combat skills. They continued to read together and have long discussions every evening.

Once, she asked him about Marge. When he demurred, she said, "You promised."

"I did. What do you want to know?"

"Everything."

"She was from Daytona. I went over there, to a flight school called Embry-Riddle Aeronautical University when I was very young. Even back then I wanted to fly. Anyway, of course what I did was go cruise the beach, like all young men and women. I liked it, so I got a part-time job as a lifeguard—I was Red Cross certified. One day this girl had a flat tire and the tide was coming in fast so no one else would help her. They were all hurrying off the beach. The short version is that we ended up marrying. Eventually, I went off to the fighting U.S. Air Force, did their pilot training and went to Vietnam. She became a travel agent, and a good one. Our children were born by then."

"So she was alone with two children while you're overseas fighting a war."

"That is what *I* thought. She wasn't all that alone."

"I'm sorry, Rudd."

"Not your fault. I understand life. Sometimes somebody else attracts you. People change, stuff like that. Go on with that new person, but don't lie about it." He shook his head. "I thought we were in love. I didn't know what love was, not back then. But now...."

"And you caught her cheating?"

"Not exactly. Not right away. What happened was, I started SIXGUN AIR and Zeke came along and became my partner. We worked hard back then. Lot's of flyboys out of the services at that time, so that's why I couldn't get an immediate job flying for an airline right away, or, more descriptively, an airline which was attractive, job and salary wise. Lot of guys in my boat, the ones getting out who had multi-engine jet qualifications. It also made the start of SIXGUN AIR difficult—all the competition. I worked long hours, I'll say that for Marge. She had to be there at home. Things got easier and Marge, her travel agent job was picking up. She was the one to be the tour guide on arranged tours. Her ticket and accommodations would be free from the airline or hotel, from Mexico to Greece, for bringing her group to their business. What she was doing, was she'd shack up with someone on the tour, some unaccompanied male. I think she'd get them a big-time discount they couldn't refuse. Mostly rich, divorced guys anyway. I don't want to talk about it any more."

"I understand. I bet she was gone more and more and you had to raise two children."

"That's the way it happened."

"How did it end?" Aloha asked gently.

"With a whimper, not a bang. Sometimes she didn't return for weeks and weeks and we wouldn't hear from her, either. She set up shop eventually in Atlanta. They say you got to go through Atlanta to get anywhere. So one day she shows up, packs a couple of suitcases and I come home from work, hot and tired and had been up the night before with Buddy who'd puked all night from the flu or some goddamn thing and I wasn't ready to be a nice guy about anything. Hell, I was cocked and loaded and not very understanding.

"She tried to tell me she was sorry, things weren't working out between us. I said she had to be here for things to not work out and I didn't care anyway and she said that was obvious, that I loved aircraft more than I loved her. Just a throwaway line, but it angered me. I said stuff like aircraft clothe and feed this family and pay the rent, too, and not only that but I haven't seen your share in the joint bank account lately, either.

"She said, 'Well, then, fuck you very much. I'm out of here.' And then she handed me the preliminary divorce papers to sign. She'd already been to a lawyer." He shook his head sadly. "Was I ever young and naive." He was silent for a long time. "Crash and burn."

"Have you seen her since?"

"I didn't see her in court. I simply signed here and there and agreed to alimony. I was numbed. I'd never done anybody dirty and had never dreamed it could happen to me." He tried to smile and failed. "Now I'm old and mean and wise in the ways of the world."

"Nuh uh," she said. "You're kind and gentle and so very thoughtful. I know sometimes I do things wrong or say the wrong thing, but you make a considerable effort—"

"That's because you're so lovable."

"You're still vulnerable, Rudd. Like a little kid. You hide it, but Denise? I can see it's killing you inside. You have tremendous loyalty to those you love and when they betray that loyalty, you die some."

His face twisted and she sensed his pain. "Everybody dies at least once; but parents die many times." His body was sad and his voice slow.

"If Marge had helped more, done her share—"

"I used to call her 'my little Marge' like the television show.

She did not like that, come to find out. One day she took a poker from the fireplace, and hit the television, and it wasn't turned on, just like Mickey Mantle going for the fence. After that I didn't call her 'my little Marge' again. She'd developed a temper."

"It's tough for some women, alone with kids."

"Don't be so damn understanding, Aloha. You're supposed to dislike Marge."

"Sure. I don't like her a lot. What she did to you. But had it not worked out that way, we would never have gotten together."

"I'm not sure," he said. "War makes you believe in fate. I didn't then, but I'm not sure I don't now. I think you and I were born to be together."

Later, Aloha was to remember that conversation. At the time, she reflected how happy she was, her life with Rudd was straight and level, in pilot lingo. Until now, her life and relationship with Rudd had not been calm, to say the least. Something was always happening, something threatening them, their happiness.

One of the jobs many small aircraft companies do is offer pilot training. Rudd and Zeke had several other pilots they hired part time to give the lessons.

Rudd took Aloha flying frequently. If he was flying cargo or passengers and there was room and she didn't have class, she'd go with him and began to learn how to fly. He also required her to learn the ground school curricula. Of course, she was a quick learner and a natural pilot. Eventually, she could fly every aircraft at SIXGUN AIR. This surprised her. She loved flying which was not the same as driving —but sort of similar. You control a huge hunk of metal. No longer was she as afraid of driving as she had been.

She was quite busy and quite happy.

One evening toward the end of summer, they were having their nightly discussion about literature and current events and flying. On the coffee table sat a bouquet of lilies. Flower Day.

The telephone rang and Rudd leaned over and picked up the instrument. "Yes." He paused and a stricken look shot across his face. "Not now—" His hand dropped and he looked at the phone and returned it to its cradle. He drained his drink.

She always worried about him when he was at work flying. She knew he was a good pilot and flying was safe; still aircraft fall or get knocked out of the sky every day. And Aloha was no exception to the worry-about-your man rule. So this time the first thing that occurred to her was that one of his aircraft had crashed—maybe Zeke.

She scooted over on the couch and grabbed his arm in support.

"What?" she asked.

"It was Marge," said Rudd.

"Your ex-wife."

"The same. She's in town and she's on the way over here."

CHAPTER THIRTEEN
HIM

Marge. He hadn't seen her in years.

"It's strange," he said. "Marge just said she's coming over. The times when she suddenly appeared in the last few years, she'd meet us, me or Denise, or both, whatever, at a restaurant. It's not like her to do this. I can't figure it."

"I can," said Aloha, getting to her feet. "Denise told her what's going on and she's coming over here to check on you and me."

He rose, too. "You could be right. I can't figure what angle she'd be working."

Aloha had her hands on her hips. "There's no way we can make all traces of me disappear in a few minutes."

"It's not necessary," he said.

"We don't know that, Rudd. From what you've told me, she's not trustworthy. She might be holding a grudge. She might want to find out for herself and call the law—"

"I'm not sure she'd do that. Why would she telephone in advance?"

"Maybe she doesn't want to find us in bed together, she'd be embarrassed. Maybe she wants to stir the pot before she gets here. I don't know—"

Rudd said, "I think maybe she's just curious."

"We can't take that chance."

"I don't know—"

"I do. I'm going to take a long walk or something. Hmmm.

She'll know you're living with someone—"

"Depending on what Denise told her—"

"If that's how it happened," Aloha said and went to look out the front windows. "Rental car pulling up. She must've called from a pay phone." Rudd could see her studying Marge as she got out of the car and came up the walk. "You never told me how good-lookin' she was—make that is. Not bad for an old broad—oops, sorry."

Rudd moved to the window and saw what Aloha was seeing. Marge was a pageboy-cut strawberry blonde, with a tight waist, narrow hips, and large breasts. She always dressed fit to kill, and today was no exception. She was wearing a peach mini-skirt which revealed long, shapely legs. Marge had always had a special walk, one reason she'd turned many a male head.

"See you."

"I don't want to deny you, Aloha. We've nothing to hide."

"Let's not take any chances."

"Maybe you're right."

Aloha went into the hallway. When the doorbell rang, Rudd heard the door to the garage open and close.

He went to the front door and swung it open. He said nothing.

"Hello, Rudd. Long time no see."

"That's a fact."

She stepped up and kissed him lightly on the mouth. "A *very* long time."

Rudd didn't know how to react. He wanted to be bitter, as he'd been after she'd left him. But now he had Aloha and could not generate that emotion. He decided that he was curious and would just see what she wanted.

"Come in and sit down. Can I fix you a drink or something?"

She never had approved of his drinking. "Coffee would be nice."

"Let's go in the kitchen and make some."

"Sure." She followed him to the kitchen. As he was digging out the coffee pot, she said, "I got to go. Back in a second."

He poured the water, added the coffee, and plugged it in. As he was getting a cup out, Marge came back in the kitchen.

"This place hasn't changed, and yet it's very different."

Marge hadn't gone to the bathroom. She'd snooped through the house.

He smiled at her. "I wanted to keep it the same just to remember you as you used to be."

"Who's Aloha?"

"What do you mean?"

"That stuff in Buddy's room. It doesn't belong to Denise. The name 'Aloha' is written in some of the books."

"Nosey. Aloha is staying here." There, he'd admitted it.

"With you?" Marge's eyebrows rose.

"With me."

"Is she making you happy?"

"Very." Something overhead creaked and he wondered if it were the wind or Aloha parking herself on the roof again.

"Why are those books high school books?"

Rudd studied her. She was staring a challenge at him.

"Let us start over, Marge. Denise talked to you, right?"

Marge grinned. "A couple of weeks ago. I just wanted to see how far you'd lie—"

"You know I do *not* lie."

Marge cocked her head, shook it and her hair rustled. "You don't, do you? You never have."

The coffee was percolating and the room smelled of it. He fixed himself a gin and tonic. "Why the visit, Marge?"

"I wanted to see for myself."

"The lovely Aloha Blaze?"

"Yessir. You're looking good, Rudd. You could attract any woman—"

Maybe Denise still cared enough about him to launch Marge at him. "What're your intentions, Marge?"

She sat at the kitchen table. "This is sort of cozy, huh? We used to sit in here and talk and plan for the future. That coffee ready?"

He poured it, added sugar and put the cup in front of her. He sat across from her, his drink lined up with her coffee. "How've you been, Marge? We never hear from you."

"I'm not one for writing. I'm always on the go. I've got a large and thriving agency. Thompson Travel." Her maiden name. "I've got an offer for it by one of the really big companies. They like my client list. Very loyal, very wealthy, very idle."

She did not acknowledge the irony of the word "loyal" and he did not mention it, either. "Are you looking for advice?"

"Nossir. I'm trying to figure what I'm going to do with my life if I do sell out."

"Hence your trip here."

"Right. From what Denise said, it was possible you might be free and we could see if the spark would rekindle."

"You always were outspoken."

"When I decided to run down here from Atlanta, I determined not to screw around. It occurred to me that you might want to trade in your teeny-bopper for a real woman."

Jesus. She wasn't mincing words. "What do you know about Aloha?"

Marge sipped coffee. "That she is very young, probably jailbait, and that you've dodged the law pretty well."

"Think what you like. I'll deny nothing."

"You look amused, Rudd. You remain pleasant and good natured as ever."

"You remind me a bit of Denise trying to manipulate. I was thankful that Denise had talked to you. You know what happened?"

"I do. Your sweetie got pregnant—at least she's old enough to have and fail to have her periods—and you got her an abortion. Witnessed in some fashion by Denise. It tore her up. How could you let Denise be so goddamn religious, Rudd?"

"How? I didn't have any help and I left the choices to her."

"From what I understand, she turned out the opposite of Aloha."

He shook his head and got up to fix another drink. "It's a long time since I've been the object of one of your backhand zingers."

"I apologize, Rudd. I have to decide in forty-eight hours whether to sell or not. This was one of my options if they bought me out, I just gotta go full steam and find out."

"You address it as if I were willing to get back together with you. You're not exploring the possibility, you're attacking."

Her eyes turned hard. "How old is this Aloha?"

"Denise didn't tell you?"

"She didn't know. She guesses somewhere under eighteen. Maybe even several years."

"I will say that it is none of your business, and it is none of Denise's business—now. Denise made her own bed and now she can lie in it." Though he admitted to himself that Denise was welcome back anytime.

"You've driven us all away, Rudd. Me. Buddy. Now Denise."

"It sure as hell appears so, doesn't it?"

"So you're serious about this Aloha?"

"Her first name is not 'this.' And whether or not I am, I say again, is none of your concern."

"You must be, I saw the for sale sign out front. I know you've bought a three-hundred thousand dollar house way out Thomasville Road—"

"About. It's under construction and not yet built. I need the mortgage deduction on my taxes."

"Great big new house. Just you and her. Way out."

"The property was expensive. Those houses are on five acre plots."

"Isolated. You're trying to hide this Aloha out, away from other people's prying eyes."

"I did not say that." But it was true, he thought. Out there you could know your neighbors or not, it was up to you. And the house was not visible from the road or other homes nearby. You could hide a ton of sins in five wooded acres, he thought guiltily.

"But it's true."

"It doesn't matter, Marge. Forget it."

She covered his hand with hers. "Look, Rudd. I'm sorry.

Hell, I've been thinking about you for a long time. I knew you were not living with anyone before her, and I kind of wanted to get back together. It just seemed—so right." She put so much warmth in her voice and hand that Rudd believed her. "Denise and Buddy are gone. It would be like old times, just you and me." She smiled, her face full of beguiling charm and he had to jerk his mind loose.

"Why, Marge? Why?"

She sat back. "After all these years? I made a mistake. I admit it. I should never have left. You're a good man, Rudd Six. I loved you once and after chasing all over the world I've realized I never stopped loving you. I remember that you were warm and fun, even when you were working fourteen hours a day or coming back from Vietnam on R & R. I miss that. I miss you."

"I admit to malfeasance on my part, working such long hours. It wasn't fair to you or the kids."

"Nowadays I understand you have to do what you have to do to earn your living. SIXGUN AIR must be doing well, money running out your ears."

"It is. Business is booming."

"Knowing you, you wouldn't spend hundreds of thousands on a house if you didn't have that much or more in the bank."

"Why this fixation on money, Marge? It's a recurring refrain here tonight."

She pushed her coffee cup at him. "Refill. No fixation. If I come back, I want to live in style. This is a plebeian development and we don't belong here."

"You might not, I was comfortable—"

"Until?" she prompted.

"The neighbors do not like my lifestyle, frankly. I've sold the place to a man who is going to rent it to college students."

"You cunning son of a bitch! Get even time."

He rose and fixed her coffee and himself another gin and tonic. The coffee smelled good. "In the old days, the pot would perk day and night, when you were here." He sat again.

"We could be back to those days. Say the word."

"Pretty soon I'm not going to be able to ignore what you're saying. Why, Marge? Are you broke? Do you have some terminal disease?"

"Rudd, I'm tired. Honest injun, I'm just burned out. If you put all your energy into the travel business, it's a seven day a week affair, week in and week out all year long. And while it seems that I'm always on vacation, that's not the case. I am flat-ass bone tired. I want out, and I need *something* to twist my metaphorical arm—"

"Thanks for the compliment."

She gulped coffee. "Don't jump to conclusions. Once I started thinking in those terms, I started thinking about you and our life. The more I did so, the more appealing it became."

"What's your offer?"

She looked startled. "You get me, fully and unconditionally."

"Marriage?"

She shrugged indifferently. "Yes, if you want. In addition, I could be your translator. I know lots of languages. French. Italian. Spanish. Mexican. Some Greek and German. A little Japanese. I can even understand some of the old guard up there in Atlanta."

"Everybody we deal with, even in the islands and in Mexico and Central America speaks English."

"Do they ever hustle you to transport drugs?"

"Sometimes. It's not hard to turn them down."

"I hope you don't turn me down. Let's go back, Rudd. Start over. I care for you. I know I can make you love me again."

"I appreciate the personal hell you are going through to do this, Marge. You must be serious."

"I am. Dump the kid. Get back a real woman."

"No."

"Are you in love with her?"

I am, he thought. Instead, he said, "You have forfeited any right you ever had to know about my private life."

"Bullshit!" She threw the half-empty coffee cup across the kitchen. It smashed on a cabinet and pieces fell on the counter below, coffee dripping onto the Gordon's gin bottle. A flash of her old temper.

He rose and began cleaning up the mess with paper towels. "Theatrics. Did you contrive that for my benefit?"

She smiled engagingly. "It wasn't very convincing, no?"

"No."

"I wanted to get under that calm skin of yours. I still can't. What are we going to do about Denise?"

Marge sounded genuinely concerned. He put the towels in the garbage and poured her another cup of coffee.

"*I'm* not going to do anything. She's old enough. She's made a couple of what I think are bad decisions, but I can't think of a way to reverse any of them. Let God look after her for a while." Suddenly, he realized that's what he'd really been thinking, he just hadn't put it into those specific terms—until now. He felt better for admitting it.

"I confess," Marge said slowly, "that I told Denise she could live with me. She laughed." Marge tossed her hair angrily and stared into her cup of coffee. "That's sort of what made me think of asking you to take me back."

"Sometimes being a parent ain't no fun."

"That's what I thought before and chucked it all, god*damn* it all." She looked up at him. "And here I am baring my soul, to you of all people. Are you really in love, serious stuff, with this Aloha?"

He didn't answer.

"It seems she's making you happy. You certainly appear so. You chose her over Denise—"

"Wrong," he said mildly, but with authority. "*Denise* chose to no longer live here."

"For a goddamn teeny-bopper."

Rudd stood. "Have your opinions. I don't have to listen to this bitterness. Please leave."

She rose slowly. "You're not the Rudd I knew—"

"I'm not. Now I know who I am and why I am that man. For once I'm at peace with myself. Do you understand how important that is? While I've grown up over the years, I attribute most of my revival to Aloha." He bit his words off. He didn't want to unload on Marge.

"*I* do understand how important that is, Rudd. Oh, dear sweet Rudd. Why in the *fuck* do *you* think I'm *here*?" She was fighting her own demons, many many of them, and obviously not getting very far.

"That's a start, Marge. You'll have to work it out yourself. Me? I have Aloha, and I'm very happy."

She went into the living room, turned and came into his arms. He felt her wet cheek against his. "I'm glad for you. I really am. I wish you well." She pulled free and went out the door into the night.

He escorted her. "Do you ever hear from Buddy?" he asked.

"All the time." Her voice was enigmatic. She got in the car and he closed the door for her.

As she started the car, he said, "Good luck to you, Marge. I do mean that."

Marge Thompson drove slowly down the street as if she were deep in thought.

Rudd stood there watching the taillights. A sadness closed in on him. He saw wasted lives. He saw much of his life was wasted. But not anymore. Yet the past assailed him, depressed him. He remained as if rooted to the driveway, images and flashes and sounds of the past bombarding him like a fucking atom smasher. His breathing became quick and shallow and pain grew in him—

And then Aloha was there, taking his arm, and he felt the electricity recharge him and his pain went away and he shook off some of his demons.

When they got inside, he saw she had pieces of attic insulation stuck in her hair. "You heard?"

"I did. I needed to know if I had to come down here and fight for my man."

"You were here," he said, "you were here."

* * * * * * *

At the end of July, Aloha Blaze had a birthday, but she did not tell Rudd. Unwittingly, this was the day of the week Rudd sent her flowers and the two dozen red and yellow roses made her feel all warm and wanted. Finally, summer ended and school began.

They moved into their new house. Aloha could catch the school bus about a mile away on Thomasville Road. Rudd bought her a motor scooter to run to the grocery store or wherever she wanted. Still frightened of driving, she declined a car. Rudd did not ask why.

Rudd was making a subconscious effort—well, half conscious, half subconscious, half wishful thinking effort—to make Aloha into his dream girl. He admitted selfishly that he'd always wanted a special lover, and Marge certainly had not filled that position. And, Rudd realized Aloha was worth the effort, by God, and he'd teach her—let me rephrase that, he thought. I could avail her of the opportunities. Not only just for his own selfish reasons, but for the fact she was so bright, so eager, it would be criminal to not do it. A nudge here, a suggestion there, and she'd learn the tools. She'd have an unlimited future. No hourly wage and baby factory for Aloha.

After all, one of the basics of life those who fly daily come to terms with is that they were mortal; Rudd knew he would not be around forever.

Their first night in the new house was a crystal clear night. Rudd had designed, and the builder had constructed, a sun deck atop the house. You could get to it by a door from the upstairs hallway. Then you climbed a winding stair up the structure.

They were sitting on a blanket under a quarter moon atop their house on the sun deck. The breeze was enough to keep the mosquitoes away. He was drinking his gin and tonic and she was drinking ginger ale from a frozen mug.

"Are you ready?" he asked.

"Always."

"Not for *that*. Just a minute." He ran down the stairs and was soon back with a bottle of champagne. He handed it to her.

"Christen the house?" she asked.

"Why not?"

"With *pink* champagne?"

"I didn't study the protocol."

"How?" she asked.

"Throw it at the chimney over there."

They stood at the waist-high railing—which had been constructed against her wishes. Aloha wound up and brought her arm forward in a sidearm motion, holding the bottle by its neck.

Naturally, the pink champagne failed to clear the top rail and exploded. The glass went forward onto the roof, but pink champagne splashed over Rudd and Aloha.

"I'll clean it up in the daylight tomorrow," Rudd said.

"Nope. I'm better on top of any roof than you are."

"Better at what?" he said speculatively.

"I'll show you." She shed her fishnet vest and stepped out of her shorts.

"Aloha!"

"What? It's night. And nobody can see through all those trees and if they could they'd have to be higher than we are."

"Oh, yeah. I forgot."

Then she was in his arms, kissing the champagne off his jaw and ear. And tugging urgently at his shirt. Soon they were down on the blanket.

As she climbed on top of him, Aloha said, "Now *this* is how you christen a house."

The last thing he thought before his body took control was how happy he was, they were, and he didn't ever want it to end.

CHAPTER FOURTEEN
HER

That fall there wasn't a cloud on her horizon and Aloha grew taller and her body became more rounded. She had excellent SAT scores and went over to the Florida State campus to get an application. There she noted all the young people—and not one knew her. It occurred to her that perhaps when she attended FSU next year that she could start a new life—or at least a new chapter in her life.

She took the application home and filled it out. With her straight A's, she knew she'd have no trouble getting accepted. She completed her application without showing it to Rudd. For she had to put her birth date on the form. Without hesitation, she signed PETER BLAZE where parent or guardian signature was required. And that hadn't been the first time either; in fact, she was quite proficient signing her father's name—a legacy of doing whatever she wanted whenever she wanted.

She liked the campus so much that she hand delivered her application. Here her streak of vanity appreciated being the center of attention of guys she didn't know. She was used to those over at Leon High; and by now the high school boys knew she was somehow removed from the dating scene. Seldom did anyone ask her out anymore; she missed the attention and the boost to her morale it gave her. Although "Lightning Lance" Gugliotta, Leon High's current all-state quarterback, did timidly ask her to the Homecoming dance. Aloha reluctantly declined his offer.

Lance was high profile and handsome, but she liked him because he was shy in spite of his status atop the school's social ladder.

This made her realize she missed the dating life, too. Oh, well, she was becoming used to skipping; great gaps were missing from her education: academic, social, family.

She walked the entire campus that afternoon, from Wescott and the Williams building to Kellum Hall. From Doak Campbell Stadium to the Student Union. She spent an hour in the Strozier Library.

The longing to attend college here became overwhelming and she chafed at the fact that she was only a senior in high school with too many months left. Maybe she could attend summer school here right after she graduated, thus not waiting until September.

As usual, to dissipate the accumulating stress, she went home and did the laundry.

The afternoon had chilled her, so while the dryer was running, she sat atop the machine cross-legged and read *Moby Dick*. She finished the book and admitted she liked the boring parts best: the cetology, where Melville was instructive and lyrical in the old ways of whaling. Then she wondered if the movie were any good, so she went back out on her motor scooter, down to Thomasville Road. At the JINX PLAZA strip mall, she stopped at the new video store.

No *Moby Dick*.

Next to the video store was a walk-in laundromat. Out of professional curiosity she went in. Two women were folding clothes and their children were crawling around on the concrete floor getting dirty. Another older woman was reading a magazine sitting in a cheap aluminum chair. The place had not been abused by its patrons; yet it had that slightly run down look of inattention. She drove home wondering.

The next day was Saturday and Indian Summer struck. It was warm and mild. Rudd had to fly to Orlando, so she was at loose ends. She went back down to the laundry and sat and watched for a while. She gauged distances and thought. While she was there, she sat in one of the folding chairs and did her homework. She wanted a soft drink, but the machine was out. She finished her homework and went home.

That afternoon, she decided to work on her tan. She found a John D. MacDonald novel she'd been saving to read and felt guilty that it wasn't one of the literary novels on her must read list.

She stripped in the master bedroom downstairs and climbed to the sundeck. She sunbathed nude for a couple of hours. She couldn't concentrate on the book, so she put it aside and resumed thinking laundry.

At one minute after three a droning noise grew from background to here and now. Aloha was face down so she lifted her head and right then a SIXGUN AIR Cessna 172 swooped directly over the house.

"Rudd!" She shouted and jumped up and waved. The wings waggled as he disappeared from sight. She hoped he wouldn't get in trouble with the FAA, buzzing residences being illegal and all. But he was a smart enough pilot to not get caught.

She sat back down then lay face up, laundry consuming her thinking again. She fell asleep.

At four in the afternoon she was awakened by an aircraft again. Rudd?

Not an aircraft, she realized and popped her eyes open. At the same time her hair began whipping around her as great drafts of air buffeted her.

A chopper. Air National Guard. Hovering right over her!
Damn weekend warriors.

Suddenly she realized she was stark naked and lying face up. Her first reaction was to leap up and cover herself with the blanket. She fought that reaction and won. Instead she rose languidly, picked up her blanket and book, straightened, appeared to see the helicopter for the first time, smiled and waved. Taking her time, she walked down the stairs and into the house. The chopper went away.

At odd times during the weekends from then on, choppers would cruise by, hover, and then leave when they saw she wasn't sunning herself. The attention discontinued when it became too cold for any sunbathing.

But when she could, she'd sit up there during sunrises, cross-legged and nude, thinking about her life or just the day ahead. Many times she and Rudd would sit there for sunsets, but these times, usually, she remained clothed. Especially as fall faded into winter.

She could dance, but he taught her more. "You're too aware," he told her one day. "Think of dancing as simulated sex." And it clicked then. She learned ballroom dancing and liked it.

She continued to read voraciously. Her flying lessons were ongoing. The garage in their new house was designed for three cars, access by one double remote controlled door and a single door, hand raised. In there, Rudd set up the exercise mat and the hanging kick bag. Aloha practiced her unarmed combat skills religiously, for at times she needed the release that only strenuous physical exertion provides.

One December evening, they were sitting in lawn chairs on the sundeck watching the sunset, dressed in jackets to avoid the chill.

"You're becoming proficient, down there in the garage. I was watching you today."

"Thanks, Rudd."

"I think you pay enough attention to life to know when to use it or not."

"It seems to me it would be obvious," said Aloha.

"It would, but some people hesitate too long and miss their opportunity. A Real Woman knows when to act."

"Sexist terminology—"

"Not at all," said Rudd.

"You've used Real Man and Real Woman before, in a couple of rare occasions." So had JJ the nurse. "Do you mind differentiating?"

"Is that a challenge, Miss Aloha?"

"Nope. A dare, maybe."

"That's the first Real Man or Real Woman rule, right there. A Real Man doesn't have to prove anything to anybody, save perhaps himself. Most rules apply to Real Women, too. Real Men don't have to beat their breast. A Real Woman doesn't have to show up anybody. See, it ain't sexist, it just applies differently sometimes."

She thought a minute. "This is not simple barstool bullshit philosophy."

He shook his head. "For a Real Man, it's not about the size of his dick or his stomach or his biceps, or how handsome he is, or about his flashing blue eyes. It's more about his values, his commitments, his character, what he thinks about children. It's about how comfortable he is with himself. There's a corollary to this: A Real Woman understands all this; but she is her own woman and is comfortable with this *and* herself. A Real Man does what it takes to get through life; he does not simply take what he wants. He gives as much or more than he takes." He fixed her with his steel gray eyes. "A Real Person knows that academic education is important; but not necessary."

For the first time in her life, Aloha realized in clear terms that she wanted to be more than she was; that she had always wanted to be more than she was, but simply had not articulated these thoughts and translated them into concrete concepts.

"Want to hear more?" Rudd asked.

She nodded.

"This is about women, but there are male corollaries. A Real Woman is comfortable in a formal dress and high heels at dinner with a senator and a CEO and a bishop and discussing geopolitics all night and gets the kids to school in the morning. Or, she is equally comfortable sitting on the hood of a pickup truck in jeans and tank top, drinking beer all night, listening to country music and talking NASCAR and eating barbecue chicken dripping everywhere and gets the kids to school in the morning. She can nurse one beer all night or drink a bottle of wine or bourbon over ice—or iced tea, if necessary."

"Okay," said Aloha. Where was he going with this?

"That's what I see in you," he said, answering her unspoken question. "You've unlimited potential; opportunity is your friend and—"

"Jeez, Rudd. That's pretty deep."

He shook himself. He smiled. "A Real Woman can shut a man up without hurting his feelings. Thank you very much."

"I reckon a Real Woman should oughta develop certain talents." She didn't know whether yet to classify herself as a girl or a woman. But for purposes of this conversation, she allowed herself to be a woman. She thought about that as they sat there quietly. She realized that for once in her life, she *was* in fact comfortable with herself, right now. She reached over and took his hand and the silence lengthened.

Rudd said, "What do you want for Christmas, hon?"

"I already have you and this wonderful house. How could I want anything else?"

"A car?"

"Not yet. I'm scared to drive." She surprised herself by her own flippancy admitting her problem.

"You ain't scared of nothing. You fly." He didn't think she was serious.

She knew he was teasing her. It had taken him a long time to get comfortable with the fact she wasn't as old as he'd like to believe. She doubted he knew to this day how old she was.

"Maybe if I get my pilot's license, you can give me a job?"

"You don't need a job. You got school, and then you have to get your college degree."

"I might, Rudd. Not wishing you ill, but you're in a high-danger profession. One day one of your aircraft might...well, you know."

"I do. It's something you think about, especially as you get older." He drank gin and tonic. "After being to war, though, I'm reconciled to my mortality. I'm not afraid of buying the farm. In fact, I'd rather go the hard way: fighting a nonresponsive stick in a nose dive, or into a mountain hidden in the clouds—"

"Rudd! Don't say that."

"Reminds me," he said, changing the subject. "If I do go, the attorney has a copy of my will. After taxes, he will liquidate everything. SIXGUN AIR, my stocks, bonds, accounts, a couple of properties I own like in Washington state, and the insurance money—a great deal. The new will splits everything in thirds, you, Denise, Buddy. Except this house. It goes to you. I've a term policy to pay it off."

"Shit, Rudd." She choked up. "I don't want to be rich at your expense."

"That's what I was saying. I've got plenty of money—"

He'd already put enough money in her personal account for her to get through six years at FSU, up to a master's. "More if you want," he'd said.

"I feel like I'm sponging—"

"No. You're my spouse, even if you won't marry me right now. It's your cut. It's us together against them. That's what it's all about."

"I don't know what to say—"

"Then don't say it. Which leads us back to the main point. What do you want for Christmas?"

"Gayfers at Tallahassee Square Mall has a couple of vests."

"Go buy 'em now. I mean significant gift."

"Really?"

"Really."

—Say it, demanded Bonnie. Shit or get off the pot.

—Done. Wish me luck.

—Luck.

"Turn and look over there." Aloha pointed. "JINX PLAZA. You can barely see the top of the sign."

"I know it," he said.

"The laundromat? It went up for sale yesterday. That's what I want for Christmas."

"A laundromat? How romantic. I was thinking in terms of a big diamond engagement ring."

"No thanks. A laundromat will do."

"Aloha, you are a weird human being."

"But I love you anyway, darlin'."

He sat still for a moment regarding his gin and tonic. "I do love you, sometimes so much I can't envision going through life without you. It might be a good investment. I will have my accountant see what kind of deal they want and insure that it's not out of line for that kind of business, and make an offer."

"Thank you. I'll pay you back."

"Nope. It's a present."

"Tonight."

"If you insist," he said. "If we find this isn't a good deal, would another laundromat do, or is this one it?"

"I'd have to case the place and it'd have to be in the right neighborhood. See, I don't want a place which gets trashed every day."

"You've thought it out."

"Mostly." There was only one problem she hadn't solved.

She leaned over and they touched mouths.

The mechanics of purchasing and running the laundromat kept them occupied until, in the spring, Buddy Six showed up, unannounced.

CHAPTER FIFTEEN
HIM

Rudd was at work, hanging up the telephone from talking to his accountant when the door opened and Buddy Six walked in.

Rudd held his breath.

"I went home and there were a bunch of fuckin' guys drinking beer out front sitting on cars which were all over the front lawn—what's left of it," said Buddy with a tentative grin. "I remember mowing the mother fucker every week against my will." His gaze was strong now.

"It was supposed to build discipline and character." Rudd met his son's unwavering stare.

"Shit, I got plenty of character."

"And likely not enough discipline to this day," Rudd said, making sure his voice remained mild.

Buddy ignored the comment. "What's the deal?"

"We don't live there anymore, and to hell with the neighborhood, it's full of hall-monitors," Rudd said and got up and went around his desk and hugged his son apprehensively.

Buddy raised an eyebrow at the hall-monitor comment. "Hello, Dad."

"Why didn't you call?" Would they fight?

"I didn't want to give you the opportunity to think about it."

Rudd stepped back. Buddy looked good. He was taller than Rudd now, and Marge's gene's had softened the rugged good looks Rudd had given him. The boy stood tall, posture ramrod straight. He had grown more than Rudd could believe, muscles rippled. He was dressed casually in jeans and a Semper Fi sweatshirt.

"Whatever the reason you're here, I am glad to see you," said Rudd even as he recalled Buddy leaving years ago, without a word; one day he was simply gone.

"I came home to kiss and make up." Buddy winked.

Rudd grabbed his son's hand and wrung it. "Done. No questions asked." He felt awkward. This was a man. The last time he'd seen Buddy, he'd been a boy. A college graduate, but nonetheless a boy. Not a man-boy like Aloha was a girl-woman, but a brat.

"Actually, Dad, I'm almost done with my four years and I have to decide if I want to stay in the Marines."

"You want *my* advice?"

"Yes and no. I had a couple of weeks leave and needed somebody to talk it over with. You were in the service and, well, I, I've kind of changed. Put me up for a week or two?"

"Hell, yes. You know I'm not living alone?"

"Mom told me. She wouldn't say anything else. She was quite mysterious."

"Marge graced me with a visit. But she never met Aloha."

"Aloha? Oh, shit, Aloha? Denise's friend?" Spoken as if denying it.

Not any more, thought Rudd. "Yes," he said. "It's the same one."

"Jesus shit, Dad, you rob the friggin' cradle, or what?"

Rudd shrugged. He didn't know what to say. Buddy wasn't the same as when he left. Almost four years in The Corps had changed him.

Buddy tsked and leered. "Let's go get a pitcher of beer."

Rudd wondered if this was going to work out. "You get promoted yet?"

"I'm a first lieutenant now. My obligation is up and that's an opportunity to quit. If I don't, I'll make captain." He ran his hand through his crew cut. He eyed Rudd's hair. "At least you're not a long-haired civilian freak. C'mon, let's hit that bar and maybe kick some ass."

Why me, Lord?

They went to a bar off Tennessee Street near the FSU campus.

Rudd kept up with his son, beer for beer, even after three pitchers of Budweiser.

Buddy surveyed the patrons. "Goddamn hot dog students. Bunch of limpdicks, still some bellbottoms, Jesus."

"You got any skills for civilian life?" Rudd asked.

"Damn straight. I can fire twenty-five or thirty different weapons. I can kill somebody by hand. I can march like a son of a bitch. I can jump out of a perfectly good fucking airplane. I can run twenty miles with a heavy pack and not even breathe hard. I can make a platoon of men follow me and do those same things." He eyed a table of girls near them. "I can also chase women, dip my wick, and raise hell."

Which reminded Rudd he hadn't called Aloha. He excused himself and on the way to the restroom, used the pay phone. No answer. Likely she was at ALOHA'S PLACE again. Damn. Ever since she started the laundromat business, she'd split her attention from him. Maybe it would level out once she got everything the way she wanted.

When Rudd returned to the table, Buddy was talking easily with the girls. He saw Rudd and stepped back to his chair. "Shit. I think I'll quit The Corps and come here and get a graduate degree." He grinned. "Not to mention gettin' laid every night."

"Remember what I always told you."

"Don't think with my dick?"

"In so many words."

"Yeah, Dad. You're probably right."

They drank silently for a while.

In college, Buddy had taken a full course load, even during summer sessions. Like many young people of his generation — or any generation, Rudd amended, Buddy had been an angry young man. He'd blamed Rudd for the breakup between him and Marge, so he joined the Marines immediately after graduation.

And left without saying goodbye. Rudd couldn't reconcile that part yet, but he could compartmentalize it, like so many other things parents had to ignore or forget, and worry about it later.

"I've kept in touch with Mom," he said, as if reading Rudd's thoughts.

"She sure didn't want to hear from me."

"Fuckin' A. That's why I did so." Buddy gulped beer. "I don't think she has anybody to care for her. Not lately."

"I'm sorry," said Rudd. He wondered at Buddy. This was more like the old Buddy than the new one.

"I checked with her a lot, you know, Dad? She was my mom and she was one reason I chucked it all and joined up. Man, this wasn't a happy family. Shit."

"I'm sorry you had to go through it with us."

"I am, too. I was really fuckin' bitter. Christ, I didn't want to have anything to do with you all. Hell, I blamed you."

"I noticed."

"I shoulda fuckin' remembered what you always told me—"

"Don't think with your penis?"

"No, not that one—"

"Always wear a rubber?"

"Not that one either, Dad. Jesus, you drank too much already. What I mean is when you say there's always three sides to every question. Yours, theirs, and the right side."

"At one time I wouldn't have believed you'd remember anything *I* said."

"To my regret, Pops. Now I been a Marine, I know what you went through over in the late lamented Republic of Vietnam. I understand. I understand what you went through with Mom."

Rudd laughed. "I admire this new sensitive side to you."

"Goddamn right, fuckin' sensitive, that's me." He poured beer into their mugs. "What's the deal with Denise?"

"What did Mom tell you?"

"That's no answer. But she said little. She hinted that your girl Aloha run her off. So I called, but Denise is long gone. I

144 | JAMES B. JOHNSON

talked to her roommate at the dorm. Who, incidentally, I got a date with Friday. Maybe I'll find out more then."

"Costa Rica, some kind of missionary trip, how long I don't know. I guess it's an open ended thing, from what I can gather from the pastor at the Church of the Redeemer."

"Fuckin' evangilistas. I oughta go over there and kick their fuckin' holy asses."

"You better start keeping a list."

Buddy touched his temple. "Got one, up here. So, I'm to gather that you and Denise had a falling out about your sweetie?"

"The Lord works in mysterious ways," Rudd said grinning. Then he winced at his making light of the problem. "We disagreed, Buddy. Dead serious. She has this religious bee in her pants that drove her." Rudd would be damned if he would mention the abortion. "She rather did not appreciate my indiscretion; not only that, but Aloha was her friend and she took inordinate umbrage at that fact. She felt betrayed."

"Shit. Just because you were dippin' your wick? Goddamn women don't understand shit. You hear about the one Marine and fifty women on a desert island? After a month, they couldn't take it any more and all of 'em died. After another month, he couldn't take it any more and buried them. After a third month, he couldn't take it any more and dug 'em up. Let's have another pitcher, and you're two behind."

"Your demeanor fails to reflect the old momma's boy I knew—"

"And loved."

Rudd cocked his eye at his son. "You're *goddamn* right, boy. I loved you then, regardless of what you thought. And I love you now. I just got to get used to the new you."

"You like the new me better?"

"I think the two will marry one day and you'll meet yourself at the middle."

"Avoiding the question."

"I like you both."

"Diplomatic. When I get to see the lovely Aloha?"

"How about right now?"

"I'm game. But I never left any beer on a table undrunk yet and I ain't intendin' to now."

"You finish it. I have to sober up to drive. Are you serious about getting out of the service?"

"Yes and no. I sort of wanted to know if things are okay here. I left things hanging, so to speak. That's why I'm really here. But, yeah, now'd be the time to bail out, elsewise if I stay in longer I got to think seriously about making a career out of it."

"Do you have any interests you can convert into a vocation."

"Not a fuckin' one."

"I've seen that in the military. It almost happened to me, except I had flying to fall back on. Being a GI was fun, you won't find anything like it outside the military." Rudd recalled how much he'd liked it: but he had a family and, well, Marge wouldn't have fit at all.

The discussion continued for a while and then they drove to Rudd's new house.

Going into the house, Buddy linked his arm with his father's and carried his duffel bag in the other. "Nice pad, Poppa-san. Shit, you doin' all right for yourself."

Aloha must have heard something. "Rudd?" she called. "I just got home. I'm in the kitchen."

They went into the kitchen.

Aloha was looking in an upper cabinet, stretching and on tip toes, hands holding the cabinet doors above her. She wore black slacks, black leather boots, a long sleeved white blouse, and a black vaquero vest. The curve of her hip was fetching and her breasts strained at the blouse.

Buddy stopped as if hitting a wall and jerked Rudd to a halt with him.

"Jesus Motherfuckin' Christ!"

CHAPTER SIXTEEN
HER

There was Rudd, drunk, and this big, handsome, beautiful lookin' guy with him. He had short hair and a familiar presence. He undressed her with his eyes, even though, she realized, that he was drunk also. He dropped a duffel bag he was carrying in his other hand and stared at her.

He turned to Rudd and said, "You old dog, you. New house, new girl. Not bad, neither one." He leered. "Not the same toot I remember."

Unaccountably, Aloha got flustered. Rudd introduced them anyway and all she could say was hello. It explained the sense of familiarity she saw about him.

Aloha felt an instant attraction for Buddy, one she'd never previously experienced. Well, he was Rudd's son. She crossed her mental fingers and hoped fervently that this was not the beginning of the end. It was something she could not imagine, not right then anyway.

But she was angry at Rudd for coming home drunk. And for bringing stay-over company without telling her.

She beat a hasty retreat while they were digging beers out of the refrigerator. She checked the guest room. It was ready. It was always ready. They'd just never had a guest. She changed the towels anyway to make sure they were fresh.

She went into her bathroom and applied fresh lipstick.

Were not Rudd and Buddy estranged? That was what she'd always thought. Was he here to stay? Was he just out of the service and needed a place to live? Aloha wasn't certain she could survive *that*.

Returning to the kitchen, she found both sitting on the counter, backs against cupboards, drinking beer, and kicking their feet against the cabinets under the counter. They fell silent when she entered and she could feel both pairs of eyes following her around.

"What would you like for supper?" she asked, faking a smile she didn't feel. "We've frozen steaks which will charcoal fine, or I could call for a pizza."

"Beer," said Rudd.

"Red meat," said Buddy.

"Steak it is," Aloha said. "The guest bedroom is upstairs and to the right." She eyed Buddy speculatively.

Which he picked right up on. "Two weeks, maybe. That's all I'll be here," he said waving his Bud longneck. "Unless we run out of beer, then I'm outa here immejetly."

Aloha managed to bake potatoes, make a salad, and grill steaks while they drank beer and talked. They were getting more and more inebriated. And that Buddy sure had one filthy mouth on him. Though, she told herself, it didn't bother her and it wasn't anything she herself hadn't said at one time or another. He was exactly opposite of the mental picture she'd drawn. Quite for the better.

During the meal, Rudd bragged about Aloha. "After school she changes from super-student into girl-entrepreneur."

"Meaning?"

"I run a laundromat," said Aloha, failing to keep the pride out of her voice.

"Run, hell," said Rudd. "She owns and operates a laundromat."

"I'm impressed," said Buddy, toasting her with his beer.

"Get her to take you down there tomorrow," Rudd said. "You won't believe the place. Used to be just another joint full of dirty clothes. Now there's carpet and a corner with plastic toys for kids and a teevee and lots of food and drink machines which she gets a cut of. Smart girl."

"She sounds like it," said Buddy. "And you go to school, while winning the American Dream."

"I do." She blushed.

"What's your major?"

"I don't exactly have one yet."

"Oh, hell. I didn't have one 'til I was a junior and I changed that twice. What year are you?" Buddy pushed his plate away.

Rudd was fully drunk now, but he was paying attention and watching her with amusement. Damn him! He wasn't going to help her out. No reason to lie. "I'm a senior," she said.

"I'll be dipped in shit," Buddy said and looked at her closer. "You're a senior at *FSU*?"

"No." She wasn't going to say it; he'd have to drag it out of her.

"Florida A and M?"

"No."

"It ain't Tallahassee Community College. Ah, got it. Out of town. Where, Auburn? Georgia Tech? Jesus, not the University of Florida over in Gainesville? Asshole Gators."

"No."

"Well, goddamnit, where, then?"

"Leon High."

"Oh, shit."

"You had to ask," she said, now enjoying herself.

"My fuckin' father. Not only did he rob the cradle, he's a fuckin' robber baron."

Whatever that meant. "You're entitled to your opinion, Buddy, and you've been drinking. So I will forgive you the slight I know you didn't mean. However, from now on, you watch what you say and how you say it." She wagged her right pointy finger at him.

His jaw dropped.

Rudd applauded. "Now you know why I love her."

"Christ, do I ever," said Buddy.

They stayed up late drinking beer, and Aloha pegged Buddy

for a healthy young marine trying to impress his war-hero father. It was obvious he liked Rudd and was making amends for his behavior years earlier.

Rudd kissed her awake in the morning and left for work. She didn't know whether he had a flight this morning or not; but what she did know was that he'd been violating more and more frequently the traditional rule of "twelve hours between the bottle and the throttle."

When Aloha got home from school, Buddy was just up, dressed in shorts and sweatshirt. "My running attire," he said with a smile. "Onliest way to get rid of a hangover is go out and run an hour."

"How far is that?"

"Seven or eight easy miles. Depends on my speed."

She made him a cup of coffee. He must run a great deal, she thought, for his legs were well sculpted and as muscular as his upper body.

—Gorgeous calves.

—Hush.

"I want to run down to the laundromat while you're out," she said.

"Show me, too."

She was secretly pleased. "Let's go."

She locked the house and began walking down the driveway. Buddy walked alongside of her. "Not far?"

"Mile, mile and a half."

"And you walk it?"

"Why not? You run eight miles, I can walk a few."

"That's not exactly what I was addressing, Aloha. You live in a big house and own a business, and you don't drive between the two?"

"No. Sometimes I take my motor scooter."

"Uh, oh," he said. "You don't *have* a car."

"I don't need one. I don't like to drive."

He stopped her with a hand on her shoulder. "I can add two and two and I don't particularly like charades." He leaned forward and looked into her face. "You don't drive because you don't *want* to? Or you don't drive because *it ain't legal* and you can't?"

"*It ain't* none of your goddamned business, Buddy." She refused to admit that driving was a personal crisis. Even though it made him assume she was not yet sixteen.

He turned and they walked for a few minutes, out of the driveway and along the feeder road to the crossroad which goes through to Thomasville Road.

Buddy rubbed his unshaven jaw. "I'm not sure you're right." His voice was matter-of-fact. "He's *my* goddamned father and that makes it *my* goddamned business."

"Just leave it alone, Buddy." She felt awkward and increased her stride and speed.

She felt better by the time they reached JINX PLAZA and Aloha's Place. Proudly she showed him the laundromat.

"Used to have bare floors," she pointed out, "now I put in that industrial strength carpet you see in high-traffic areas in public-access buildings. Even a sandwich machine." Along with a snack machine, a candy machine, a cigarette machine, and two soda machines.

A railing separated the business portion of the laundromat from the recreation area. The carpet there was thicker. On one side were plastic toys and such for children to play with and on the other, a sofa and some chairs all facing a television. Two men were watching "General Hospital."

"I wonder if Doctor Steve Hardy is still on there?" said Buddy.

"Beats me," Aloha said. "Too bad nothing's on for kids right now. It's a slow time. More mothers would be here otherwise."

"Go out and get one of those video tape machines," he said flippantly. "Play Bugs Bunny."

"Yeah, but—" And the answer to the problem she'd been worrying struck her. She leaned against the railing, excited. "That's it! That's what I've been searching for. Thanks a million, Buddy." She grabbed him and pulled his head down and kissed him on the lips without thinking. When she realized what she was doing she tried to pull away, but he'd wrapped his arms around her and was kissing her back passionately.

"Awright," said one of the two men watching "General Hospital."

They disengaged, both showing guilt.

But Aloha soon regained her thought process. "My problem is that laundromats are usually *unmanned*, unless they're attached to a dry cleaner or something. I have to watch my hours and lock up the television and the toys for fear somebody'll steal them. I've lost a few anyway. But I can't afford to hire some-body when I'm not here, it just won't pay—not to mention the government required paperwork." She pursed her lips. "But just suppose we had a Betamax or VCR in here. Right?"

"If you say so."

"We'd have to come up with videotapes and they'd be at risk, too. But not, I say again, not, if they are part of the business."

"What the hell are you talking about, Aloha?"

She walked ten feet and banged her fist on the wall. "On the other side is a *video* store. It has a full-time clerk. They run tapes over there on their television all day and night, anyway."

"Makes sense to me. Look, it's getting very late. Let's go back. I got to do my run before this hangover kills me."

She thought guiltily that he didn't taste like a man with a hangover.

The sun was quickly dying as they arrived back at the house. "Rudd called earlier," she said. "He had a late charter to Jacksonville and won't be home until after eight and he'll bring pizza with him."

"Great. We got enough beer?"

"You are your father's son." She made her voice saucy, but she knew they better have beer because she sure as hell wasn't mobile enough to buy any.

She let herself in and he went running.

Aloha was excited about the video store. She had to think. Even though it was a warm day, the spring chill was still there.

But she needed pure thinking time and, by God, she was going to do it the way she always did it. Besides, Buddy wouldn't be back for an hour.

She stripped in her bedroom and, just in case, threw a terry cloth robe over her arm. She went upstairs and out onto the sundeck. The sun was falling quickly into the horizon behind the trees.

She sat cross-legged on her robe, facing the sunset, as she did occasionally, in a meditation position. It did help her think. She folded her hands in her lap and shrugged off the oncoming chill. It would help her thought processes.

The thing was, if the video store was together with the laundromat, then one clerk could handle the whole thing. She'd seen them next door. Except during rush times, they had little to do. It took little time to check people in and out and to file videos. And housekeeping was nothing.

The cash register could provide change for the washers and dryers and snack machines—that was always a problem at laundromats. The clerk could run a movie, or cartoons for the kids, for watching while people did their laundry.

Not only that, but each business wouldn't be mutually exclusive: one would generate cash for the other.

Suddenly, a flock of squawking ducks flew overhead through the growing dusk, heading for a lake or going back north. She waved at them and returned to her thinking.

She determined to get Rudd—or Buddy—to drive her to every laundromat and video store in the city. She doubted any were operating jointly as she was proposing. But she had to check it out; it was very feasible, for no other reason than each business was feasible on its own, and together there would be less overhead. She'd have to learn about employees and paperwork and all, but SIXGUN AIR was a business with many employees and Rudd's accountant, Handy Hank Hartwell, acted as business manager, too, and could tell her all she needed to know.

The air became disturbed momentarily, but she stared off onto the horizon anyway, the chill forgotten. The sun disappeared in a golden swarm.

The main thing, she worried, was coming up with the money. Buy the video store out? Make it a joint venture, a partnership; that way it would be a shared risk. But also a shared profit and she knew nobody would want to be partners with a teenage girl. There had to be an answer. She didn't want to hit Rudd up for the money again.

The only real expense would be knocking down the wall between the two. Nothing to it.

She rubbed the chill off her bare shoulders.

What was the answer? Mortgage the laundromat?

Well, it was an idea. Maybe she could buy the video store with a down payment from her account. The Blaze house rent was adding up and Rudd had stuffed a bunch of money in there for her college expenses and then some. She could borrow against that and the laundromat.

But she didn't have to decide right away. Or this week or this month.

But she knew she would. The idea was perfect and it was already eating away at her. She'd talk it over with Rudd.

Who might be home soon with the pizza. She was starving. And cold, too, she realized.

She shook herself out of her reverie and rose to her feet and stretched happily. She'd solved a major problem.

When she bent over to pick up her terry cloth robe, she saw Buddy leaning against the railing behind her, arms crossed and gaze fixed directly on her.

"You are the most beautiful woman—girl—female—creature—I have ever seen."

Flustered, she threw her robe on.

"Silent as a shadow, that's what they said about me in the jungles and all those advanced survival schools." He uncrossed his arms. There was a light sheen of sweat on him from running.

"How long have you been watching?"

"Not long enough, love."

"Rudd will kill you."

"I don't think so. I won't tell him. And I doubt you will." He grinned boyishly. "If you did and he killed me, it would still be worth every minute of it. Let's keep it our secret."

"Fine with me." She stepped past him.

He grabbed her elbow. "One thing, Aloha? I see what he sees in you. And it is more than the incredible body. You got a mind up there won't quit." He released her and bowed, extending one arm out. "After you, ma'am."

He turned to go after her. "The only thing is, sweet thing, is that you are indecently young."

CHAPTER SEVENTEEN
HER

Rudd was gone to work the next morning and Aloha was brushing her hair when a banging came on their bedroom door.

"Hey, girl, you decent?" Buddy. He came in before she answered. "I seen it all anyway."

Aloha tightened her robe. "Crude and rude both."

"I found an old bicycle in the garage. Come ride with me while I run."

She didn't even think about it. "Be down in a minute."

She pinned her hair and chose a particularly brief pair of shorts and a skimpy, tight, and revealing tank top.

When she climbed on the bike, she said, "Wanna race?"

"No chance, purple spotted underwear pants. Youngster like you would run me ragged." His references to her age were getting pointed.

She took off and he raced to catch up.

Oddly, Aloha enjoyed the experience. Buddy ran easily, not even breathing hard. And they talked the whole time until Aloha realized she had to get back or be late for school.

That Friday night, Buddy had a date with Denise's ex-room-mate.

Aloha was up late trying to finish Fielding's *Tom Jones*, toasting her feet propped up on the hearth. Rudd was long asleep.

When Buddy came in, she was in the reconciliation part between Tom and Mr. Western and Mr. Allworthy.

Buddy was drunk again and he smelled like sex. Aloha fought an unaccountable twinge of jealousy.

He sat next to her feet on the hearth, back to the fire. "Hello, young lady." The smell of sex and beer was stronger.

"Buddy, you remind me of Tom Jones, born to be hanged."

"Born to be dipped in shit or shot by a jealous husband, maybe." He leered at her. He took the book from her hand. "That fuckin' Western, man, what a asshole. Ready to sell off his daughter—Sophia?—to the highest bidder."

"I am supposed to think you are well read?"

"I am, my lady. Dad's influence." He tried to bow and almost fell over and she reached out to steady him. He held her hand against his chest. "I can feel your heart beating, and now it's right here next to mine."

"That's logs settling in the fireplace."

"Oh." He rose unsteadily. "I got to get to bed. Me and Dad are going skydiving *mañana*." He checked his watch. "I mean today."

"Nobody told me."

"It's a guy thing."

"Oh yeah?"

"Uh oh," he said. "I think I just fucked up."

"You ain't kiddin', buster."

"You a goddamn handful, sweetheart."

"More. It takes a Real Man." She eyed a challenge.

"Try me, Aloha dearest. Then you make the call." He grinned. "I've heard that lecture. Real Man, Real Woman, number forty-seven."

* * * * * * *

"You could get killed." Rudd gestured.

"You, also," Aloha said. "If you die, I want to die, too."

"It's different chutes, it's not like one dies, we all die together kind of a thing."

"I fly your airplanes."

"It's not the same thing. Why do you want to jump out of a perfectly good airplane?" The old refrain.

Buddy interrupted. "We've both had a lot of jumps and ground training and practice."

"There had to be a first time. And all you do is jump out, that's gotta be the hard part, and pull a D ring or whatever."

"Yeah, but—" said Rudd.

"She's got a point, Dad."

"It's settled then," said Aloha.

"No, it ain't. You need the training in case something goes wrong. You need to learn canopy control, how to land. There's official stuff you're supposed to learn—"

"Oh, pooh. Zeke's going to fly you off toward Marianna, nothing official about that. You're not going to jump at an approved location, just some place he can pick you back up."

"Yeah, but—"

"Rudd, you knew full well my penchant for heights when you arranged this. That's why you didn't tell me. Well, Buddy blew it. I'm going."

Rudd turned to Buddy. "Do something."

Buddy smiled. "You're doing bad enough all by yourself."

The whole time driving to SIXGUN AIR they briefed her.

"We're not using a static line—" Rudd started.

"That means you aren't going to be attached to the aircraft," said Buddy. "You're going to have to pull your own ripcord."

"The main ripcord handle," added Rudd. "In front, at waist level, easy access."

When they got to SIXGUN AIR, Rudd went into the equipment room and got each a rig. "This whole rig has the harnesses and the main and reserve chutes." A helmet, gloves, an altimeter, goggles, and a flightsuit. Aloha almost burst out of the one which fit her best. Buddy eyed her appreciatively.

Aloha found the main ripcord handle yellow and plastic, one she could easily pull with a gloved hand.

The whole time flying to the drop-off location, they briefed her.

"When you pull the ripcord handle," Buddy was saying, "then the pilot chute deploys—it's spring-loaded. This pulls out the main canopy which is usually still contained in its own bag. It goes on up so the suspension lines don't tangle. When these lines are finally tightened, that causes the main canopy to deploy." He looked at Rudd. "No AAD?"

"Not in these chutes. That's an automatic activation device," Rudd explained to Aloha. "It'll deploy the chute at a preselected altitude, works on barometric pressure. A safety device. They're generally on the rigs when you punch out of military aircraft because a lot of times you don't have a choice when to punch out and you might become unconscious."

"And we don't have this," said Aloha. "Great."

"You don't have to jump," Rudd pointed out.

Aloha looked at the ground two and a half miles below. "Like hell I don't."

"Okay. Pay attention now," said Rudd. "Two other handles. This one," he indicated a pad on her right side, "is very important. It's called a Cut-away Handle. You use it to get rid of your main chute if it fails."

"I'll know in time?"

Rudd shrugged fatalistically. "I hope so. But you might not. One of us will accompany you and signal."

"What's the signal?"

"I'll get to that soon. Once you've jettisoned your main chute, pull this handle," he touched one on her left side, "to deploy your reserve parachute."

"Got it. What could go wrong?"

"You pull the rip cord and it comes off in your hand and nothing happens." Rudd was frowning, but ticking off fingers. "A streamer, the canopy won't inflate. Bag lock, meaning the canopy won't deploy from its bag. Line over, that's where one of the rigging lines gets hung up over the top of the canopy. Steering lines tangled."

"You won't have long to ID the problem and take action," said Buddy.

"You are *so* encouraging," Aloha said, knowing they were trying to discourage her. She grinned. "Tell me more."

"Remember to arch like we told you," Rudd said. "It's called the Stable Position. Arms and legs out and face down."

"They taught us it's like a frog leaping, all fours spread out, back arched. Don't get into a reverse arch, or the air could flip you on your back." Buddy bent forward to show her. "That's a no-no." He held his hand in that position, wrist and fingertips higher than the back of his hand. "That's one of the signals, it means arch." He held his first two fingers out like the scissors in the game and said, "This means straighten your legs." The same two fingers up and pulled back at the knuckles. "Raise your legs." He extended his pointy finger. "The most important signal. Pull."

"Got it," said Aloha.

"Spit it back, quick," demanded Rudd.

Aloha went through the hand signals.

"Good," he said. "So pay attention to whoever is accompanying you. Identify the main ripcord handle, the cutaway handle, the reserve handle."

She did so.

"Again."

"We should have done cut away drills," said Rudd.

"Beginners have all the luck," said Buddy dryly.

"Why do I need a helmet?" asked Aloha. It seemed to her that if her chute failed, a helmet wouldn't help much when she hit the ground.

"Your head could bang on the doorway on the way out, or into the head of another diver." Buddy knocked on his own helmet on the floor alongside him.

"Twenty-five hundred feet is usually the deploy chute limit," Rudd said to Buddy. "Let's do three thousand."

"Agreed," said Buddy. He turned to Aloha. "At first we'll be falling about the speed of the aircraft and in ten or twelve seconds we'll reach terminal velocity, maybe a hundred twenty miles an hour."

"Depending," said Rudd, "that's right near two miles in one minute. Figger it out if you jump from twelve to fifteen thousand feet and deploy around three thousand."

Not long, thought Aloha. Not long enough.

There was more.

"A couple minutes," Zeke called.

One final time, Rudd tried to dissuade her. She ignored him. The excitement was building in her. The more she anticipated it, the more excited she became. A glance around told her that Buddy was like her; he wanted to live on the edge, challenge death, some manly BS. She was simply excited to death. Rudd was worried to death. Let him sweat, it was her life.

Zeke circled the drop zone. "When I level out, anytime."

Rudd held the door open.

Buddy checked their harnesses one last time.

"Now!" Zeke shouted.

Rudd gave her a pleading look as she moved to the door.

She paused over the abyss, wind whistling past her and the Earth beckoned her and she dove out, arms outstretched, and the feeling was so intense she had an orgasm as she fell, spinning slowly, down down down. Later she found there was a term called "airgasm" explaining the feeling of free-fall. But she knew her reaction was much more intense. Through her goggles she saw Buddy floating down and over, watching her. She didn't look for Buddy or Rudd, for she was enjoying herself. Buddy was supposed to have gone at the same time to be her partner.

Awright! This wasn't going to be the last time, no way in hell. She moved her arms experimentally, cupping her hands and tried to learn the flight dynamics of the human body in the few seconds she had. Arch, she remembered.

—Breathe, too.

—Oh, yeah, thanks.

She heard a shout and there was Buddy gesturing with one finger. She checked her altimeter strapped to her chest and it was winding down past three thousand.

Reluctantly, she tugged on the Main Ripcord Handle and wind whistled through nylon lines as the pilot chute deployed, the main chute popped open just like clockwork and she jerked upright, swinging like a pendulum. She guided her canopy like she'd learned once at the beach over in Panama City behind a speedboat.

Buddy had not deployed his own chute, doubtless showing off, then she realized that he would reach the ground first to assist her in landing.

She saw Buddy land, running along and then spilling air from his chute.

Aloha headed toward him, tugging on the steering lines, and she recognized that what they'd called ground rush was occurring.

—Great! Do it again for me.

—I will. And again, and again, and some more agains.

Buddy stood calmly waiting as she sped toward him. At the last moment, she dumped air, hit the ground, stumbled, and Buddy caught her, spinning, and they went down together, tangling chutes and lines. Somehow he contrived to end up with her body atop his, grinning his pleasure.

She struggled to her feet and extended a hand to help him up. "Let's do that again!" Next time she better wear a panty-liner, she thought and wondered if there was a wet spot showing.

Suddenly it was so quiet; she realized she missed the whistle of the wind. She removed her helmet and goggles.

They both turned to look for Rudd and he was still airborne, circling professionally above them. Gradually, he came down, checked up just before landing, spilled air, and settled gracefully to the ground, not taking even one step.

"Shit hot!" shouted Buddy. "Of course, he's done that while under fire and bleeding and returning fire. This was nothing."

They gathered their chutes and trudged to the side of the field.

Aloha B. Blaze vowed to skydive often.

"She wasn't bad, for a youngster on her first jump," Buddy told Rudd.

* * * * * * *

Sunday, Aloha went to the Strozier library at FSU, determined to do some long needed research. After a couple of hours, she thought she had enough material.

That evening, they were sitting and talking in front of a fire in the living room, Buddy drinking beer, Rudd gin and tonic. One hell of a comfortable family situation, Aloha thought.

—Time to stir up some shit.

—I been waiting; it's about time, said Bonnie.

"May I have your attention?" Aloha announced and moved in front of the fire and faced them. "This aforementioned 'youngster' has some facts to relay."

"What's up?" Rudd asked.

"Me. I would like to present some famous people to you." She had their attention and curiosity. She picked up a notebook and opened it. "Does Frances Folsom Cleveland mean anything to you-all?"

Buddy shook his head.

Rudd shot her a knowing look. "The wife of Grover?"

"President Cleveland. She was the youngest First Lady in history. He was forty-nine, she was twenty-one. They married in the Blue room of the White House. People called her 'Frank.' Her father was Grover's law partner, and died; Frank became Grover's ward *at the age of ten*. Eventually, she bore him five children."

"What a woman," said Buddy.

"A mere youngster," said Rudd dryly.

"Yep." Aloha flipped a page in her notebook. "Exhibit two. Jerry Lee Lewis married his thirteen-year-old cousin in 1957. Exhibit three: Loretta Lynn was thirteen when she married Mooney, fourteen when she had her first child. Exhibit four: Bogie and Bacall. Lauren Bacall was nineteen, Humphrey Bogart forty-five when they met. Different accounts have him forty-four."

"I didn't know that," Rudd said, eyes bright.

She went on relentlessly. "Mike Todd was twenty-three years older than Elizabeth Taylor—another account has him twenty-five years her senior. Frank Sinatra was fifty and Mia Farrow was twenty-one when they married, only nineteen when they met. The ceremony was four minutes long in 1966, July 19 to be specific."

"More?" said Buddy.

"Pat Henry, famous orator and turner-downer—"

Buddy started to interrupt, but Rudd held up his hand. "She'll tell us when she gets to it."

"Old Pat held many positions, and while this isn't part of tonight's lecture, it is interesting to know that he turned down in one five year period, positions such as Secretary of State for George Washington, Chief Justice of the Supreme Court, a seat in the U.S. Senate, posts as minister to France and Spain. In 1796, they elected him Governor of Virginia for the *sixth* time and he refused to serve. Now where was I?"

"About Henry's private life," said Rudd.

"Nothing. I was researching and ran across that. I thought it was interesting."

Rudd grinned.

"I have more. Let's do politics, historical figures. My favorite: Thomas Jefferson was thirty years older than Sally Hemmings and she stayed with him the rest of his life."

Rudd looked very introspective then. An uncharacteristic tear in his gray eye?

And Aloha knew the similarity, that's why she'd buried the TJ reference in the middle of her report. She went on. "Juan Perón, forty-eight; Eva, twenty-four. Ike was eighteen years older than Kay Summersby. William Randolph Hearst was thirty-four years older than actress Marion Davies and their affair lasted thirty-six years. Nan Britton was twenty-one in 1917. Warren Harding fifty-two, and *their* affair lasted the rest of *his* life—in fact, after his death, her name occasionally and mysteriously appeared in the guest register at the Harding Memorial."

"They should have put that stuff in the history books," Buddy observed, "it would have been a hell of a lot more interesting and I wouldn't have slept through so many classes."

"Now some literary references, for the avid readers in the Six family," said Aloha. She shuffled her notes. "Charles Dickens was a randy old goat. He was twenty-seven years older than Ellen Ternan when they had an affair, and he was twenty-three years older than Adah Isaacs Menken. Now this same Adah also had an affair with Alexandre Dumas who was thirty-three years older than she—"

"Maybe the lesson there is that she liked older guys," said Buddy, and Aloha couldn't tell if the emphasis was a joke or sarcasm.

She continued relentlessly. "H. G. Wells was forty-six, Rebecca West only twenty. Here's a killer: George Bernard Shaw was sixty-five, Mary Arthur Tompkins twenty-four. Here's a flip-flop: Thomas Wolfe was a babe of twenty-five, Aline Bernstein was forty-four and had two grown children." She paused for effect.

"Likely, there's more," said Buddy dryly.

She smiled. "Yep. From the world of entertainment. John Barrymore forty-two, Mary Astor a mere eighteen. In 1941, Charlie Chaplin was fifty-two and Joan Barry only twenty-two. W. C. Fields was twenty-nine years older than Carlotta Monti. Other categories. Casanova was thirty-two when he robbed the cradle, Manon Balleti only seventeen—"

"That's more like it," Buddy interrupted.

"And everybody knows about Aristotle Onassis. He was sixty-two, Jackie Kennedy thirty-nine. Before that, he and Maria Callas when he was fifty-seven and she thirty-four." She looked at Rudd. Rudd raised his glass to her in a mock toast.

Aloha put her thumbs in the arm holes of her Indian vest. "Any questions, class?"

"I learned a lot," said Buddy.

"Well done," said Rudd quietly.

She basked in his praise and all was well thereafter for a while.

Monday after school, Buddy drove her to every laundromat and video rental store in Tallahassee. It took several hours. She found none of them together. Video stores were relatively new back then, and there weren't many to visit. One thing Aloha observed was that few people had VCR's or Betamaxes, so the better video store rented the machine along with the movies.

Daily she rode the bicycle alongside Buddy as he ran. She enjoyed the outdoors, the exercise, and the company. Rudd was seldom playful; Buddy the opposite. Aloha recognized that was an age thing. She began to confide in him. She told him her dreams of expanding her laundromat to include the video store. She hinted that she'd like to expand her businesses. And she shared that she was not happy with the conflict of school, now high school and next college, and her personal interests: her business, sky diving, and flying. There just wasn't time enough to accomplish all she wanted. Not yet. She knew it would get worse next year when she went to FSU.

She knew in her heart of hearts that all this would take her attention from Rudd, and she regretted that in advance. But it was her life and she was going to go about it in her own way. Until recently, they were able to go about their life in a slow and easy fashion. Rudd liked to come home, have a drink, do something, go to bed. Routine, necessary, but routine. Sometimes, she just wanted to party. Thus she welcomed Buddy's presence: it was new and different.

One day the conversation wound torturously around to Rudd.

"Buddy? I know Rudd flew in the war, but he won't hardly ever talk about it." She stopped pedaling and coasted.

"That might also have something to do with my lovely mother." Buddy shrugged, an awkward thing while running.

"I don't want to hear about her."

"Don't get all pouty, cute thing. See, Dad had a couple tours in The Mystic Far East. The first tour, he flew F-100's. Supersabre it was called. It's mission was mostly close air support of ground troops. Bombs, napalm, guns, rockets. They were sometimes directed by what's called a FAC—a forward air controller. FAC's can be airborne or on the ground. When Dad was shot down in his F-100, it was because the FAC didn't do his job right." Buddy was getting ahead of her.

Aloha started pedaling again and caught up. When she reached him, he slowed down, so she had to brake. "Stop screwing with me."

"I ain't started yet, good-lookin'." He matched her speed again. "Anyway, that's when he punched out and Charlie and him had a firefight while he was floatin' down—"

"I've seen a couple scars."

"Yep. Purple Heart. Silver star. On account of the mistake by the FAC, Dad volunteered to be one. Because they needed experienced pilots to do that thing, and also since he was a pilot before joining, the Air Farce bought off on his checking out and training in FAC aircraft. He flew O-2's, same as the Cessna 337—"

"I know it. Twin-boom and in line engines."

"That's the one. And he also flew its cousin, the Rockwell OV-10 Bronco. Night observation, counterinsurgency. He did some of that kind of stuff all the time. Got shot up a lot, crashed a couple of their aircraft. Hadda fight his way to the Friendlies. He, my dear Aloha, is one tough son of a bitch."

"I've seen the steel," Aloha said and thought: And I've seen the tender part of him, too, and the twain have met.

"The VC killed a couple of other officers trying to poison him. He had a hell of a reputation. They targeted him with snipers. They put a price on his head. He was so good at vectoring in air strikes, and artillery sometimes, too, that Charlie went all out to get him. Cut to the chase, now sexpot. Because of this undue attention, the USAF rotated him early just to save lives of those around him." At her glance, he explained. "Rotated. Shipped out, back to the land of the big BX, the states." Buddy paused for several moments, his brow crinkled in thought.

"What are you thinking, Buddy?" His look of introspection gave her voice an unusual urgency.

"Maybe that's why I ran away and joined The Corps."

"To emulate your old man?"

"Could be. Jealousy? Prove I could do same, but better?"

"And?" she prompted.

"You learn, you grow. The older I get, the smarter he becomes."

Aloha didn't know what to say to this admission, so she didn't say it.

Almost home, he turned to her. "I thought that was illegal."

"What?"

"You, right now."

"*What?*" she demanded.

"Pedalling pussy."

She shook her head in disgust.

One day after school, Aloha was on the exercise mat, radio on an FM station, and she was spinning and kicking the heavy bag. Her foot smashed from knee height to head height, and then she'd follow up with backhand chops.

Again, she never heard him, but during a spin, she saw Buddy sitting against the wall watching her. She ignored him and continued her workout with more vigor. She made a couple of mistakes in her anxiety to not make any mistakes.

Finally, she broke off. "Next."

"All right." Buddy rose languidly and stood in front of the kick bag until she was out of the way.

"See—" he began, and suddenly he was all action, exploding. The sandbag rocked and banged aside, and he followed it in a circle, slashing, hammering, kicking, head-butting, and pounding with fists. Timbers above the garage groaned in protest.

She stood in awe. If she hadn't known what he was doing, she wouldn't have been able to follow it, he was so fast.

He quit and grabbed the bag to steady it.

"Jeez, Buddy, you're *good*."

"Bet your cute curvaceous ass, sweetie. Notice the start?"

"I did. Sudden. Explosive."

"Exactly. For you, that'll be the whole battle. Surprise is

your key element. C'mere and show me how to break some rear holds."

She went to him and turned. From behind, his arms circled her chest, careless of where his hands lay. Immediately, she grabbed his left little finger which was automatically sticking out and proceeded to bend it backward. If he didn't let go, it would break. Buddy jerked his hands away. "I was prepared for a double elbow strike. Try this one." He encircled her torso, including her arms, from the rear. He fit against her buttocks so well that it was akin to a sexual position.

Not hesitating, she locked her hands and lower arms over his, ducked, bent, twisted and knelt at the same time while pulling on his arms. He lost his center of gravity and went over her right shoulder, dragging purposefully across her body, hit the mat and rolled so that when her hand slashed at his throat, he was no longer there and her soft blow bounced off the mat.

She knelt there watching him grin, went through it again in her mind, and realized he'd let her do that to him for the body contact he'd had.

"Bastard."

"Likely, but I enjoyed every split second." He rose and held his hand out to her.

Suspecting the old trick, she took it, prepared to react.

The radio station played "Theme from a Summer Place" and Buddy surprised her. He swept her into his arms and began dancing, left arm tugging her right closed, jammed between them.

She was learning to love dancing from Rudd, and she didn't break it off right away and when it occurred to her to do so, it was too late. So she danced away with him in a variation of the two-step.

"You're squeezing me, dear."

Buddy growled deep in his throat. "You, sweet thing, are built to be held tight."

His body was hard and she felt his muscles along her entire body.

"You're good, Menu Girl," he said into her ear.

"Do I even want to know?"

"The menu, full of wonderful and intriguing dishes. Even the hamburgers are good. Get to prime rib and beef tenderloin. All kind of things to choose from. Smells good, tastes good, looks good, eat a lot or a little. Appetizers, full meals, extensive wine list. Never, ever disappoint you. The wine cellar has the best stuff buried deep and dark and way inside. Some things don't cost much, like a dance. Other items are expensive, cost you a lot. Sometimes more than you can afford."

"You can stretch a metaphor," she said into his chest, very comfortable.

"Wish I could stretch time."

Just then, a Ford van pulled up into the driveway and the delivery man climbed out, saw them and headed for the garage.

"Hey, Aloha. It's that day." He held out a dozen peach-colored roses from Rudd.

Flower Day.

She pushed away from Buddy. Reluctantly.

"Goddamn," said Buddy.

* * * * * * *

Buddy's leave was running out and he was to depart on Saturday. Aloha resented the fact he was going away. She'd finally found a friend close enough to her own age, and now she was losing him. It did not escape her that she merely had to acquiesce and the relationship would be deeper, intimate.

Rudd dropped Buddy and Aloha off at the terminal and drove to SIXGUN AIR for a few minutes.

Buddy processed his ticket and duffel and they went to the waiting area.

"I'm going to miss you, Buddy."

They stood next to each other looking out at the flight line through a large plate glass window.

He threaded his arm through hers. "Thanks, Menu Girl. I'll

accept my next assignment and stay in the Corps. Semper Fi, by God. I think I'm due for sea duty; it's something you got to do sometimes. But if I get some leave and we're within shouting distance, I'll hop a flight and come visit."

She looked up at him. "No, you won't."

He looked down. "No. I won't."

She turned her head and watched a 707 taxi. "Sometimes you wonder if things were different...."

"Me, too." He put his arm around her shoulders. "You're a girl, but a lot of woman. You're the most intriguing woman— aw, shit. Listen, Aloha. You ever need me, you call. Any time, any place, any reason. I be there."

She could not look at him.

"Next week," he said, "next year, five years, ten, twenty years."

She turned to him and stood on her toes. Her lips brushed his, side to side and lingered and regretted. She couldn't speak. She broke loose from him and sat alone in an empty lounge.

After a few minutes, she composed herself.

She sighed, rose, and headed back for the gate.

She didn't want to disappoint Rudd.

Rudd was there and she was silent while father and son talked.

When they called the flight, she gave Buddy a perfunctory hug and he walked up the ramp alone. And did not look back.

And Aloha knew that her life was changed now. Irrevocably. Melancholy crept over her. Now there was a void in her which she knew she'd never be able to fill.

CHAPTER EIGHTEEN
HIM

Though Rudd didn't know it then, Buddy's visit triggered a bad case of empty nest syndrome which in turn triggered his midlife crisis which would last a couple of years. And cost him dearly.

Denise had moved out only gradually, and Aloha had been there when Denise severed her ties with Rudd, so it wasn't apparent. Then when things were settling down with Aloha, Buddy came back into his life and Rudd realized he really liked his son; consequently, when Buddy left, Rudd felt an immediate sense of loss. Bang. Gone. Something he hadn't known he possessed, gone. He'd invested too many years in his family; now they were gone and he didn't know what the hell to do about it or how to deal with it. It was becoming painfully obvious to Rudd that his life was at a dead end.

The depression ebbed and flowed for months. He thought he found gray hairs, but didn't—or so Aloha convinced him. He knew he had more lines around his mouth and eyes. He drank more and felt worse the next day, his body not recovering as it once had.

Life wasn't all that fun anymore.

Except for Aloha. One single bright star in the night.

He was given to reliving the past and decided his accomplishments were not significant enough to suit him.

So he threw himself into work and his investments in stocks and bonds.

Not knowing how to deal with his depression and recent lack of a family, he responded by lavishing all of his attention on Aloha.

He made money. Against her protestations, he paid off her mortgage on the video store. He deposited a hundred thousand in her name, because he felt too mortal and worried that Denise or Marge would lawyer Aloha out of her part of the will.

Lavishing his attention on Aloha became more difficult, although he continued to send her flowers once a week. He made it more difficult by working harder and longer hours. She made it more difficult by growing up and having varied interests of her own. She was accepted at FSU, now she was simply finishing high school. She was pursuing a reading list of her own devising, one so she'd have all the literature read for a major in English. Additionally, her business interests were consuming more of her time. She was spending a lot of time shadowing his accountant and business manager, "Handy" Hank Hartwell, trying to learn everything she could about the workings she needed to know. She spent most Saturdays doing necessary business chores for the video store and laundromat. She continued to practice her unarmed combat skills; Rudd could tell by some of her techniques that she'd learned well from Buddy. The heavy bag was taking a beating. After her workouts, Rudd liked to lick the sweat off her neck.

Her ground school flight studies suffered some, but she still pursued them. She did love to fly and went with him whenever she could. She pestered him to death about taking her skydiving; he made her go through that ground course and join the skydiving club. Therefore, she was gone many Sundays, but she was building an impressive number of jumps to her credit.

Rudyard Kipling Six was constantly in awe of Aloha's ability to learn and absorb new information. She'd have made a great systems analyst because she not only wanted to do something, she wanted to know how that thing came about and the mechanics involved in it: from quarterly tax filing to how aircraft work to packing her own parachutes.

Rudd knew something radical was wrong with his life; he shied away from self-examination because he was a man and men didn't do self-examination. Otherwise, he would have recognized the empty nest and the midlife crisis symptoms.

Monday after Buddy left, Rudd was at work early.

Zeke came in late, as usual. He stood in the door and regarded Rudd. Finally, he whistled. "If you wasn't such a stud, I'd steal Aloha from you. Every time I see her, I want to tell you what a lucky guy you are."

"Thanks for the compliment."

"How does a old guy like you keep up with a young thing like her?"

"It takes me all night long to do what I used to do all night long."

"Yeah. Buddy told me to rib you one last time after he left. I promised him. Now, I'm not so sure—"

"Tell me, Zeke."

"I'm positive he was trying to be funny, you know?"

Rudd nodded.

"He said to tell you fifteen will get you twenty. I think I know what he means."

Rudd shook his head. "That's Buddy."

"Rudd, is he right?"

Rudd pretended not to understand. "Buddy's just playing a game." Rudd still stubbornly avoided learning Aloha's age. Don't want to know? Then don't ask.

"I didn't tell you, but some months ago there was a lady cop nosing around out here, asking questions."

"Oh, shit." It had to be Sergeant Ebert. He wondered if her inquiries were before or after she'd talked to him at home. "What'd she want to know?"

"About you. Reminded me of one of those FBI checks they used to do on you for top secret clearance. Background stuff. Shoot the bull long enough to find out if whoever they're talking to got a hard-on for the subject and get them to spill any beans need spilling. I was very complimentary of you and your morals."

"My morals?"

"Of course the conversation got around to your divorce and current lady friends. I pled ignorance." He checked his watch. "One of us needs to make that courier run over to Pensacola so we don't lose the contract. I got one question."

"Which is?"

"Can I still send my laundry out, or am I morally obligated to take it over to Aloha's and do it myself?"

Rudd did not tell Aloha about the lady cop's investigation. Since he'd heard nothing further, he assumed they had avoided the law for at least the time being. Whether they passed muster or Ebert couldn't get anything on them, Rudd could only guess.

One spring evening, they were swimming in the solar-warmed pool, suitless as usual. Rudd was playing a little grab-ass, preliminary to making love, pushing and splashing, underwater touching.

"I'm wondering about night skydiving," Aloha said, paddling around the deep end.

"Jesus. Only if you have to. Not me."

"Rudd, you know what I've found about myself?"

"What, hon?"

"Ever since Buddy visited, I don't cuss as much."

"There isn't much left for the rest of us." Rudd was exceedingly happy that Aloha had liked Buddy and they'd got along so well together.

He was hanging on the lip of the pool, facing her. She swam over to him and clenched his hips with her legs. Her arms went around his neck and she took him fiercely and it was all he could do to hang on.

Afterwards, they sat chest-deep on the shallow-end stairs, Rudd drinking a Tanqueray martini.

"Remind me," he said. "To shock the pool after we get out. I had to go out of my way coming home to that pool supply place over off the Apalachee Parkway to get chlorine."

"Don't forget to shock the pool," she said automatically. She cocked her head in that engage-thinking mode of hers. "What did you say?"

"Chlorinate the pool, shock it."

"No. Before that."

"Apalachee Parkway, work, home, what?"

She was silent, then took his glass and sipped the gin, spat it out into the pool, and made a face. "Uh, oh."

Oh, shit. "Uh, oh, what, Aloha?"

"Remember Thomasville Road over there? It used to be way out of town. Now the growth is exploding, sort of in a pie slice from the city outward."

"And?" He drank gin and felt good about his life for the first time since Buddy left. Maybe it was post-coital somegoddamn thing, that and straight gin, and Aloha, who was climbing onto his lap, facing him.

She squirmed on him. "The residential growth out here is more affluent. These wealthier people all have hot tubs, spas, swimming pools. All of which eat chlorine, muriatic acid."

He groaned. Now he knew what the "Uh, oh," was about. Her squirming was arousing him.

"These people don't want to drive all the way over to Gaines Street or Apalachee Parkway, I bet."

"Doubtless," he said dryly, "they'd much prefer to stop right over at JINX PLAZA for their supplies." Her increasing movement splashed water. He put his glass down on the lip of the pool.

"Exactly! And equipment. That yogurt store isn't doing the business it needs to keep on keepin' on."

She rocked urgently on him and he entered her. "Twice in a row?" His hands roamed.

"Proves you're a *real* man."

"If I'd known pool supplies turned you on—"

"And patio furniture, knickknacks, the whole spectrum, that yogurt store is too large for simple pool supplies." She was bouncing up and down on him. "I want you *now*, Rudd."

Fortunately, their privacy was assured by five wooded acres, including a shrubbery hedge surrounding the pool cage.

Later, when they had showered and got in bed, Aloha snuggled up against him and held him tightly. "Let's do it again."

"Three times?"

"Do you know what today is?"

"Pool supply store day?"

"No, silly. It's our anniversary. Sort of."

She rolled over on her back and pulled him on top of her. "Wow. I *knew* you had it in you."

Rudd thought fleetingly that she was making love today as if they were running out of time.

CHAPTER NINETEEN
HER

It was their anniversary and *he* didn't know it. That was discouraging. However, she was the one who didn't want him acknowledging her birthday, so she had little room to complain.

The sense of melancholy that had been her companion since Buddy left lifted when she engaged her thinking-mode about a pool and patio supply store.

Her sessions with "Handy" Hank Hartwell, Rudd's accountant and business manager, had taught her many things and a way of thinking. She could convince the pod of doctors who owned JINX PLAZA to lease her another storefront. Not a problem. Her problem was too much income and not enough out-go.

Now, if she *owned* JINX PLAZA, she could pay a mortgage, deduct it, *and* grow equity in the property. Since it was in an expanding part of the greater Tallahassee area, it would not be worth less, it would always appreciate. One of these days one of the big boys like Publix would need another location out here.

It didn't take much to convince the yogurt store guy he wasn't going to make it. He was ready to quit anyway, he'd just been putting off the decision. The final straw that pushed him over the edge was Aloha's promise that if she succeeded in buying the Plaza, she'd make him the manager of Pools & Patios.

Then she went to the operating officer of the doctors' real estate group. She took Hank Hartwell with her, not only because of his expertise, but because of his reputation. His name was familiar in the money circles of Leon County.

Doctor West was a gynecologist. He was balding and Aloha characterized his eyes as very alert.

"I've had the plaza appraised," Aloha told him. She put an offer sheet on West's desk. "This is my offer."

"How's your financing?" West asked.

"We have preliminary approval from the bank," Aloha said, putting another document in front of him. "Their okay is based on this offer, though."

"Your offer is under your own appraisal," he pointed out. He looked at Hank.

Hank said nothing. It was Aloha's show.

"It *is* under appraisal," Aloha said. That was one reason the bank had been easy.

"We're not interested in selling at this time."

Aloha said, "I'll bet your books could be made to show you lost money on the deal, and you'd get a great tax break." Hank had assured her that would likely be the case.

"It's still insufficient reason to sell," said Doctor West. "We're making money on the plaza now. The future of that part of town is rosy."

"Not any more," said Aloha, trying to project regret in her voice. "I'm sorry," she said. She reached over and picked up the papers. She stood. She handed him a letter.

"What's this?" West asked.

"A letter of intent to vacate. Our lease is up soon. We've got another location in mind—nearby—for the laundromat and the video store. We've a super client base and don't want to go far."

—Way to go! Bonnie said. You got him good.

—I did. He knows it won't be easy to rent those locations to another laundromat or video store because *we* have the customers.

"I see," said West, appraising her.

She stepped away from the desk. "I can no longer afford to pay rent; I've got to own for tax purposes. Surely you understand that." She shook her head. "Thanks for your time, Doctor." She turned to leave, then snapped her fingers as if she'd forgotten something. "Oh. By the way? The yogurt store is closing down. He won't be renewing his lease, either."

West stood. Aloha could see him thinking.

—You got his attention, said Bonnie.

"That makes three of the five tenants gone," she said. "The other two won't last without the walk-in trade we three provide."

One was a used bookstore that Aloha had had her eyes on for a long time. If this deal went through, she'd own that bookstore eventually. She'd always loved books. The final tenant was a mom and pop pizza place which did benefit from the customers at the other stores. "Thanks for your time, Doctor."

"Just one minute, Miss Blaze. Hank, is she serious?"

"As a heart attack."

West ran a hand over his shiny head. "Let me take it up with the board, and perhaps we'll be amenable and present a counter offer."

Aloha turned to face him. "Sorry, Doctor. That's the one and final offer. I do not wish to go in hock for more than that amount." She held out the papers to him. "Take it or leave it. I withdraw the offer Friday, close of business."

West sat heavily back in his leather chair. "Hank, who the *hell* is this? She got a gun and robs banks part time?"

"She's, ah, involved with SIXGUN AIR," Hank said.

West sighed. "Heard of 'em, but that's at the airport on the other side of town. Out of my territory."

Aloha was still holding out the papers. "Yes or no, Doctor?"

West stood heavily. "I can't commit. I'll pitch it to them." He took the papers from Aloha.

"That will be fine, Doctor. It's all you can do. I'll hear from you Friday?"

"I don't think I can get a consensus, for or against, by that time."

Meaning, Aloha thought, that they'd jump through hoops and see if they could either locate more tenants to replace the ones they'd lose, or find out if they could sell the property to a higher bidder. That was why she had established the Friday deadline.

"Friday four o'clock I withdraw the offer. You must know the offer is a fair one, given the circumstances."

West winced. "It'll be tough, I'll try."

Hank handed her another sheet of paper.

"By the way," Aloha said, "I took the trouble to get an estimate for remodeling the laundromat. Since you'd not be able to rent to another one after we leave, something has to be done with all that plumbing." She gave the estimate to West. "There would be your minimum costs."

West glanced down at the page. He shook his head. He glared at Aloha. "I'm a professional gynecologist. And I can't figure out how old you are. It's been bothering me."

—It always comes down to this, said Bonnie. Men suck.

—Not Rudd, Aloha told her.

"Is that a question?" Aloha demanded. "Do I have to be a certain age to negotiate a sale?"

—Cool it! yelled Bonnie. You'll blow the deal.

—I don't care. Fuck it. Fuck him. Fuck them all.

—Jeez, girl, you *are* in a funk.

"Well, no—"

"My money is old enough, Doctor. That's all that should concern you. Good day." She stormed out.

Hank drove her back to Aloha's Place. "I think you sold him. Then, right there at the end, I've a feeling you slam-dunked the poor sod."

Friday at three forty-five in the afternoon, Dr. West called Aloha.

"They want me to make a counter offer."

"No way, thanks for the call."

"I told 'em you'd say that. I told 'em to accept your offer. They said do it."

—I'm proud of you, dear, said Bonnie.

JINX PLAZA was hers. She already had a list of suppliers, and she began calling them to see what kind of deals she could get for Pools & Patios. Then she'd call her new manager and turn him loose on it.

That night she wanted to celebrate with Rudd. She was so happy. She was finding that *accomplishments* were just as fun as *pleasures*. It was a new world and she was looking forward to meeting it head-on.

She phoned for reservations at the Silver Slipper.

But Rudd didn't come home until eight that night, and he came home drunk. He and Zeke had been to happy hour at some bar.

Aloha put him to bed and carried the old paint-splattered ladder up to the sun deck. She climbed atop the ladder and watched clouds cover the night.

* * * * * * *

She finished her reading list. She also tasked herself to improve her cooking. Rudd was a good cook and was helpful. She wanted to take a course on taxes, but postponed it until she had more time.

School was rushing to a close and summer was looming.

"Lightning" Lance Gugliotta asked her to the senior prom. He was shy for a star quarterback and proud possessor of a full athletic scholarship to FSU in the fall.

"Sorry, Lance," she told him. Regret flooded her. "I'm going with someone."

"Is what they say true?" he asked, still tentative. It was not an accusation.

"I don't know what they say, Lance. And I don't care."

He smiled. "That's one of the things I like about you. Maybe some other time?"

"Maybe."

He fixed her eyes with his. "If you and whoever ever break up, you'll let me know?"

She touched his cheek. "I will."

That summer, she finished all the ground school curricula for her pilot's license. All she needed was hours. And she got them, single and double engine.

She also attended summer session at FSU, taking some of the basic courses such as English. This was so that she could make time in the fall and spring semesters for a couple of business courses. She was no longer certain she wanted to major in English. But she still loved books and literature and wanted to know more. Twice she saw Amanda McMullen in the halls of the Williams Building. They smiled uncertainly at each other. Aloha knew damn well Amanda recognized her. She remembered Amanda had asked her to take the American Lit survey class she taught. Aloha determined to do so, if for no other reason, just for the hell of it. She had a full academic scholarship.

On the first of September, Aloha B. Blaze was in the living room, stereo on full blast, when Rudd got home from work. She was singing along with The Crests, belting out "16 Candles," one of the few birthday songs she knew the words to. It didn't then occur to her that this was all so misleading. She was using an empty champagne glass as a mock microphone.

The music and her off-key singing was so loud, she never heard Rudd come in. When she performed a pirouette, she spied him, but she was so ebullient, she continued on and finished the song.

"I never knew what day it fell on," he said, and swept her into his arms. "Happy birthday, darling." Later, she realized that particular song doubtless reinforced his possible misbelief of her age. Why, though? Why had not Rudd checked her birth certificate? He was smart enough to find her age one way or another. He could have asked her or addressed it cleverly in passing. Why why why?

—Maybe he's afraid of the answer, said Bonnie.

—"If you don't want to know the answer, don't ask the question" Aloha quoted Rudd.

—Exactly. He appears to be comfortable with the situation now, so why look under rocks?

—Likely you're right, dear, said Aloha.

—Except....

—Except what?

—Except one thing.

—Bonnie, you're exasperating. What in the world is it?

—Okay. Except: What you gonna do, girl, when he finds out you've been misleading him?

—Not exactly, Aloha replied thinking—

—Exactly, Bonnie emphasized.

—Well, sort of...Aloha's thoughts trailed off. Why hadn't *she* volunteered the information? *She* could have brought it up, just in passing, without making a big deal out of it. She knew part of the answer: she wanted him to love her without reservation or condition. And she wasn't comfortable with her age anyway, just as she was not comfortable with driving. But, she amended, there was more to it than those simple answers.

Her parents had even sent her a card, all the way from Mauritania. They had another year and they liked doing the work because they thought they were making a difference for a change. They were the area reps for their foundation; they covered Mauritania, Mali, and Upper Volta.

The next afternoon, Rudd brought home a brand new Ford Thunderbird. "Like I said, happy birthday."

"Oh, Rudd, I don't know what to say." She shaded her eyes from the setting sun and walked around it.

"How about thanks and take us for a spin?"

Fear clutched at her gut. "You mean drive?"

"I do." An unusual inflection in his voice made her stare at him. His mouth was smiling, but his eyes weren't. And she knew that he knew—or he guessed something. Age? Unwillingness? Fright?

"It's new, um, I don't want to mess it up," she alibied.

"It's insured."

"I might scratch the new finish."

Rudd held up the key. "I will key the side of the car and then it won't matter."

"Rudd! You wouldn't."

"Wouldn't I?" Now, his lips weren't smiling either.

"You would."

"Well?" he prompted.

She was undergoing a major panic attack and splitting her attention with him.

—Bonnie! Help!

Rudd's eye's were boring into hers, commanding her full attention. He tossed the key idly into the air.

"Leather seats are sweaty in Florida." It even sounded lame to her.

"I like you all sweaty."

"The car's too big. I don't need something big as a battle-ship. I need something small, just to run around town in." "I'm beginning to wonder at the note of desperation in your voice, Aloha." His own voice was studiously neutral.

"*All right*, goddamnit, gimme the goddamn keys and get out of the goddamn way." She snatched the key out of his hand and pushed past him. She jerked the door open and slid in.

It wasn't even difficult to put the key into the ignition and start the car: she didn't even have to apply the gas. It was automatic and she didn't have to worry much about shifting, like on the goddamn Volkswagen."

He'd followed her to the side of the car.

She looked up at him. "How do you turn on the goddamn air-conditioning?"

He leaned over her and slid the lever. "It's on."

"Then get out of the goddamn way." She stabbed her foot at the brake, knowing at least whatever was to happen, she could stop it. She couldn't reach the brake comfortably.

Rudd reached down silently and pushed a lever and her seat slid forward.

"Oh," she said in a small voice. She took a deep breath and reached for the shifter. The car was purring healthily.

"In your frame of mind, it'd be safer for you if you had your seatbelt on," Rudd pointed out. "And adjust the mirror."

"Shit," she said and did those things. "Now get out of the

goddamn way." She slammed the door and he stepped back apprehensively as if reconsidering.

"Goddamnit!" she said aloud. Foot on the brake, she slid the shifter into Drive. And then saw there was nowhere to go forward. "Shit." She hit reverse, stood on the gas and burned rubber backward in the driveway. She ripped the steering wheel to turn and plowed into the grass, stopping the car after about twenty feet.

She went back into drive, goosed the accelerator, and sprayed grass, sod and rock across the yard, jumped back onto the driveway and headed down the slope, screeching the tires and slewing the back end from one side to the other. Without thinking, she was pulling backwards hard on the steering wheel.

—This ain't an aircraft, Bonnie's sane and quiet voice intruded.

As the T-Bird accelerated toward the main road, Aloha realized what she was doing.

"Oh, shit!" she said and stood on the brakes. The car slid the fifty feet to the end of the long driveway. She smelled burned tire smoke even inside the closed car.

"Awright!" What a thrill. Damn, this was gonna be fun. She turned on the left blinker, looked both ways, and drove sedately onto the thoroughfare, accelerated properly and began enjoying driving. "Nothing to this. I'll be damned."

—Ninny nanny boo boo, said Bonnie contentedly.

"But it ain't me," said Aloha.

—Explain.

—It's too pretentious, Bonnie. Too big for one young lady. Too hoidy toidy, maybe.

Aloha turned right, remembering to signal, and merged into more traffic.

—Ah, got it, said Bonnie. The T-Bird is new and beautiful and *you* don't wish to share any stage.

—My modesty will not let me dignify that with a response.

After driving around for an hour, she went and bought a pizza for dinner. The longer she was gone, the more Rudd would worry.

—You're nasty, Bonnie observed.

—After what he did to me? I want him to sweat a bunch.

—Um, sweetie? Note that Rudd bought you a brand new top of the line car.

—There's that, admitted Aloha.

—And in a very few minutes he made you conquer you fear of driving.

—Now *I'm* feeling guilty.

—On the other hand, you've reestablished some control and gotten mobility and you're less dependant upon him.

—Shut up, Bonnie, and lemme drive.

When she returned to the house, driving sedately, he was no longer outside, but as she drove up the driveway, she saw Rudd hurrying out of the garage as if he'd been watching for her.

Aloha made Rudd take the T-Bird back and exchange it for a pickup truck, fire-engine red. She reasoned that the pickup would be more useful in her business. And she could write it off.

Rudd shook his head in amazement, but he did that thing.

She thought about naming the truck "Buddy," but a few minutes consideration told her that wouldn't work.

The following day, she was at the driver's license bureau. She had the driver's handbook memorized. And she'd driven the pickup for a couple of hours of practice. By four o'clock she had her license.

Driving home from getting her license, she spoke aloud to her alter ego.

"Bonnie, wanta know something I just realized?"

—Spill it."

"I am in college, something I've always dreamed of. I'm legal to drive. I own my own transportation, this darn truck. Of which I'm not afraid to drive, I might add."

—Go on, Aloha."

"Don't you get it? *I'm free!* By God Almighty, I'm free!"

—Don't forget, you have money in the bank, too."

"There's that."

—And a good man. You got one of those."

"I do."

—It's all gravy.

"Nobody can touch me now."

—It took hard work on your part.

"And I ain't done, yet, sister. Just you watch me."

She had some immediate plans and some hazy long term plans. But she realized secretly that the way she'd shaped her life to date and what remained in the planning stages left out one thing: a social life. She'd love to party and socialize with those of her own age—or near it, anyway.

The age disparity between her and Rudd also led to an interest disparity. He didn't want to go to after-football game parties with a bunch of kids—and she didn't blame him. That was one of the reasons she loved going to college. The interesting things you learn, the challenge, and the other kids.

FSU was such a big place and was so far removed culturally and academically from Leon High, that she found her reputation had not followed her. She was just another new girl on campus. But a new phenomenon occurred: many of the boys in her classes hit on her. She deflected their attempts with humor, double-talk, or pleading studies came first. She didn't know why she didn't just tell them all she was shacked up.

She felt like she'd been with Rudd a million years. All in all, it had been grand.

Anyway, as a freshman, she was all but lost in the crowd. Except for the fact that she was drop-dead gorgeous. And the fact she drove a brand new red pickup truck. And the fact that she usually wore a vest, even with shorts. And the fact that she always got A's on tests, papers, labs. Because of Rudd, she was very private: Nobody knew about her business interests, or her flying or her skydiving. She was pushing five nine and she wore her champagne hair long.

As the fall semester unfolded, Aloha did become a more social creature. Now that she had he own transportation and didn't have to depend on others, she accepted invitations, not dates. If someone were having party, she'd sometimes stop in. Occasionally, she'd even dance with some of the boys. She didn't know it, but these occasions squashed the rumors she was gay. When one of the girls told her this later, she laughed, for she could deal with rumors about her personal life.

With Rudd working longer hours and often staying out late drinking with Zeke and others, it freed her. She studied with student friends, attended parties, football and basketball games. But she never had a date. Sometimes—no, all the time—boys got fresh with her at parties, but she fended them off easily and developed a tough persona and her behavior became natural in the circles she traveled.

Aloha liked her new self, her newfound freedom, the fact that she was now her own person. She'd always been fiercely independent: evidence her behavior in high school. But now she had her own money, her own income, her own transportation, *her own hopes and dreams*. While she did live with Rudd, she was no longer dependent on him for a roof over her head.

These were the things she'd wanted; these she'd targeted to have before she would accept Rudd's marriage proposal. Now she had them.

Now he had given up asking her to marry him.

Now she knew she could bring up the subject, even do the asking, and he would marry her in a split second. But for some reason she couldn't identify, she did not do so. She stayed away from the subject.

Bonnie observed all this.

—Sweetheart, you are fighting the nesting instinct big time.

—How do you know?

—All that reading you do? I pay attention. That ain't all.

—Ain't all what? asked Aloha.

—It's growing in you. That itsy bitsy tiny bit of resentment of Rudd. He made everything you got so easy. He footed the bills, came up with the seed money you built on.

—Nuh uh. I resent him a little, only a little, because he

doesn't seem to need me as much any more. I know he loves me to death. But he's not exclusively mine any longer. He likes drinking. He likes his work—

—*You* like accomplishments, not drinking. Same same. You like your business interests and schooling, same same with his work.

—It's different.

—If you say so. You're learning he ain't the geographical center of your universe and, worse, *you* ain't the exact center of his universe. Or if so, there are other planets, galaxies, stars to deal with.

Aloha secretly admitted she was restless sometimes.

* * * * * * *

It was inevitable. At the end of the semester comes a flurry of activity. Papers, reports, presentations, all due. Tests, finals. Aloha had a certain group of friends, mostly girls, with whom she studied.

One day there was nowhere else to go, so she invited them to her house. Rudd was going to be home late, so she felt safe— not that, she castigated herself, she was hiding him, concealing their relationship. Which in fact she was, but she didn't admit it to herself. She was afraid some such announcement or public awareness of this would somehow hinder her school life, academic or social.

"Gawd, nice place!" said one girl, named Tina.

"And I share a dorm room," said another, whose name was Judy.

The third, Faith, pointed out, "My apartment building could fit here."

They sat at the dining room table, books spread out, Cokes on coasters.

"Your parents must be rich," said Tina.

"Nope," said Aloha without thinking.

All three looked at her.

"I mean," she said, flustered, "this isn't my parents' house."
Oops.

"It's *your* house?" said Faith with wonder.

"No. Um, it belongs to, to, well, my boyfriend."

That shut them up.

"He's not a student?" Judy asked innocently a few moments later. The other two waited expectantly, all studying forgotten.

—In for a penny, or a pound, it doesn't matter, said Bonnie. "No. He's a pilot," Aloha said.

"How glamorous. Betcha he's handsome." Tina.

"He is that," Aloha said. "Let's study? You're making me feel uncomfortable."

That shut them up.

Until the inevitable happened and Rudd came home earlier than expected. He walked in, took in the situation at a glance. "Sorry. Didn't mean to bother you." He ducked back out and Aloha could hear him go the other way into the kitchen.

"Aloha!" whispered Judy.

Tina said, "I toldja he was handsome."

Aloha considered asking them not to say anything, but then she figured do that would only exacerbate the situation.

It didn't matter. The word that Aloha had a sugar daddy spread at the speed of light. No one knew that she had money of her own.

Christmas came and went, as did the end of the first semester. Aloha B. Blaze got straight A's again, maintaining her perfect 4.0 average.

Between school and business, her melancholy fell away. She was too busy to fret. Her new and enlarged social life washed away the final vestiges of the ennui.

The spring semester ended and Aloha got straight A's again.

She was invited to a sorority party and told to bring a date. She said her "boyfriend" was out of town but she would come anyway.

It was over on Park Avenue. She had to park her truck down by the old cemetery.

She walked in and the music was already flowing and so, too, was the beer. After a couple of hours, she went outside to get some fresh air. Those sorority girls smoked a lot.

She sat on the steps leading down to the sidewalk and sipped a rare beer.

Next door was a fraternity, music flowing, and so, too, was the beer. Just another Friday night at FSU.

Sitting outside in the splash of light, nursing a beer, was a familiar figure.

Unable to stop herself, Aloha got up and walked to him. "Lance?"

"Lightning" Lance jumped up. "Aloha!"

"Hiyou, Lance?" she held up her beer at him.

He tinkled his against hers. "Everybody inside is smoking. I'd rather be out here."

They sat and talked for an hour, neither wanting another beer.

He'd been "redshirted" by the football team, meaning he couldn't play, but could practice; and would spend five years instead of four, but would have a one year jump in experience when he began playing. He was "the quarterback of the future."

"How are you doing, Aloha?"

"I'm doing very well, Lance."

"You know I've missed you."

"You're just saying that." She shook her hair self-consciously.

He stared into his empty beer bottle. "I've had three beers tonight. Most I ever had in a month. Tonight they taste good." He took her hand. "I'm not just saying that. Everybody knows I was carrying a torch for you—"

"I wish you wouldn't say any more, Lance."

"Okey dokey Okeechobee. Wanna dance?"

"Here? On the steps?" Music was conflicting between the sorority and the fraternity.

"If you want. I'd prefer down there on the sidewalk."

"Why not?" Why in the hell not?

He took her hand and led her down the stairs. He put his right hand on her waist and she took his left in her right. He did not grab her tightly, as others did when dancing with her; he simply held her close. Then their out arms folded in. He led her in a slow dance to the sounds of Willie Nelson singing "Blue Eyes Crying in the Rain". Country music came from the fraternity, rock from the sorority. They danced back and forth between the two, depending on which had the more favorable slow music.

Ten minutes later, he asked her, "You still spoken for?"

She dropped her head to his shoulder. "I am." She felt his strong maleness.

After a little while, he said, "Well, I am enjoying the shit out of these stolen moments."

"Me, too."

She was tall, but not as tall as he was. Her head nestled perfectly between his shoulder and his neck.

Once, she saw Tina and a few of her other friends standing on the porch of the sorority watching them. The word would go out, she knew. Lance was a major catch, the object of many women. Jesus, just what she needed.

She suppressed her thoughts, her worries. These were magic moments, and she was going to savor each one.

This was the life she was missing. It wasn't the same as jumping out of an aircraft at ten thousand feet, or pulling hard, positive gees flying. It was something she'd dreamed about for years; it was something she'd missed for years. Sure, she loved Rudd Six, but she was swept away this evening, intoxicated on life itself. A caged and prized jungle cat finally free.

The two melted together, raw biology driving them. Among their social circles, it would be the topic of conversation for months, Aloha Blaze and Lance Gugliotta dancing up and down the sidewalk of Park Avenue, from sorority row to the grave-yard.

Once, he sought her mouth and she could not resist him. They danced, no longer within the sound of the stereos, because they were leaning against the fence surrounding the cemetery, jammed against each other.

He tasted good, clean, beer flavor long gone. His kiss was

long, gentle, and demanding. He *smelled* good, no artificial fragrance like many guys used. His hands roamed only on her back.

Aloha thought she was going to die.

Bonnie was clamoring for Aloha to break it up.

—No way in hell! the essence that was Aloha said.

But it wasn't her choice.

Lance stopped, as if he'd been told to. He gently disengaged them. "If this goes on, I am going to howl at those gravestones. And I am going to go home and cut my throat, for you are committed to another."

She caught her breath. "Everybody says you're tough, Lance. I think you are tender, sensitive."

"Don't tell 'em. I need my reputation."

"Shit, I don't care, not right now, about my reputation."

His hand brushed her right shoulder, then her left. "No ice here." He grinned. "You're too hot, Aloha, for all that ice they talk about."

"I have to go," she said. *Or I never will.*

"I want you to."

"You do?" She was dismayed.

"I do. I have to go run about ten miles to cool down."

"Oh. Thanks."

"'Member what I told you once?"

"Yes," she whispered. He'd said if she ever broke up with whoever, to tell him.

"I'm still here. It's been over a year and I'm still here."

She had to stop what was happening. "I have to go, Lance."

"One thing, Aloha?"

She stepped back to him.

He grabbed her, jammed himself against her, kissed her roughly and passionately, drawing the very breath out of her. Then he pushed her away. "If we're not to be, that's what I want to remember."

He walked away into the night.

CHAPTER TWENTY
HER

She went home and swam two hundred laps. Then she rode her bicycle around the neighborhood in the dark for an hour. Then she sat nude in her personal version of the lotus position on the sun deck until dawn.

"Bad girl rising" she thought, a parody on the CCR song. Like I used to be, before Rudd.

—You just didn't have any direction, Bonnie opined.

—I didn't care. And I was a bad girl. Now I have guilt, I didn't used to have that.

—Now you can afford guilt.

—I tried to swim it off, and that didn't work. The bike didn't work. This is helping.

—Reason being, Bonnie said, is you *enjoyed* tonight. Lance is a dreamboat—

—I don't care about that. I like him.

—Do you ever!

—How do I reconcile it with Rudd? How, Bonnie, *tell me how.*

—Simple answer is: *you don't.* You a oversexed chick. You fighting a million years of biological imperative.

—I don't wanna hear that.

—Because you know it's right on the money.

—I love Rudd. But, Jeez, Bonnie. Lance is attracting me, I can't believe it. Being with him is so, so exciting.

—Quoting Antoine' Bret, Aloha, pay attention: The first sigh of love is the last of wisdom.

—Pooh. But the thought made an impression on her. Please, Lord, lead me not into temptation.

* * * * * *

But it was so.

She was the pilot of the *Titanic* and knew she was heading for the iceberg and could not change course.

She went to summer school again, business courses mostly.

Her investments at JINX PLAZA paid off well and trade was growing. She was beginning to look around for another investment in which to sink her accumulated cash.

She got her multi-engine pilot's license. And was working on a commercial license.

The annual birthday card from her parents informed her that they had gotten a one year extension on their tour.

And for her present, Rudd flew them to Key West where they spent the three-day weekend.

Getting away from it all was worth it. She hadn't realized how involved she was and how much she and Rudd needed this escape.

"Gotta regenerate your batteries sometimes," Rudd said.

Like all tourists, they went bar hopping and visited Hemingway's house. They watched the sun set from the quay. Shopping, she found three new fashionable vests.

The trip seemed to rejuvenate their relationship.

And once again, she was happy, her life bubbling along as she'd planned.

Until the fourth FSU football game of the fall.

Lance Gugliotta had played well the first three games. Aloha had stayed away from him since the night of the cemetery. But she knew it wouldn't last. The *Titanic*, the iceberg. The iceberg was not just Lance, the iceberg was also a wildcard inside her, driving her.

So she invited all of her friends, and Lance and his friends, to an after-the-game party at her house.

She was up front with Rudd. "Since you don't fit in with all these kids, it'd be kind of you to disappear until after midnight."

"Not a problem, hon. Do whatever you want."

She'd guessed he'd be easy to deal with. He really was a dear, understanding man.

—And you, accused Bonnie, have one giant death wish.

—Go away.

* * * * * * *

Saturday night. After the game. The evening was cool.

Aloha had arranged for two of the guys to bring a keg of beer. She had lots of food and a live four-piece band.

She opened up all the windows and doors so people could party on the patio and around the pool and still hear the band.

Aloha was apprehensive about two things, the first being this ostentatious display of wealth; and the second being how to explain her living circumstances. Most knew that she was living with an older man, a pilot.

So she was gracious and accepted compliments about what a nice house you have and where in this giant place do they keep the airplanes.

When Lance arrived, she said, "You were great this afternoon. I was so proud of you."

When they were dancing the first dance together, he whispered in her ear. "I'm not sure this is a good idea, Aloha."

"You deserve recognition. You're very good."

"I don't care about football. I mean, me coming here. You know how I feel about you. This kind of rubs my nose in it."

"I did not intend that, Lance." Damn! She dropped her voice and whispered into his ear. "This is the only way I could think of to get us together without seeming to slink around behind everybody's back." She used the word "everybody" as a code word for Rudd.

"I don't want that. I want you free and clear, Aloha." They

danced on, getting closer each passing minute. "Oh, God, I'd kill for a minute with you like this. Even if it is a stolen moment."

"Thank you," she said into his ear, her tongue flicking.

Aloha Blaze and Lance Gugliotta stayed in each other's arms most of the night. Much of the time they danced in a dark corner of the pool patio.

After breaking a long kiss, Aloha said, "I often wondered what to call guys here in college. Boys or men? There must be a point where it changes."

He kissed her forehead.

"I think I know the answer tonight," she said, and pulled him to her lips again. Sexual urges overwhelmed her, those same feelings she did not understand and had not yet learned to harness.

At one-fifteen the band was on its last set. Half the people had already gone home.

Of course, it was fated to happen. Bonnie knew damn well it was inevitable.

—You asked for it girl, with your eyes wide open.

Rudd came home, and he was drunk.

The iceberg loomed and the *Titanic* accelerated inexorably.

CHAPTER TWENTY-ONE
HIM

Nobody noticed him; they thought he was just somebody else invited to the party. He went into the kitchen and got himself a glass of gin and went to join the party.

He walked around unsteadily until he spied Aloha and Lance in a corner, locked in an embrace, barely pretending to dance.

He stopped next to them.

And winter blew into his heart.

"I tried to convince myself to stay away longer," he said, startling them, "but I couldn't."

"Rudd, I—"

"Somehow, I've always expected this." He tipped his glass and drank half of the gin.

Aloha seemed to grow bigger. She stepped forward. "It's my fault, I shouldn't ha—"

"Who the fuck is this?" Rudd asked. He peered into Lance's face. "I know you?"

"I don't know, mister. Do you?"

"Hot dog quarterback. Goddamn, Aloha. You stray, you stray far. Fuck me to tears."

The band had stopped and ten or twelve people were standing there watching the confrontation.

Lance surprised them all. "It does not matter who I am, Mister. I ask you to remain civil."

"*Remain civil*? How the fuck I'm 'posed to do that, you cuttin' my nuts off."

"To hell with what you think," said Lance, anger seeping into his voice. "I was trying to be—shit. Aloha doesn't *belong* to you."

"This ain't a fuckin' debate, boy—"

"Before I leave, I want your assurances you'll not mistreat her."

"This is *my* fuckin' house, and you *will* leave." Rudd was trying to become angry. His alcohol clouded mind told him he should be a man. But the only thing he really wanted was to stop the hurt. He'd never *caught* Marge cheating in person, now he'd caught Aloha.

People were leaving, the band packing their equipment.

Rudd choked down the rest of the gin. "Betrayal, Aloha. God it hurts. Right here in my own house—"

Her resentment must have finally boiled over. "Yes, sir, Sugar Daddy. It's all yours." He could tell she was fighting back the tears.

"I will say you never were like the traditional fuckin' gold digger."

"I was everything you wanted me to be," said Aloha, now wounded.

"Not yet." He reached and took Aloha's arm and pulled her away from Lance.

Lance shot his own arm out and broke Rudd's hold on Aloha.

"Lance! Don't," said Aloha. "I've seen Rudd in action. He'll kill you, even when he's drunk."

"This *old* guy can take *me*?" asked the football star incredulously.

"He can and you'd never know what hit you. I saw him take out five grown men with one hand." To Rudd, she said. "Why don't you go have another drink? You do that well, too."

"Never mind my goddamn drinking. We're talking betrayal. A fuckin' young guy, Jesus, Aloha. I always thought you had more class than that. Shit, I *raised* you to have more class than that."

Aloha drew herself up. "You're right, Rudd. I have more

class than this. I was going to yell at you for being a drunk. I was going to yell at you for *owning* me. *Raised me*? Go to hell, Six. Lance, take me out of here, will you please?"

Rudd knew he was losing her but didn't care in the heat of the moment. He whispered hoarsely. "I lost Denise because of you. I turned down Marge again because of you. I let Amanda go because of you. God how I loved you. Take her, Lance, and good luck to you. I think you are a fine man to catch Aloha Blaze, it speaks well of you. I hope she doesn't betray you like she betrayed me. Go away, Aloha, and don't ever come back."

Aloha was crying openly now.

And Rudd was crying on the inside.

"Lightning" Lance Gugliotta took Aloha B. Blaze out of Rudd's home.

Rudd spent the rest of the night cleaning up after the party and blaming himself. He'd allowed the mental chaos of his midlife crisis to boil over and, consequently, his normal iron control had failed him. He'd lost the one thing he loved more than life itself. He had really loved her; fuck, he still loved her. He was angry as hell and didn't know how to deal with it.

He slept from three Sunday afternoon until six, Monday morning. He packed a suitcase and locked up the house.

He drove the thirty-five miles to Thomasville, across the Georgia line. The FAA being what it was, he knew they'd contact the FBI. He didn't think the FBI would search this far.

He made his purchases at different grocery stores and drug stores in Thomasville so the quantity wouldn't raise questions.

He drove back to the Tallahassee airport, and loaded his suitcase and purchases into the Cessna 172. He knew SIXGUN AIR could do without the Cessna more than another aircraft. He fingered his key ring. In case of emergency, he always carried a spare key for the 172. Just in case. If he was cross-country and lost the original. Or if he wanted to fly the aircraft without going to the office where they kept all the keys.

He found Zeke preflighting the Beech.

"Zeke, I need your help."

Zeke looked at him. "You look like shit, Rudd."

"It was a bad weekend. Listen. It blew up with Aloha Saturday night, and I need to get away for a while. You can get one of the part-time guys to take my flights."

"We'll work it out."

"I'm going to Panama City. When I get a motel room, I'll call it in and the phone number in case you need to contact me."

"If I can do anything—"

"Thanks, Zeke. Just hold the fort."

Rudd flew the ninety miles to Panama City, tied down the Cessna, rented a car and went hunting for a motel. He found the Pelican Hightower at the end of the beach where it changed into high dunes and scrub brush. The Hightower was an exclusive hotel and very expensive, but he ignored the cost because it was isolated from other beach motels. He could easily afford it anyway.

Anger still boiling, he decided to make his move that night.

He drove back to the airport, filed a flight plan for a night instrument training flight out low over the Gulf. They probably thought he was going to run drugs or something, but he didn't care.

He worked on the aircraft and set up the cargo until eleven, when he gauged it late enough.

He took off and headed southwest, away from land, dropped below radar and turned back east. He vectored to Thomasville and flew low, likely scaring the feds into thinking, if they were tracking by radar, he was in fact making an illegal airdrop. He gained altitude at Thomasville and headed to Tallahassee. If he was on a screen, it looked as if he had come from Thomasville. And it was better to approach Tallahassee from the north as he would not interfere with any possible air traffic going into the Tallahassee airport.

Over Tallahassee, he dove and commenced to buzz Florida State University. As he did, he forced rolls of toilet paper out the window. Rudd had already removed the paper wrappers and started unwinding the rolls to insure they would streamer out as they tumbled down. He circled the large campus, crisscrossing it for the nearly ten minutes it took to drop his entire load. They'd wake to a papered campus in the morning.

Cabin empty of the toilet paper, he headed back for Thomasville, ducked down, and flew low to the Gulf, emerging over the coast at Panacea. He headed out into the Gulf, turned north, and regained the proper altitude. He landed uneventfully at Panama City and drove his rental car to the Pelican Hightower.

If caught, the FAA could suspend his license. Buzzing is illegal. Not to mention littering.

But nobody would be able to figure Rudyard Six was the culprit.

Well, *one* person would, and she wouldn't tell.

But she, By God, alone would understand the message.

CHAPTER TWENTY-TWO
HER

She was angry, ashamed, guilty.

She got in Lance's car. "I want out of here bad."

"I live in the athletic dorm, but there's an apartment owned by a Seminole booster, he lets me crash over there when I want." Lance grimaced in the dome light. He closed the door. "It's one of the questionable benefits of being a starter on the team." He touched her arm. "You all right?"

"I don't know." Her voice was small.

"The apartment sound okay?"

"Fine." It beat the hell out of sleeping at Pools & Patios in a lounge chair.

Aloha had always been driven by sexual urges she was just now beginning to understand. She welcomed what was at hand, but not without some guilt. She suspected those sexual urges were subconsciously responsible for her predicament right now.

—You bet, sis.

—Shut up.

—You'll regret this later, said Bonnie, but he sure is oh, so good looking.

Lance drove across town, to an apartment on a new street out past West Tennessee Street. Aloha liked the area. They'd saved the trees.

Once inside, they were undressed and in bed before she could think. She threw her leg over his hip and they made love face to face, urgently and with no preliminaries. She remembered reading avidly Erica Jong's book. This, then, was your basic "zipless fuck." Then they repeated the act more slowly and more conscious of each other's needs.

Aloha couldn't get enough of him. His body was hard and muscled from football conditioning. And he apparently couldn't get enough of her. "I've wanted you for years," he told her after the second time. "And I find now I want you more than I did before."

"That's so sweet."

He ran his mouth over her entire body, trying to learn it. It drove her crazy and they made love again; this time it was longer, and more satisfying.

They drowsed until dawn, when he awoke her with a seemingly endless need matching her own.

She appreciated Lance, for he did not make small talk. Not now. He knew she was lying there thinking about what had happened with Rudd.

Her guilt had risen and risen until Lance had wanted her again, that pushed her self-recrimination to the back of her mind.

But afterward, he fell asleep, and she just curled up on her side and wished she could be on the sun deck in her lotus position to think this through.

—You were right about your subconscious, said Bonnie.

—I blame myself.

—In fact, upon review, *I* think you wanted to screw Sir Lancelot so much that you went to all the trouble of planning and having that party, knowing, just knowing, you'd probably be caught.

—Could be, Aloha agreed. God, she felt—fulfilled.

—And, Bonnie continued, you were terribly lucky Rudd was drunk.

Aloha almost sat up in bed.

—Make sense, will you? Aloha said

—Had he been sober, he'd have been the ultimate gentleman as he usually is and let you go about your girlie games you were playing. No big scene, no public split. As it was, the scene was *not* a screaming show-down.

—No, it wasn't, was it? Harsh words, but—

—And you got what you been wanting for a year or so, didn't you?

—I always liked sex—

—You could say that, said Bonnie, sarcasm dripping.

—It's not dirty. It's an act of love, of caring.

—Right, sweetie. And you know enough not fall in love just because you fell in bed.

—Buddy told me, Aloha said, something that Rudd always hammered into him. "Don't think with your dick," said Buddy.

—You bein' the female version of that, said Bonnie, thinkin' with your vagina again.

—I miss Buddy, Aloha realized unexpectedly.

—Jeez, girl, keep you pants on! One at a time.

—Uh, oh, said Aloha. Here he comes again!

They stayed in bed most of Sunday.

Aloha realized something about Lance: he was not very experienced in the techniques of making love. Oh, sure, he knew how and what he was supposed to do, and he was a natural. But he was awkward at times, and at other times he delighted in her creativity.

Monday morning, Lance said, "I can cut my classes today. But I have to be at a team meeting at three."

"Go to school," she said. "I haven't missed a class yet, and I'm not about to start now." Though she dreaded seeing some of her friends. Certainly the whole school knew about her big fight with Rudd and her consequent humiliation.

—Do you think it was worth it? asked Bonnie.

—After having an orgasm before school on Monday morning? Hell, yes it was worth it. You remember what a morner is? she asked Bonnie.

—It's a nooner, only sooner, replied her alter ego.

She called Rudd's number and got no answer, so he was already at work. She had Lance drop her off there. She packed a suitcase quickly, got her books and vests, threw it all in her truck and left. She'd come and get more of her things later in the week when she was settled.

—Settled? Where?

—Beats me.

Lance had assured her they could stay at that apartment without repercussions. The athletic booster who owned it ostensibly had the apartment up for rent, but let Lance stay there when he wanted. It was a good tax write-off, Aloha recognized. Unrented apartment, take it off the top of your taxes. There was even a for sale sign out front, the listing of the entire building obviously legitimatizing the fact the apartment hadn't been rented.

Aloha attended her classes that day. She discovered the Strange Things Happen Rule. While she was the subject of conversation, most people applauded the fact that she and Lance were together. It seemed to have enhanced both of their reputations.

After classes, she went to the post office and submitted an individual change of address from the house to Pools & Patios, where she had a small office in the back. Then she went to Lance's apartment to unpack her suitcase—and stack of vests.

As she carried the vests in, she saw the one on top was one of the three Rudd had bought her in Key West, a khaki sort of thing with big pockets, probably supposed to evoke a Hemingwayesque look.

On her second load, she took her suitcase inside and saw the FOR SALE sign as if seeing it for the first time. "Uh, oh."

The building contained four two-story apartments, one in each quadrant.

She called the realty number and they gave her the runaround. "You don't want to sell it, do you?'

"We do, it's just, well, we're representing the owner and he's out of town."

"Yeah, right."

Next she called her appraiser. She explained about the realtor being evasive.

The appraiser, by now her good friend because of all the work she'd brought him, looked up the listing in the Multiple Listing Service. "That sounds inordinately high an asking price," he told her. "Let me check recent sales of similar property in that area. Gimme ten minutes, I'll call you back. I have your number."

"Not anymore, I'm at a different number for now. It's at the building itself."

Ten minutes to the second he was back. "The price is a bit more than ten percent over market. The comps prove it."

"The owner doesn't want to sell—unless he can make a killing," Aloha replied. "Go ahead and do a formal appraisal, will you?"

Lance returned late from football practice. Aloha had the apartment cleaned, and supper organized.

"You cook, too," he said, eying the Cuban yellow rice and chicken.

"I'm a regular domestic engineer," she said. "I met some of the people in the other apartments today. They're kind of nice. I like it here." Scouting the property.

"Great. I called the owner and cleared this with him—"

"Cleared what?"

"Um. Golly, Aloha, don't make it hard on me."

"You are referring to a living arrangement, namely you and me?"

He smiled shyly and she liked that in him. "Yes, ma'am, that's what I mean. I was hoping, sort of, you know—"

"Jeez, Lance. Ask me first?"

"Aloha, would you like to stay here in this apartment with me?"

"I'd love to, Sir Knight." She dimpled.

Lance ducked his head in a self-deprecating manner. "Thanks. This kind of stuff is new to me."

He thought nothing of his statement; but it did imply that she was more used to sexual arrangements and the appropriate protocols. —That one hurt, said Bonnie.

—But he was right, Aloha pointed out.

—Not by much.

As if by mutual consent, they went to bed early that night.

Something else Rudd used to say? What was it? The bit about taking him all night long to do what he used to do all night long.

—Well, said Bonnie. Lancelot is just an overgrown boy. Just because he's quick doesn't mean he's bad.

—Quick and often, you could say.

—Don't fret, dear. You'll teach him.

After breakfast that Tuesday morning, she made Lance give her the name and phone number of the landlord.

"Why do you want it?"

"I might want to talk to him."

"What about? This is kind of an under-the-table deal."

"I know, sugar. I'll smooze him. I just want to feel him out, sort of a courtesy call, make him feel okay about our arrangement."

"Well, okay."

"What's his name."

"Ralph Rucker. Rucker Insurance. He played football for FSU, too. Years ago."

They each went their separate way to school that morning. Aloha couldn't find a place to park and finally went to Doak Campbell Stadium and walked to the Williams Building. Two television news crews passed her on Woodward Avenue when she went to the Strozier Library to drop off a book.

Walking across Landis Green, it became obvious what the television newshawks were after. Much of the campus had streaks of toilet paper lying all about. It was especially thick in the Westcott and Williams Building areas. Someone had done a major TP job. A whole fraternity? No—

Rudd! That sonofabitch!

There was only one way so much toilet paper could have been delivered.

In the middle of Landis Green, she turned a full 360 degrees, admiring his work. Even the library.

Unmindful of other students walking past, she looked up in the clear morning sky and said aloud, "I got your message, you son of a bitch."

After school she went to her tiny office in the back of Pools & Patios and called the appraiser.

He gave her the numbers he'd come up with. "I went in your apartment only," he said. "All four are alike."

"Thanks. The check's in the mail."

"I love doing business with you, Aloha."

She dialed the owner's number and got Rucker Insurance Agency. It was easy to get him on the line.

She introduced herself and said she was a prospective buyer.

"I don't handle that. The realty—"

"Your real estate agent isn't very cooperative."

"I'm sure you're mistaken. I'll talk to them."

"I know where your office is downtown, Mr. Rucker, I'd like to come down there and make you an offer for the building. You can have your agent with you if you like."

"No, ma'am. It's not for sale." Bang. He hung up on her.

Aloha sighed. She was in a very short aqua dress and did not bother to change. She got in her pickup and drove downtown.

As she walked into Rucker Insurance Agency, she passed through a small garden guarded by a ceramic "colored jockey" in a green vest and arm outstretched holding a lantern. "Wish me luck," she told the statue. She touched his hand holding the lantern.

She found Rucker at a water cooler. He was tall and florid and looked very much the ex-jock of twenty years. The office was lined with FSU paraphernalia, banners, photos, signed footballs.

She introduced herself. "I'm the one on the phone?"

"That's good rental propity out there, honey. Why'd I want to sell?"

Honey? "Because you have it listed and there's a big old sign in the yard."

"Oh, I forgot. I meant to withdraw that off the market."

"That doesn't sound quite fair," she said mildly.

"Oh, well. Bidness is bidness."

"Get a pencil," or crayon, you cretin, "or something to write with. Write this down. You know how much it's listed for? I had it appraised this afternoon." She told him the figure. "And this is *my* offer." The appraisal was twelve percent lower than the asking price. She took another ten percent off that figure to make her own offer.

"Jesus, little lady. You're crazy. Now, if I can get back to work?" His face was red.

Little lady? Right. "Ralph. I'm going to give you three reasons to sell me that building."

"This is a joke, right?" His face became redder.

"Reason number one. Tax fraud. I don't have to look at your records to know that you're not making an effort to rent apartment A. Yet it's occupied much of the time. Your income from the building only reflects apartments B, C, and D. If I were the IRS I'd want to know how many years this has been going on, if it's ever been rented."

"Nothing says I have to rent it out—" His eyes darted as if afraid the office staff was listening.

"If so, then you cannot write it off like that. Let me call the IRS and ask them about it. Want to hear reason number two?"

"No, I don't. I think this is some kind of extortion—" He leaned on the upside down water bottle and it burped.

"That's a heavy accusation, Mr. Rucker. Reason two: The NCAA."

"Well, shit—"

"Who can and does slap probations and suspensions on member schools' athletic programs because of booster rule violations—"

"Now, now, little lady—"

"Reason three. I'll bet you don't remember my name. Write this down. Aloha Blaze. Do you know Handy Hank Hartwell?"

"Hell, I do. Everybody knows Hank."

"Here's what I want you to do. You call Hank and you tell

him my name. You can talk to him if you want, whatever. But Hank is my bona fides. Then you will likely want to sell to me. Have your realtor call me and I'll do the paperwork with them and get my own financing."

"But I—"

"You just call Hank. Since I don't need to, I won't bother him with my first two reasons, he doesn't need to know."

"Thank *you* for small favors." He glared at her. "You play fucking hardball."

She did not respond and turned to leave.

"I never want to see you again."

"Me, neither," she said and went out the door.

She stopped in front of the ceramic jockey. "This fifties sexist and racist shit pisses me off," she told the statue.

She hiked up her dress to her waist, exposing her powder blue panties, spun and did a side kick. The lantern went flying and bounced off Rucker's plate glass window

People were staring at her through the window.

A sliding ball kick took off the jockey's outstretched arm. A heel thrust knocked off one leg. She spun into another side kick and the other arm went. She kept spinning and kicked off the head next. It flew up and crashed into a gurgling fountain.

She rotated and delivered a full vertical punch to the torso and it exploded into shards and dust.

Her final strike was completely show off, but she couldn't stop herself. Leaping in the air, she performed a perfect heel strike to the crumbling remains of the jockey and the explosion of the thigh and last leg peppered the window. She saw people surge backwards. But the plate glass must have been safety glass.

She tugged her dress down to its proper position. She saw Rucker standing inside, aghast. "Rucker! This little lady wants to kick your ass!" She couldn't tell if they heard her inside or not. But no one hurried out, so she just waved them off with her right hand, adjusted her dress, and walked away feeling oh so better.

Wednesday, on her way to class, she stopped by the Student Union and bought three newspapers. The TP episode was headline in *The Tallahassee Democrat*, and below the fold in *The Tampa Tribune*; and in *The St. Petersburg Times*, it was in the state section.

After class, she called Ralph Rucker's realtor.

"What did you do to Ralph?"

"I talked like a Florida Cracker," she said. She told them the name of the title company which would handle the transfer. Then she called her banker.

"Not again, Aloha."

"Yes, again. All that money burning a hole in your vault, I need to do something with it. Borrow against it—for now."

"How much?"

"Can you float a mortgage for three hundred?"

"With your account and assets we could go up to five hundred thousand, no questions asked."

"I only need three, your best customer rate." Which should be a quarter under market. "Incidentally, I got the property at ten percent under appraisal."

"Done. We have the latest on you?"

"This is it since JINX PLAZA."

"Money will be available whenever you need it."

"Oh. One thing more. I'm going to write a check for one hundred thousand dollars in the next day or two."

"That cuts things a bit closer, but you still come in under the wire."

Aloha next called Hank Hartwell. "Hank, thanks for helping with Rucker. I didn't hear from him, but his realtor agreed to my proposal."

"It's the least I could do, Aloha. I don't know what you did to old Ralph, but you did not make a friend."

"I had to twist his condescending arm."

"You know, Aloha, if you turn ruthless, you'll own this town."

That gave her pause to think. "Not me. Thanks for being a

dear friend."

"Anytime. I tried to call Rudd today, and Zeke said he's out of town for a while. What's up?"

She didn't want to disavow Rudd. And she needed to keep on Hank's good side. Her mind figured out what Rudd had done immediately. "Oh, he needs some time off by himself. He'll be back and up to speed soon."

After she hung up, she felt an immediate concern for Rudd. Jeez, he must have taken it hard.

—You bet, sweetie. When you dump somebody, you don't let them down gently, you hang them by the balls.

—That's not what happened.

—It worked out that way.

The following day, she went back to the house and removed most of her stuff. At least the apartment had two bedrooms, one of which she appropriated as a room for herself and her stuff.

When Lance came in after practice, he remarked, "The FOR SALE sign is gone. Hope they didn't sell this place."

"They did and we won't be out on the street, don't you worry."

"What do you mean?"

"I mean somebody I know very well bought it and we're gonna live here rent free."

"That's why you wanted Ralph's name and number." He said it half accusingly.

"Yes, dear Lance, I did. Now you are safe. If somebody ever tells the NCAA about you and this free apartment, you'd have lost your eligibility right then. No eligibility, no more football. No NFL in your future. That's probably the important thing to you. The important thing to me is that you'd lose your scholarship and consequently your schooling. There's a few other benefits, for instance you won't get FSU in trouble with the NCAA."

He stared at her. "Jezus, Peezus, Aloha. You only been here a couple days and already you're saving my ass. I don't know what to say."

"Don't say anything. Just hold me."

"I'll do more than hold you."

Surprise, surprise.

* * * * * *

For weeks, Lance Gugliotta and Aloha Blaze were insepa-rable. They ate out at pizza restaurants, met for lunch, and were seen all over campus. Everybody said they were a natural couple.

Aloha attained a certain amount of notoriety from this; a few thousand people knew her or knew of her. And it did not escape anybody's notice that she was a 4.0 student. Lance remained the same, even though most of the male population now considered him a super stud. After all, he'd hooked the most beautiful girl on campus—and the most difficult catch in that sea.

Being fall and football season, Lance was busy all the time. And gone most Saturdays. Sundays he nursed his bruises and rested from the beating he took from the games the day before.

So, Aloha sometimes went skydiving on those days. She no longer flew, because she didn't have free access to aircraft. And most of the guys out at Rudd's competition would recognize her and the word would go straight to Rudd. And maybe she didn't want to embarrass him by paying money to his competition. On the other hand, if she needed to fly, she could probably call Zeke and arrange a flight without Rudd knowing.

One late Saturday night, she picked up Lance at the airport when they returned from an away game in North Carolina. She'd driven past SIXGUN AIR out of curiosity and a bit of nostalgia—

—And because you miss him, interjected Bonnie.

—I do, admitted Aloha. Hell, I still love him. I just don't like him.

—Spin me another tale.

There was a light on in the office part of his hangar and she had to fight herself to keep from stopping. She didn't think she could face him. She shook herself.

After she picked up Lance, she told him she'd listened to the game on the radio and he done good.

Lance beamed in her praise. "I'm a lot better since you came into my life, Aloha. Coach even noticed a difference."

"Practice makes perfect," she said.

"What'd you do today?"

"Went skydiving," she said without thinking, because she was driving her red pickup past SIXGUN AIR and the light was off in the office and a car was pulling out of the parking lot. She stepped on the gas and sped off, not wanting to be seen by whomever....

"Skydiving? You're kidding."

"Nope."

"Well, I didn't know that about you."

A lot you don't know about me, dear. "It never occurred to me to tell you. There's a lot we still don't know about each other."

"There's a lot I *do* know about you," he said salaciously.

"I know a guy who trains skydivers; he'll train you if you want."

Lance trembled. "Me? No thanks. I'm not crazy."

* * * * * * *

In the weeks that followed, Aloha kept busy.

She completed the transaction for the building and was now the owner. And now *she* got the tax break.

She continued to practice her unarmed combat.

One day she was irritated.

—Where the *hell* are my flowers?

—You killed them yourself.

—Oops. Right. I miss 'em, though.

She thought often about Rudd. What he'd said about Marge was bilge; but he'd been right about Denise. Denise had disowned Rudd because of Aloha; and now that weighed on Aloha's conscience.

So she sat down and wrote a check for a thousand dollars to The Church of the Redeemer. In the note section on the check, she wrote "Charitable donation, Rudd Six."

—You've sunk to a new low, Bonnie observed. Buying off your own conscience.

—Not exactly. Though it helps. There's a madness to my method.

—Convoluted, as usual.

Even though the athletic program provided tutors, Aloha helped Lance with his studies and his grades improved significantly.

—I'm glad you have *some* positive impact on your men, said Bonnie snidely.

—I'm thinking about banishing you, said Aloha. You're getting more and more caustic.

—That's called a conscience, honey.

One day, Aloha picked up Lance after school. "I've got to make a quick stop and get my checkbook," she told him as they drove to JINX PLAZA.

"Aloha's Place?" Lance asked as they pulled up.

"My laundromat."

"You *own* a laundromat?"

"I do. I also own this whole plaza, the pool store, the video store. Next, I'm going to buy out the book store. The only thing I won't have is the pizza place; I don't want to mess with food and health codes, they're too much trouble."

"There are depths to you that I never guessed at."

"You've probed some of 'em."

Color rose in his cheeks.

She showed him all the businesses, finally going into Pools & Patios.

"Hey, Aloha," said the manager. "Zeke's been trying to get a hold of you."

Fear stabbed into her heart. Rudd? Was he okay?

"Did Zeke say what he wanted?"

"You're supposed to call him. If you're free Saturday, they need you to fly the mission relief supply run down to Haiti."

She went in her office and called Zeke.

"Everybody's either out of town or committed," Zeke told her. "I thought of you. You're supposed to have a commercial license to fly cargo, but nobody checks paperwork on these relief flights."

Lance had a game down in Miami Saturday. "Sure, glad to help, Zeke. I'll be there." And SIXGUN AIR and Zeke would owe her a favor, so later if she needed to fly she could borrow a plane. Then something occurred to her. Could Zeke be doing this to get her back with Rudd? To talk to her?

She sat back thinking, ignoring Lance.

"Let me get this straight, Aloha." He sat on the corner of her desk. "You're going to fly an airplane?"

"Right. Down to Haiti and back."

"That's something else I didn't know about you." He didn't sound happy.

"I'm a person of many talents."

"You are not the same girl I knew back at Leon High, Aloha. You've changed. You're so, so *grown-up*. You got it together big time. You're in charge of everything you do. Including me." This last, he got out sounding strangled.

—Shit. I've overwhelmed the poor kid.

—Kid? He's older than you. Think emasculation.

—He's young, he's just feeling threatened.

—*Rudd* was never threatened by you.

—He shouldn't be. He opened all these doors. It's because of Rudd that I know these things.

"Lance? I don't know what to say. I'm me. As Popeye says, I yam what I yam. I try to do the best possible in everything I do." She put her hand on his knee and rubbed it.

"It bothers me you're so far out of my league. I remember little Aloha Blaze."

Lost Aloha Blaze. "You're one of the top quarterbacks in the country. You're the best you can be. It's just that we each have our own areas of interest."

"Well, yeah. I guess."

That night, long after he'd fallen asleep, she stared up at the ceiling.

Something had been bothering her, too. She wanted to show Rudd she could do without him.

The next day she wrote Rudd a letter.

Dear Rudd,

You put $100,000 in my account as a gift. I thank you but I cannot accept it, considering our new circumstances. Be advised I'll have to pay a large gift tax to Uncle. However, if you want to consider the sum a loan, then all you have to do is pay taxes on the interest I'll pay you; and, in turn, I can deduct my interest payment.

Enclosed, please find one check in the amount of $100,000 and another in the amount of $7,500 interest.

It's your choice, cash whichever strikes your fancy.

Best wishes,

Aloha

She thought a long time before she decided to end the note with "best wishes." That was neutral enough. She folded the letter and put it in an envelope to be mailed tomorrow. She wrote the two checks and put them atop the envelope to remind her.

Naturally, Lance discovered the checks.

Aloha was reading Dumas and Lance was highlighting his notes from his history course.

"Golly, Aloha. A hundred thousand dollars? In one check? I've only dreamed of this. I'd have to be a first round selection in the draft."

Patiently, she explained. "The IRS tracks large amounts of money. Banks, financial institutions have to tell them. If I get a hundred grand, I either earned it, in which case I pay income tax or royalties depending how I got it. If somebody just gave me the money, then I pay a gift tax. But if I borrowed the money, I still have it, don't pay taxes a bit. *But* I should be able to prove I'm using the money legitimately for business purposes in this case. If so, I can deduct the interest payment as a legitimate expense."

He was bright enough to follow her. "The legit expense being?"

"Partly this apartment building. Other investments."

"Aw, not again! You told me somebody else bought it."

"I said somebody very close to me. Listen, Lance. I didn't want to upset you."

"Upset? You overwhelm me a lot." He slammed the history book closed on his notes, shoved his chair back and went into the bedroom. Aloha heard the television go on very loud.

She sighed. She stood. She went to the bedroom door. "Lance?"

She stood expectantly for two minutes and finally the television sound went off.

"Lance. I invoke the Popeye rule. I am what I am. I am me."

"I adore you and I love you," he said, sitting upright against two pillows. "I am afraid of you."

"We each have our own lives to lead. Once we get used to each other, these things will fall in place."

He didn't respond.

"Want to see if we both still fit in the shower at the same time?"

"No."

Aloha went back to Dumas, which was depressing in itself.

She knew this was the beginning of the end.

CHAPTER TWENTY-THREE
HIM

The first time Rudd saw Colette Duval, there was something wrong with this picture, but he couldn't put his finger on it. Both were staying at the Pelican Hightower. And both were out jogging on the beach at dawn.

He was running behind her, going faster than she, and as he caught up he identified what it was. She was running with an athlete's smooth and effortless gait, but her graceful motion had a hitch in it. There. Her arm, her right arm was a bit out of synch in the traditional runner's circular pistoning. He wondered why.

The Gulf of Mexico warmed the chill of fall breeze and Rudd felt good for a change. As long as he was physically active, he could put Aloha out of his mind.

Yes or no, he debated himself. The answer would chart the rest of his life.

He didn't want to pass the woman, so he slowed his pace. Any diversion to distract him from the ache.

She was very slender, he could see, athletic legs, tight derriere, small breasts, nice shoulders, and a rounded face which was singularly attractive, framed by auburn hair that wasn't quite shoulder length.

He followed her appreciatively for a half mile.

Then she slowed and motioned him past her.

"*Bonjour.* You can go ahead?" French, pure and simple. Her accent was so out of place on the beach of Panama City, Florida at dawn, it was striking.

"I'm in no hurry," he said.

"It is so beautiful here," she said. "The Riviera, where I go, it is so many rocks."

He fell in step beside her. "The problem with this beach is when the tide is high, you have to run in the softer sand."

"I have seen you at the hotel. You are on vacation, no?"

"You could say that." More like a retreat from the battle front.

They ran comfortably together for a few minutes.

"How far do you run?" she asked.

"Forty-five minutes, an hour." The longer he ran, the greater the interval he avoided the hurt savaging him.

"Me, too."

As if by mutual consent, they turned around and headed back for the hotel.

"I am Colette Duval," she told him.

"My name is Rudd."

"That is unusual in America."

"It is. My father loved the writings of Rudyard Kipling. He collected old first editions, he read everything Kipling wrote. He was an expert on the writer."

"I do not read much; my friend, she reads."

Rudd saw they were within a mile of the hotel, the sun shining over his shoulder.

Colette took off at a surprising speed. "Race you." She ran like a graceful animal, full long stride, arms pumping but not heavily. As he reached her, he saw her right arm motion more pronounced. "I always run hard the last mile."

Rudd saved his breath to match her pace. Buddy used to sprint the last mile, too; Rudd simply maintained the same rate until he finished. Only because his legs were longer and they did not have to run farther than the final mile was he able to stay with her.

Rudd went to his room and changed to a bathing suit, grabbed a towel and headed back to the alabaster beach. He swam for a little while to cool off.

Colette Duval came out a few minutes later. Another woman

was with her. Colette walked into the Gulf gingerly, for it hadn't warmed enough yet today. She saw Rudd, waved, and swam her own way.

The water temperature was too cold for him to swim long, so he went back up the beach and retrieved his towel.

Colette saw him and hurried to do likewise. She came over to him, drying her hair. She wore a modest two piece suit and Rudd saw how slender she really was. Her hair was now stringy and wet and she was busily drying it with a hotel towel.

"*Aimez-vous nager*? Do you like to swim?"

"I love it. But it's too cool this morning. The hotel pool is warm."

She motioned from him to the other woman. "Come, I would like you to meet my friend." She led Rudd to the other woman.

The woman was sitting on a towel, regarding the two of them. She scrutinized Rudd closely as they approached, then she rose. She reminded Rudd of a fireplug, but none of her largeness was bulky or fat; it was all muscle, legs and arms especially. She wore shorts and a pullover shirt and her hair was black and very short.

Colette introduced them. "Simone? I present mister Rudd—?"

"Six," he said.

"And, Monsieur Six, I present Mademoiselle Simone Gauthier."

Rudd shook hands with the black haired woman and guessed her to be perhaps forty years old. He prepared for a crushing handshake, but Simone's grip was perfunctory. There was something familiar about Simone Gauthier.

"I am Simone's assistant and travelling compa—"

"I remember," Rudd said, "tennis champion. Won some Grand Slams, Wimbleton. Maybe ten years ago."

Simone was smiling now, her broad face broken by the fissure.

"She is retired then," said Colette. "Now she performs exhibitions, *n'est-ce pas*?"

"Yes, I understand. I've seen in sports magazines endorsements—"

"That is so," said Colette. "Simone, she speaks English well, but she wants me to talk for her, for practice."

They were on vacation, between exhibition matches. Simone apparently also acted as spokesperson for some products and made personal appearances for them.

Then Rudd had to explain his presence. He made it as simple as possible: vacation.

"You have no wife?" Simone asked pointedly.

"Not any more."

"I am sorry," said Colette, reading hurt in his eyes and face.

He wasn't going to explain his double meaning. "It's been many years."

She brightened, which cheered him immensely. He liked Colette, for she did not appear to be a complicated person; simply a curious, healthy young woman.

He explained that he intended to go spelunking up in Marianna today, near the Georgia border. Impulsively, he invited the two French women.

Colette glanced at Simone.

The ex-tennis star waved her right hand magnanimously. "Not for me. You may go."

It turned into an all-day trip, and they returned dirty, muddy, and tired.

The next morning when he went to jog on the beach, she was waiting for him. He was beginning to like Colette a lot. She was very attentive and not assertive at all—unlike Aloha Blaze. The comparison was inevitable.

After the run, they swam in the Hightower pool and sunned themselves for most of the morning. Rudd welcomed her company, for he could ignore his inner demand to address the yes or no question. He had to make a decision, but flat didn't want to. Aloha's defection hurt him so much, he was seriously considering a major change in his life.

He was merely putting off making himself decide.

That evening, Rudd was going into the dining room when

he encountered the two women. They ate together and Simone Gauthier paid for Rudd's meal, which made him uncomfortable. Simone drank four-star brandy constantly and it did not seem to affect her. Colette drank three glasses of burgundy. Rudd had his usual gin. Twice autograph seekers interrupted them.

After dinner, they moved to the lounge, where Simone continued to toss back brandy. Rudd wondered if and when it would catch up with her.

They drank for a while and watched people dance and the band play.

"Why not you two dance some?" said Simone.

As Rudd was shrugging off the suggestion, Colette jumped up and said, *"Oui."*

She wore a beige sheath dress and he was glad he'd opted for a jacket and tie. Colette's hand and arm clasped him under the jacket. They danced slowly and he found her naturally agile and she followed his lead perfectly.

"Vous dansez très bien." She looked up at him happily. "I mean you dance well."

"Thanks." An ache lanced through him. He'd taught Aloha the fine points of dancing. On the other hand, Colette was lighter on her feet than Aloha.

He glanced at Simone. She was still practically chugalugging brandy, eyes roaming the room. He'd noticed that some people recognized her. They were more familiar with tennis circles than he was. Once or twice people, mostly women, came over for autographs.

After two slow dances, they went back to the table. Simone's eyes were beginning to glaze over. She spoke in rapid French to Colette and sat back with an empty glass.

"My Colette. She was one who was going to be the next superstar," Simone said. "Fifteen years of age. The younger ones were taking over. Colette, too. In three years she would have been a champion, ranked in the top five." She flagged down a waiter for more brandy.

"I was so ashamed," said Colette. "At the *aèroport*, Heathrow, in London, my first time at Wimbledon. I fell down went boom over a suitcase. My right arm, poof."

Which told Rudd the reason for the discontinuity in her arm movement.

Simone took her brandy from the waiter. "The break did not heal well. Colette was right-handed and her career finished not long after it began." Simone drank some brandy and her eyes roamed the room. "She would have been greater than I, ever."

"Merci."

The band was playing another slow tune.

Colette said, "But the injury does not hinder my dancing."

Taking the hint, Rudd stood and pulled back her chair.

As they danced, Rudd watched Simone move to a table against the back wall and join two women there. He sort of got the idea that Simone was pushing him and Colette together. He reviewed their friendship so far and he admitted you could construe what had happened as such. At that moment, Colette melted against him, no longer the formal dancer. Rudd did enjoy her wiry hard body against his. He found the experience distracting from his sense of loss.

He wanted to drink only a little, for, the more he considered it, the more it was obvious Colette was staking him out from the crowd. If he stayed sober, he'd be able to handle rationally whatever she threw at him.

But he didn't fight it; he didn't care. He drank plenty of gin. Whatever happened, so be it. It was a measure of how much Aloha's defection had done to his psyche.

Late that evening, what was supposed to happen, happened.

They were walking on the dark beach, past the hotel's well-lighted grounds, to air out. The lounge had turned very smokey.

An unexpected rain squall blew in off the gulf and Rudd led her to a cluster of palms and slash pine between two towering sand dunes.

"It shouldn't last long." He took his jacket off, ruefully seeing how wet it had already become, and draped it over her shoulders. Then he put his arm around her shoulders to further protect her.

"Merci." She huddled closer to him.

The cold rain made her shiver and he enclosed her in both his arms and she tilted her face to him and the natural occurred.

Rudd was surprised, for he didn't think he'd react sexually to the French woman. But he found himself aroused and he crushed her to him. All four hands roamed, seeking, as their hips ground together.

Then she pushed him away and slipped her dress over her head and in an instant she was nude. Her small breasts were perfectly round and rock-hard. She watched him speculatively for a moment and then stripped him.

In seconds they were lying on the soft mat of pine needles, rain beating on them. She pushed him back and climbed atop him, poised, then impaled herself. *"Chéri!"*

Rudd flipped his jacket over her shoulders as she rode him desperately. She was lithe and gripped him with strong legs. She was athletic and rhythmic.

Surprisingly, it was over quickly, both climaxing together, straining rigidly at the end. Then she collapsed on him and covered his face with kisses. He ran his hands over her breasts, her back, her buttocks and thighs.

In a few minutes, she broke contact, rose, and held her hand out to him.

He took her hand and she pulled him up with surprising strength. She dropped his jacket, turned and ran toward the Gulf. "Come."

He followed her into the surf and past the waves cresting from the storm. Since it was low tide, the water wasn't very deep. He discovered the temperature of the Gulf of Mexico was more than the ambient air temperature and it warmed them.

The warmth was a relief and Colette swarmed into his arms, locking her lips onto his and lifting her legs to capture him. She sank down on him and they rocked hips for a moment and then froze together, heat burning between them, the only motion slight hip twitching. They remained still for minutes as the passion between them grew and grew until they exploded together. He held her tightly against him as her heels dug into his hips. Then she writhed, moaning in his arms. He held on for the ride while she had multiple orgasms.

Back at the hotel, they went to his room and took a scalding shower together. They fell into the big king bed that was standard at the Pelican Hightower. Colette curled against him contentedly and promptly fell asleep. She snored softly, a comforting sound.

His left arm cradling her, his mind whirled.

Yes or no?

He didn't know for sure, but he suspected most men were like him in one respect. That being each man had a place already selected—a town, a city, a rural area, one or more—which was geographically far removed from where you were at the present.

A place to which you could escape and start over.

The place identified because it was somewhere you'd encountered along the way and liked a great deal. The main criterion was that this special place was way and the hell removed from wherever you are when the trouble mounts too much and you know you got to bail out or something bad wrong could happen.

One such place Rudyard Kipling Six had identified for himself was Yakima, Washington. A growing city, yet throw a rock and you're out in the country. It had its own small airport where he could run a flying service like SIXGUN AIR, or fly crop-dusters, or charters. He even owned a few empty acres there.

Rudd had determined that this respite in Panama City would be for the purpose of getting away from his life in Tallahassee and thus giving him a sample of life away from there and time to make the decision whether or not to bail out.

He had no one left. Buddy, Denise, Marge, all gone, involved in making their own lives work. Aloha.

Aloha. Sadness settled into his soul. He'd loved her so much. This time in Panama City was also designed to help him get over her.

It wasn't working. The ache remained.

Colette shifted in her sleep and Rudd realized he was

becoming exceedingly fond of the woman. He couldn't help it. She had such a refreshing persona, honest and frank in her needs.

But he wasn't intellectually attuned to her as he was to Aloha. Between Aloha and him had been a link which was more than sex, more than common intellectual interests, more than simple getting along.

Colette was slender and unassuming; Aloha was full-breasted and more substantial, lusty, bawdy, randy.

Colette was beguiling, Aloha was intriguing.

Colette was an enchanting fantasy; Aloha was bold and sensual reality.

It was becoming obvious to him, moving from the back of his mind to the front, that he was using Colette too, as she was using him. At first he'd considered Colette his way of getting even with Aloha. But now he knew that wasn't exactly the case.

Colette was his key to breaking Aloha's spell over him. And he was going to continue the affair with Colette for however long possible for the very same reason. Aloha had bewitched him and he was just now realizing how thoroughly.

He was becoming too analytical. He rolled over and spooned with Colette. She sensed the move and snuggled backwards so she was jammed against him.

Rudd fell asleep fighting demons and decisions.

They ran again in the morning.

A tall, powerful blonde woman was running, too. The blonde passed them going the other way and struck fear into Rudd's heart for the way she held her head and her build and deep, determined stride evoked the image of Aloha Blaze.

After a moment, Rudd looked back over his shoulder and the woman was gone.

But a wave had ridden up the beach. All that remained was the woman's deep footprints; his and Colette's were erased as if they'd never been there.

The metaphor bludgeoned him. Few people make a significant impact upon the world and Aloha was one of the few.

CHAPTER TWENTY-FOUR
HER

Aloha Blaze had to find somebody who'd get Rudd out of her mind. And Lance wasn't the one.

The end of football season had come and gone. The Seminoles had done very well. Consequently, now she and Lance were spending more and more time together and, because of that, she was finding they had less and less in common. The physical part was good, of course, and dear Lance tried. At her urging, he tried to read, but reading wasn't his strong suit. At least he tried, she thought.

Also, he'd never gotten over his resentment of her success and self-reliance. Their social circles tended to be different; but her reputation grew as a stunningly beautiful sky diving pilot entrepreneur superstudent with a 4.0 average and a body to kill for. With her now full-blown sense of self-esteem, she no longer concealed her intellectual abilities as she had done in high school.

Four sororities and the cheerleading squad wanted her. But she realized they wanted her for either her looks or her status, and neither, therefore, interested her.

Her parents were still working in Africa. They were happy she was doing well; they were ecstatic she didn't need any money. Aloha gave up her scholarship and grants, for Rudd had long ago given her money for tuition and she didn't need the money: perhaps someone else needier could go to college now. This gave her another thought: so many students needed financial help that she made it policy to hire only FSU students for part time help in her businesses. All of which led her to thinking of ways to help more students than she was capable of hiring. Thus the repo house concept.

In the spring session, she changed her mind on her major again. She'd gone from English to Business Admin to Finance. Now she was back with English, but taking a finance course. She was learning that while many of the professors and instructors over in the Business building knew and taught the theoretical well, most hadn't been exposed to the real thing. Some of her friends in Education told her similar stories. English in the School of Arts and Sciences was different. There, theoretical was actuality. An interesting difference she'd encountered was that peppered throughout the Arts and Sciences disciplines were professors for the reason of being professors: they'd stayed in school themselves through and past undergraduate studies to avoid being drafted into the Vietnam War by maintaining student deferment. When the birthday-lottery draft came along, they just hung out and some made it past the age cutoff and many of the rest were lucky enough to miss the draft entirely before they became too old. So the staff of many departments was decidedly liberal or ex-hippie, speaking generally. Most of them had a wife (or ex-wife now) and at least one kid for the same reason: draft deferment. Consequently, Aloha preferred female instructors and professors.

This dynamic provided Aloha with what she later called "Aloha's Renaissance".

She took a Shakespeare course.

One day the professor was sick and, to fill in, a blind man named Nathan Ex substituted. Nathan Ex was a foremost Shakespeare scholar; but he was not a professor. He was an eclectic.

Next to the Williams Building where the English Department was ensconced, rose Dodd Hall, home of WFSU. WFSU was Florida State's public television station and their campus/public radio station.

On the radio side, the station played mostly its own format, from classical to album rock late at night. And their premier disk jockey was one Nathan Ex. Ex was thirty-five years old and working for the seventh year on some kind of advanced degree in broadcasting. Which meant he took a course or two every year. But he was employed by the station itself and had, over the years, generated a cult following. And he just happened to have a Ph.D. in English, where he'd studied Shakespeare almost exclusively.

One Wednesday spring morning, he walked into the classroom, led by a German shepherd guide dog. He groped his way to the lectern and placed upon the table in front of the podium a briefcase. He was dressed in jeans and a Seminoles sweatshirt. His long hair was casually caught up in a ponytail.

He felt a watch on his left wrist and said, "Time to start. From whence comes this quote: 'Love looks not with the eyes, but with the mind'?"

This bit of wisdom struck an arrow into Aloha's heart.

No one answered.

"Well, dammit, take a guess."

"It wasn't me," said a girl with a giggle.

"It wasn't Ray Charles, either," said Nathan Ex.

"Maybe *Midsummer Night's Dream*?" offered Aloha.

"Excellent," said Nathan. "What's your name, young lady?"

"Aloha Blaze."

"Yours is the most poetic name I've encountered outside of literature. It has its own internal rhythm. My compliments to your parents."

Aloha didn't answer.

"The takeoff point of my lecture," said Nathan Ex, "is that you don't have to have eyes," he gestured at his own under dark glasses, "to love something. In my case, I love the work of William Shakespeare, the Swan of Avon."

As Nathan Ex continued his lecture, Aloha became lost in Shakespeare. She did not think about Rudd or Lance or fantasize about skydiving, or worry about her business interests.

The next week, she went to a poetry reading at a cafe downtown on Monroe Street near the capitol to hear him read.

After he read, she went over and introduced herself.

"Blaze. I remember you," he said.

A woman was preparing to read and so they sat quietly together at a table and listened. Aloha bought him a beer and herself a coffee.

And that was the start of it.

* * * * * * *

Lance Gugliotta moved back to the dorm. "It's not working, you know? It's my fault, really, Aloha. I just need to be with someone more like me."

She kissed him goodbye and depression washed over her.

Aloha Blaze, dumped. Aloha, the beauty, dumped. What the hell was wrong with her?

She was the one who was supposed to dump the male. *She* was supposed to pick and choose, not the other way around.

After going to coffee with Nate Ex, she knew the answer to the question. Lance had loved her for her looks, her body, and her outward personality. Not for herself, not for her intellect, not for her accomplishments.

—Rudd did.

—That's different.

—Yeah, if that's what you *want* to think.

—All Lance wanted was a trophy.

—You are one hell of a trophy, everybody says.

—I don't wanna be a damn trophy. I wanna be loved for me. Lance didn't appreciate me not doting on him. I didn't follow him around with adoring eyes. I had my own life and interests and was *not* dependent on him for those things. He wasn't mature enough to handle me.

—You want to be handled?

—Metaphorically. A poor choice of words. Accommodated, perhaps. Nay, make that *accepted.*

In the spring, the pizza restaurant folded and Aloha took the opportunity to open a dry cleaners and knocked out the wall between that and the laundromat. It was a natural marriage. She arranged to buy out the bookstore and put in a door between the laundromat-video store-dry cleaners so that people could wander through. Don't want a video? Go buy a book to read. Then she included Pools & Patios. She coordinated sales and specials. Business increased in all her stores. The whole plaza was hers. The money she made was more than enough to cover expenses and help pay off bank loans.

She visited more and more with Nate Ex. At first he'd impressed her with his knowledge of Shakespeare, then his wisdom, crusty as it was. And lastly, because he seemed to genuinely like her. And since he couldn't see her, what she looked like was not important to him.

They began dating. At first their social life consisted mostly of long walks and conversation. Aloha loved this. She finally had someone with whom she could discuss books and literature. Their relationship was platonic; not one she enjoyed, but endured.

One day they were walking past Kellum Hall, Nate's arm linked to hers; the seeing eye dog was left at the office.

Aloha was damning her new least favorite book of all time, *The Last of the Mohicans*. "Not only stuffy writing," she said, "but incomprehensible plot mechanisms. One minute you're involved in a shooting war, then the next you've got an alien fog body-snatching dead people and a television-fantasy-surreal landscape. And how could you care about the characters? Whatever got into Cooper? And they call that crap literature."

"The tale has lasted a couple of hundred years," Nate pointed out.

"Likely because nobody can believe how really bad it is and therefore it must be real literature," she said. "There are so many better books we could study—"

From an open window, a young man saw Aloha and gave a loud wolf whistle. Automatically, she turned and smiled and waved.

"Everybody's told me how attractive you are," Nate said.

"Well, I—"

"But it doesn't matter to me. It's your mind and character which fascinates me."

"Obviously, you don't care about my vanity either."

Suddenly, he stopped. He disengaged his arm from hers and put his hands low on her hips and cupped her butt. Then he ran them up her side, along her breasts, over her shoulders, and framed her face. "As The Bard sayeth, thou havest an hour-glass figger, dear lady Blaze. And I feel the beauty exudeth from thy face."

"Nathan!"

They resumed their walk, turning and heading behind the math building and the tunnel under Woodward.

"Our star quarterback has found his way home," Nate said. "You're no longer attached?"

Strangely, this made Aloha feel uncomfortable. "No, I'm not." Her voice was small.

"Ah, you pine for him yet," said Nate.

"Not one damn bit."

She felt him stiffen and they walked silent for a few moments. "From *As you Like It*:

"'If ever—as that ever may be near—
You meet in some fresh cheek the power of fancy,
Then shall you know the wounds invisible
That love's keen arrows make.'"

"What am I supposed to make of that?"

"From *Midsummer Night's Dream*: 'The course of true love never did run smooth'."

"Jeez, Nate, you're giving me the willies." She shivered.

"You *are* suffering the wounds invisible. I am God Damned near psychic, and I can sense those wounds invisible."

She squeezed his arm. They were passing behind the student

union now, paralleling Tennessee Street. "Nate, I've so many slings and arrows of outrageous fortune, I can't stand it. Though, when I'm around you, it's not nearly so bad."

"One of my talents, repairing people. If you want, come and live with me. I'm very gentle."

Nathan Ex lived in a rambling old two-story affair off Jefferson Street, between the Capitol and the university, and within walking distance of school.

Nate had thousands of books in Braille, and a stereo system set up through the entire house.

Aloha found that Nathan had the most agile and zephyr-like hands, incredible hands, which drove her into sexual frenzy. His love-making was not demanding, like Lance, but more of a sharing.

Afterwards, Nate would say quotes like, "'Love comforteth like sunshine after rain.' *Venus and Adonis.*" Or, "'The kiss you take is better than you give.' Meaning you, Blaze. From *Troilus and Cressida*. You give better than you receive."

"Not only are you wonderful, but you're modest, too."

"'For love delights in praises.'"

"Two Gentlemen of Verona?"

"It is, and you are a quick student. And an excellent teacher, for I have learned from you this evening."

"Thanks, I think," said Aloha.

Aloha moved in with Nate Ex, for there was plenty of room upstairs. She rented out her apartment in the condo. She threw herself into her studies and into her work.

Never one to miss an opportunity, she had Nate teach her to read braille. One result was that he was impressed with her and her willingness to learn from him and join him in his endeavors. Which was all true, but it had occurred to her that she could sit cross-legged in the night atop a building outside and watch the stars and read with her fingers: no light necessary. Anything to read. She didn't bother to learn to write it. She graduated quickly from grade 1 braille to grade 2. She never went to grade 3. She applied herself assiduously. The basic braille cell of up to six dots was easy. This provided 63 patterns: all the letters, numbers, some common words and speech sounds. She did not need to write braille with a stylus on a slate or a braillewriter. If she had to leave Nate a message, she simply used a cassette recorder.

Governor's Square Mall was growing fast, and BLAZE VESTS & ETC. opened. On the second level, it sold vests, scarfs, and, for men, vests, too, and ties, suspenders and the like. Her specialty was vests, both in store stock and catalog. She had the most comprehensive selection of catalogs from which to order which had ever been assembled in one location. A specialty which became quite popular was her extensive selection of leather vests. And ahead of time, she managed to set up a section of holiday theme vests, such as green and/or red velour vests for Christmas, black and white Pilgrim models for Thanksgiving, and red, white and blue for Fourth of July. A major problem she encountered was that she wanted to buy hundreds of vests for herself. She steeled her mind against the temptation and her merchandise sold well. Another profit making business. Her businesses thrived, for she was innovative and encouraged employees and store managers to be the same.

There was one fly in the ointment, however. Besides the fact she was no longer getting flowers every week.

Othello.

The seeing-eye dog.

Try as she might, Aloha couldn't seem to make friends with the animal. She supposed that the dog was jealous, for now Nate relied much more on her than the dog.

Aloha learned that just about everything had its place in the household, from the pepper shaker to footstools. Out of necessity, they must be in the same place day in and day out. She learned that he arranged his money in his wallet in a certain sequence, as with the clothes in his closet.

When he did a deejay shift late at night on the radio, she would study or read and listen. Often, he spoke to her without identifying her. By dedicating songs or music and by quoting literature, mostly Shakespeare. She'd climb out an upstairs window and scramble up to the peak and sit and read or simply contemplate.

One day she realized how really good he was at conversation and never at a loss for an intelligent word or thought. "Why don't you do a radio talk show?"

"Specifically?"

"They call you and you talk to them. You're a natural. It's an up and coming thing, sports radio call in shows are taking off. Larry King. Do it on your late night shift here where people won't be so inhibited."

He did that thing and became an immediate campus and local celebrity. Which he wasn't certain he liked.

* * * * * * *

By now, half the school knew she was your basic entrepreneur-sky diving-pilot-stunningly beautiful-straight A student. Some guys still tried to get into her pants, but the only one she was comfortable with was Nate Ex.

Othello was a thorn in her paw. Whenever they were in the same room, his eyes followed her everywhere. This made her very uncomfortable which, likely, the dog picked up and reinforced his behavior. Aloha suspected Othello felt threatened on some basic level; she knew what the animal felt herself: no one seemed to need her much anymore. Oh, sure, Nate needed her for eyes sometimes; but that was mere convenience—he was self-sufficient and sometimes it seemed he only tolerated other people, her included.

Even though her businesses were doing very well and growing, she went into another period of melancholy.

One afternoon, Nate came home to find Aloha drinking pink champagne. She hardly ever drank anything alcoholic, but this Wednesday afternoon, she simply had a craving for the sweet bubbly. She was dressed in a black leather vest and short, lacy, black silk panties. Not that you'd notice, she subvocalized at him.

"Hey, Blaze, what's that smell?"

"Pink champagne."

"I sense your mood is more mauve than pink." He released Othello and felt his way to her sitting in an overstuffed chair, her right leg thrown carelessly over the arm. He touched her on her knee, her chest, her chin. "You feel good." He backed until he encountered the couch and sat carefully. "What's wrong?"

Othello settled down alongside the couch, his eyes locked on her.

"Ion't know." She didn't know.

"While champagne fails the grade as strong drink, nonetheless, you are not accustomed to any drink."

"Fuck it."

"Ah. 'Tis worse than I thought."

"I say again in pilot lingo, fuck it."

"You find it difficult to care any longer," he said perceptively. And he did one of the things which annoyed her. He looked elsewhere, not at her. From habit, a trait of his own personal blindness.

"That's about it. I don't give a fuck anymore."

"You've nothing left to accomplish—"

She finished her glass, picked up the bottle from the coffee table and drank from it, holding it awkwardly by the neck. "I don't give a fuck if the world catches on fire and burns up. In fact, gimme a match and I'll light the motherfucker."

"I will say you always march to your own drummer and apparently do so during PMS—"

"It's more than that, goddamnit."

"Fluent thou art in salty language."

"Fuck it, it never bothered you before."

"And still does not. What it also does not, is it does not become you."

"I'm no fuckin' lady anyway."

"Could have fooled me," he said softly.

She thought about that. It was one thing she'd worked hard on. "Um, thanks, Nate." She pulled her leg down and tucked it under her.

"There is a great deal left for you to accomplish. You're not done yet, Blaze." He swiveled his head and looked directly at her. As a gesture, it was ineffective because of his sunglasses.

"Like what?" she asked studying the champagne's label.

"Beats me. That's up to you. Always has been."

"Aw, fuck me to tears." Where'd I get that?

"Blaze, do you want a dime's worth of psychoanalysis?"

"No."

"Good. You're going to get it anyway. Remember it's worth what it cost you."

Aloha was interested even though she pretended not to be. Nate didn't ordinarily talk about her or them. "Well?"

"I've extrapolated this from what you've told me and what I've observed. You're changing. You were an extraordinary girl and now you're on the cusp of becoming an extraordinary woman."

"Aw, fuck. I can't deal with this shit."

"The problem now is you have an infinite capacity for love, and that part of you is unfulfilled. I'm no macho he-man, nor a sensitive and responsive partner. I'm me and I cannot change. For you, I will try, but it will not work. I'm too gruff—"

"That's okay—"

"No, ma'am, it is not. You needed someone to help you over the transition, and I became it, maybe by default—"

"Never."

"Stop interrupting. I do not have any idea where you came along with that infinite capacity for love, but you've got it. You don't love me—"

"I do." She waved the bottle at him.

"Sure. To an extent. But something eats at you in your quiet time; you are pensive, preoccupied—"

"Not when I'm flying or jumping out of aircraft—"

"That's all part of the package which is Aloha Blaze. You

consume life. Your capacity for love should be filled, especially now. But I will tell you one thing which may surprise you."

"What?"

"Ten years. Twenty years. When you are full woman. Thirty or forty years old—"

If only you knew.

"—you will not believe how fulfilled you can be. You've an *infinite* capacity, I keep saying. Add on those ten and twenty years. My Christ, what will you be like?" He shook himself like a dog. "I don't often see the future and it doesn't often scare me like this."

"I don't know what to say."

"Then don't be like others and say it. Be you. You are special as any human being's ever been, Blaze. Do what you and only you do best. Be Aloha Bonnie Blaze. See, the world needs you. It doesn't know it, but it needs you bad. Give me some of that wine."

"Champagne." She put the bottle into his outstretched hand.

"Problem is right now," he said as he lifted the bottle and drank from it, "you don't know how special you are and you don't know the world needs you and the motherforpin' world doesn't know it needs you. Shit, I need you."

"You never told me that before."

"I am not especially romantically inclined. But *love delights in praises*, sayeth the Bard in *Two Gentlemen of Verona*. I know you're not in love with me—"

"I do love you."

"You might love me and my old crusty ways, but you are not *in love* with me. Your aforementioned infinite capacity needs something, somebody, which doubtless you are aware of, if nowhere else, in your subconscious—"

"And I think, Nathan Ex, *you* have an infinite capacity for understanding."

"You know what, Blaze? I know that, that's why I took you in. But right fucking now I'd trade it for your love, your devotion, your complete attention—"

"I'll try."

"You'll die trying. I knew when I took you in it was a repair job. I did not expect to fall in love with you; alas and alac, I have. It was never my intention, now it is my regret, for I know ye be with me but an ephemeral second." He sighed.

"Nate, you're full of shit as a boiled owl."

"I am that. You and me, Blaze. It has to work itself out, without all this focused attention."

"I know, Nate. Boy-girl stuff. Biology. I like you more, now that you've explained yourself and where you are."

"And we've digressed from addressing your blue funk."

"Mauve *is* better. And life sucks."

"See, you're not even to the halftime of life, yet, still the first quarter somewhere." He finished the bottle.

"Enough with the metaphors already, Nate. I do feel better. I have a great deal more to understand about me than I thought. I thought I knew all about me."

"Not hardly. Likely you knew *too* much *too* soon. Found out the hard way."

She nodded though he couldn't see it. "And maybe it was *too* easy and *too* soon. The understanding sometimes came, sometimes comes, after the fact. It's a strange sort of temporal disorientation. At times I just have to stop and wait for the world to catch up.And then go on again."

"And sometimes exorcise demons."

"There's that," she admitted.

"'Our doubts are traitors,' from *Measure for Measure*."

—I always thought growing up was easy, Aloha told Bonnie.

—Nope. You thought you *were* grown up already. You have done some of that thing today.

—It fucking hurts.

—You, my dear Aloha, are having a midlife crisis right now and you are yet very young.

—I feel a hunnerd and teen.

"A couple of observations," Nate interrupted her reverie. "You are resilient. And your best days are ahead of you. Remember what I said about ten, twenty years hence."

"I do. I will remember, always," said Aloha.

"Beware, though," Nate went on, "because, as Will said so well in Hamlet, I think act four, *'We know what we are, but not what we may be.'* Sharp guy."

"Nobody knows the future," said Aloha.

"I have seen you attack the future and you aren't even there yet. Figure that one out."

"I can't. I'm too sleepy and worn out. Hold me?" She slid onto his lap and fell asleep.

* * * * * * *

As the weeks flew by, she gradually emerged from much of her melancholy. There was a pocket of darkness in her mind, one from whence came demons sometimes, which seemed to maintain a root system for her melancholy.

Nate was trying desperately to make her love him without reservation; and that was one thing she thought she wanted to do, but found she could not. She realized Nate was very good for her. Until recently, she had *not* been the center of his universe: he was the center of his own universe. He liked sex, but it wasn't important, he could take it or leave it. He did appreciate her magnificent body by feel, but it didn't seem to matter that *she* had an incredible shape.

During this period, she was still not fully happy, unaccountably, she thought, but managed to get along with her life. Maybe it was lack of time to fly and jump out of airplanes, she thought. She sent another check to the Church of the Redeemer in Rudd's name.

One night she met Nate at WFSU to walk him home after his shift. It was just after four in the morning and they were walking along Jefferson Street a few minutes from home. A half-moon gave her enough light to see.

"I've started a new company," she was telling him.

"Oh? Another?"

"Yep. UNIVERSITY REPO, that's what I call it."

"You repossess universities?" he said.

"No, silly. See, I find repossessed houses. Then I have my appraiser check it out. Not only does he figure what it's worth now, but he tells me what's necessary to fix 'em up and then how much they'll be worth after that repair is done. Stuff like repainting, new carpets, carpentry, plumbing work, the like. I bid low on the houses using his appraisal, and if I get it, I send in my FSU crew."

"Which is?"

"Students who have the necessary technical abilities, electrics, carpentry, painting—good thing Florida is a right to work state."

"Now more needy students owe you—"

"Nobody *owes* me anything. They earn their pay."

"Okay, Blaze," Nate said holding up a hand in mock surrender, "cool down. You're still touchy. I didn't mean it like that and you know it."

"I'm sorrrreeee."

"Apology accepted."

Othello growled low in his throat.

"What's wrong boy?" said Nate.

"I don't see anything," Aloha said.

They continued walking, her right arm linked in his free left arm. His right held onto the dog's harness.

"Knowing you," said Nate, "you've already leapt into action with UNIVERSITY REPO."

"I have. I've done it twice."

"And it worked, obviously." The dog stopped and Nate urged him on.

"Yep. I cleared nine grand on the first and fifteen grand on the second. I can do one or two a month. I'm also doing a profit sharing with my guys—." Another thought occurred to her. "I might even start my own real estate business to handle the action. And it could operate as the manager for this project."

"You are an idea person, Aloha. Everything you touch turns

to gold. The talk show thing works so well that an AM station downtown wants to hire me for a morning gig."

"Super, Nate. I'm so proud of you."

"I don't know if I'll accept the offer or not, I got my own little world here and I'm pretty secure."

"Don't we all—"

Othello balked and growled.

Three men appeared behind them. One took a baseball bat and swung. Othello went down yelping and crying. Another blow silenced him in mid howl.

Nate had immediately clenched his arm tight, pinning Aloha against him. "What the hell, Aloha?"

She struggled urgently to free herself as she turned to face the threat.

The three men stood in front of them, one still holding the bat.

"Jesus," said one. "This is a blind guy."

"I'm not," said Aloha, shrugging Nate off and stepped in front of him.

"Fuck it, honkies anyway," said the one with the bat. "See, babe," he spoke conversationally to Aloha, "we got to take out a white guy every month, put 'em in a hospital. It's one of the things about our gang. Nothing personal, okay?"

A Real Woman knows when to act.

"Why certainly," said Aloha, "if you don't take this person-ally," and kicked him in the balls with the basic sliding ball kick. She chopped his neck as he went down clutching the bat.

Continuing the motion, she spun and slammed her right elbow into the abdomen of the guy in the center. He bent double and spewed projectile vomit on the sidewalk and crashed into his own vomit as she nailed him with a reverse elbow strike to his right kidney and dropped him like a stone.

Number three was much quicker. He didn't waste time shouting or warning. He simply came up with a switch blade locking in place loudly as he stepped toward Aloha. And he was smart in knife fighting to come in underhanded, not over-handed.

But Aloha was still moving and slapped the knife arm partly into his side. This bought her the time she needed.

She grabbed his wrist, still continuing her momentum, and ducked under his arm while holding his wrist. She twisted, her hands holding his wrist with all the strength she possessed and spun twice more, not letting go, a macabre dance, just like turning your partner in the jitterbug.

Never, ever, would she forget his scream as sockets broke at the elbow and shoulder and his arm rotated completely around three times. She had moved so quickly and sharply that his body never flipped like he might have. Tissue and bone had broken and stretched in a split second and he stood anchored to the ground, eyes big as dinner plates.

The knife fell and he stared at his arm hanging there by tendons and torn muscle alone. Then he fainted, falling where he stood, the horror still in his eyes and the scream still on his lips.

Then it hit Aloha what had happened. She stepped into the street and vomited herself.

The first man, the one with the baseball bat, was rising, pushing himself up using the bat as a crutch. His eyes were locked on her with deadly purpose.

Aloha stepped over to him, and she was out of control. "You son of a bitch! Why did you do this to me?" She kicked him in the face as he struggled to rise. He flipped all the way over and fell on his back, his head thumping ominously on the sidewalk.

"Aloha?"

"Hang on a second, Nate. It's okay now." She saw he was kneeling alongside Othello.

Nate's hand rose from the dog's head. Blood and gore and brain matter. "He's dead, isn't he? Tell me he's not dead." Tears burst from under his sunglasses.

A red, roaring tide overcame Aloha. She vomited again realizing what she'd done, what had happened. The world had suddenly changed. It would never be the same place again. She threw up again and again until nothing was left.

The second man was the only one moving, and he was trying to crawl away unnoticed.

The red roar overcame Aloha again. She went to that man. "I didn't even like the dog, God*damn* you." She kicked his exposed kidney expertly with the point of her shoe and he collapsed yelping like Othello had and rolled into a fetal position. Aloha stomped his bottom knee onto the pavement until she felt it crack and splinter like ice.

Nate was sobbing uncontrollably now. "Othello? Somebody please help him. Oh, my dear God in Heaven, please help Othello?"

Aloha Blaze surveyed the havoc she had wreaked. She looked up. "God help us all." Odors of vomit, dog piss, and fear from the attackers threaded through the scene.

She went over and sat heavily next to Nathan Ex and took him in her arms. He held the dead body of his dog and continued to weep.

"It will be okay, you'll see, Nate," she crooned. "I promise, it'll be okay." Then she held him silently as he wept.

Ten minutes later a patrolling Tallahassee police officer found them like that.

One dead, one would never walk again, and one amputated right arm at the shoulder.

After they got home from the police station, it took her two hours to get Nate to sleep. She waited for shock to hit her but it did not. She knew she was strong enough to handle this, but—. Still there was a dead guy. She felt a sense of disorientation, something naggingly undone and unable to do. She couldn't express it concisely. She needed to talk to somebody. And there was only one person she knew with the experience and background to understand and put her problem in perspective. And she could not call Rudd. No way in hell.

It was a natural thing to do and the right person to talk to, but a mistake nonetheless. For a change Aloha wasn't thinking clearly.

She found Buddy Six in Hawaii. When he came on the line, she realized he'd have questions she could not or would not answer.

Too late.

"Hello, this is Captain Six, sir."

"Buddy, it's Aloha—"

"What's wrong. Dad crash?" he said immediately.

"No, um, I need to talk to somebody."

"Nobody's dying or dead or emergency?"

"No," she shook her head unaccountably, and glanced to Othello's empty spot and sobbed for the first time. Then she breathed deeply and regained control.

"You okay, Aloha? What's wrong?"

Aloha said with a strangled voice, "You ever kill anybody, Buddy?"

"A few. Fuckin' guys attackin' our relief convoy over in Africa. And a couple Arabs playing sapper in Lebanon. And a drugged Filipino trying to chop me up with a machete in a bar in Olongapo, Zambales Province on the island of Luzon— What the hell is going on? You never call. C'mon, Aloha, spill it."

"I haddakillaguythismorning." There, she said it.

"Tell me." Buddy's voice was commanding, in charge, alert.

She felt better already. She outlined what happened. She finished, "Without the training from you and Rudd, God knows what would have been the outcome."

"Leaving aside the questions arising from the fact you were out at four in the morning with a man not named Six, I'd say you done good. This blind man, he got a name?"

"Nathan Ex."

"And he ain't doin' good?"

"He was really attached to the damn dog. But Nate's tough, he'll come around."

"So we got to reconcile the fact you killed that man."

"Sort of, Buddy. I feel weird about it. But I don't have as much remorse as I thought I should."

"I see. Let me put on my psychoanalyst hat for a moment. Ah, got it. Ready?"

"I am," said Aloha.

"Here's the lesson I've learned. Fuck the son of a bitch. He killed himself. Fuck him big time. You did not allow him to get to you when he was alive, don't let him do so now that the cocksucker's dead."

"Point taken. I feel better just for talking to you anyway."

"Dad would've told you the same thing. You know when he crash-landed, VC's and NVA's went after him and he killed a bunch of them motherfuckers."

Aloha let silence reign for moments. Her mistake in calling Buddy. Finally, she said, "I couldn't tell him, Buddy. We're, um, estranged."

"Oh, shit."

"Buddy...."

"What went wrong?"

"I don't know. Two headstrong people."

"You're young," said Buddy. "You got to sew your wild oats, all them clichés, see what life's like. It happened to me."

"Would that it were so easy."

"I know it ain't none of my business, but—"

"Good, let's keep it that way for now. I love you lots, Buddy."

"Say the word, I'll be there."

"No. Not now. As it is, just talking to you, I feel a hundred percent better."

"Under the circumstances, you obviously know you're a marked exhibit for the world and your own circles if this goes public."

"I've thought about it already. I'm going to try to at least keep our names out of the press."

"Tell 'em your pseudostepson mean fuckin' Gyrene will come and break their fuckin' legs."

Aloha smiled for the first time in ages. "I'll tell 'em you were the one taught me how to kick ass like that—"

"And you made me so proud, darlin'."

"You-all," said Aloha, meaning Buddy and Rudd, "were right as usual. I knew it as I did it. You only get one good chance and that's right off, when the situation is still developing. Had I tried to talk them out of it, we'd have been goners. Most of all, immediate situation assessment. The element of surprise and immediate action."

"You sound like an unarmed combat instructor. Lissen, hon. If you're going to be out a night a bunch? Think about gettin' something light, maybe a small .25 automatic. Derringers are cute and handy, but there ain't enough rounds in 'em for three guys. .25 Auto does, and you can just start hosing off rounds and that'll scare the shit out of 'em."

"That's a good idea."

"How's business?"

She told him about her projects and new stores.

He whistled his approval and that made her feel wonderful.

"Bein's as how you're a rich broad and all, please remember I'm saving myself for you."

"Yeah, right."

"I didn't say I was celibate. I just gonna not get hitched." His voice dropped low at the end and it scared her. He meant it.

"What a nice compliment," she said lightly.

"Take it any way you want. What's the deal with you and Dad?"

"Ion't know, now, Buddy. Talking to you has helped me immensely. I am glad you were here for me when I needed you."

"And I always will be."

"Done, Buddy. Thanks a million."

"Yes, ma'am."

"Love you, Buddy. Bye."

He hung up without answering.

Aloha Blaze used every connection she had to keep their names out of the press. Nate even called in favors from the president of the university to get his help. Finally, the thing that convinced the one television news organization which had the most of the story, to forgo using names was the fact that the three attackers were black. The station agreed so that racial tensions would not be fanned. Aloha didn't give a damn; she just didn't want the episode around her neck. People were afraid of and in awe of her enough already. The newspaper was on one of its save-the-150-year-old-oak-tree crusades and didn't follow up the story.

However, some people in the know talked, and rumors flew through the university faster than the speed of light.

And the entity that was Aloha Bonnie Blaze, student with major reputation, became a legend, not spoken loudly or publicly, yet talked about with awe and reverence. People treated her with respect and at arm's length where before she was just another odd student with a reputation.

At least Rudd would never know. But somehow he'd known years before the event, for he'd given her some basic training in the martial arts, the stuff she'd need to know in an emergency.

And the dark place within her mind grew to incorporate the fact that she'd killed a man. She kept it locked tight. She had some initial remorse; however, when remorse threatened to overcome her, she recalled the vision of Nathan Ex, and his anguish over Othello's death.

Aloha wondered if this episode in her life meant she was now a woman and no longer a girl.

—Bonnie, do you reckon that was my personal rite of passage?

—If so, you've had a bunch of them already.

—I didn't know I'd have to fight my way through life.

—Now you know it, dear. And you're worried. How many parts woman and how many parts girl are you?

—Ion't know. But I'd give anything for some of those girl parts back.

—Aloha, you just wanna be a kid at heart.

—Not exactly. But I still dream like that girl-child.

She bought him another guide dog. They drove down to Palmetto which is just south of Tampa, to Southeastern Guide Dogs, to train Nate and pick up the new dog. Lady Macbeth was a two-year old golden retriever and Aloha almost liked her.

And to ease her conscience another notch, she sent another large check to the Church of the Redeemer.

To change her image, not only her public image, but her own personal view of herself, Aloha begin to wear her hair in braids or a pony tail. It certainly changed her look, for her hair was way down her back. She knew she'd cut it back to just below shoulder level when she stopped with the pony tails.

The new semester started and she signed up for Professor Amanda McMullen's American Literature Survey Class. They were studying Henry Miller, Mark Twain; books by Truman Capote, Melville, Hawthorne, Nabokov, James Dickey, and John Steinbeck.

If Amanda recognized her as a friend of Denise and from the episode with Rudd at the Silver Slipper, she did not show it. Aloha thought it unlikely Amanda did not know who she was. Hell, *everybody* knew her. Not to mention that she was an English major and *that* was a small world. Not mention that Nathan Ex was more than well-known in the English Department.

With the new semester, Aloha hoped fervently that nothing untoward would happen to her. So she could tend to her businesses and studies.

Of course, nothing doesn't never happen in the life of Aloha Bonnie Blaze.

Not in the life of the well renowned karate expert sky diving entrepreneur pilot drop-dead gorgeous four point zero student.

One day Nate told her. "Sonnet 60.

> "'Like as waves make towards the pebbled shore,
> So do our minutes hasten to their end.'"

"Let's go to a party."

CHAPTER TWENTY-FIVE
HIM

Rudd landed the 172 at the Panama City airport and taxied past the terminal. He swung toward the 727 where passengers were boarding. They'd just spent three days on Gasparilla Island and while landing he'd coordinated this drop off so that Colette would not miss her flight out.

"There's Simone," said Colette.

The stout figure emerged from the end of the line of passengers climbing a boarding ramp and waved imperiously and impatiently at the Cessna.

A ground crew member trotted over to the 172. Rudd set the brake. "I say again, you're welcome to stay."

Colette Duval put her hand on his arm. "I thank you, but I cannot, n'est-ce pas?" She paused. "Perhaps one day we can meet again, no?"

Rudd knew it would not be so. "Sure."

"Dear Rudd, she must be crazy, I think?"

"Who?" asked Rudd as the ground guy tugged open the door to the Cessna.

"The one your eyes see only. Au revoir."

The door opened and the prop noise and wind blew away the moment.

Colette leaned over and gave him a wet, lingering kiss and he saw regret on her face as she climbed out, handing the maintenance man her carry-on. The door closed and Colette walked toward Simone like she was going the last hundred feet to the electric chair.

"Goddamn life," Rudd said aloud and released the brakes. He gunned the engine, swung 180, and headed for the runway.

Their ten days together had not done what he'd hoped they would: give him a head start getting over Aloha. The ache returned.

Spending that much time with the French girl, it had not been difficult figuring out the relationship between Colette and Simone. Colette was a kept woman, a designated lesbian partner of the famous tennis player. The two French women had used Rudd to satisfy Colette's heterosexual cravings. He wondered sadly if he were but one among many. It didn't matter. Though he had tried to talk Colette into leaving Simone and staying with him in Tallahassee. But Colette would have none of that; Rudd suspected Colette liked her current lifestyle. Not to mention her association with fame and spotlight.

The tower cleared him for takeoff and he wished he had a couple of J-79 jet engines he could punch into afterburner and perform a vertical climb until the G-forces made him grimace and almost pass out.

But the Cessna simply floated off almost of its own accord and he savagely pulled the nose up to right next to stall speed and the engine labored and he regained his senses and leveled out and headed for Tallahassee.

He'd decided not to bail out and go to Washington state, to Yakima. He knew you learn the most when life is at its lowest ebb, like right goddamn now. Fuck it, he thought, I ain't quitting. That's something Rudyard Kipling Six does not do, and that's that.

Especially since his time with Colette Duval had showed him that he still loved Aloha. The one lesson he'd learned in the last ten days. And he wasn't going to dodge the problem by packing up and moving to the West Coast.

Well, he'd been down before and likely would again. He'd fight his way out. Life must go on. But this ache wasn't going to go away easily, that he knew. He'd never had that kind of feeling before in his life; there was a vast emptiness within him which beckoned him. If he kept busy and his mind occupied, he could barely tolerate the feeling. At least Colette had helped him over the first and worst part. He'd hoped desperately that the girl would help him break Aloha's spell.

Nope.

The episode with Colette also helped him make his decision to not run away from his problems.

Back in Tallahassee, he discovered Aloha had moved most of her belongings out of their house. He thought about changing his will, but thought that if he died in the near future, that the house would be hers and a constant reminder of him. For some odd reason, this cheered him up.

He found she'd stored a dozen cartons of books in the garage. She must not have much room where she'd moved. Aloha had also left him copies of newspapers regarding the toilet papering of the FSU campus. Of course she would have figured it out.

Rudd threw himself into his work. He flew more flights and hustled more clients. Zeke was dubious, but said nothing.

One day he received a letter from Aloha.

"'Best wishes'?" he said aloud to no one on his five acre secluded home site.

There was no question as to which check to cash, and cash it he must. He tore the one for a hundred thousand in half, then taped it back together. What a souvenir, a check from Aloha B. Blaze in the amount of $100,000. He determined to put it in a frame and hang it on the wall somewhere. He cashed the interest check.

Under the heading of "Life Must Go On," he rekindled his friendship with Amanda McMullen. Amanda still liked him enough to resume seeing him and soon the flame of passion grew between them. It was such that Rudd had a sincere hope that their relationship could grow to such proportions that Amanda could replace Aloha. The fact that their names were so close seemed to fight against his wishes, for he had to concentrate so as to not say "Aloha" when he meant "Amanda."

Amanda liked to walk, and she especially liked to walk at night or before dawn. He enjoyed walking with her. Since he was an avid reader, including the classics—had he not imbued Aloha with that trait, after all?—the English professor and the well-read pilot got along famously, and could discuss great works of literature or the latest from Louis L'Amour. He suspected Amanda read spy novels and new-release westerns because he did and thus she could be conversant with him.

One cool night, they'd walked for two hours from his house and around his neighborhood. Rudd realized one of the reasons her legs and butt were so tight and attractive was from all the walking.

They'd settled in his living room, Rudd with the obligatory gin and tonic, she with a glass of white wine. She was sitting on a couch facing the hearth and he stood warming his backside to the fire.

"I learned to drink gin and tonic," Rudd was saying, "over in the Mystic Far East. It was mostly quinine water over there, chock full of quinine, and it was supposed to keep you from getting malaria—or so we kidded ourselves. I doubt a malarial mosquito checks to see what you've been drinking. Though quinine is one of the things they used to treat the disease with—"

"Rudd," Amanda interrupted, staring over his head, "you and I are going to have to get our relationship squared away or kiss me goodbye." She continued to stare.

He followed her gaze. Eight hundred dollars and change, that's what it had cost him.

From a photograph, he'd commissioned a well-known artist in Miami to paint the picture.

Thirty by thirty-six, the painting showed Aloha cross-legged on the sundeck, reading a book in her lap, champagne hair cascading all about her, sun setting in the background. She was dressed in jean cutoffs and a brown leather vest with silver buttons. You could see a swell of breasts through her hair and on the left side of the vest alongside her arm.

"Oops," said Rudd lamely. "I forgot about that."

"Sure," said Amanda, "something that eye-catching just sort of hangs around and you don't notice it."

He shrugged. "You're right." He put his glass on the mantle and, stretching, lifted the painting off its hook and took it out of the room. When he returned, he had a painting of the nearby St. Marks lighthouse. "Right down by the coast, in the St. Marks National Wildlife Refuge. During the Civil War, troops from the South tried to blow it up, but failed. It's been rebuilt and all and they put it on the National Register of Historic Places." He snagged the wire on the hook and settled the painting in place.

Amanda toasted him with her still half-full wine glass. "One of your superb talents, Mr. Kipling, is your ability to change the subject and divert attention from one matter to another. Like a kid whose homework ate the dog?"

"I want to be fair to you. Go ahead." Rudd went and sat on the floor, his back still to the fireplace, and captured Amanda's legs with his own. It was a comforting and open gesture, revealing his vulnerability. He saw she recognized his intention to be open and honest.

"Who is Aloha Blaze?"

"She used to joke we were high school sweethearts."

"With the age differential? You were sweethearts? I recall a certain dinner date at the Silver Slipper, and odd going's-on, and shortly we were no longer dating."

Rudd leaned back, bracing himself with his hands on the floor behind him. "Technically, I guess you could call her my ward—"

"Legally?"

"More or less."

"You are saying, then dear man, that this girl is young enough to be termed a 'ward,' are you not?"

"I guess—"

"Which means she *has* to be less than eighteen—"

"Well, maybe, at the time—"

Amanda was firing away like a prosecutor in court. "The high school sweetheart comment leads one to think in terms of an affair."

"Well—"

"Not to mention rumors and whatever the hell that was about at the Silver Slipper."

"Um—"

"Speak up, Rudd." Amanda drained her glass and mock-threw it at the fireplace. She leaned forward and rubbed his knees. "I will say that you and I were not at the time involved and thus that gives me little right to act the inquisitor here. I hereby withdraw my questions, for it sounds to me as if I am being a shrewish bitch which, for reasons of my not-so-recent divorce, I do not wish to appear."

He gave her a highly edited and condensed version of the Rudd and Aloha story, leaving out references to ages.

"Oh, shit," Amanda said when he was finished. "You had it bad for her, didn't you?"

"I did." He told Amanda about Aloha's business interests. "She's very bright."

Amanda slid to the floor in front of Rudd, jamming against him and stretching her legs out beside him in a V. "Aloha is an English major, you know that?"

Rudd nodded.

"So people in the department sort of know what's going on."

"And?" Rudd prompted.

"Do you know an instructor named Nathan Ex?"

"No."

"He's a blind man. A premier expert on William Shakespeare."

"And?"

"Maybe I shouldn't have brought it up."

"Then don't tell me," he said, knowing what Amanda was going to say.

"The quarterback is out."

Good, thought Rudd. The young stud, gone. Aloha had learned quickly.

"And Nathan Ex is the new man in her life."

The wound which had not yet healed, opened again, and

fresh blood leaked out.

Amanda scooted closer to him and her dress rode up around her hips. She rubbed her crotch against his leg. "Let's go to bed. All this talk makes me horny."

Through her panties he could feel her heat. He rose and turned off the lamp on the table. "A fire's more romantic, cheri." Oops.

"Good. Hurry, darling." She was looking up at him hungrily and tugging down his slacks.

A few days later, on a Saturday morning, Rudd answered the doorbell and there stood the matronly Sergeant Ebert.

"Shall I show you my badge again?"

"No."

"I went to where you used to live. I follow up, see? And you don't live there anymore."

"I know."

"Your old neighborhood is going downhill. Mind if I come in?"

"Do I have a choice, Sergeant?"

"You do. I don't have a warrant or anything. I'm just doing my job and trying to save the citizens of Leon County from the Saracens."

"Come in."

"Nice house," she said as they walked through the downstairs. "You flyboys do all right for yourselves."

"Are you satisfied now, Sergeant?"

"I see evidence of a female. Who all lives here?"

"Me, mostly. Alone."

"And who else?"

"Occasionally I have overnight guests. Nothing illegal."

Just then Amanda came in the sliding glass doors from the pool patio, toweling herself off. Rudd was thankful Amanda was not like Aloha who loved nudity. Amanda was a bit old fashioned except when making love. Then she was eager and aggressive and wanton.

"Well, Mr. Six. Times have changed."

"Who is this, Rudd?" asked Amanda.

"The self-appointed morals enforcement agency witch-hunting barbarians," Rudd said, unable to keep the anger from his voice.

"That's me, you bet," said Ebert, bowing slightly. "Pardon the interruption, ma'am. I got to go line a name off the list."

With that, the sergeant turned and walked out. Rudd didn't even have to face the dilemma of making the introductions between the two women.

"What was that all about?" asked Amanda.

Rudd could see he had to tell the truth. "It's about Aloha. That lady cop thought she had us committing crimes, and came over one time trying to catch us in illicit sex or some damn thing."

"Illicit sex?" said Amanda, rubbing her body against him. "Tell me more." She pulled his head down and began kissing him passionately. Amanda snapped the clasp on her top and removed the bottom of her bikini swimming suit while still kissing him. To do so she had to squirm a great deal. He pulled her tightly against him, some of her wetness soaking his clothing. Which he soon had shed.

As Amanda lifted her legs over his shoulders, Rudd heard a car drive down and out of the driveway.

A few weeks later, Rudd and Amanda were taking another of their long walks from her apartment. Located off Blairstone Drive near Governor's Square Mall. At Rudd's suggestion, they finished by going through the mall. Handy Hank Hartwell had told him of Aloha's new store selling vests. He saw it and was impressed. Yep, vests galore.

"It belongs to Aloha Blaze, doesn't it?" asked Amanda.

"It does."

"We need to get out of here quickly," said Amanda. She turned and marched toward the exit with a purpose.

Rudd caught up with her. "What is it?"

She glanced at him. "Seems every time we mention Aloha we end up making love. I've some juicy gossip and this is a very awkward place to screw."

They threaded their way through the parking lot and got on a sidewalk headed for Blairstone Drive.

Rudd had to hold his impatience.

Finally, Amanda took his hand. "Rumor, rampant all over the Williams Building, in fact, all over our part of campus. Did you read the paper, a story about a mugging gone bad, all very mysterious?"

"They passed it off as a gang-related kind of thing. One killed and a couple of others maimed in the melee."

"That's it. Guess what—no, guess who?"

Aloha? He gathered himself and imposed an iron control. "Tell me?"

Amanda must have heard something in his voice, for she looked at him for a moment, then said, "Aloha and this radio guy, Nathan Ex? They were walking home in the middle of the night—"

Home? Rudd didn't want to hear about that.

"—when they were attacked by three men. They killed the guide dog and Aloha Blaze went ape shit and killed one of them and hurt the others badly."

Aw, shit. The iron control almost broke but he bore down. Aloha. He wondered if she needed him. The ache exploded within him again.

"Either one of them hurt?"

"Only the dog. It's dead."

Relief washed through him. Aloha was safe and uninjured.

"I taught her some martial art fundamentals. Karate kind of stuff you learn in survival schools. Buddy did, too."

They made it halfway up the stairs from the living room to Amanda's bedroom and no farther. Rudd was so relieved that Aloha was safe, he was more amorous than Amanda and they did it on the carpeted stairs, her panties dangling from the hand railing.

When Rudd got home late that night, the phone was ringing.

He picked it up. "Six."

"Me, too," said Buddy. "I'm at the O'club at Hickam right now, don't try to figger out the time here." Near Honolulu International. "I couldn't not call you."

Rudd waited. Buddy never called. This could mean only one thing. "Your mother or your sister?"

"Wrong, Dad. They're fine. It's Aloha."

Uh, oh.

"She had an incident."

"I heard."

"Did you talk to Aloha?" Buddy's voice was leading.

"Why do you ask?" said Rudd.

"You two are no longer living together, true?"

"It is."

"Anything I can do, Pops. Shitfire, two people made for each other, it's you and Aloha. Tell me how to help."

"By keeping your nose out of it."

"I guess you told me, father dear. Maybe you don't know, but Aloha is the finest woman you'll ever—"

"Buddy? Do you know the whole story of our separation?"

"No, but, goddamn—"

"Then do not jump to conclusions. Okay?" Rudd had to reassert his crumbling iron will. "She called you?"

"She did, Dad. Said she couldn't call you."

"Tell me what she said."

Buddy did so. Rudd was alternately proud of Aloha and angry he hadn't been there to protect her.

"That's about it," Buddy finished.

Rudd said, "If she calls again, tell her—"

"*I* ain't tellin' her nothin'. You want to send a message, you call Western Union, just don't get me involved."

"Sorry, Buddy. Maybe you're right on this one."

"Fuckin' A."

* * * * * * *

Then one day Amanda called Rudd at work. "Rudd, I have a

major problem."

She was obviously agitated to a high degree, for they never called each other at work to talk other than to make a date or some such.

"What is it?"

"You're aware the new semester started today?"

"I am."

"Guess who showed up in my American Lit survey class?" Amanda continued, not waiting for his response. "Your sweetie, my rival. Darn it to heck."

Aloha seemed to have a second presence that shadowed his every move.

"What can I do, Rudd?"

"Be professional," he advised. "She's just another student."

"It's so hard. People all the time are talking about her. Something like the Kung Fu Killer Queen Straight A Flying Beauty Sky Diving Businesswoman Beautiful Pilot."

"That's just talk, gossip—"

"But it's all true! See whose shadow I have to exist under? Everybody knows it was her, now me. The comparisons. Oh, Rudd."

"Amanda? You are your own person, separate and unique." Rudd wished for a time out so he could gather his thoughts.

"My name and her name are similar; they both begin and end with A's. Every time I hear her name I'm scared to darn death. I'm attracted to you so much Rudd. She took you away from me one time before. I came back to you because I liked you so much. I still do. Every time I hear her name, I die a bit inside. And now she's going to be in my survey class three times a week for months? Rudd? I don't want to lose you; you are the most man I've ever known; gentle and sensitive, yet strong and rough; you're cultured and well-read, and a war hero. Sometimes I contrive sex when *she* becomes the subject. Then you turn me on and I do it and love it because it's you—I want you so much all the time—"

"Amanda! Calm down. Tell you what, it's late and I'll close

up here and pick you up in twenty minutes. Okay?"

"O-okay." She sounded like there were tears in her eyes.

He hung up slowly. Amanda was much farther into their relationship than he was. He shook his head sadly. Goddamn Aloha anyway. Not only does she weigh on my mind day and night, but now she was getting to Amanda. Damn, damn, damn.

And what about Amanda's unsolicited declaration. He reviewed what Amanda had said. The word "love" had not appeared in her phone call. But it was there anyway. Rudd knew she'd be calmed down by the time he got there; but that didn't solve the long range problem. Amanda was right. Every time one of them turned around, some reminder of Aloha popped up.

Rudd realized that it was time to either take the relationship with Amanda to a higher level or cool it. And, by God, he didn't know which. He liked Amanda enormously. The sex was good, and she helped fulfill one of his basic needs: intelligent female companionship. In a moment of clarity, he knew that his marriage to Marge had begun to die when they no longer connected on an intellectual level; their intellectual interests had diverged, were no longer even in the same ballpark. Apply that to Aloha. Their intellectual interests remained constant and hungry, they each wanted to know everything about the world and the community in which they lived, consequently the only times they fought was over the front page or the local section of the paper. That was one reason Rudd had all the newspapers available in Tallahassee delivered. He also saw that he did have an intellectual connection with Amanda; but that ran more to the arts and literature; Amanda didn't care about local politics or business or what was going on in Portugal or Bolivia. Aloha was the only one whose interests were as catholic as his.

He sighed. He knew all this had to be resolved. He couldn't keep going through life wondering every minute about Aloha. And he couldn't let the growing legend that was Aloha Blaze get to Amanda and kill off the wonderful thing that was growing between him and the lady from Gainesville.

Rudd sensed momentum gathering and knew this was a

wreck hurtling toward impact.

The only answer was to get over Aloha and do so sooner rather than later. It had been long enough for the healing to begin of its own accord; yet it had not done so. Maybe he should get professional help.

Or maybe he should just go home, get drunk, and re-read a Donald Hamilton book. Fuck the world, lemme off.

A while later, he turned left off Jefferson onto North Copeland Street and saw Amanda waiting for him at the intersection of College Avenue.

Amanda slid into the car and slammed the door. "Thanks for the ride." She slid over and pecked him on the cheek.

Rudd turned right, heading for Monroe. "Feel better?"

She smiled wanly. "Some." She waved a fancy envelope at him. "The chairman of the English Department is having a party Saturday night. We're invited and the protocol is we better be there."

"*You* have to be there; I haven't been asked."

"Rudd, will you go with me Saturday night?"

"Sure."

CHAPTER TWENTY-SIX
HER

Aloha drove them to the party in her red pickup.

Nate was talking about Lady MacBeth, his new guide dog and Aloha was only half listening.

The episode with the three gang members had turned into a seminal event: It made her think a great deal about who she was and who she was going to be. And she wasn't certain she liked what she saw of the future. She knew where she wanted to go professionally; she wasn't certain where she wanted to go personally.

"...expensive personal training you paid for thank you very much," said Nate.

Professor Woloch had a big place out on Lake Jackson, to the northwest of the city.

"You reckon Amanda will be there tonight?" Aloha asked.

"Likely: attendance is mandatory."

"She's been very formal with me lately," said Aloha. "Maybe I can find out what's wrong."

"Maybe it's her new boyfriend, the pilot—"

Oh, shit. "Rudd Six?"

"Sounds like it."

"Nobody tells me nothing," complained Aloha, her mind racing.

"Probably because you are usually the subject of most talk," said Nate amiably, not detecting her distress. "And they don't tell me because I don't give a damn and I'm never interested in this gossip business—it's like incest, see, but sometimes I overhear things."

Would Rudd be there?

It occurred to Aloha that it would be grand if he were: for they had not seen each other since.... It was time. They'd both be in Tallahassee for some time yet to come and the inevitable might as well happen sooner than later.

Aloha thought she could deal with it.

That's what she thought.

After all, she'd changed. She recognized a metamorphosis within herself. Rudd had triggered it, teaching her to stretch her mind. He'd certainly expanded her horizons; while she'd always been very bright, she just hadn't applied her intelligence to higher pursuits such as learning from all the reading, including two or three newspapers a day, and her cultural upbringing guided again by Rudd. She could dance, cook, kick and kill, discuss exotic locales and obtuse ideas, and be awesome in bed. Yet, she'd been a snotty teenager. But now she knew she'd grown up swiftly, and she couldn't have handled it the way she did without the foundation Rudd helped put in place. She thought of all the clichés. Midlife crisis. Forty and crazy. Seven year itch. Others. She'd gone through the tough parts of all of them. She swung around a Volkswagen and, since night was falling, she turned on her lights. She took the spur road toward the shore of Lake Jackson where Woloch lived. Coming around a curve, the lights caught a doe standing at the tree line. For a brief moment, the deer froze, then shook itself and jumped into the woods.

—That ain't you, babe, said Bonnie.

—For a moment, I, too, was frozen. It happens.

—Don't forget Rudd triggered your renaissance, your metamorphosis, in other ways. You learned a lot about yourself soloing at fifteen thousand feet or leaping unbidden into the void with a chute you packed yourself.

—Why do we always talk about me? asked Aloha.

—I don't know. Therapy? Maybe you need help more than you admit, Bonnie said. Look, dear, think more and deeper.

Why is it Rudd did all that stuff? Why'd he make you into the entrepreneur sky diving karate kid pilot and so on?

—He did not *make* me into it, he pointed me. And I don't know. Because he loved me?

—And?

—And, I suppose, neither Marge nor Denise turned out the way he wanted—

—Or dreamed, Bonnie inserted. He fantasized a perfect woman and you were clay at the right time and place.

—You think?

—I do.

—Me, too, thought Aloha. But I don't think it was a specific plan with that endgame in mind. I think it worked out that way.

—You are so modest, dear Aloha.

—Keep me straight, hon, I hate arrogance worse than anything you can name, and I don't wanna be it.

—There's the house, Bonnie pointed out.

—I hope Rudd's there. We can get this all over with. Wish me luck?

—Luck.

She slowed down, turning into the gravel drive.

"Are we getting close yet, Blaze?"

"We're there, Nate."

When she stopped, he got out and walked to the front of the truck running his hand along the front right quarter panel. She came around and took his arm and threaded it through her own.

Dr. Woloch and his wife, Mrs. "Doctor" Woloch met them at the front door. He was a curly haired man running to gray with a permanent frown. He introduced his wife by saying, "This is my wife." Consequently Aloha thought of her as Mrs. Doctor Woloch.

Woloch spent a few minutes with them, primarily talking to Nate until someone else rang the doorbell.

The house was a sprawling ranch style with rooms open to each other.

Aloha and Nate wandered through speaking occasionally to

people they each knew. Aloha would whisper whom they were encountering and he'd pretend to recognize them without a cue. It was a good intro bit and warmed the atmosphere. There were already perhaps forty people wandering around drinking punch and beer.

Many of the women gazed jealously at Aloha. She was stunning as usual, braided hair stretching down the back of her tangerine shift. She'd chosen it because it went with her eyes and her hair and it was new. The only problem was that a vest didn't go with the outfit. Oh, well.

Of course, no music, not even FM background. Aloha wondered about the Doctors Woloch.

When it happened, Aloha and Nate were standing in front of a rectangular dining room table. She had just handed Nate a cocktail weenie on a toothpick and picked up a nacho for herself.

Amanda McMullen strode up and stopped on the other side of the table. She was wearing a low cut blue dress which was tailored to accent her breasts and hips. "Aloha! Wonderful seeing you here!" Her voice was full of forced sincerity. She stepped around the table and hugged Aloha.

Aloha did not expect the hug and was startled for a moment. A dollop of cheese had fallen on Amanda's shoulder. Aloha ate the nacho and picked up a napkin, stepped to Amanda, said "Hold still," and wiped most of the cheese off. But a tiny dark stain remained. "Sorry," she said even though it wasn't her fault.

"Er, thanks," said Amanda.

"Hey, McMullen," said Nate. "Nice to see you."

"Thanks, Nate."

"It is your misfortune, Nate, that you *cannot* see her," said Aloha.

Amanda cocked her head at the compliment. "Thank you, Aloha. Are you going to steal Rudd from me again?"

"No. And that wasn't a fair question, either, Amanda."

"What the hell is going on?" asked Nate Ex.

At that moment, Rudd Six walked up and stood across the table from all of them.

"Aloha? A pleasant surprise." He was wearing slacks and a casual blazer with an open shirt.

She died inside. "I miss you," she managed to say. Her knees shook.

"I miss you more," he replied.

And Aloha Bonnie Blaze froze. Like the deer. Her blood pounded and hurt her eyes. Her jawed ached. She was conscious that her knees were locked and each one of her nerves was jangling and frying individually. She couldn't speak. Her mouth was as dry as the Sahara. Her eyes locked onto his and she had to consciously direct herself to start breathing again.

And she knew the questions and the answers.

And she saw that he knew that she knew.

"I've been hearing the words to the song of life," Rudd said to her, "but the music has been gone."

"I pledge to work hard to rebuild it," said Aloha.

He turned to Amanda. "Amanda? I'm sorry, I truly am. You deserve a better man than I am." His voice was wistful but not apologetic.

Aloha was breathing shallowly and her heart thudding like a stampede of buffalo.

"Aloha?" said Rudd. "Will you come back to me?"

She tried to speak and her voice came out strangled. She gulped air and tried again. "If you will marry me and we can try and have children."

"Aloha Bonnie Blaze," said Rudd, "Will *you* marry me?"

"I will if you can forgive me." She paused, thinking furiously. "I withdraw my request, I will come back to you, no conditions."

"I have asked for your hand in marriage."

"I accept."

—*Hot damn!* said Bonnie.

"Don't *do* this to me!" wailed Amanda.

A murmur went through the gathering crowd.

"I'll be go to hell," said Nathan Ex.

"Amanda, I'm sorry," said Aloha. "There is a demand, an

urgency within me I cannot control."

"Goddamnitall!" whispered Amanda.

Nate reached toward her voice and found her shoulder. His hand squeezed on the nacho cheese stain. "Me, too, Amanda. I think I need a ride home. C'mon, let's find some liquor and get drunk."

"O-kay," said Amanda tearfully.

Nate said, "Aloha, it has been grand. Every minute."

Aloha leaned over and kissed his cheek. "I am sorry, Nate."

He shrugged. "Hell, I knew it was coming, didn't I tell you?"

"You did."

He nodded and drew Amanda with him. "Do you recall what Shakespeare said in *All's Well That Ends Well*? 'No legacy is so rich as honesty.' I believe we have just witnessed and been a part of the ultimate honesty."

—We're going home! said Bonnie.

CHAPTER TWENTY-SEVEN
HIM

He knew he should be apprehensive about their arrival.

He stood alone on the flight line. He walked around the PA42 Cheyenne III. It was new from Piper; he eyed the T-tail and tip tanks. It had come out first in 1980 and was comparable to the Beech Super King Air.

Rudd thought about his schedule. It would have been so much easier if Aloha hadn't decided she wanted a big, formal wedding. He didn't disagree, but a preacher or a trip to Vegas would have sufficed for him. Aloha certainly has grown up, he thought. Cream rises to the top. And she'd let her hair out again, no more braids or pony tails.

He looked at his watch. Where was she?

The Cheyenne had cost him two legs and an arm but the most difficult part was finding a ribbon wide enough to look good when tied around the body of the aircraft. Zeke had helped him wrap the red ribbon around the fuselage. Then he attached a large bow.

The side door of the SIXGUN AIR hangar opened and Aloha Blaze shouted at him, waved, and walked over. She was wearing slacks and loafers and a white ruffle shirt with a brown leather vest designed to look like his brown leather flight jacket.

When she reached his side, she looked at the Cheyenne appreciatively. "Nice machine. Whatcha got the ribbon on it for?" Her voice was coy.

Rudd handed her a large envelope. She tore it open eagerly.

"Your wedding present."

"Rudd! You didn't." She pulled out forms and paperwork from the envelope. Ownership and registration paperwork in her name. She grabbed him and hugged him and the papers got crushed between them. He followed her as she walked around the aircraft. "Zeke flew it in last night. I want the guys to go over it thoroughly before we start checking you out in it."

"Rudd, I'm out of words."

"That's a first," he chuckled.

He handed her a large pair of scissors and she formally cut the ribbon. It snaked off the fuselage.

They climbed in and she sat in the pilot's seat, he in the copilot position. "It was designed as a business-size aircraft, note the low wing, and is exceedingly fast."

"How fast?" She was running her hands over the controls.

"Three hundred eighteen miles per hour advertised cruising speed."

Aloha whistled. "Twin turboprops will do that."

Rudd sat back enjoying her enjoying the aircraft. "Let me tell you what I'm thinking. It's configured for executive seating for six people. Easily changed to carry eleven, if you want. Once you get your management company in place, assign the aircraft to Aloha Enterprises or whatever you decide to call it."

"I'm still thinking on that." Aloha was consolidating her business interests and designing an operations company as an umbrella management concern to run and coordinate all her businesses and projects. It would also provide the support all needed: payroll, taxes, personnel, accounting.

"Anyway," Rudd went on, "since you aren't going to fly this all the time, you lease it to SIXGUN AIR. There are plenty corporate and government leaders in Tallahassee clamoring for first class transportation. And SIXGUN AIR has more business nowadays than our fleet can handle."

"So I make money, have a tax write-off, and own my own twin turboprop?"

"Well, yes. I knew you'd appreciate that part, too."

"Six, you are a man after my own heart." She grabbed him and kissed him enthusiastically.

"Wow," he said afterward.

"How about we do a Mile High Club Flight? We could charge a bunch."

"Rascal. You'd need something bigger with more privacy."

Aloha sat back. "I'm not certain about traditions and protocols here. But, dear Rudd, I would like to give you my present here and now."

"Just having you is enough for me."

"That's sweet. But, listen Rudd. I've thought about this long and hard; it's been an obsession. There's nothing you need—"

"Just you."

"Nor could I think of anything exotic or even outlandish that you couldn't go out and buy yourself if you wanted it."

Rudd couldn't think of anything he wanted or needed either. "Go on."

"Therefore, my gift to you is a pledge. I promise to love, honor, and cherish you so long as you or I shall live."

He caught his breath. "You're going to say something similar tomorrow during the wedding."

"I know, Rudd. But you do understand why I say it now?"

"I do."

She told him anyway. "I was young and I strayed and hurt us both and others badly. That I cannot undo. And Lord knows I've lost my youth somewhere along the way. But I can and do promise unequivocally that I do love you and I always will."

The level of emotion in the Cheyenne was so high he felt his heart racing and skipping. "Then I shall be happy for the rest of my life."

With her finger, she wiped a tear from his cheek and tasted it.

Rudd recalled the day she'd moved in with him: a lovely young lady, ragged around the edges. He'd decided that rough cut girl could stand a little polishing. Now look at her.

For a while they sat holding hands, silent, and looking out the windscreen. He drank in the smell of a new aircraft.

"I do have a small token for you, but I'm saving that for later."

"Animal, vegetable, or mineral?" Rudd asked.

"It's a surprise. Forget it for now." Aloha took a deep breath as if she were going to plunge into something. "I would like you to have a long and fruitful life," said Aloha slowly. "Therefore, I have a request."

"Shoot."

"I would that you stop working so hard, Rudd. I want you around for a long time and I do *not* wish for you to work yourself to death."

Rudd saw she was dead serious. "Agreed." Was she saying he was too old? "If you will agree to do the same."

"I, too, agree," she said with a smile, and he knew she wouldn't cut back unless she got pregnant. "I'm off the pill and you can never tell what will happen." She was reading his mind.

"Just concentrate on school," he said.

She sighed. "It's been difficult. I can't believe I didn't drop Amanda's American Lit class." She shook her head. "I'm no quitter, but that's a struggle. She's still very stiff and formal around me; it's got to be awkward for her, too."

"She and Nate didn't work out?" asked Rudd.

"No," said Aloha.

Rudd cleared his throat. "Amanda is one of the good people in the world. She'll find the right person eventually."

"She did when she found you," said Aloha. "But your point is taken." She looked at her watch. "Mom and Dad are due in about twenty minutes." She pointed across runways and taxiways at the terminal.

"Let's go."

"You don't have to, they just want to talk to you sometime before the wedding."

"I'll go with you, and you take 'em to the motel and we'll pick them up later for dinner."

* * * * * * *

After dinner that night, Rudd and Aloha drove Peter and Mary back to their motel. The dinner had been awkward, with periods of silence. Aloha was forcing laughter and familiarity which she obviously didn't feel in order to make the evening work.

Both had changed their appearances greatly. Mary had slimmed down significantly, from a long term illness of some kind of African tropical parasite. "The only thing got me through it," she confided to them, "was smoking marijuana. Otherwise, I don't think my sanity would have lasted." Her illness had been treated as if it were amoebic dysentery.

Peter was now sun browned, a bit less hair, yet he was healthier than Rudd remembered. His body was built up from working outside. He was quiet but Rudd could see he had changed, perhaps grown from his experiences in Africa, some of which he related.

When they arrived back at the motel, Peter said, "I think the girls would like to talk alone. Can I buy you a drink?"

Rudd nodded and the two went to the motel bar. They took a table in the back, away from most of the smoke.

They settled back, Rudd with a gin martini and Peter with a pitcher of draft Bud.

Rudd prepared himself for what was coming.

Peter drained half the glass, set it down, and eyed Rudd. "So. You took my little girl to bed." His voice dripped with accusation.

"I'm not sure it's any of your business, now, Peter. You went away and left me as a surrogate parent. You dumped her like a red-headed stepdaughter."

Peter shook his head. "It doesn't matter. I love my daughter. You took advantage—"

"Well, I did not, just so you know."

"What happened then?" demanded Peter.

Rudd paused. Then he shrugged. "We fell in love."

"You must be twenty years older than she."

Thirty, thought Rudd. "Love conquers all," he said with a

wry smile. He'd recently decided to learn her age—not ever difficult, but less so with a driver's license. He'd only done that thing because he'd reconciled it and was no longer worried about how really young she was or wasn't.

Peter finished his glass and poured it full from the pitcher. "I'm not sure I can impart to you my sense of frustration and disappointment. You violated a trust, our trust—"

Rudd sighed. "Peter, listen carefully. You abandoned that girl. Plain and simple. She was in your way. An opportunity conveniently appeared and you leapt at it. Let me tell you more. You were not raising her—um, correctly—or as well as you could have."

"I, we—"

"Didn't do shit, Peter. Now look at your daughter. She is not only the smartest student on that giant campus, but the best. She's never missed a class, while she had the flu, after being attacked by a gang and surviving, after plenty more complications. Let me tell you what Aloha has done with her private life. It started with a laundromat." Rudd picked off fingers one by one as he described her businesses. "Now she's worth several million. And she hires needy students. Most communities cry for assets such as her. The editor of the business section in the newspaper is hounding her for an interview. So far she's successfully dodged him."

"Well, I—"

"I am not yet finished. Now Aloha is a very bright person and doubtless would have made the big time herself without me. But not as soon or as well. And I ain't bending over to pat myself on the back. I taught her to read the right stuff. She already liked school, but without me I doubt she'd have gone to college. She'd be a single parent some goddamn place right now with a shitty wage-scale job. I taught her to cook, to dance, how to fight and how to kill. I taught her to fly and to sky dive. I proudly showed her horizons she'd never dreamed of. Then she not only dreamed of what was on those horizons, but what was over those horizons, and then went out and did those things."

Rudd was leaning forward and his voice was low and deadly. "What did you teach her?"

"What do you mean you taught her to kill? And sky dive?"

"I'm talking unarmed combat survival skills. And they paid off. She jumps out of airplanes just for the hell of it, just because she likes it."

"She's not pregnant?" asked Peter.

"No." Rudd sat back and signaled for another martini.

Peter grimaced. "I will say she appears to genuinely like you and that she is marrying you of her own free will."

"Nice of you to notice."

"I was just so surprised. Mary is trusting me with this dialogue. We had to be sure."

Meaning Aloha's mother is currently giving Aloha the third degree, thought Rudd. Well, Mary would learn a thing or two.

"Let me tell you another thing," Rudd said, still angry, "Aloha is occasionally mentioned in the society pages these days. And the business section and the fashion pages. Hell, she *sets* fashion trends. She has parlayed a single laundromat into several million dollars, cash and assets. In just a few short years. And she is a *real lady*, young but a lady nonetheless. Now I would say that you don't have any bones to pick with me."

Peter drank a full glass of beer, slammed it on the table and wiped his mouth. "Goddamnit, man! I am a *parent*! If I want to pick a bone or raise hell about my child, I shall. I do not care if she became queen of England, I still have not only the right, but the personal obligation to do my job as I see it."

And Rudd Six was glad, for there was hope for Peter yet.

"In addition, Mr. Six, I would make the point that when we did *allow* Aloha to stay with you, I believed you to be a man of character and caliber, elsewise we would not have given in to her request to finish the school year. And, you will recall, the deal was supposed to be that Aloha was staying with her best friend and your daughter, not you."

Rudd nodded. "We both have valid points."

"I need more beer," said Peter.

Rudd waved for the waitress.

After they got refills, Mary and Aloha appeared. One look told Rudd that Aloha had gone through a similar grilling. Neither of the two looked bloody, so it must have turned out all right.

They sat and drank for a while, Aloha sipping ginger ale, and Mary had a white wine and sneaked a cigarette. This gathering was more comfortable than dinner at the restaurant.

Rudd paid the bill, and while they were waiting for change, Aloha took her father for a few minutes' talk, leaving Rudd with Mary.

"Mary, I really would like to know the origin of Aloha's name. Tell me?"

Mary stood and nervously stubbed out her cigarette. "I did not want a child; I was afraid of abortion and didn't really believe in it anyway. Can you see that in me? Me a sixties refugee being against abortion?"

"I'm glad you didn't."

"Yeah, sure. So, I wanted to be rid of her, from my body, and did not want the responsibility of a kid. So I called her Aloha, for 'Hello and Goodbye.' When I thought of that, I almost changed it to Stephanie or Debbie or Peggy Sue or Julie or Lindy or Brenda or Kathy or Mike or Judy or Susan or Colleen or Karen or Linda or Anita or Joni or Liz or Nancy or Mary Ann or Jeanette or Sylvia or Heidi or Patty or Estrella or Lori or Kim or Tricia or Sarah or Barbara or Dawn, but the more I thought of Aloha, the more the internal poetry started to ring, and it seemed so right, so I stuck with it. By then it had matriculated through my mind and came to mean more than hello and goodbye. I sort of thought of it last as 'Hello, world, here, by God, I am and you better watch out and stay clear of my wake when it's goodbye.' And that's that."

"And the Bonnie part?" he prompted.

"Symmetry. Aloha was on one ocean, Hawaii, one side. To fill out the yin and yang, I chose Bonnie from the Beatles' song called 'My Bonnie.' From England, the other ocean."

After dropping them off, Rudd and Aloha returned home.

Aloha sighed. "We overcame that obstacle."

They had departed home before sunset and had left no lights on.

Now most of the lights in the house were shining and there was a rental car in the driveway.

"What do you think this is all about?" said Rudd.

"It's my other present, and, I think, a bonus."

"Maybe it's Buddy," Rudd said hopefully.

"That'd be the bonus," said Aloha.

They parked in the garage and went into the family room.

"Buddy!" Aloha shouted and ran to him and swarmed into his arms. "Aren't you happy for us?"

"Yeah, sure." Buddy put Aloha down and hugged his father. "You one lucky son of a bitch, you know that?"

"I do," Rudd beamed.

And in from the kitchen walked Denise.

"Dennie," said Rudd. He couldn't believe it. He went to her and she held her arms open and Rudd grabbed her and could never have been happier. He saw Aloha smile knowingly. Somehow Aloha had gotten Denise back. He released Denise and stepped back.

"Aloha," Denise said simply.

Buddy took Aloha's arm. He nodded to father and daughter. "Let's leave 'em alone and go somewhere and talk."

CHAPTER TWENTY-EIGHT
HER

Aloha led Buddy to the sun deck. They settled in lawn chairs.

"You done good, step-mom-to-be. Denise told me you've been sending checks to her church in Dad's name."

"I felt guilty being the cause of their split."

"And are responsible for them resolving their differences."

"It took a long time," said Aloha.

"You so—well, I've never loved anybody like I love you at this minute," said Buddy conversationally.

"Thank you, dear," said Aloha.

"It appears you can do anything you set your mind to, Menu Girl."

"I needed a bridesmaid and Denise was my only choice."

"Keep it in the family, I guess. I'm the best man. Here." He drew an envelope out of his pocket and handed it to her.

"It's dark and I can't see anything. Tell me."

"A wedding present, from that biological mom of mine, to you and Pops. It's a cruise. Airline tickets from here to Seattle. Cruise tickets up and down Alaska."

Aloha groaned. It was a super gift, but now she'd have to somehow thank Marge and that, perhaps, was Marge's intent when she gave them such an expensive gift.

—You've done more difficult things in your life, Bonnie pointed out.

—Shut up.

"I have to know, Aloha. How old are you?" Buddy leaned

forward, elbows on knees.

"Plenty old enough." She paused. "But your question really is, how old *was* I? When Rudd and I started. To assuage your curiosity: seventeen."

After a moment, Buddy said, "I know you too well; you ain't lying."

"Nope."

"Some things don't add up. You didn't drive. You were very secretive about your age. It was almost as if you were pretending to be older than you really were."

"It almost became a game," she said with a smile at fond memories. "I think Rudd finally figured it out and played along. It's something we've never addressed. I was, in fact, frightened to drive. Rudd hustled me into that; not to mention the fact that flying is more difficult and dangerous and I did that fine. The flying actually made the driving easy, once I decided to conquer my fears."

"You kind of blew past that real quick, doll."

Buddy was quick and picked up that she skipped a beat.

"Well, Buddy, after a while, it became a matter of principle. I wanted people, Rudd especially, to take me as I was, no matter what their perceptions of me were. It's really simple: I didn't have much else going for me."

"Not counting beauty, brains, resourcefulness, determination, and a bunch of other stuff?"

"Well, I guess."

"You, dear Aloha, are a rascal. A cunning rascal."

"And that's one of my endearing traits."

Buddy shook his head. "You bet your cute ass, sweetheart." He paused. "The menu has more intriguing pages in it now, Menu Girl. I—"

"Buddy? Don't get maudlin, okay?"

His face darkened, perceptible even in the night from the splash of light at the door. "I'm tryin' real fuckin' hard not to, Menu Girl." His voice strained. "Do you understand there's not *any* fuckin' time left for me to tell you how much I love you?"

Aloha leaned forward and took his hand. She put her face right in front of his. "You don't *have* to tell me."

"Oh." He squeezed her hand and his hand was warm and pulsing.

Her eyes turned hard. "My wedding is tomorrow, less than twenty-four hours from now."

"Yeah. I'm happy for you." He pulled his hand from hers. Then he stood and went to the railing and stared at the glow of Tallahassee to the southwest.

The dynamics of family took over and the door opened and Rudd and Denny came out, and everybody tried to talk at once.

Aloha was glad it was night and Rudd couldn't read her expression.

After a while, Rudd said, "My life has not shown me to be much the traditionalist. However, I'm happier than I have ever been to this minute, and this minute is pushing midnight. I've decided I can't see my lovely bride on our wedding day until the ceremony. So I bid all goodnight."

Aloha rose quickly and went to him. She threw her arms around his neck. "Goodnight, Rudd. I love you," she whispered and kissed him gently.

She spent the night in the master bedroom. The big house had three other bedrooms so there was a room for everyone.

At five in the morning, Aloha walked into Buddy's room. She flipped on the overhead light.

"Buddy! Rise and shine, soldier."

He was awake immediately. He sat up. "What?"

"You go running. I'll ride my bike?"

"What the hell, Aloha?"

"We, by God, are going to get stuff straight between us. You, my dear, are not going to fuck up *my* wedding day."

He reached out and put his hand on her hip. "I wouldn't do that. I'm okay now." He yawned.

Suddenly, she pushed his shoulder hard and he tumbled off the side of the bed, dragging the sheets to cover his nakedness.

"Don't matter," she said mimicking his voice, "I seen it all now anyway."

"Shit, Aloha!"

On his torso, she saw scars from wounds. "Get your tennie pumps on; I'll meet you in the garage in ten minutes."

She was busily engaged in kicking the shit out of the sandbag when he came into the garage. She wore shorts and a bulky, sleeveless FSU sweatshirt.

"About time." She grabbed her bicycle, hit the garage door button and took off. "C'mon."

When they'd accompanied each other in the past, she'd ridden casually alongside of him, matching his pace, and they'd talked.

This morning, she pedaled faster, and he had to run hard to keep up. After thirty minutes of him running seven minute miles, she slowed and he jogged beside her. She couldn't help but notice he wasn't even breathing hard.

He looked at her in the dawn and grinned the boyish grin she remembered. "Well?"

"So we have to come to some arrangement on your behavior." Aloha let the bike coast for a moment.

"Well, I see you're no longer teasing me with skimpy outfits," Buddy said easily, as if he were not running. "I can read messages as well as the next guy."

"Last night—" Aloha started.

"Last night was an aberration. I was feeling sorry for myself."

Aloha resumed pedaling. "Buddy? I do love you. You have to know that."

"You pick a funny way to show it, darlin'."

"I love Rudd, too. I love him a hell of a lot. I have always loved him. I will always love him. To the exclusion of everybody else."

The sun was climbing faster.

"I could tell," said Buddy, voice tight.

"So," Aloha said, "is there going to be a problem?"

Buddy stopped abruptly, unbelievably almost in midstride. He grasped Aloha by the shoulders and she and the bike halted immediately in his grasp.

He stuck his face in hers. She could smell his metallic runner's breath.

"See, Aloha dear, I do love you. Your happiness is more important to me than anything, including my own happiness. Strange as it may sound, I love my dad, too. I'm fuckin' happy as a pig in shit that he's fuckin' happy as a pig in shit. You both are fuckin' happy, so I'm fuckin' happy as a fuckin' result, goddamnit. I would walk the fuckin' plank for you, Menu Girl. Do I fuckin' make myself clear?"

Surprised, Aloha said, "Um, absolutely clear."

Still holding her against him, he jammed his face against hers and his torso against her. He kissed her hard, not passionately, but thoroughly.

The handlebars dug into both of them and then he broke the embrace.

"Goddamn, Menu Girl. See, now I can live with myself." He let go of her and she had to shoot her left foot out to maintain her balance.

"Jeez, Buddy."

"Now let's get your cute ass back to the house and dressed and married off."

"Buddy? I understand." Her voice choked and filled with tears. "I do love you."

"Yeah, sure, Menu Girl. Race you back to the house." He turned and sprinted the other way and it took her five minutes to catch up with him. He ran like he was escaping a horde of demons.

* * * * * * *

She wore a cream colored sheath dress, street-length, not full-length. She would not wear a veil, but carried a wreath of baby roses and baby's breath. Her hair was pulled back and tied with a black satin ribbon. She wore matching silk pumps. Aloha regretted that the occasion did not call for a vest. Which led her to think about designing a wedding vest.

Rudd dressed in a formal dark blue suit.

Denise wore a simple sheath pale rose dress.

Buddy was dressed in his Marine Class A uniform, badges, medals, and ribbons abounding.

Over a hundred people were in attendance.

When he got to that part, the preacher was saying, "And do you, Aloha Blaze, promise to love, honor, and obey—"

Aloha said, "I promise to love, honor, and cherish—"

A murmur went through the crowd and after that it held its collective breath.

"But," the preacher said, "the words are—"

Rudd spoke. "I agree with her."

"Well, okay."

And the crowd sighed as if one and most of them applauded, for they knew Aloha well and then the ceremony continued to its conclusion.

Aloha found the sheets of her wedding bed covered in rose petals. They were cool, smooth, and sensuous on her skin.

And....

CHAPTER TWENTY-NINE
THEM

...they lived happily ever after.

Sort of.

When Aloha Blaze, now Aloha Six, is involved, nothing ever doesn't not happen.

They tried and tried, but could not duplicate Aloha's earlier pregnancy. Tests showed her fertile, though she'd known that already. Often, she regretted her long ago abortion. Very often.

Denise went back to school, married, and had six children. When they were young, grandfather Rudd ritualistically taught each of them to say their prayers at bedtime. "Now I lay me down to sleep," he would intone, "I pray the Lord my soul to keep." Amanda McMullen went to the Tallahassee Civic Center and saw the circus. She liked it so much she ran away with the Ringling Brothers & Barnum & Bailey Circus, went to Clown College in Venice, Florida, worked for the circus for two years when she fell in love during a performance where she had to fill in as Ringmaster, in Houston, Texas. She married a man who had his own oil equipment supply company and moved to West Columbia, Texas where she happily landed a job, which she didn't really need, as the head librarian.

Lightning Lance Gugliotta received good grades, much better than he had at Leon High School, throughout his career at FSU. The academic advisor was constantly surprised at Lance's academic perseverance. When his eligibility ran out, he actually graduated. He was selected in the second round of the NFL draft, played backup for three years with the Kansas City Chiefs, became a starter in his fourth year, played two games, and was injured permanently and never played another down. Having his degree, he went to the University of Florida at Gainesville, earned a law degree, and was hired immediately as a corporate lawyer and began at a higher salary than he had earned while in the NFL. Upon his hiring, he sent Aloha a copy of his law degree certificate with **THANK YOU!** written across it in red magic marker.

Nathan Ex earned a few more degrees and moved to Atlanta where he sometimes reports for CNN, an experiment by Ted Turner, and where he broadcasts his syndicated radio call-in show from midnight to five thirty Monday through Friday nights.

Zeke, Ward Zekowski, was killed trying to land his Beech in a thunderstorm. He and Rudd had reciprocal key-person insurance policies dedicated to each other. Rudd reluctantly accepted the money from the agent and used it to exercise a buy-out clause with Zeke's mother, who was his only heir. Rudd now owned all of SIXGUN AIR. Aloha had received her commercial pilot's license, single and multi-engine, so sometimes she helped out by flying for Rudd.

Denise was able to talk her mother, Marge Thompson, into accepting Jesus Christ as her savior, and Marge became a Born Again Christian, went to several Baptist schools and landed a job as the preacher in a small community church off Old Myakka Road in far eastern Sarasota County, where she tended her flock, a graveyard, and grew vegetables in the sandy loam at the back of the property.

Mary and Peter Blaze became roving ambassadors for their foundation.

Upper Volta endured several coups and became the country now known as Burkina Faso. Mauritania went through several coups of its own.

Buddy Six came and went in and out of their lives. He became a major, then a lieutenant colonel, then a full colonel.

He had assignments in the Pentagon where he became one of the "fast-burners" destined to become a general officer. His other assignments included NATO, a stint on a nuclear carrier as commander of the Marine contingent, a tour as military assistance group commander to a secret Republic of Korea training base. Where he got into a fight with, and almost killed, a CIA trainer which should have ended his career, but strangely enough because the rivalry at the time between the Marines and the CIA only enhanced his career. He barely admitted to himself why he did it, except that he knew it was for the same reason he'd killed the Filipino wielding a machete so long ago in Olongapo when he could have disabled the crazy man: he was madly in love with Aloha which pushed him over the edge sometimes. Because of his death wish, he courted danger and volunteered for all the lousy missions. Bosnia. Rwanda. Zaire. The Saudi. Kuwait. Iraq. Somalia. He ran and won several iron man triathlons. He'd just pinned on his colonel's eagles when Rudd suffered his first heart attack.

Aloha got her B.A. with straight A's. Immediately thereafter she became a graduate student and received her M.A. in English Literature. Her thesis was on Herman Melville. She continued on with her studies and earned a Ph.D., also from Florida State, and her dissertation was on Plutarch and three of the men of destiny he'd written about in *Lives*: Solon, the Lawgiver; Alcibiades, the Traitor; and Cicero, The People's Advocate. By 1995, she was entrenched in Leon County business circles as a heavy hitter, and a big-time fundraiser for FSU and several charities. She was also elected to the county commission and had been appointed to the State of Florida Board of Regents, a powerful and respected position.

She still flew and jumped out of perfectly good airplanes.

Rudd and Aloha liked the cruise to Alaska so much, that every year on their anniversary they took a long cruise. They went to Samoa, the Antarctic, around the Horn and through the Indian Ocean, Southeast Asia, the Marshall and Mariana Islands, Fiji, Greece, the Mediterranean, Japan and Korea, Russia, Thailand

and Burma and many other exotic locales.

They were never able to have any children.

One day she realized her metamorphosis was complete. She knew she was far different than the person she would have been without Rudd.

She bought him a Harley-Davidson for his birthday.

* * * * * * *

Every year on their anniversary, Rudd made sure their bed sheets were covered with rose petals.

When Rudyard Kipling Six turned sixty-three, he had his first heart attack. He was still strong, virile, and ruggedly handsome. Though his eyes were more muted and there were some age lines at the edges of his eyes.

The doctors told him, "Too many years of too hard work and stress. After all, you *fly* for a living."

"Yes, but I cut back," he told them.

"Cut back more."

He did and did not have another heart attack for four years.

While in the hospital recovering from his second heart attack, he had a stroke. He had just told Aloha, "Looks like I'm down to the worm in the tequila bottle of life." Then it happened. Doctors and nurses were quick and busy for a while.

Aloha took up residence in the hospital. While he lay in a coma, she held his hand and told him: "I said I will love, honor and cherish you until you or I shall die, and I do. By God, I do."

Doctors explained the telltales: weakness on one side of his face or body. And Aloha could tell that very thing was occurring in Rudd. But since he was unconscious, the medical staff could not determine how major his stroke had been. They did perform a computerized tomography scan and diagnosed his stroke resulted from blood clots, not hemorrhages. They gave him drugs to help keep the existing clots from growing larger and try to prevent new clots from forming.

Week after week she sat there.

For the first time in her life, she missed classes. She was enrolled in law school and finally had to drop out for the rest of the semester.

One day she went home to do her laundry and check the mail. When she returned to the hospital, Rudd was gone.

Security details were running all over Tallahassee Memorial Hospital and the nurses and doctors were shaking their heads. The nurse on his floor showed Aloha the IV and drug needles and monitoring attachments hanging where they'd been ripped out.

"He must've regained consciousness and simply walked out."

Aloha checked the closet. Slacks and a shirt were missing, as was his flight jacket, wallet and keys.

"Somebody stole a Harley from the parking lot," one of the security men advised.

"Uh, oh," Aloha said. A spare key to the old Cessna 172 was on his key ring.

Aloha was afraid to call, so she ran down the stairs, jumped in her car and outran chasing police cars to SIXGUN AIR on the opposite side of Tallahassee from the hospital.

The outside gate was swinging loose where he'd failed to relock it. An old Harley sat pinging alongside the fence. The muted brrr of a propeller echoed between the hangars.

She ran into the office and snatched up the microphone. The office and maintenance staff were staring at her and one mechanic was standing there waving his hands. "He just got in, cranked it, and left. By the time I got there it was too late."

Aloha keyed the mike. "Rudd? Can you hear me? Come in Rudd."

A voice came on the ground control frequency. "Cessna 172, identify yourself, I say again identify yourself and announce your intentions." A pause. "You have no clearance. Please respond or I'll have to alert security and your life could be forfeited."

Jesus, thought Aloha. She clicked the mike. "Who's in the tower? This is Aloha over at SIXGUN."

"Roger, Aloha, this is Wilson. Hey, what the hell's going on?"

"It's Rudd. Pick up the hotline, will you?"

Aloha set the mike down and grabbed the adjacent hotline telephone which was starting the automatic ring, meaning Wilson had picked up on his end.

"Tell me quick, Aloha; he's fixin' to take off."

She told him what she knew. "I don't know what kind of shape he's in," she finished. "He's at least lucid. He stole a motorcycle and drove it over here and got through the gate and he's taxied the aircraft."

"Aloha, I don't have any choice. We gotta report it to the FAA right away."

Aloha thought furiously. She covered the receiver and barked orders at the SIXGUN AIR mechanics, "Get my Cheyenne ready for immediate takeoff. Start the engines. Pull the chocks. Now."

The command authority in her voice shocked them and two men ran out the side door toward the Cheyenne.

The radio next to the mike squawked, "SIXGUN AIR Cessna, I say again, you are not cleared, do not go airborne. Rudd, damnit, *listen* to me."

Aloha lifted the mike and keyed it. "Rudd, it's Aloha. Listen, hon, it's dangerous to other people. You have to think of them. Please come back."

The Cessna surged forward on runway 27 and Aloha watched through the big window in horror as he tried to rotate too soon and when he finally got airborne the wings wobbled dangerously and almost caught on the runway, but he straightened out, and climbed steeply, heading west.

"Rudd!"

She spoke into the hotline again. "Wilson?"

"Aloha, if he flies over Tyndall, or Eglin or any of them military bases, they can launch somebody to shoot him down. They probably won't, but they can."

Damning herself to probably losing her licenses permanently, Aloha Bonnie Blaze Six said, "You tell those sons of bitches if they try anything, I will ram them with the Cheyenne."

"Christ, Aloha! Don't you go off the deep end, too."

She dropped the phone and sprinted out the door and ran to the Cheyenne.

Thank God, they had the aircraft running already. She jumped in, somebody slammed the door, and she ran no checklists, simply checking for emergency warning lights and fuel level. Everything okay.

She turned on the radio to the tower frequency, 121.9, Ground Control.

Wilson was already squawking. "Aloha, my supervisor refuses you clearance. Security is on the way—"

"I understand," she said, talking into the mike and not bothering with a headset. She listened over the radio's speaker. Wilson was telling her to hurry because they'd try to prevent her taking off. She slammed the throttles forward on the taxiway, took the cutoff and hit runway 27 heading in the opposite direction of traffic. She almost flipped the Piper then and there for her speed was too high for a ground turn.

Never mind the call letters, protocol no longer mattered. She keyed the mike. "Thanks, Wilson. Clear traffic please, I'm taking off."

"I already did. Go with God, Aloha."

Airborne, she headed west, buckling her seatbelt as she made a ninety degree turn searching for the Cessna. She got to five thousand quickly. The Cheyenne was much faster than the Cessna. The Cessna could hit 140, maybe 150 miles per hour, depending on headwinds. She could push the Cheyenne well above the 318 mph cruise.

She spotted the Cessna a thousand feet below her flying straight and level. "Once you know how, it almost flies itself," she said aloud, quoting Rudd.

—Oh, sweet Jesus, what I'm gonna do?

—Steady, girl. You got this far. Use your brain.

She did and starting flipping channels on the radio. "Hello, Rudd, can you hear me?" She said this on every channel she could think of. She scraped her brain clean, there had to be an answer. *Wilson!*

Once, she recalled, she'd taken Rudd to Atlanta to ferry an aircraft back to Tallahassee. They'd picked a seldom used frequency, 123.45, so they could talk aircraft to aircraft without much chance of others overhearing or complaining because they were clogging more used and public freaks. She remembered fondly that flight, for they'd both just read *On Human Nature*, by Edward O. Wilson, the Harvard University curator and professor. The work had earned a Pulitzer Prize. They'd discussed the book off and on for the entire flight.

Quickly, she dialed in 123.45 MHZ.

Immediately she heard his voice. "—went this way on our first flight together, remember?"

He was talking to her but had his mike keyed and she couldn't answer. She waited as he talked.

"...was the day I knew I was in love with you forever and ever and ever and ever and ever...."

She had slowed the Cheyenne as slow as she could, but had overtaken him and went into a steep 360 turn to keep him in sight and fall behind him again. She dropped the flaps and reduced power to slow down. Better.

"...and went sky diving over there twice."

She heard Rudd's transmission terminate and instantly keyed her mike. "Rudd, hello Rudd, this is Aloha, do you read me?"

"Hello, darlin'. Nice day to fly, ain't it? Over."

"It is that. Listen, think about heading back for Tallahassee. Okay, dear?"

"I got places to go and things to see."

"You okay?" She found herself crying for the first time in years.

"Damn right. Never better. Except part of my face doesn't work too well. See, we went way out over the Gulf—say, where are you?"

She pushed the yoke forward and dived five hundred feet and appeared on his wing. "Right here, dear, right side."

He leaned over and looked out. He smiled and waved and keyed his microphone again. "You be my wing person. What's goin' on? What the *hell* is goin' on?" He kept the mike open and after a minute, said "Tell me."

—God help me!

—You can do it, said Bonnie confidently.

Aloha decided the truth never hurt. She transmitted, "Rudd, you were sick in the hospital and unconscious. You woke after a long time, got in the Cessna and took off. Now you're heading off into the Gulf of Mexico."

"How'd I get here?"

"You are one hell of a pilot, Rudd. If I make a big, wide turn, can you follow me?"

"Sure thing. We gonna go home?"

"We're going home, Rudd." By God, we are. No more fucking hospital.

"Okay. Lead on, love."

She made a gradual 180 and he followed.

—He's a better pilot in a coma than most of these idiots are with all their faculties.

—I can tell, said Bonnie. You ain't doin' bad yourself.

—Well, you monitor *me* for a heart attack, Aloha said, because I don't think I can take it much longer.

—*You do what you have to. You always do.*

—I'm trying, oh, Jesus, I'm trying.

Coming back east over the coast, she transmitted, "You're doing beautifully, Rudd, keep it up, dear."

"Aloha?"

"Yes, dear?"

"I just woke up a little. What the hell I'm doin'?"

He sounded better. She told him again. "Just let your natural reactions have control. You've flown so long and those things almost fly themselves."

"I used to tell *you* that."

"Yes, dear." She paused. "Just follow me. I have to contact air traffic control for just a sec."

"Sure."

She hit the preset button and transmitted immediately. "Hello, Miami Center, this is SIXGUN AIR Piper Cheyenne 673. I am declaring an in-flight emergency. Request all traffic divert from Tallahassee, over."

"What's your status and the Cessna, 673?" Professional. They knew what was going on. She tried to gauge if another airfield was closer, maybe Panama City? Not now. It'd be easier and safer for Rudd to land where he was most familiar.

"I have the Cessna on my wing and he's flying with me. We'll be there in less than ten minutes, please clear the area and call out fire and rescue."

"Done."

"I've got him on 123.45 and I can't get off it again, so if you want to monitor it, do so. But *do not* interrupt, my control is tenuous."

"Ah, roger, copy, 673. Are you going to land with him?"

"I'll bring him down, wing to wing, if he'll cooperate, but I'm afraid my airstream might upset his aircraft." And he might need the whole runway, side to side, to the end.

"Roger, understand. I'll be with you. They got somebody else to run my board."

"Thanks. What's your name?"

"Fitz. Good luck, Miss Aloha. Changing frequencies now."

Fitz. She didn't even know him, but he knew her.

She flipped back and called Rudd. "How you doing over there?"

"Grand, just fuckin' grand. There's blood all over my arm."

"That's where the IV's and stuff were."

"Hell, I knew that."

"We'll be back in five minutes, how's your fuel?"

"Half a tank."

Great. Enough for a nice sized explosion.

"Rudd, do you think you can land okay?"

"Hell, I don't know, hon. I'm gettin' woozy, kinda."

"We're almost there."

"I'm awake now. Know what?"

"What, dear?" Aloha trimmed the Cheyenne a bit.

"I think I was gonna just fly to places you and I been, you know? Sorta a farewell tour."

Aloha started crying again.

Rudd went on. "I always thought it would be better to die in a steep dive you can't pull out of you know and fighting it all the goddamn way down until you slam into the ground and they can put you in a martini glass."

"Rudd, we're almost there. I'm starting a descent. Nice and easy. Then we do about a ninety-degree turn and we'll be lined up on final. Understand?"

"Yes, dear. I can land this son of a bitch in my sleep."

"Good."

—He can, said Bonnie.

—I know.

"I love you," said Rudd.

He followed her down and through the turn.

"Just put it down like usual," Aloha transmitted. "I'll be fifty feet above you and behind you."

"You gonna land with me?"

"Yes, I will."

"Aloha? This be my last landing, lemme do it by myself?"

Oh, dear Rudd, do not please do not kill yourself. "Yes, dear. I love you."

"You can peel off now."

"Yes, dear." She surveyed the airfield. "*Fitz! Wilson!* Tell them to kill the emergency lights! And get those fucking teevee trucks the hell out of there."

"Roger."

They couldn't, of course, but anything would help.

"And, guys? Nobody touches him when he gets down, understand?"

"Roger," Fitz and Wilson replied simultaneously.

To her surprise all the emergency lights went out, but the vehicles remained strung along the runway.

She pushed the throttles forward, retracted the flaps, pitch nose up, and the Cheyenne leapt forward. She climbed and banked with more G's than the tech data allowed, a "yank and bank," a tighter turn than you're supposed to. She came down losing altitude and airspeed at the same time and at the last second leveled the wings.

Then it was she saw the Cessna execute a perfect landing.

"Awright, Rudd!" She keyed the mike and talked as she touched down, not applying brakes, and only reverse thrust momentarily, so that she could outrun the emergency vehicles, emergency lights now flashing like the Fourth of July at D-Day.

"Rudd, you're slowing well, when you want, just go ahead and kill the engine. I'll get one of the guys to bring the Cessna back to SIXGUN AIR."

"Like hell," he growled. "My job ain't done 'til I'm home."

She couldn't answer because her own landing hadn't gone as well as his. She was bouncing all over the damn place, too fast, blowing past the fire trucks and security vehicles. She got it to stay on the ground, chopped at the throttles again, and took off across the grass, slipping dangerously and digging the left wing tip-tank into the ground and smashing into a ground light fixture. As she headed for SIXGUN AIR like a juggernaut, dried grass, clumps of dirt, pieces of tip tank, and plumes of dust rooster-tailed behind her. She skittered across the taxiway with at least one flat tire shredding and pulling her hard left and slammed to a stop, killing the twin turboprops, no checklist, no procedures, seatbelt unbuckled and diving out the door even before the Cheyenne stopped near the Cessna 172.

She outran security, fire, rescue, and police to the Cessna.

She lunged at the pilot's door and opened it.

Rudd was staring down calmly at her. "Let's go home?"

"Come on, dear, yes, we will go home." She held out her hand to him.

A crowd had appeared, maybe a million different kinds of uniforms, including all the SIXGUN AIR people. Cameras whirred in the silence.

Rudd climbed tiredly out and took Aloha's hand.

She walked them both toward SIXGUN AIR and the crowd parted like the Red Sea. No one spoke a word.

Aloha's Cadillac was sitting in front of SIXGUN AIR, driver's door still open. She got Rudd into the passenger seat and hurried around to the driver's side.

Every cop and Fed in the world was going to be after her.

Fuck it, fuck them. Thank you, Lord.

CHAPTER THIRTY
HER

Rudd dozed on the way home.

No more hospital.

Aloha drove across town following traffic rules and regulations this time. Two deputy sheriff vehicles followed her sedately.

Aloha pulled out her cellular telephone and punched in the doctor's phone number. Of course, nobody calls a doctor's office and is allowed to talk to the doctor. "Just tell him I have Rudd now and I'm taking him home. And that I *will* see the doctor there at his earliest convenience."

Then she called the Leon County Sheriff's Department Communications number.

"You have two cars following me, what are their intentions?"

The lady deputy replied, "To insure public safety, Ms. Six. When you get to your destination, they'll return to patrol."

"Thanks. I'll settle up my traffic violations from earlier today some other time."

"There are none, Ms. Six. We saw your landing on television. We wish you all the best."

"Thanks," said Aloha, somehow touched by a stranger.

"Almost home," said Rudd shaking his head.

When she turned into the driveway, she ran the window down and waved at the two patrol cars. They flashed lights and continued on down the road.

Aloha helped Rudd out of the car.

Flowers at the door? He'd remembered and ordered them before he stole the motorcycle and went flying.

"Jeez, Rudd, we have to get you bathed." Blood was seeping down his arm. Briefly she wondered where his flight jacket was.

"Later. I want a drink."

"Well, why not?" said Aloha.

She sat him down on the couch in front of the fireplace and he stared at her portrait while she went to the kitchen.

The answering machine was blinking with a thousand messages. She'd deal with those later. Quickly, she made a gin and tonic. She was going light on the gin and thought about that. "Fuck it." She made him a stiff drink and took it to him.

He sipped on it silently, but his face showed appreciation.

Aloha sat at Rudd's feet. "How do you feel now?"

"Better," his voice rasped. "How long has it been since I've had a drink?"

"Maybe thirty days."

"Too long. This is just like old times."

Tears were leaking out of her eyes and blood was leaking out of his body.

He sipped his drink. "That's good. Right now I think I know what is going on. You'll be up to your ass in alligators because of what we did today. But I had fun." He cocked a knowing eye at her. "I guess the umbilical is on the other foot now. You can handle it all." The left side of his face didn't move with the right side.

Aloha's throat was choking and she couldn't speak.

He drank again. "I believe it is my time. Gawd, I feel woozy." He leaned backed.

"Let's get you to bed." Her words came out strangled.

"In a minute. I do not know if I will be able to express myself again. The dark rushes over me...."

Aloha took his hand, his cold, cold hand, and still could not speak.

Rudd enunciated each word as if launching them. "You... are...young...yet. Take...the...world...by the throat. There."

Except the ice, his glass was empty. He held it out slowly to Aloha. "One more for the road?" His smile was wan, but pure Rudd.

Aloha scrambled up and ran into the kitchen, afraid not to fulfill his final wish. She was terribly frightened of what she'd find when she returned. She made the drink swiftly and hurried back.

Surprisingly, he was breathing and his eyes were open.

He waved off the drink.

"Want to lie down?" she asked.

He nodded.

She pulled him up and he walked by himself, tiredly and slowly, into the bathroom and stepped into the shower. She stripped him and turned on warm water. She saw where the catheter had been and his bleeding had slowed to a mere seep. Maybe his heart wasn't pumping strongly enough.

Then she dried him off and got him into pajamas and into bed.

He fell asleep and she ran into the kitchen and speed-dialed the doctor's office. "Where is that fucking doctor? You call him on his cell phone and tell him to come straight in and don't ring or anything, I won't be able to answer."

She hung up and looked at the bottle of Gordon's gin on the counter. For the first time in her thirty-seven years, she opened the cap and drank four swallows. It helped open her throat. It occurred to her that no matter how much she aged, he'd always been thirty years older than she was. They'd been together twenty years—mostly good ones.

She went back and sat with Rudd.

When the doctor came in, he had a nurse with him.

Aloha left them alone. In the kitchen she went through all the phone messages and made her own calls.

Doctor Neely was a slim man in his thirties. The best in Tallahassee.

"He should be in ICU."

"Not anymore," said Aloha. "He stays here."

"He will die."

"Yep." Her heart dropped. The death sentence pronounced.

"I'll send over a hospital bed and we can connect back the IV's—"

"Nope."

Neely eyed her. "You got ice in your guts, Aloha."

"It's his last wishes, Doctor."

"I've read about people like you in medical journals."

"How long's he got, Doctor?"

"Without intravenous fluids, he'll dehydrate quickly, the shape he's in. That is, if his heart doesn't fail or he gets more blood clots and another stroke—"

"How long, Doctor?"

Neely shook his head. "Could be ten minutes, or ten days. My guess would be two days, not much more."

"His will to live is gone," Aloha said, and those were the most difficult words she'd ever said in her life.

"Two days. I'll leave the nurse. Call me if there's any change. The nurse can do CPR or what's necessary."

"I just want her to help me physically handle him. I'll be sitting with him."

Aloha sent the nurse to the family room to watch television. When Denise arrived, Aloha briefed her.

"Where's Buddy?" asked Denise.

"He's coming. He'll be here in a few hours."

Rudd was still alive when Buddy arrived. They sat with him until midnight. Buddy went to take a nap and Denise fell asleep on the living room couch.

Aloha Bonnie Blaze Six sat there hour after hour.

She thought about the young Aloha plotting to seduce Rudd. About her machinations to move in with him. She thought about Rudd's insistence that she read. About him teaching her to dance, to fight, to love education for its own sake. And how to love. She remembered fondly how happy they'd been when he'd bought her the laundromat. She remembered he never badgered her into or out of anything; just how he'd appealed to her intelligence. She remembered his monologues on horizons and how to expand them. She remembered jumping out of airplanes with him. She remembered learning to fly and what a wonderful thing that had been. She remembered the good times they'd had, and she died a little inside.

She squeezed his hand tighter and felt him move.

Rudd's eyes opened!

For a minute he looked confused and then he saw Aloha.

He smiled at her.

She wrung his hand and leaned over him as his lips moved.

"Now I lay me down to sleep, I pray...the Lord...my...soul...to...keep—Aloha?" A hoarse whisper. His eyes tried to open again but they wouldn't. Then they flicked open for a scant moment and clouded and closed with finality.

"I'm here, Rudd."

—*He's going!*

She clenched his hand with all her strength. His hand was getting colder and stiffer and colder and stiffer.

She couldn't hear him breathing.

She would not call the nurse to resuscitate him.

Suddenly, she remembered. She bent over him and covered his mouth with hers. Flocks of memories swarmed through her. His mouth twitched and was still. She continued the kiss, desperately hoping it would revive him, save him.

Finally, she knew it was too late.

Their last kiss. At his long ago request.

"I love you, Rudd. Now go kick down the gates of hell."

That final kiss provided her a sense of closure. The pall of gloom still flooded her, but she felt she'd sent him off properly.

She must hurry. One more thing left.

—*Bonnie!*

—*Here.*

—*Ready?*

—*I am. It's been years since I've been useful.*

—*It's time.*

—*Just a second. Aloha? I love you.*

—I love you, too, Bonnie. I'll miss you.

—There he goes! Now-I-lay-me-down-to-sleep-I-pray-the-Lord-my-soul-to-keep—Bye!..........

—Take care of him—

Then they were gone. Rudd and Bonnie. Irrevocably and forever. When he died, Rudd took a major part of Aloha with him.

Aloha sat holding his cold, dead hand for an hour.

And another hour.

And another.

Both of her hands were around his.

The bedroom door opened and, in a moment, a warm hand took one of hers.

She turned her head and looked up at Rudyard Kipling Six, Junior. "Buddy? He's gone."

"I know."

Buddy's hand was warm and familiar.

Her eyes were locked onto his. "Buddy? Did you ever feel empty? Oh, so empty? The world no longer matters. Nothing matters?"

"I understand."

"I'm not sure I want to go on."

"One person in the world who will persevere, it's you."

"Thank you, dear," said Aloha.

"I'm here for you."

Aloha felt a surge go from her right hand still holding Rudd's to her left hand, now gripping Buddy tightly.

"For how long?" Her eyes were still locked onto his.

"For as long as you want."

"That will be a long, long time," said Aloha, knowing it was so.

"'Til death do us part," said Buddy Six.

"I do," said Aloha, "and maybe after that."

She rose and folded Rudd's cold, dead hands together. She touched his cheek one last time. She threaded her arm through Buddy's. "Let's go. I've lots to do."

ACKNOWLEDGMENTS

Many thanks to Captain Dan Hubly of Chicago and environs, and U.S. Airways pilot John Evans of Sarasota for flight protocols and guidance. For narrative flow, I abbreviated and smoothed over some of the technical details. Any errors are mine.

ABOUT THE AUTHOR

JAMES B. JOHNSON has written seven novels: *Trekmaster*, *Habu*, *Mindhopper*, *A World Lost*, *Daystar and Shadow*, *Counterclockwise*, and *When the Pirate Prays*, all of which are being published by The Borgo Press. *Mindhopper* was optioned twice for a movie, and three of his books were translated into French and German. He has also penned numerous short stories and articles. Jim has sold advertising, worked for the Post Office for fifteen years, and spent eleven years in the Air Force. He lives in Sarasota, Florida, with his wife Beverly.